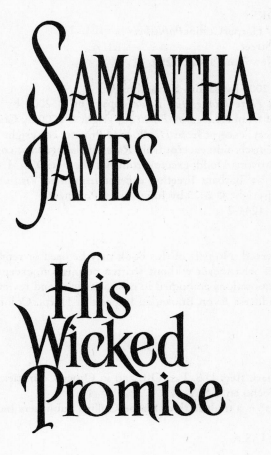

SAMANTHA JAMES

His Wicked Promise

AVON BOOKS

An Imprint of **HarperCollins***Publishers*

This is a work of fiction. Names, characters, places, and incidents are products of the author's imagination or are used fictitiously and are not to be construed as real. Any resemblance to actual events, locales, organizations, or persons, living or dead, is entirely coincidental.

AVON BOOKS
An Imprint of HarperCollins*Publishers*
10 East 53rd Street
New York, New York 10022-5299

Chapter 1

Dunthorpe Keep, Scotland
Early 1200s

"She's leaving," the lad whispered.

"Nae, Drummond," scoffed the thin-faced lad next to him. "Me mum said she won't leave. She won't go back to . . . to—"

"Blackstone Tower," supplied Drummond, the elder of the pair who perched behind the tooth-shaped crags of the high stone wall that overlooked the chapel. A dirt-stained hand pointed toward the forest. " 'Tis there, far yonder in the Borders. My da told me so."

"The Borders," repeated Gordon, a wide-eyed, scruffy-haired lad of ten. "But there are thieves in the Borderlands. Thieves and"—his voice plunged to a whisper—"and Englishmen."

Drummond's mouth turned down. "Aye, you are right. Thieves," he repeated, his air clearly disdainful.

The sweet scent of wild flowers drifted through the air. Far afield, a hound bayed, and three horsemen followed the animal in fervent pursuit. But it was not the excitement of the hunt that claimed the two lads' attention. Instead they peered over the high stone wall toward the pair of women who sat on a blanket far below. Clinging tendrils of ivy climbed ever upward to where the lads strained to hear their voices.

"My aunt says the mistress will miss Glenda terribly if she leaves. Glenda cured the ache in my tooth, y'know. What if it should return?" Gordon's tone had turned mournful. " 'Twill be a sad day if Glenda leaves us."

Such was true, not just for the young lad Gordon, but for many . . . including the woman to whom the boys referred. For in truth, the thought of leaving the home Glenda had known for these past eight years roused a piercing sadness in her . . . yet it was forged by a resolution she could not forsake.

For this was a task that was hers alone—and the decision had been hers alone to make.

"So. You will go to Blackstone Tower."

Meredith, wife to Cameron, chieftain of the Clan MacKay, repeated the words Glenda had uttered but a moment earlier.

"I will," Glenda said simply.

The brightness of the warm spring sun reflected in Meredith's hair, turning it into a bright halo of fire around her head. She tipped her head to the side and regarded Glenda. "You will not be swayed from this course, will you?"

Glenda shook her head. "I fear not, Meredith. My father and my uncle are dead. I doubt my sister's husband would consent to moving Eleanora and their children from Ireland. Of a certainty I cannot ask her to leave her family."

Meredith's reminder was gentle. "But *we* are your family now, Glenda."

Glenda smiled slightly at the flame-haired beauty. Aye, she *was* a MacKay, for she had married Niall, eldest son of Ronald, the clan chieftain, more than eight years ago. She had shared the clan's many joys in that time, as well as the crippling grief when Ronald and six of his sons had been slain by the Munro clan . . .

Among them was Niall.

It was a day that would haunt her forever. A day that had wrought not just one blow, but two . . .

Taking a deep breath, Glenda wrested her mind from the empty bleakness of those days . . . and every day since. "Aye, I am a MacKay, just as you are now, Meredith. Yet Blackstone Tower is where I spent my childhood. 'Tis different in the Lowlands—different than the clan way—the Highland way. With my father and my uncle gone, with my sister Eleanora and her husband so far away, there is no one left but me. I fear that if I remain here, if I do not step forward and Blackstone Tower were to fall into ruin, my poor father would surely turn over in his grave."

Before she could explain further, there was a high-pitched shriek across the bailey. Both women turned their heads toward the sound, in time to see Brodie Alexander MacKay crawl out from beneath the skirts of Myrna, the washerwoman. In an instant the lad had scrambled to his feet. He darted to the left, sending the chickens scattering and squawking before him.

"Now, there's a rogue who likes the ladies—och, and but two years old!" someone called out.

The laughing jest roused the attention of the lad's father, who stood near the stables, talking to a groom. His head came up and Cameron groaned.

"Brodie! Brodie Alexander! Come here, you scamp!"

He took off in pursuit of his son. As if the child knew precisely how to elude his father, Brodie ducked under the hay cart, which sat idle.

Cameron dropped down on his belly and peered beneath the cart.

"Brodie! Come here, lad."

Brodie giggled and stretched out a chubby hand. "Come hide with me, Papa!" he demanded.

Cameron sighed. "I cannot fit beneath the cart as you can, lad."

"Try, Papa!"

"Another time, laddie. For now, please come out."

It took no small amount of pleading and cajoling before the child crawled out. The instant he was snatched high in his father's strong arms, Brodie planted a wet, noisy kiss on the broad sweep of his father's bristly cheek.

Spying his wife, Cameron strode toward her, ruffling hair as dark as his own before carefully easing the boy into his mother's lap.

"Can you not teach your son some manners, lady?"

Glenda looked on as the chieftain of the Clan MacKay dropped a kiss on his wife's nose.

"*My* son?" A slender brow rose askance. "I but gave you the son you demanded of me, sirrah, and now you would complain!"

"And I but gave you the daughter you demanded of *me*, wife—and most insistently, as I recall, which reminds me . . . where *is* our daughter, love?"

"Sleeping most soundly, my lord." Shifting slightly that he might see, Meredith lifted a corner of the plaid that lay between the two women, revealing the crown of a tiny oval-shaped head swept by the gauziest layer of silky blond hair.

Cameron's features grew soft. He shifted his gaze to his wife, whose lips now carried the faintest of smiles. Their eyes met and meshed, both Cameron's and Meredith's. And in that moment spanned by aught but a breath, Glenda watched as something passed between them—an enormous pride, a bond that only two who shared the creation of a child could share.

An odd sensation pierced Glenda's breast. Mayhap it was wrong, but she could not help it. Though Glenda dearly loved Cameron and Meredith, there were times—times like now—when she saw the pair together with their children, and it hurt to be near them. She could not banish a twinge of envy. For it was at once a feeling she had never truly experienced . . . and a feeling she understood in full measure.

Dimly she heard their light-hearted banter. "Ah," Cameron groaned, "but I should have known. So tiny in size, yet still she mocks me, this daughter of mine. For she sleeps the sleep of the undisturbed, the sleep which forsakes her father night after night."

"The sleep which forsakes her father . . . what, do you protest? Most certainly she did not wake you last night. Indeed, while I agree she shows no signs of forsaking her nourishment, the last three nights you've sounded like the veriest hog in the pens as she takes it!"

"Not I, madam," he returned mildly.

" 'Twas you indeed, sir."

"Mayhap you heard the snores of the soldiers sleeping in the bailey, the ones who drank a dram too many last eve."

"I heard most distinctly the snores of the man who lay beside me!"

Glenda summoned a faint smile. Ah, but the path of fate was unpredictable, she decided reflectively, for who would have foreseen that Cameron would fall in love with Meredith of the Clan Munro? The MacKays had feuded with the Munroes for generations. Yet 'twas only these last few years that the feud had been set aside—for the most part, at least—and now Meredith and Cameron had both son and daughter. Indeed, their daughter Aileen had been born but a fortnight earlier!

Hands placed boldly on his hips, Cameron had planted himself squarely before his wife. "We shall settle this later, my love. For now, before our son decided to make his usual mischief, I could not help but note you appeared gravely serious."

The laughter faded from Meredith's eyes. "I was indeed." Her gaze flitted to Glenda, who bit her lip rather guiltily.

Cameron blinked. "What is this? Why, 'tis Glenda who is usually your champion, not your tormentor!" Cameron spoke only half in jest. "Indeed, if not for her, I might never have come to my senses and married you!"

As a sudden breeze arose, lifting a strand of the reddish hair from Meredith's temple, Cameron bent down to tuck the lock behind his wife's ear.

Cameron frowned. "The sun has shifted to the west and it grows chill here, love. Why do we not move to the solar and continue this discussion?" he suggested. "Glenda, would you take Aileen?"

His hands carefully solicitous, Cameron assisted his wife to her feet. Glenda obligingly reached for Aileen, settling the infant into the curve of her arm as she straightened. Oh, but it felt so right to hold a wee one snug against her breast! As if she knew exactly what was in her mind, the child in her arms stirred. Her cheek plump and flushed with sleep, her body warm, the babe yawned and nuzzled her breast. Her tiny little mouth made sucking motions, yet Aileen slept on.

Anguish ignited deep within her chest. A branding of the soul, a burning of the heart. A thousand times she'd battled this feeling when she'd held Brodie . . . and now with Aileen. Glenda could have screamed with the wrench of pain that ripped at her insides, a pain that left no outward sign, no bruises. Holding a child in her arms—especially a bairn so new to the world—brought mixed emotions. The longing she was usually so adept at controlling rushed to the fore.

"Glenda?"

The soft, musical notes of Meredith's voice reached her ears. Only then did she realize that Meredith awaited her daughter. For the space of a moment, conflict raged deep within Glenda. Her arms were reluctant to release the slumbering bairn, yet a part of her was almost anxious to surrender the child to her mother's waiting arms. Memories battered her, memories of Niall and the son she'd borne . . .

With a deep breath, she laid Aileen in her mother's arms.

"Such a lamb," Meredith murmured.

"Aye," Glenda agreed. "Like her brother." For indeed, it was true. Brodie had been the sweetest tempered of babes, never fussing or fretting, crying only when he was hungry or wet.

At that precise moment, Brodie slipped a chubby hand into Glenda's. Glenda smiled down at the lad as his parents crossed the bailey. Her heart twisted as they entered the great hall. She sought to will away the feelings tearing at her chest. Life was hard, she told herself as they mounted the stairs. Many a child never lived to adulthood. They succumbed to disease, she reminded herself as she stepped into the solar, or the harshness of life. But for Glenda it had never been easy to accept.

She seated herself on the wooden bench perched against the wall, then pulled Brodie onto her lap. Burying her face in the silky dark strands of the lad's hair, she couldn't help but wonder . . . what would her own son have looked like? Would his hair have lightened to the same sun-kissed henna as his father's? Would his eyes have been golden as her own, or as green as the misty hills of the Borderlands . . . as green as his father's? Would he have been small and stout? Tall, with gangly limbs, like Niall? Would he have been full of playful deviltry and laughter? Ah, but had he been here, he might be even now playing in the bailey, with his cousin Brodie chasing after him.

It was hard, knowing that never again would she hold her own.

Swallowing the ache in her throat, she saw that Meredith had placed the babe in her cradle. With a rustle of her skirts, Meredith turned to face her husband, who had taken the seat before the fire.

"Now," Cameron said with an arch of his brow. "Would someone please tell me what is amiss?"

Glenda raised her head. "There is naught amiss," she said softly. " 'Tis simply that I have decided I must return to Blackstone Tower."

For the longest time Cameron said nothing. Glenda had the feeling she'd startled him. Brodie had slipped from her grasp to play with several small clay balls beneath the shuttered window. Cameron's gaze never left her. Dark brows knit together almost fiercely, he stroked the squareness of his jaw with his right hand, a gesture that reminded her piercingly of Niall, for in just such a way her Niall had been wont to ponder.

She could not stop it. She could not *help* it. Niall's visage swam before her, squeezing her insides like a giant vise . . .

"I see," Cameron said slowly. His gaze was steady on her face. "But I wonder, Glenda . . . do you go by choice"—a faint pause—"or by duty?"

Glenda took a deep breath. "Does it matter?"

"Nay." An unswaying resolution echoed in the word. "Not if it is truly what you wish."

The ache was back in her throat. "It is," she said, horrified to hear her voice wobble, then all at once feeling compelled to explain.

"In these last three days since I received word that Uncle is dead, I've thought of little else. My father would have been horrified were Blackstone Tower to fall into someone else's hands. I—I cannot let that happen. So you see, the duty is mine ... as well as the choice."

Once again Cameron said nothing.

Glenda took a deep breath. "I pray you will not discourage me, Cameron. For this is something I must do, you see ... I must."

The look he gave her was deep and probing. Ah, but it appeared he knew her too well and too long! "It's not only your uncle's death, is it, Glenda?"

Her head ducked low before she could summon the strength to answer. "Nay," she whispered, and then again: "Nay! Oh, Cameron ... Meredith, I am not certain I can explain! The happiest days of my life have been here at Dunthorpe."

"And the most painful as well."

Glenda's smile was bittersweet. "Aye. And I have been restless of late. Oh, I pray you understand! I have made my home at Dunthorpe these many years. But 'tis time I returned to Blackstone Tower"—she took a deep breath—"to make my home there."

This time it was Meredith who spoke. "Never tell me," she said faintly. "You will not return?"

Glenda said nothing.

Meredith must have gleaned the answer in Glenda's silence. "There will be no changing your mind, will there?"

"I fear not, Meredith." Glenda's tone was gentle, for she'd glimpsed the betrayingly bright sheen of tears which welled in Meredith's eyes—and all at once those tears were her own as well.

Cameron sighed. Rising, he squeezed his wife's shoulder, then crossed to Glenda. Gently he kissed her forehead. "Ah, but if I remain much longer the two of you will have *me* weeping," he teased. The laughter faded from his expression. "You wish to leave soon, don't you?"

Glenda nodded. " 'Tis a long journey to the Borderlands," she said quickly. "I would leave on the morrow, if possible."

Cameron was quiet for a moment. "I'm certain it can be arranged," he murmured. "But one thing troubles me. You are Niall's widow, and 'tis *my* duty to take care of you, but 'tis a long journey to the Borderlands, just as you've said." He hesitated. "Glenda, I do not mean to dissuade you, but I hate to leave Meredith with the babe so recently born—"

Glenda was already shaking her head. "And I would not dream of asking that you do," she told him firmly, "nor would I allow it."

Cameron nodded. "Would that I could take you myself," he murmured, as if to himself. "But I cannot, and there is only one man to whose care I would entrust my own sister-in-law."

Glenda's heart seemed to catch. Somehow she knew what he would say, even before he said it . . .

"Egan," he decided with a satisfied nod. "Aye, Egan will take you."

The midnight haze of nighttime still blurred the edges of the sky when Glenda slipped from her chamber. Sure-footed and intent, she left the walls and sprawling towers of Dunthorpe behind to climb toward a grassy knoll. A solitary tree devoted a lonely, endless vigil over the seven graves that stood in a half-circlet before it.

Glenda was on her knees in the dirt. At her back was the breathtakingly dramatic sight of Dunthorpe Keep and the granite valley below; Glenda paid no heed to the view, for it was here that Niall, his father Ronald, and five of his six brothers now found eternal rest . . . along with his son.

He'd been buried with his son in his arms . . . the son he'd never known he had.

How long she remained, she knew not . . . yet the first warming glance of the sun on her head reminded her it was time.

She pushed herself to her feet. There were no tears, though she knew not when she might return to this place. In truth, a voice within her head resounded, most likely she would never return. She pressed one last, fleeting kiss to the tips of her fingers . . . and then to the grave marker of her husband and son.

"Farewell," she said softly.

Not once looking back, she retraced her steps to Dunthorpe. When she reentered the bailey, she saw that all was in readiness for her departure—and it seemed there were more farewells to be said, for she had scarce appeared than two women, Meghan and Adele, ran up to her.

Adele gave her a quick hug. "Oh, but we will miss ye sorely," Adele sniffed. From the look of her, she'd already been weeping.

Meghan's voice joined hers. "Aye, and terrible though it may sound, we hope ye dinna stay in the Borders. We hear 'tis a terrible place, full of thieves and rogues!"

Glenda couldn't help but smile. "That's what I was told before I came to the Highlands. And look how long I've remained—why, 'tis nearly eight years."

"But ye couldna leave," someone cried. "Yer husband was 'ere."

The day was long past since the mention of Niall ensured a hollow silence when Glenda was present. Yet somehow today was different. By subsiding degree the air fell silent. A stark pain tore through her heart, yet somehow her smile never faltered.

There was a tug at her skirts. It was Brodie, bright-eyed and cheery as always. He held up his arms in mute appeal.

Glenda reacted instinctively. She whisked him high and close, pressing the softness of his cheek against her own. Then Meredith was there, appearing at the fringes of her vision.

Slowly Glenda lowered the lad to the ground, and turned to his mother.

"So. You will leave us." Meredith made no effort to disguise her wistful regret. "Alas, I shall simply have to content myself with the hope that mayhap in the Borderlands you will find another man to love."

Glenda shook her head. "Nay, do not hope, for I shall never marry again."

"Never?" Meredith chided her. "Do not be so certain, for you are too much a beauty not to sway some man's head."

"A beauty! Nay, Meredith, I think not."

"Och, but you are," Meredith insisted. She twirled a gleaming red lock that hung over her shoulder around her finger and stuck out her tongue. "I've always been envious of your smooth, honey-colored waves," she said with a sigh, "and so have all the other women."

Glenda pursed her lips. "Nonsense," she said crisply. "What is to envy? I am old."

"Old? At five-and-twenty? You are not so much older than I!" The spark of laughter gleamed in Meredith's eyes. Yet in the very next instant it was gone. "I shall miss you, Glenda. I shall miss you dreadfully!" At the very same moment, the two women reached for each other.

Glenda hugged her friend almost fiercely. "And I you," she whispered, and all at once she thought she had surely gone mad.

God in heaven, she thought achingly, how could she do this? How could she leave Dunthorpe and the people she had come to love so deeply? These past few days, both heart and mind had told her this was the right thing to do. Yet now that the moment was upon her, all at once she was not certain—not certain at all!

Yet it was just as she'd told Cameron. She must. She *must.*

"Come back soon," Meredith told her. Her words were laden thick with the blur of tears. "For if you do not, then we shall have to find you."

"And I shall hold you to it." Glenda's voice wobbled every bit as much as Meredith's. Reluctantly the pair released each other.

By now Cameron had appeared as well. Glenda turned to him, and for an instant, he caught her snug in his embrace. "When you turn your eyes to the north, remember us," he said. "And should you need us for any reason, you have only to send word."

"I know." Her throat ached so, 'twas a miracle she was able to speak at all. When he released her, blindly she turned toward her mount, Druscilla, dreading the moment she was gone, yet hasty in her wish not to prolong this painful farewell any farther; for if she did not, she was afraid she might disgrace herself by weeping openly.

Hands closed about her waist and lifted her to Druscilla's back. They were warm, those hands, hard and tanned and strong, sweeping her high aloft, seemingly without effort...

It was Egan. He was there, as always, ever-present ... lending a word or his sword if needed, yet never intruding, his presence stoic, his demeanor quiet.

For just an instant, a strange little quiver shot through her, in a way she couldn't quite control... in a way that was disturbing and utterly vexing. She had known him for years, she told herself, almost as long as she'd known Niall. Yet the reminder did naught, for in truth she'd never felt the way she did of late when Egan came near. She knew not why... and she knew not how to stop it!

For that very reason, Glenda did not look at him. Instead she kept her gaze fixed upon Cameron, who stepped before his friend, now mounted on a stallion as silky black as his master's hair.

"Guard her well and deliver her safely," Cameron stated simply, "for she is one of us."

Egan's reply was lost on Glenda. Wildly it spun through her mind that she would have much preferred that Finn escort her. Finn, with his whiskey-blurred voice and great, shaking belly laugh...

Instead it was Egan. Egan... with eyes the color of blue steel. Egan... who seldom smiled. Egan...

with the deepest-timbered voice she'd ever heard in a man.

His hand descended sharply on Druscilla's rump. The mare started, then began to prance through the gates. This was it, Glenda realized dimly. Just before they passed beneath the iron-gated portcullis, an odd feeling arose within her. A momentary panic assailed her, briefly taking her breath. She felt as if she were about to venture forth on a perilous journey into a land of the unknown, a land of some dark, vast uncertainty.

And aye, so she was. For this was a journey that would now snatch her from all that had been familiar to her these past eight years . . . and deliver her to the realm of the future.

But she was not alone. Nay, she was not alone, and she was not sure whether the knowledge brought comfort or a fledgling fear. 'Twas a journey that began with . . . merciful heavens, but she could still hardly believe it! . . .

With Egan.

Chapter 2

Cameron had sought him out in the great hall last eve.

"Glenda will travel to Blackstone Tower."

Glenda. For an instant, the beat of Egan's heart picked up its rhythm, as it always did, 'ere the mention of her name . . . the merest chance glimpse of her. In his mind's eye, her features flashed before him—large, wide-set eyes the color of golden flames, framed by rich chestnut waves that curled below her hips.

Slowly Egan raised his head and gazed at Cameron, his chieftain and long-time friend. "Indeed?" he inquired. "To see to affairs at Blackstone Tower?"

Cameron nodded. "She wishes to leave at morningtide."

It was Egan's turn to nod. "And how long will she be gone?" The inquiry was made with no hint of his feelings.

Cameron was silent for a moment. "A very long time, I fear."

Egan could not help it. He stared. "What? You mean she will not return?"

"She will not. She means to make her home there."
Cameron chuckled. "You needn't sound so astounded, my friend. Blackstone was her childhood
home—indeed, Blackstone was her home far longer
than Dunthorpe has been."

Egan felt a dull flush creep beneath his cheekbones.
He prayed he hadn't betrayed himself; thankfully
Cameron didn't seem to notice anything amiss. Yet a
slow curl of darkness crept round his heart. Never to
see Glenda again. Never to hear the sweet, low ca-
dence of her voice . . .

As if from a distance, he heard Cameron sigh.
"Mayhap 'tis for the best after all. Meredith will miss
Glenda sorely, but . . . she grieves for Niall still. And
mayhap it will always be so if she remains here at
Dunthorpe." There was a small pause. Cameron
glanced over at him. "But with the babe just born, I
fear I cannot take her. So you see, I must find someone to take her to Blackstone Tower—"

Nay, Egan thought. *I pray you, Cameron, do not ask
me. Ask me anything but this . . .*

"Will you, Egan?" The faintest of smiles curled
Cameron's lips. "Will you take my sister-in-law to
Blackstone in my stead?"

For one full second Egan could say nothing. The
full import of Cameron's request washed through
him. To be alone with Glenda . . . God's wounds, it
did not even bear thinking about . . . !

His mind screamed inwardly. *I cannot. Dear God, I
cannot!* The words threatened to spring free. Reason
told him it would be best. For this was the last thing
he wanted . . . the *only* thing he wanted.

Yet everything inside had gone utterly still. This

was not wise. By the bones of Christ, not wise at all. He should tell Cameron the truth. Tell him why he could not take her . . .

The words would not come.

For they *could* not. Niall had been Cameron's brother, and Cameron was his truest friend—and he dare not take the chance that such a thing might forever come between them.

Nay, Cameron must never know that he—Egan— had long hidden his feelings for Glenda. When Niall had brought home his bride, Egan had envied him, for Glenda was a beauty of a kind he'd never seen. He had come to admire her quiet serenity, her shy courage as she'd gradually gained acceptance into the clan; indeed, he'd been smitten almost from the beginning. Her brows were darker than her hair; there was a piquant slant to them that but hinted at the laughter beneath . . . a laughter that had been all but extinguished by the death of Niall, he admitted soberly. But Egan could scarcely confide in anyone, even his greatest friend, Cameron, for Glenda was Cameron's sister-in-law. And so he had buried his feelings deep inside, in a place that he seldom acknowledged. There were times he'd even managed to convince himself they didn't exist.

Now he knew better.

Yet, as if from a very great distance, he'd heard himself say, "You know I will, Cameron."

It was done. He had agreed. He had given his word, and he would keep it.

Yet Egan could not withhold the faint bitterness that seeped into his soul. He had watched Glenda leave early this morn, when the mists still shrouded the earth and the coolness of night still hovered on her breath. He knew she'd been to Niall's grave. He'd watched her return, and he knew he had not imagined the sadness that lingered in the depths of her eyes.

Forever it was so, it seemed, that he had watched her.

Brutally he chastised himself. They were on their way and there was no turning back. He had given his word, and by all that was holy, he would keep it.

Had Egan but known her thoughts he would have been startled; in truth, he'd have been shocked to the depth of his being.

For Glenda was not so unaware of him as he was convinced.

She allowed Egan to set the pace of their travel, which was hard but not grueling. Near noonday they stopped to water the horses at a tiny loch that glistened like a jewel in the sunlight.

Standing behind Egan, she found her gaze inexorably drawn to him. He stood next to his stallion, his hand carelessly curled around the reins while the horses slurped noisily from the calm, crystalline waters, his booted feet braced slightly apart. When he turned his head to the south, the direction in which they traveled, she was afforded a view of his profile.

Unaware of her perusal, she examined him more thoroughly. Had she not known him, he would have frightened her. He was big, broader than any of the MacKay brothers had ever been, more than two hands taller than she—and, oh, aye, the hands of a man!—and not a diminutive one at that. His skin was weathered a deep bronze which never faded, even in the deepest chill of winter.

He was, she found herself admitting, an arresting sight. Even when she'd come to Dunthorpe as a bride with eyes for no man but Niall, she'd always thought him attractive. His handsomeness was marred only by the thin white scar angled on his cheekbone just beneath his left eye.

Glenda swallowed. Had she but one word to describe Egan, what would it have been? *Intense* was the only word that sprang to mind.

Suddenly a memory rose high aloft in her mind, the memory of a night not so very long ago . . . the scene in the hall that night at Dunthorpe was one of merriment and gaiety—Daniel, one of Cameron's men, had wed Alinda earlier that day. Though it was not the first wedding since Niall's death, there had been a poignant ache in her heart that day. Lilting music filled the air and dancers swarmed the center of the hall; she'd been idly watching the celebration when someone had pulled her to her feet and swept her into the circle of dancers. Moments later, laughing breathlessly, she felt herself whirled around.

She came face to face with Egan. He did not reach for her, nor did she reach for him; it was as if neither of them knew what to do, as if . . . as if each were brought up short by the sight of the other. The moment passed in but an instant, for she was seized by another partner.

It was later she spied him near the hearth with Patsy, the alewife's daughter. Patsy had smiled invitingly up at him, her arms twined familiarly around his neck . . .

When next she looked, he was gone . . . and so was Patsy.

She did not see either of them again that eve.

Sleep was elusive that night. A stark, wrenching loneliness spread through her; the ache was nearly unbearable. She thought of Daniel with Alinda . . . Egan with Patsy . . .

And her beloved Niall.

She cried herself to sleep that night . . . cried as she had not for so many, many months.

'Twas odd, the sensation aroused by that remembrance. Her gaze strayed to Egan again and again that day—just as they had that night.

Her earlier wish was all at once renewed . . .

Why couldn't it have been Finn she was with?

Glenda couldn't withhold the yearning any more than she could stop the sudden clenching of the muscles of her stomach. Ah, but she should have known Cameron would want Egan to escort her!

In truth, she had known Egan nearly as long as she had known Niall. Though Niall and Cameron were brothers, the three of them had been so very close— Niall, Cameron, and Egan. Indeed, Egan had almost been raised as one of Ronald's sons. Glenda knew that Niall had always regarded Egan as one of his own brothers. Yet somehow *she* had never thought of Egan as a brother—nay, never in this world . . . not in the same fond way in which she had always regarded Cameron. With Egan, it was never so easy to laugh and tease . . . indeed, had she ever laughed and teased with the same carefree abandon that she had with Cameron and his brothers? Nay, she thought slowly. Somehow she had always been far too con-

scious of his masculinity. Yet it was not only that—
Egan was not a man of secrets, yet he was never one
to confide freely of his mind or his mood. Nay, he
was not an easy man to know . . . indeed, when they
had first met, for a time she'd been wary of him, convinced that Egan disliked her. When she confided it
to Niall, he'd laughed and said that Egan's quiet reserve was simply his way.

"Are you ready?"

It was him—Egan. In her absorption, she hadn't
noticed that he'd turned to face her. His countenance
was unsmiling, his mouth a thin straight line. Coolly
their eyes met; Glenda knew then that he was aware
of her regard.

"Aye," she said, shaken, though she could not have
said why it was so. "Let us be on our way."

The hours passed. Glenda rode a few yards behind
him, for her palfrey was not so swift and long-legged
as his stallion. Throughout the remainder of the day,
the proud, straight line of Egan's back never faltered;
he was an excellent horseman. Yet he remained almost broodingly silent.

In time the sun dipped below the hills to the west.
A murky haze began to fill the western horizon. Egan
did not speak, but slowly brought his stallion to a
halt near a stand of tall gray aspen surrounded by
towering firs.

Druscilla dutifully trotted behind his steed, slow-
ing down as well. As soon as his mount stopped,
Egan swung down from the saddle. In but an instant
strong hands closed around her waist; she felt herself
lifted effortlessly from the saddle to the ground. At

the feel of his hands, both hot and cold flashed inside her. Saints above, why did he make her feel so uncomfortable? The question had no more than tumbled through her mind than one of her knees gave way, a betrayal of the long hours astride.

A sound of distress emerged—she couldn't stop it; the grip on her waist remained staunchly firm.

"Steady now."

Her gaze tripped up to his. " 'Tis all right. I am fine." The words were breathless, even to her own ears. Quickly she stepped back, breaking the contact between them.

His hands fell to his sides. His expression seemed to tighten . . . or was it but the deepening shadows of twilight?

Unable—or mayhap unwilling—to examine it just now, Glenda made her way toward a stout-limbed oak tree. Lowering herself to the soft, mossy ground, she leaned back against the hardy trunk and stretched out her legs. The gurgling sounds of the brook nearby filled her ears. She closed her eyes, thinking to rest just a moment.

Precisely what woke her, she was not certain. The next thing she knew, her eyes snapped open. The clearing was steeped in darkness, but the light from a blazing fire revealed Egan standing directly before her, arms crossed over his chest. A dark brow slashed upward, as if in vehement disapproval.

"If you were so tired, why did you not ask me to halt earlier?"

Glenda was not obliged to excuse his shortness. In all honesty, she hadn't realized how exhausted she was until they stopped. "And if you did not wish to escort me, you need not have done so. Cameron could have found someone else . . . Finn, mayhap!"

"Now, why would you say that?"

"Because you are angry."

"I am not."

That was Egan. Ever direct. Ever spare of words. Ever calm, never one to ponder and puzzle. Only then did she realize she was the one whose temper was short. Perhaps she was more tired than she realized.

"I'm sorry," she said softly.

"There is naught to forgive, Glenda." His gaze was steady. "Are you hungry?"

Her chin bobbed. "I am," she affirmed.

He turned and strode toward his stallion, returning with a small pouch. Lowering himself to the ground nearby, he rummaged through it and handed her a wedge of cheese and bread. Glenda ate hungrily, finishing off her portion of cheese before he did his own. Without speaking, he passed her a horn of ale. Glenda drank thirstily, then daintily wiped her mouth with the back of her knuckles and handed it back to him.

Glenda found herself unable to look away as he tipped the horn to his mouth. The muscles of his throat worked as he swallowed. That he drank from the very spot she had just abandoned seemed to bother him nary a trifle. Ah, if only Glenda could say the same!

His lips touched where hers had touched. And when next she drank, hers would touch where his had touched. 'Twas an intimacy she had shared with but one man . . . Niall. And within a very short time, with Egan, for indeed, her thirst was not slaked. 'Twas an awareness that sent heat flooding to every pore of her skin.

In one lithe move, Egan rose to his feet, then moved to drop another handful of branches on the fire. When he resumed his place beside her, her gaze had yet to leave him.

Hair of black swept back from the broadness of his forehead. So near to him, she saw that his lashes were short and thick, curling slightly upward at the ends. A most handsome man, she thought anew, yet the scar lent him a decidedly dangerous look.

Something seemed to tremble inside her. It wasn't that she didn't feel safe. She had come to know Egan as a man of unquestionable loyalty—a man of unquestionable strength. She could never have been afraid of him. Never in this world. Had there been a need to choose a man to defend her, it could only have been Egan. She trusted him as she would trust few men . . . as Cameron trusted him.

" 'Tis ugly, is it not?"

His tone was wholly matter-of-fact. It took an instant for Glenda to realize he referred to his scar. She flushed then, embarrassed that she'd been caught staring at him yet again!

"Nay," she said quickly, "truly it is not." It struck her then . . . there was something almost sad about Egan . . . of course they had spoken, many a time over the years, for they sat at the table together almost nightly. They had talked about others . . . but never about themselves. Never had she revealed to him her thoughts or feelings or emotions . . . why should she, a part of her rationalized, when she had been married to another? Nay, she realized vaguely, never had she been given to wonder . . .

To her surprise he gave a dry, raspy chuckle. "I am lucky I'm not called Egan the One-Eared. Were it not for Ronald MacKay, I would not be here at all."

Glenda tipped her head to the side. "I didn't know that. Tell me how."

"When I was a lad, I stole a sausage at a market fair in Inverness. The vendor did not take a liking to being robbed, and he was determined that I pay. He set out after me and caught me by the scruff of my tunic. As he pulled me back, he struck at me with a dagger. It glanced down my cheek."

Glenda was appalled. "How vicious! And for such a trifling item—a sausage, yet!"

One corner of Egan's mouth turned up. "You must understand, Glenda, 'twas hardly the first time I'd stolen from this particular vendor. In truth, I had a fondness for his sausages—and I was usually quick enough to elude him." He paused. "Ronald chanced to be nearby and saved me from further harm."

"Lucky for you. Your parents must have been most grateful."

"My mother died when I was but a wee bairn. I have no memory of her. And my father, Marcus MacBain, seldom knew where I was. He was more often sotted than not, you see." He shrugged. "When I was a lad of ten, I grew tired of the ache in my belly, so I left my village for Inverness. I ate much better on my own than I did waiting for my father to put food on the table."

Glenda blinked. "You mean you stole it?"

"Much of the time, aye. It was either that or go

hungry." Again that matter-of-fact tone.

So. Egan had been a thief. That, too, was something she hadn't known. "And what of your father? He never came after you?"

"Ah, no doubt he never even knew I was gone!"

"But . . . where did you sleep?"

"Wherever I could. If I was lucky, in a doorway. If not, beneath the open sky. In either case, as far away from the firth as I could. 'Twas cold there!"

"And what of Ronald? Did he take you back to Dunthorpe?"

"Aye. He kept my belly full and saw to it that I had a warm place to sleep, and trained me as well as any of his sons."

Glenda listened intently to his tale. This, then, was how Egan had come to live with the MacKays. She had never even thought to ask the details until now, and suddenly she felt almost guilty.

There was a moment of quiet reflection before she spoke. "You are lucky," she said soberly, "that you did not lose your eye." She paused. "What of your father? What happened to him?"

"Once, when I was older, I went back to the village to see him. He had long since perished."

"I'm sorry." Glenda knew not what else to say.

But Egan was already shaking his head. "Do not be. I was lucky that Ronald found me when he did, else I might never have completed my journey to manhood. Ronald was more a father to me than my own." He was silent for a moment, then glanced up at the sky. A frown pleated his brow, for dark, threatening clouds had begun to gather high above. "The hour grows late. We should rest. We've a long way ahead of us yet."

A short time later, Glenda crawled into the tent he had erected. Though she was weary both in body and spirit, sleep did not come easily that night. For she could not stop thinking of the little boy Egan had once been.

And the man he had now become.

Chapter 3

Each day took them further south toward the Borderlands. It was a tiring journey, both for beast and man, for the countryside was a vast sea of steep, undulating hills and valleys. Egan had cursed himself soundly that first night, for pushing Glenda so hard when she was unused to the travails of travel.

She had been right. Though he'd denied it, Egan had indeed been angry, though not with her. Nay, never with her. 'Twas himself he was furious with . . .

For now that he was alone with her . . . Egan could not help it. He'd longed for her from afar for years now. He wanted her. He wanted her as much as ever. More. For now she was free . . .

And yet she was not. Mayhap she would never be free.

I shall never marry again.

There had been no jest in the statement, naught but the fervor held deep in her being. Nay, there was no doubt she meant it, he decided bitterly.

He had always hated it when Meredith would occasionally tease Glenda that she must marry again.

An occasional prospect had appeared now and again at Dunthorpe; Egan had been secretly glad when Glenda spurned those who would have courted her. Indeed, Meredith had teased her yet again the morn they had departed Dunthorpe.

But now . . . his mouth twisted. Sweet heaven, but he was a fool! *She grieves for Niall still,* Cameron had mused sadly. Little wonder that she claimed she would never marry again!

Aye, but he was a fool—and would ever be one, it seemed!

On the third afternoon, they stopped to rest. Egan helped her down, resisting the urge to allow his hands to linger. It flashed through his mind to wonder what she would have done had he dared. But already she had pulled away, as if she were anxious to be quit of him!

He watched as she moved away to seek refuge beneath the soft, mossy ground of a shady tree. Laying back, she dropped off to sleep. Egan couldn't stop himself from stretching out beside her. Propping himself on an elbow, he stared yearningly down at her. Though they did not touch, he could feel the warmth of her body. His imagination took flight. Were he to touch her, what would he find? Heat mingled with softness. Unaware of his perusal, her breathing deepened. Her chest filled with air, yielding a supple, rounded shape that her clothing but hinted at . . .

One he'd dreamed of many a night.

That shape drew his gaze endlessly. When she had awakened and they were off once again, he fixed his eyes upon her anew. What was it, he found himself puzzling, that made him burn so? Her breast was primly covered. Her legs . . . he'd never seen her legs, though he somehow knew instinctively they would be slender and shapely, like the rest of her. Was it her smile? 'Twas a dazzling smile, he reflected almost somberly, not because 'twas flashed so sunnily and so often—nay, just the opposite. Nay, in truth her smile was sweet and demure . . . much as the woman herself.

'Tis not her smile, but the lushness of her lips that hold you entranced, whispered a voice within him.

Her lips. Ah, he acknowledged wryly, but it was too true!

That night as she ate, he could hardly tear his gaze from her lips, moist now with the juices of the hare he'd roasted. Her mouth was small, the lower lip slightly fuller, naturally tinted a ripe rose. He watched as the tip of her tongue came out to savor the last bit of flavor. The ache that started in his middle was almost a physical pain. What would it be like to kiss that sweet mouth, to let his own tongue run wild across that very same path?

Christ! He was abruptly disgusted with himself, for he was a man who always kept tight rein over his primal urges. What the devil was wrong with him? Were he a believer in such things, he might have been convinced that he was bewitched. That she, or some other, had cast some nebulous spell upon him!

They had been traveling for nearly five days when Glenda noticed her mount began to limp. At first she thought it was the uneven terrain, for the hill they traversed was uneven and dotted with rocks. She glanced over at Egan, who rode several feet away.

"Egan." Softly she spoke his name.

"Aye?"

Glenda pointed to the palfrey. "Something is wrong with Druscilla."

Egan's gaze sharpened. "She's favoring her left foreleg."

"Aye. I noticed it but a short time ago."

"We'd best stop and have a look." He pulled his stallion to a halt, while Glenda did the same. Swiftly he swung her down. Glenda felt her cheeks heat as she placed her fingertips on his shoulders. Egan did not dally; as soon as her feet found purchase on the ground he turned to Druscilla.

Yet it was not the palfrey who commanded Glenda's attention, but him . . . *Egan*. He bent over Druscilla's hoof. As he lifted it toward her belly, she blew out a snort and tossed her head skittishly. Immediately Egan raised a hand. Long, lean fingers ran over Druscilla's dappled skin; it rippled, then stilled. Softly he spoke, but the words did not reach Glenda's ears.

Satisfied that the palfrey had been quieted, he resumed his task anew. This time Druscilla remained calm as he bent over her hoof.

Glenda's throat grew dry. The fabric of his tunic stretched taut across his back, clinging to the muscled span of his shoulders. Glenda could not help but think that never in her days had she seen a man's shoulders as wide and sweeping as a bold new land.

He straightened. Glenda's gaze jerked back to his face. She prayed he wouldn't notice the intensity of her regard. It took a moment to realize he was speaking.

"I suspect there is something lodged in her shoe, but I cannot tell for certain." He patted Druscilla's neck. "She should be examined further."

Glenda nodded. "Aye. But where?" The last village they had passed through had been early yesterday afternoon.

Turning slightly, Egan shielded his eyes against the glare of the sun. "I believe there is a keep in the next vale. Mayhap there will be a blacksmith there who will oblige us."

He whistled, and his horse trotted forward. 'Ere she could discern his intent, Glenda found herself atop his stallion's back.

Glenda blinked. "Egan! I can walk—"

Her protest might never have been uttered. Egan had already taken up the reins in his hands and was walking briskly forward. Glenda's mouth pursed, but declined against further argument. Druscilla trailed obediently behind.

It took nigh unto dark to reach the keep Egan spoke of. Pale yellow light flickered from high in the tower when at last they crested the top of the hillock. From his perch aloft, a sentinel hailed them.

"Ho there! Who ye be and why are ye 'ere?"

Egan called up to him. "I am Egan MacBain and I travel with Glenda, sister-in-law to Cameron, chieftain of the Clan MacKay. We ask a boon—the assistance of your smithy for the lady's mount—and then we will be on our way."

"Wait there!"

The echo of running footsteps down the tower

stairs were heard. Glenda guessed the guard had dispatched someone to seek permission. The minutes seemed to drag by before he shouted down to them again.

"Enter!"

The gate creaked open. Glenda gave a sigh of relief, for if they had been refused admittance, who knew how soon they might find another smithy?

Egan led his stallion through the towering arch. Glenda glanced around and saw that they were within a large bailey. Tufts of grass grew sparsely. Egan halted. Strong hands caught at her waist and she felt herself lowered to the ground.

By now several figures had appeared. In the glow of a torchlight, she saw that a man strode toward them. Just ahead of him trotted several lads. He was clearly in charge, for he beckoned to the lads.

"See that the horses are fed and the lady's mount attended to!"

Glenda smiled at the pair of youths, who reached for the reins. "Her name is Druscilla," she said softly.

By now the man had reached them. Some years Egan's senior, a sprinkling of gray dotted his hair and beard.

"Welcome, Egan MacBain!" he greeted. "I do believe I have heard of you."

"Have you, sir?" Egan's gaze was as steady as his tone.

"Oh, aye! I am Dugan." He swept a hand wide. "This is my home. And you, fairest lady, must be Glenda."

He took the hand Glenda offered and bowed low. When he arose, he glanced between them. "Forgive me my curiosity, but my sentry said you were sister-in-law to Cameron of the Clan MacKay. A pity"—he shook his head—"the deaths of his father and brothers."

Glenda's smile seemed to freeze. "I am Niall's widow," she said quietly.

An awkward silence ensued. Egan cursed inwardly. Quickly he said, "I must thank you for allowing us entrance."

"I can do no less for someone in need." Dugan stroked his beard. "But come now. You are just in time for the evening's feast. If a hot meal and a soft bed are to your liking, they are yours for the night."

Glenda had already taken a long, slow breath. Dugan's invitation nearly made her sigh with yearning, for the thought of sleeping on something other than the damp, hard ground was tempting indeed. Though Egan never seemed to tire and always appeared fresh and alert no matter the hour, Glenda could not claim the same hardiness.

In truth, Egan had no knowledge, either bad or good, of Dugan of Ragmoor. It was Egan's first instinct to refuse, for it was not his way to embrace a man of which he knew naught, but then he glimpsed the undisguised longing which Glenda couldn't quite hide.

Softly he addressed himself to Glenda. "What is your wish? Would you like to stay?"

"I would indeed." His breath caught, for her smile was as radiant as a blazing summer sun.

"Excellent!" Dugan rubbed his hands together. "Come into the great hall and I'll see that you are settled."

"Let us go then."

Egan placed his hand between her shoulder blades. Glenda's heart leaped with quickening awareness. This was hardly the first time he'd touched her, she chided herself. Many a time he'd helped her from her horse. But as they followed Dugan up the stairs and into the great hall, his hand fell to the nip of her waist. His palm seemed to encompass her as well; she felt the warmth from his body, and now her heart was beating so hard she feared it would choke her. Why it was so, Glenda could not say. Yet this time it was different, and she knew not why. For this time his touch was almost . . .

Possessive.

There was no help for it, she thought, no help at all.

'Twas the only word that came to mind.

Once they reached the great hall, Dugan summoned several servants to show them to their respective chambers. The chamber to which she was taken was small but comfortably furnished. Though Glenda longed for nothing more than to crawl deep within the depths of the feather bed on the far wall, she knew the proper respects to their host must first be dispensed. Indeed, by the time she'd washed the coating of dust from her body, hunger gnawed at her belly.

When she returned downstairs, Egan was already seated at table. Dugan rose and seated her several chairs to his right, while Egan was placed directly opposite her. Nor, it seemed, were they the only guests. Glenda nodded and murmured greetings while Dugan introduced various guests—his cousin

Clarice and her husband Alpin, an Englishman, Robin of Chadwick, his knights David, Michael and Edward.

Very soon the table overflowed with food. There was an assortment of fish, whole roasted hen and hare, stuffed piglet, stewed fruits and an abundance of wine.

The man next to Egan was Robin of Chadwick. Dark-haired and dark-eyed, the neck and sleeves of his tunic were trimmed with fur. As the meal progressed, more and more he fixed his unbending scrutiny upon her; so piercing was it she grew uneasy. When at last he propped his chin upon his hand and stared, Glenda could abide it no longer.

She turned her own regard upon him full tilt.

"Must you stare at me, sir?"

His teeth gleamed against the darkness of his beard. "How can a man help it when there is such beauty to behold?"

" 'Ah, but 'twould seem there is an abundance of beauty here this night." Egan cut in smoothly, then gestured toward the far end of the table, where several ladies were engaged in conversation. "In particular, the one gowned in red velvet."

Three pair of eyes swung to the far end of the table. As if she knew she was the subject under discussion, the woman threw back her head and laughed, displaying the arch of her slender white throat. In the very next instant, she chanced to glance at them . . . it was Egan upon whom her attention resided the longest.

Without breaking the hold of their eyes, she inclined her head with a ruby-lipped smile, in silent acknowledgment of him.

There was a strange pinch in Glenda's chest. She turned her gaze away, but Robin's disclosure reached her ears.

"That is Elfrida." He laughed softly. "She gives her favors quite freely, I fear. Not a quality one wants in a wife, eh? Ah, but when it comes to entertainment for a night, 'tis oft precisely what a man needs."

His meaning was clear. Startled by such boldness, Glenda felt a hot tide of color rush to her face. Egan's response was lost on her, for just then Dugan spoke her name.

Very soon the last dish was served. Glenda was vastly relieved, for she was suddenly anxious to quit the repast and seek her bed. Rising, she thanked Dugan for the meal and his hospitality.

'Twas then that she felt the touch of Egan's eyes upon her. He had risen to his feet as well.

"Glenda, wait. I will escort you to your room."

She adopted a smile. "There is no need. I can find my way to my room quite well." Though her tone was pleasantly even, she did not look at his face as she spoke—she *could* not, for something within her did not wish to know what Egan thought of the lady Elfrida's conduct.

Yet just before she turned from the table, a swirl of red velvet flashed in her line of vision. She saw that Elfrida was at his side, deftly slipping a hand into the crook of his elbow. It seemed the lady returned his interest in full measure.

"We've not yet had the opportunity to speak. I should like to rectify that, sir. Will you tell me of the rugged Highlands?" She gave a clear, tinkling laugh and ran the tip of a finger down his sleeve. "I daresay they are as rugged as you, are they not?"

There was an odd constriction in her chest. She told herself both were entitled to pursue their pleasures, but deep inside, she did not approve of such displays of wantonness before others.

She didn't wait to hear Egan's reply, but moved toward the stairs, her head held high. Her chamber was on the third floor, and that was her destination. She had just cleared the landing when there came the sound of footsteps behind her. Her own hastened, for the corridor was dark and shadowed, lit only by several meager candles. Their light wavered eerily against the stone walls.

"Glenda. Glenda, wait!"

Glenda halted. A hand at her throat, her heart pumping madly, she turned just as Robin of Chadwick emerged from the stairwell.

"Robin, thank heaven 'tis only you! Why, you very nearly scared the life out of me!"

"No need to be afeared, lady." He gave an exaggerated bow. "Indeed," he said upon straightening, "before long you may well think of me as your rescuer."

A prickle went down Glenda's spine. "I do not take your meaning, sir."

"Oh, I've no doubt you'll take me quite well."

The gleam in his eyes served as a warning. Oh, but she'd been right to be wary! Somehow she stopped her gaze from veering to the stairs and giving her away; she prayed it was not too late and that the wine he'd imbibed would slow his reactions.

Alas, before she could move, he snared her arm in an iron grip.

Glenda gasped and struggled to free herself. "Release me!"

His laugh sent another chill through her. "Nay, sweetings, not just yet." He dragged her into a darkened chamber. His fingers digging like claws into her forearm, he slammed the door shut with his heel. Glenda sought to wrench away but he was too strong.

He seized her wrist and dragged her up against him. "Ah, but I knew it as soon as I saw you. A widow, eh? How long has it been, I wonder?" He gave an ugly laugh. "Too long, I vow. No doubt you are in need of a man. Well, I shall oblige, lady. I shall oblige."

"Let me go!" She twisted anew, but she couldn't avoid his moist, wet lips. An insistent tongue jammed between her lips. Glenda gagged and jerked her head back.

With a twist and a turn, he slammed her body hard against the wall, pinning her against it with his own. Hot breath struck her full in the face. "We can do this my way, or we can do it yours. Either way, I warn you I will have what I want."

As he spoke, he seized her gown and dragged it toward her waist. Glenda filled her lungs with air. "Egan!" she screamed. "*Egan!*"

Black eyes glittered down at her. "Your Highlander will not help you now," he sneered. "If I know the lady Elfrida—and I know her quite intimately, I might add—your hearty Highlander is even now seated to the hilt inside her."

He thrust a leg between hers, seeking to pry hers apart. Glenda sought desperately to keep them together, but his bulk was more than she could handle. Damn, she thought. Damn! The drink had not dulled his senses after all—

All at once Robin's body went bone-stiff.

"The next time you wish to be alone with a lady, you really should bolt the door."

It was Egan, his tone ever so pleasant. Glenda's heart rejoiced.

"Raise your hands and step slowly away from the lady."

Robin's lips pulled back from his teeth in a snarl, but he did as he was told.

Moonlight streamed through the window. It was then Glenda saw what had made Robin go still. Egan held the point of a dagger poised against the back of his neck.

"Excellent. You see the chair in the corner? Fetch it for me, if you please."

"And if it does not please me?" Robin's expression was as black as his tone.

Egan shrugged. "As you so recently pointed out, it matters little. I will have what I want . . . one way or another."

His voice was still pleasant, but in the deadliest kind of way. Robin must have sensed it as well, for again he complied, though not without comment.

"You are a bastard."

"The subject of my birth is not in question." For an instant, Egan smiled tightly. Then, for the first time since he'd entered, Egan spoke to Glenda. "Glenda?"

"Aye?" To her embarrassment, her voice was naught but a hoarse croak.

"Are you all right?"

"Aye," she said, this time more firmly.

"That's a good lass. Now, there is a knife in my right boot. Can you get it for me?"

Glenda blinked, but knelt and quickly did as he asked. Slipping her fingers beneath the soft leather, she encountered a cool metal handle. She pulled it from its berth. Weighing it in her palm, she started to hand it to him, but he shook his head. " 'Tis not for me, 'tis for you."

Glenda blanched. What was this! Would he have _her_ use it on Robin? Saints, but she could not! "Egan," she said faintly. "Please! I cannot."

Robin of Chadwick's eyes had bulged.

One corner of Egan's mouth turned up. Throughout, his gaze had yet to stray from Robin's face. "Nay, not that, lass. I would have you fetch the sheet from the bed. Use the knife and cut it into strips for me." With a nod he indicated the chair. "You, sir, may sit."

Hurriedly Glenda gathered up the sheet and dropped it on the floor. Robin sat. Several times while she worked, Robin's gaze darted toward the door, but Egan barred the way. Though he glowered, he made no attempt to escape.

At last she was done. She glanced uncertainly at Egan. "Will this do?"

"Aye. Now lay the strips before him."

Glenda did as she was bidden, then stepped back.

Egan had already tied Robin's hands behind his back. "If he dares to move," came the grim order, "gut him." Only then did she realize she still clutched the knife.

A flick of the wrist and Robin's tunic fell away. Glenda's jaw dropped as well. What on earth . . . ?

His chausses followed in short order. His boots were tossed out the window.

He was left completely naked.

Too astonished to avert her gaze, Glenda could only watch as Egan proceeded to truss a naked Robin with the strips of the sheet so that he could not move. His legs were bound snugly to the wooden legs of the chair, his arms behind his back, his torso to the high, straight back of the chair, as well as to the seat.

Robin cursed. "You will not get away with this! By all that is holy, I shall—"

Whatever threat he might have made was crammed back in his throat. Egan shoved a wad of cloth in his mouth, then tied it with another.

"Are you primed with ale or primed with lust, I wonder. Mayhap a little of both. Either way, you are lucky you yet live. Luckier still I've decided you may yet sire children"—Egan drew the tip of the dagger down his belly to his navel—"so let this be a lesson to you, Robin of Chadwick. The next time you would bed a lady, make certain you procure her consent as well."

Robin's eyes blazed. Garbled sounds came from deep in his chest. Glenda had no doubt that were he not so tidily trussed, he would have sprung straight for Egan's throat.

Egan paid no heed, but drew Glenda from the chamber. Closing the door firmly behind them, he held a finger to his lips.

"We must hurry lest we run afoul of the men of the keep. I know now what they will do when he is discovered—with luck that will be well into tomorrow. If they decide to follow, I think it best that we are as far away as possible."

There was a note of urgency that demanded both silence and compliance. Glenda nodded.

Mercifully, there was another entrance to the bailey that did not demand they pass through the great hall. They crept noiselessly past, keeping their heads ducked low—though from the sound of the revelry within, no one would have noticed their passage.

In front of the stable, Egan rose to his full height. "We've decided to journey through the night," he told a sleepy stableboy when he asked that their horses be readied.

Glenda marveled at his calm. Her heart seemed to crash against the walls of her chest; her stomach churned so that she feared she would lose the contents of her earlier meal.

He repeated the very same to the guard at the gate.

Once the tower was out of sight, they took flight, giving the horses free rein. The light from the full moon shimmered down from above, as if to light their way.

Throughout the night, they pressed ever onward to the south. The morning came and went. The afternoon sun beat down on their heads. They stopped only to water the horses. When the moon once again cast a flowing circlet in the sky, the night without sleep and the rigors of the day began to take their toll. Her lashes grew heavier and heavier. Her head drooped. A strong hand on her arm prodded her awake—and it was all that stopped her headlong tumble from the saddle.

She raised her head. "Egan, please. May we rest a while?" The plea emerged before she thought better of it.

His expression was grim. For a heartbeat, it seemed he would refuse. Then the taut line of his mouth softened slightly. He gave a brief nod. "Aye," was all he said. He pulled his stallion to a halt. Glenda followed suit.

Glenda was numb and exhausted. When her feet touched the ground, her knees buckled and her legs refused to hold her weight. Egan caught her beneath the arms and steadied her. Glenda murmured her thanks and made her way toward a tall stand of aspen. Beneath one of the trees, she lay down, curling her knees against her chest and pulling her mantle over her shoulders. Though hunger gnawed at her belly, she was too tired to care.

Exactly when Egan stretched out beside her, she never knew.

When next awareness struck, sunlight had vanquished the night's darkness. She knew it, for there was brightness against her closed eyelids.

She stirred, but it was so warm and cozy here, she had no desire to waken. Caught between the fringes of sleep and wakefulness, she cringed at the thought of riding yet another day. With a sigh she inched closer and burrowed against that cozy warmth, rubbing her cheek against the solid strength of a man's shoulder. She knew it instinctively, for the sheer bulk of the form beside her could only have been a man's, she decided hazily. Yet as the knowledge penetrated her tardy mind, she felt herself pause. A man's shoulder . . . ?

Ah, she realized sleepily, it was only Egan against whom she nestled.

Only Egan . . .

Chapter 4

The realization tumbled through her mind.

Her eyes flew open. In but a heartbeat, Glenda was fully awake. Yet somehow her body seemed frozen. She couldn't move. Could not even *think*.

Egan had turned his head ever so slightly.

Their eyes locked inevitably. Stunned, she couldn't move as his gaze roamed slowly over her face. Glenda felt her throat go dry, for it was in a way that made her feel as if he touched her . . .

Ah, but they were close, so very close that had she but lifted her head, their lips would have brushed. And it was there his gaze now dwelled.

Heat seemed to sizzle and pulse between them. Yet 'twas not a feeling akin to the sharing of warmth between them.

This was a heat of a far different sort.

Time stretched unending. Glenda's breath caught fast in her throat. She thought she would surely die of waiting, waiting for what might happen next . . .

In one swift move, Egan was up and on his feet. "The hour is late. We can ill afford to dawdle."

He extended a hand to assist her, and with that,

the moment vanished. Indeed, as she glanced at Egan again and again throughout the day, 'twas almost as if it had never happened. The cast of his profile was somber and remote, his manner almost formidable.

He had wanted to kiss her. She knew it, and she could think of little else. Ah, but she was no innocent maid who knew naught of the fire in men's eyes. She had been married, and not unchastely. Oh, aye, she could almost taste it . . . her thoughts meandered and she could not stop them. Would his kiss have been like the rest of him? Hard and strong . . . and cold? Nay, she thought. Not cold. Never cold. Somehow she knew it with all that she possessed.

He had wanted to kiss her.

Nay. The idea was preposterous. Impossible. She was mistaken. Why, that such a thing should ever cross his mind . . . for this was Egan—Egan, whom she'd known for many a year.

She could not forget. Her mind would not allow it. For he was the one who had pulled away. He . . . not she.

She churned inside just thinking of it. Dear God, what would she have done if he *had*? Would she have stopped him?

Near noonday, they stopped to water the horses. While they drank, Egan moved to the top of a small hillock. He stood for a moment, booted legs braced wide apart as he gazed back in the direction from whence they had come. Glenda knew he was looking for signs that they were being followed.

He returned a moment later. Glenda heard the crunch of gravel as he stepped beside her.

Wide golden eyes turned upon him. "Do you think we are safe yet?"

"There is no way of knowing for certain. They know not where we are headed, but I will not rest easy until you are behind the walls of Blackstone." His statement was as succinct as ever.

Glenda shivered, all at once reminded of Robin's mouth on hers, the way he'd jammed his leg between hers. If not for Egan, he might well have succeeded in his quest.

"I'm sorry, Egan. I truly did not wish to—to rob you of your pleasure with . . . with your lady."

Glenda heard his sharp intake of breath and sensed she'd startled him. In truth, she'd startled herself, for the confession tumbled unbidden from her lips.

"My lady," he repeated blankly. Then: "You mean Elfrida."

"Aye, the very one." She swallowed. "I must thank you," she said, her voice very low. "If you had not heard me—"

"I had already left her."

Her heart began to pound. The way he was looking at her . . . There was a smoldering in his eyes, some-thing she had never seen before this morn. Some-thing that made her tremble inside, something she was afraid to put a name to. Something that made her gaze slip away, only to return an instant later.

"What do you mean?"

"I had already left her in the hall."

"But . . . why? Why did you leave her? Robin said she—she gives her favors quite freely."

"That may well be true. But no matter, for I did not wish to partake."

He made the admission so readily, Glenda was stunned. Her gaze lowered. "But she is quite the beauty."

Egan neither agreed nor disagreed. Softly he said, "I had not the inclination. I am only sorry I was not there with you sooner. I can only assure you that it will never happen again."

Her eyes flashed back to his. "It was not your fault, Egan."

"And if I say it was?"

"You would be wrong. I am . . . beholden to you."

With an effort, she held his eyes. His gaze sharpened. This time . . . nay, this time she did not imagine that his gaze dwelled long and hard on her mouth.

Glenda was confused as never before. She'd been near him, aye, of a certainty! But now it was different. Different and . . . disturbing.

But all he said was, "We'd best be off."

Nay, she was not mistaken.

Over the next few days, Glenda was conscious of him in ways she'd never thought might happen. Their clothing had only to brush, and fire seemed to leap inside her. In their haste to leave Ragmoor, he'd forgotten the tent. Though he was always careful to put several yards between them at night, sleeping with him so near at hand, she was disturbingly aware of him as a man.

When it had happened, she knew not. She knew only that it was so, and there was naught she could do to stop it.

Early one morn, she tiptoed away from the place where they'd camped for the night. They were near the shore of a small loch, and Glenda found the lure of a bath, however brief it might be, irresistibly appealing. Now, in the hour just after dawn, nary a ripple marred the surface, dappled with a gossamer sheen of gold cast by the rising sun. Shedding her clothes, she waded into the loch.

She soon discovered that if she stayed where it was shallow, the water was not so cold that it was unbearable. The water had just reached her waist when a sound reached her ears. Glenda ducked into the water and snapped her head around, but it was only the shifting of leafy branches in the breeze. It felt heavenly to cleanse the dust from her body, and she dunked her head beneath the surface to rinse her hair.

It was with a wistful reluctance that she finally left the loch, but she was anxious to be finished before Egan arose. Goosebumps rose as the chill morning air met her wet, naked flesh. Shivering, she ran from the water to the place where she'd left her clothes hanging on the outstretched branches of a tree.

She was wholly unaware of the blue-eyed scrutiny that tracked her progress as she scampered from the loch. White limbs flashed as she reached for her linen smock. She did not know that Egan stood next to a willowy tree that lined the path to the loch.

He groaned inside for the temptation aroused by the sight of her. When he awoke to find her gone, he'd leaped to his feet with a curse. 'Twas then he'd heard the splash from the loch. On silent feet he ventured near, for by now he'd guessed what she was about. He'd arrived just in time to see her duck her head beneath the glimmering waters of the loch. Not wishing to disturb her, he had eased down to the soft, damp earth to wait while she finished her bath.

'Twas the fairest of mornings, with the sun turning shimmering pinwheels of light across a cloudless sky, and the loch sparkling like the brightest of sapphires, nestled between the shoulders of green-draped hillsides.

But no more fair than the sight before him now.

She had no cloth to dry herself, and so her skin dampened the linen smock she'd just donned. With the sun at her back, the light of day rendered the material almost sheer; clearly visible were the round circlets of her nipples standing high and taut with cold, tinted the deepest rose, the color of the dawn. Her legs were long and graceful, her buttocks deliciously curved as she bent and provided him with a view so enticing he could almost taste it.

It was willpower, sheer and simple, that kept him rooted to the spot. Indeed, 'twas all he could do to stop from surging to his feet. From striding to her and pulling her entire sweet length against him, capturing those lips that would part in soft surprise, only to feel her melt against him. To make her forever his, as he longed to . . .

But never would.

He should have looked away. Merciful heaven, if only he could! He should have allowed her her privacy. Mayhap this was God's way of punishing him, he acknowledged distantly, punishing him for wanting his friend's wife. For though his insides were twisted into a hundred knots, he could not look away.

She turned, only to stop short before even taking a single step.

"Egan." Her tone reflected a startled wariness. "What are you doing here?"

It was on the tip of his tongue to tell her that he could not protect her if he could not see her. Instead he said, "I awoke and you were gone. You should have told me where you were going." Somehow the admonishment held no sting.

With her fingertips, she smoothed the folds of her gown. Even from here he could see the faint distress in the depths of those golden eyes.

"How long have you been there?"

"Not long," he said smoothly. "Indeed, I have only just arrived."

It was a lie.

The most blatant lie he'd ever told. For in truth he'd been there long enough to know that his dreams had not lied. Just before her smock had dropped into place, he'd seen her . . . every inch of her. She was slender, yet supple and curved, with the ripe fullness of a woman, not a young girl. To Egan, she was the most beautiful creature imaginable. Gazing at the flatness of her belly and hips, it didn't seem possible that she'd once housed a child there.

Yet it was not as she thought. He'd never have forgiven himself if anything else happened to her. Though he'd not denied himself the vision of her loveliness, he hadn't meant to spy on her, and so he stated.

He both saw and heard the deep breath she took. "You've only arrived . . . just now?"

"Aye."

Her gaze faltered beneath the steadiness of his.

"Then why do you look at me so?" she asked, her
tone very low.

His heart skipped a beat, for she refused to look at
him. He knew then . . . she felt it, too . . . the pull between them.

It seemed she could control it no more than he.

Egan did not answer. Instead he tipped his head
toward the horses. "Come," he said. "We've not so
very far to travel now."

Glenda prayed that he was right, for in truth this
journey was the longest of her life.

Not only had he wanted to kiss her, but she was
very much afraid there was a goodly chance he had
seen her naked . . . *naked.*

By noon the next day they had entered the low
country, the Borders. Shafts of sunlight pierced the
clouds, spotlighting an endless sea of grassy hills that
swayed with the rhythm of the wind.

High atop a bluff, Glenda reined in Druscilla.
"Wait," she said. She raised a hand and pointed.

"There is Blackstone Tower. Do you see it, just beyond the bend in the river?"

For an instant Egan gazed down where the river
seamed the width of the valley. A stone bridge
stretched across its span, and he followed its course
as far as the eye could see. He caught just a glimpse
of a round stone tower.

"Tell me. Are these not the greenest hills you've
ever seen?"

There was a keen note of excitement in her voice
that hadn't been there before. Egan glanced at her.
"You're glad to be back, aren't you?"

"Aye. It seems I am. I hadn't realized it until now." She smiled, a smile she could not have withheld if she'd wanted to. Yet in the very next breath, a pang caught at her heart. It had been quite some years since she'd visited her father here—Niall had not been able to accompany her and she'd missed him dreadfully. With stark, vivid clarity, she recalled how she had vowed that the next time she returned to Blackstone, it would be with her husband.

Instead she was with Egan.

A trail wound down the hillside. Egan guided his stallion down. Glenda followed just behind. At the foot was a small wattle-and-daub cottage. But there was no door, and only the charred remnants of the thatched roof remained. A frown pleated Glenda's brow, but she said nothing.

Within the hour, they came upon another charred cottage, and within the next, still another. It was here that Glenda stopped and dismounted. Egan followed her into the hut, where weeds now poked through the dirt.

Outside in the sunlight Glenda shook her head. "Something is wrong, Egan. A man named Peter lived here with his wife and family, and his sister. She could not walk, and she often sat there." She pointed toward the door. "Papa and I would often bring honey." Her worried gaze met his. "What happened to him? To his family? Where did they go?"

"Perhaps he died and they moved elsewhere."

"Aye," Glenda said slowly. "That must be it." Yet her mind was buzzing with unanswered questions. He'd had four stout sons and a daughter several years younger than she; her name was Jeannine.

Where were they? Wouldn't at least one of them have remained with the land?

Their pace quickened as they pressed on. Glenda fought down her alarm, for there was something dreadfully wrong. She could feel it in her bones. For this was not the land she remembered. Many a field lay fallow. Many a garden was overgrown; many cottages were empty or burned—or both. And there was nary a soul outside the donjon, and there was no one in the guardroom inside the gatehouse.

Egan said nothing, but his mouth compressed tautly as they trotted beneath the towering arch. Glenda glimpsed an empty cart with a broken wheel that had been abandoned in the center of the inner bailey. Her breath hitched in shock, for Blackstone Tower was not teeming with life as she remembered . . . as it should have been.

It was then they spotted a man hidden in the shadows. He sat on a stool with his head tilted back against the stone wall. Lank, greasy locks plastered his forehead. His mouth was open and noisy snores emitted from his throat.

Egan dismounted. "You there!" He planted himself squarely before the guard, then poked him in the chest with a finger.

The man snored on, unmindful of his audience. Glenda would have laughed were it not for the awful feeling wedged tight in her chest, nor did Egan appear amused.

It took two more prods before one eye opened sleepily, then the other. He appeared dazed, then with a snort he jerked awake. His bloodshot eyes widened when he saw the dark giant towering above him.

"Who do ye be, then?" he gasped.

Egan stepped back, his expression distasteful. Even mounted atop Druscilla, Glenda could smell his sour breath.

"Your name, sir," came Egan's terse demand.

"I-I am Milburn. Who the devil are ye?"

"I am Egan. This is your mistress Glenda."

"Glenda," the man repeated dumbly. "But Glenda is the daughter of Royce." His gaze moved slowly to Glenda. "Are ye Glenda then?"

"Aye," Glenda said gently.

"But . . . what do ye here? Ye live in the Highlands now!"

"She is here because she is the mistress of Blackstone Tower!" Egan looked ready to explode. "Is there anyone in authority here?"

Milburn scratched his head. "I suppose 'twould be Bernard ye want."

"Fetch him for me then."

Milburn rose to his feet, grabbing at Egan's arm as he stumbled. Once upright, he swayed dizzily.

Egan's face was as black as a thundercloud. "When you're done fetching Bernard, go wash yourself of the stink of ale. And if you report to this post again when you are sotted, I vow you'll regret it most assuredly!"

Milburn thrust a wet lip out. "All right, then," he grumbled. "Have patience, man, have patience." He ambled toward the keep.

Egan's patience was clearly not in evidence just now. He helped Glenda down from Druscilla's back.

Together they advanced several steps into the bailey.

An old man descended the stairs of the keep, stooped nearly double with age. His pate was bald but for a few gray hairs standing on end.

"That is Bernard," Glenda said, "one of my father's men-at-arms. I did not know he was still alive."

When at last he stood before them, he looked Glenda up and down. "Saints!" he said loudly, "but ye look just like Glenda!"

"She *is* Glenda!"

The old man turned toward Egan. "What's that, laddie?"

Laddie. Never in her life had she heard anyone refer to Egan as *laddie*. Glenda laid a hand on his arm and spoke then. "Be tolerant, Egan. Methinks he cannot hear." She stepped close to Bernard and cupped her hand around his ear.

"You are right, Bernard. 'Tis I, Glenda."

"Glenda!" His eyes filled with tears. "Och, Glenda, but yer father died," he said mournfully. "And then yer Uncle Rowan. Now there is no one left."

"Oh, but there is, Bernard. I am here now." Her tone overly loud, she smiled at the old man, whose features were still awash in amazement. "Is Nessa still here?"

"Oh, aye, she is still here. She is there, within the hall." A bony finger pointed toward the keep.

Glenda squeezed his hands. "Thank you, Bernard." She nodded toward Egan. As they crossed the bailey and mounted the stairs into the keep, Glenda explained that Nessa had been nurse to her and her sister when they were children.

The inside of the hall was dimly lit by only a few

high, narrow windows set into the walls. The rushes on the floor smelled stale and moldy. Glenda did not hesitate, but stepped within.

"Nessa?" she called.

In the midst of throwing a handful of twigs onto the fire in the hearth, a figure stopped cold. Slowly the woman's head turned to view the newcomers. She straightened, yet even then she was nearly as stoop-shouldered as the old man Bernard.

She hobbled closer, assisted by the staff clutched in her other hand. As a beam of sunlight lanced through the window, the twigs dropped from her grasp, scattering upon the floor. "Mother Mary," came the rasping whisper, "never say 'tis you!"

Glenda smiled and held out her hands. "I am here, Nessa. I am here and—and this time I've returned for good!"

In but a heartbeat, the two were embracing. Egan stood awkwardly, feeling rather out of place. The old woman wiped tears from her eyes and finally drew back.

"And who have we here?" Egan could have sworn though a hundred lines scored her cheeks, her eyes and voice were surprisingly keen.

"This is Egan MacBain, Nessa. He escorted me from Dunthorpe."

Was it his imagination, or had Glenda's manner grown a trifle stiff? The old woman, Nessa, fixed her gaze upon him. Hair that had no doubt once been a bright red was now a wiry gray and covered with a wimple. Her frame was gaunt, skin stretched taut over bones. Yet though she gave the presence of frailty, her voice cracked like a whip.

"Safely, I presume?"

Glenda smiled slightly. "We are here, are we not?"

Egan had the feeling he'd just been weighed and measured—and judged decidedly lacking. The feeling was mutual, he decided darkly. Thus far, he'd yet to be impressed by anything he'd encountered here at Blackstone Tower.

Nessa turned back to Glenda. "I heard of Niall's death. And yer babe. I grieved for ye, child, losing both husband and son."

"Thank you, Nessa." Glenda's smile slipped a little.

"Come," Nessa said. "Sit." She drew Glenda to a wooden bench against the wall. She lowered her staff across her lap, but still clutched Glenda's hand. " 'Tis a poor welcome we give, I know. Bernard is half-blind and half-deaf. I am half-crippled, and a good many of the servants have fled." She held out her hands. Her knuckles were bony and misshapen. "I fear these old hands cannot do what they should."

" 'Tis no matter," Glenda said. "But tell me of Blackstone, Nessa. So much has changed since I was last here! Many of the cottages we passed had been abandoned or burned."

Nessa shook her head. "Much has changed indeed," she said sadly. "The Blackstone ye once knew is no more. Nay, this is not the place where ye grew to womanhood, child. The laughter has fled, along with many of its people."

"Tell me what happened, Nessa." This was something Glenda had not anticipated—had not even *begun* to anticipate.

"It began after yer father's death. All was well for

a time, but then yer Uncle Rowan began to sicken, much the same as your father had done. Little by little the keep has fallen into disrepair. The soldiers began to desert, and many families fled to the north."

Glenda could not hide her dismay. "Why did no one send word? If I had known—"

"Rowan would not allow it. He would not tell ye, for he would not burden ye with yet more heartache. He did what he could, but he was too ill to do more." Nessa folded her hands in her lap. "That is not all," she said after a moment.

"What? Tell me, Nessa." Glenda was determined that nothing be kept from her.

"This last year—och!—but it has been like a pestilence. A band of men have been terrorizing the countryside—no one knows when they will strike. They have trampled the crops, driven off cattle and oxen, rousted people from their huts. Sometimes weeks go by and nothing happens. Just when all begin to feel safe—that it is over—it begins anew."

Glenda was numb. "Who would do this? Do you know, Nessa?"

Nessa hesitated. "No one knows for certain, for oft they strike at night, when it's too dark to see them clearly. Even if they did, they hide their faces with cloth."

Egan's eyes narrowed. He had listened intently to all that Nessa related. "Someone must have *some* idea," he injected.

Nessa's lips pressed together. At first he thought she would refuse to comment. Then she said finally, "There is talk," she admitted, "that Simon is responsible."

Glenda's brows drew together. "Simon Ruthven?"

"Aye," Nessa confirmed. "Some call him Simon the Lawless behind his back. Even before his father died, he was always one to do as he pleased with no regard for anyone but himself. Indeed, I know not a man who would dare say such a thing to his face! Nay, no one dares speak out against him, for fear of being retaliated against."

Egan's eyes had narrowed. "Who is he, this Simon Ruthven?"

It was Glenda who answered. "He is an English baron with lands across the river."

"England lies just across the river?"

"Aye. The lands of Blackstone Tower run to the north of it, Simon's to the south."

Her use of Simon's given name was not lost on Egan. "You know him well then?"

"Nay, not well. We are of an age together, and I knew him when we were young, but . . . that is all."

"Do you think him capable of such atrocities as Nessa has told of?"

"In truth I could not say either way! I've not seen him for many years. He was at the English court when I married Niall."

Immersed in thought, Egan rubbed a hand against his jaw. "Perhaps 'tis possible he wants more lands."

Nessa made a sound of disgust. "He already has lands aplenty and wealth aplenty. Far more, I daresay, than Blackstone has ever had. I know not why he would want more. I know only that while it is mischief that is sowed, 'tis heartache that is reaped."

"Then perhaps 'tis a case of ill will. Perhaps he bears some malice against your father or your uncle."

Nessa snorted, a distinctly unladylike sound. "There is no malice against either Royce or Rowan," she stated flatly. "Whether it is Simon the Lawless or another who preys on the people of Blackstone, 'tis the way of men to covet what is not theirs, to ever covet more! 'Tis their nature, just as it is oft their nature to be evil and mean-spirited toward any and all!"

Egan raised a brow. "Have you a husband, Nessa?" he asked pleasantly.

"Nay!" That single word was as gritty as stone scraping against glass.

"I thought not."

Nessa's dark eyes blazed. "Why, of all the arrogant . . . I can see ye're a Highlander to the bone—"

What else she might have said was cut short, for Glenda's gaze had traversed beyond Egan's broad shoulders. Glenda rose to her feet. Nessa turned to see what had captured her attention.

The old woman raised a gnarled hand and beckoned the newcomer forward. "Come, Jeannine. Come, girl."

"Jeannine! Oh, I knew it!" Glenda exclaimed. "The man whose cottage we passed—Peter," she explained to Egan. "The daughter I spoke of. This is she. This is Jeannine."

Jeannine had slowly crossed the rushes to stand before them. She was shorter than Glenda but heavier through the hips and shoulders. Golden brown hair was tucked beneath her wimple. Cradled in one elbow was a small bundle.

Glenda would have thrown her arms around the other woman, but something stopped her. At the last instant she realized there was no flare of recognition in Jeannine's large dark eyes.

"Hello, Jeannine," she said quietly. "I am Glenda, daughter of Royce. Do you remember me? My father and I often visited your cottage when you were younger."

Jeannine shook her head, her manner reticent.

Glenda advanced a step closer. Her gaze dropped to the bundle Jeannine held. The ache in her heart was swiftly banished. "You have a bairn, I see."

"Aye." Jeannine brightened. "Would ye like to see him? His name is Thomas. He greatly resembles his da." With her free hand she parted the swaddling. Glenda stepped close, thinking to admire the babe.

There was no babe.

Puzzled, she lifted her eyes to Jeannine, whose expression told her she awaited her reaction. Glenda gave a tiny shake of her head. "Jeannine," she began, only to stop short. Her gaze chanced to alight on Nessa, who was shaking her head adamantly and holding a finger to her lips.

Though she did not understand why, Glenda realized she was to say nothing.

"A handsome lad, is he not? Just like his da."

Glenda smiled. "Just like his da," she echoed.

Jeannine beamed.

Minutes later, when Jeannine was gone, Nessa explained. "Once the trouble started, Peter and his boys were among the first to leave. Jeannine stayed behind, for she and Colin had just been wed." Nessa's tone grew heavy. "Colin and their babe were killed in a raid last harvest. Since that time, Jeannine is . . . different. She will not speak of their deaths. Once I tried to speak with her about it, to ask why she will not accept that they are dead. Others have tried as well." Nessa's stooped shoulders lifted. "She cried so long and so hard I feared she might well perish herself! And now, should anyone mention it, 'tis like she does not hear . . . *will* not hear. She carries the swaddling in her elbow always; always she talks to it, sleeps with it close to her side, as if her bairn were still cradled within. There are many who jeer at her and call her daft, but I could never be so cruel."

Glenda's eyes were drawn to the corner where Jeannine now sat, crooning to her bundle. She couldn't help but wonder why Jeannine refused to accept the truth . . . Was it easier to simply believe that husband and child still lived? Something twisted inside her, for her heart well knew the ache wrought by a pair of empty arms.

Their meal that night was a meager one—boiled turnips, day-old bread, cheese, and watered-down ale. The table was lit by a few stubs of tallow candles. Glenda made a note to check the castle stores the next day.

Under Glenda's direction, several bedchambers in the east wing had been prepared. One was the chamber Glenda had always occupied; the other was several doors away, the lord's bedchamber. The bed there was comfortable and large, and would suit Egan's big frame. Besides, she told herself, it was just for one night.

Egan nodded his satisfaction, and Glenda started toward the door, only to turn back.

Shaggy black brows arose. "Is there something you would like to discuss with me?"

"Aye, there is." His invitation was just what she needed, yet somehow the words she sought eluded her.

"Then do not be reticent. We've known each other for years now. There should be no secrets between us."

"And indeed 'twould seem there are none." At last she drew upon some wellspring of courage inside her. "I must know, Egan. That morning at the loch. You—you saw me, didn't you?"

"The loch? I know not what you mean." He chose to deliberately misunderstand. Even as he regarded her with a decided gleam in his eyes, she fixed him with a glare.

"I think you do. You saw me"—she floundered—"you saw me . . ."

"Naked?"

"Oh, God." She looked away. The breath she drew was deep and ragged. "You did, didn't you?"

Her dismay made the veriest smile curl his lips. "What if I did? Is that so terrible?"

Her eyes swung back to him. "You said you did not!"

"Nay." His tone was smooth. "I told you I had only just arrived." His eyes snared hers. "Would that I could see you so again," he said softly.

Glenda felt her face grow hot. "Do not say such things!"

"Why not?"

"Because it is wrong."

"Why is it wrong?" His smile vanished. "You are free," he pointed out. "So am I."

"I am not free. I am . . ." She stopped short.

"A widow," he finished for her. "You are no longer married, Glenda."

"Oh, but I am. I am wed in my heart as surely as the day I left here a bride. And that is all that matters." If she was deliberately cruel, she couldn't help it. Whatever it was that was happening between them, it must end!

Only now it was his turn to be deliberately cruel. "Is it? I find I am curious, Glenda. You and Niall were wed for many years, and now that he is gone, surely the nights are endless. Do you not feel very alone?"

Glenda started. What was this? How could he know the heartache she felt without Niall? The way the nights stretched long and lonely and empty—especially those nights since Daniel's wedding. For the space of a heartbeat, it was as if he delved deep inside her mind, her very heart.

She drew herself up to her full height. "What would you know of it? You are not married."

"Nay, I am not. But that does not mean I will never wed. That does not mean I don't harbor the same desires as other men."

Glenda's chin came up. "Aye, I know about men's desire," she said stiffly. "I know about *your* desires. Indeed, we *have* known each other for many years. And in those years, you've hardly led a celibate life, have you?" She tapped a finger against her lips and pretended to consider. "Ah, I have it! I believe Anna was the first I knew of. Then there was Mary, and Louise—she was madly in love with you, you know. Ah, and the most recent . . . Patsy. You were with her the night of Daniel's wedding, were you not?"

Egan's teeth came together hard. He stared at her, wondering how the devil he was supposed to respond. He disliked knowing that she was aware he'd been with other women. God's teeth, but it made no sense that he should feel guilty! He owed her no loyalty. He owed her nothing, for she had been another man's wife.

Not his.

Nay, he'd not been celibate. But if he had not, it was because he'd had to find a way to somehow forget about *her*—if only for a time! But he couldn't tell her that! Instead he said only, "I am not a monk, nor did I ever pretend to be."

The sound she made low in her throat made it abundantly clear she quite agreed. With a swirl of her skirts, she whirled and started toward the oaken door.

Egan was already there, planted squarely before her. "Do not be so hasty, lass. It occurs to me perhaps we should settle this."

Glenda looked from him to the door. "What are you doing, Egan?"

"Ah, I think you know very well what I'm doing." Softly, deliberately, he said, "There is much between us. Perhaps we should tend to it here and now."

Panic wedged deep in her breast.

"There is nothing between us." Her gaze flitted away. Her voice sounded nothing at all like her own. She had to force the words past the dryness in her throat. "I feel nothing for you, Egan, save what I have ever felt these many years."

"And what is that? I confess, I'm eager to hear."

His directness took her by surprise. From somewhere she summoned the courage to meet his gaze anew. "I—I admired you," she stated without thinking.

His eyes began to gleam. "Ah. So you admired me."

Oh, how dare he appear so pleased! "Not in that way!"

"In what way then?" He remained undaunted.

Not so with Glenda. "You—you are a man of honor. A man of pride and respect, of strength and valor. I-I admired that," she said breathlessly. "Indeed, I still do."

"And that is all?"

Her pulse skidded. In truth, she'd revealed far more than she'd meant to. "Aye," she said unsteadily, somehow managing to sound more desperate than forceful. "What more did you expect?"

He did not answer, not directly. "This journey," he said softly. "The two of us alone"—he shook his head—" 'tis not the same as before, Glenda."

There was that in his tone which made her heart begin to hammer . . . that . . . and the way he looked at her.

"I know not what you mean." Her mouth was so dry she could barely speak.

"And I think you do. I know you fight it, lass. Indeed, I have fought it, too."

Damn him, she thought. Damn him! He was so sure of himself, while she felt scattered to the winds of a storm. Nor could she meet his eyes any longer. The air was suddenly close and heated and intense. *He* was so intense. Her gaze slipped to his mouth . . . ah, dangerous territory, that! Her regard finally settled on the bronzed column of his throat.

"You are wrong, Egan. There is nothing between us." She despised herself, for now her denial was even weaker than before.

He stepped close, so close her breasts brushed the front of his tunic. "Of a sudden you are reluctant to look me in the eye," he observed. "Indeed, if that is true, then look me in the eye and tell me so."

Egan saw the way she swallowed, sensed her struggle as she finally lifted her gaze. And as their eyes tangled, he saw the leap of fear, heard the labor of her breath, felt the rise and fall of her breasts . . . and knew her anxious panic.

Dear God, was he elated? Or as terrified as she was?

For Egan had just discovered that she could not tell him, *would* not tell him . . . for it was not true. He'd wondered if she felt what he did, and now he knew. Oh, she could talk of honor and respect and admiration, but he was not fooled. She'd not be so skittish if there was nothing, as she claimed so righteously.

It was too soon. Deep in his soul, he knew it. But if he could not have her lips, he would at least have this. He raised a hand, intending to trace the delicate line of her mouth, just for an instant.

Her lashes fell, hiding from him what he craved so desperately. She turned her head away in the heart-beat before he would have touched her.

"Do not, Egan. I beg of you, do not."

Her voice was so low he had to strain to catch the words. Her plea hung between them, like stale smoke in the air.

Egan's hand dropped slowly to his side. He stared at her, while she stared into the shadows across the room. Time stretched into eternity. Neither of them moved.

It was Glenda who broke the tense, ringing silence. "I'll see that there is food ready when you leave in the morn."

His jaw tensed. "I'll not be leaving."

Her eyes flashed to his. "I beg your pardon?"

"I'll not be leaving in the morn," he reiterated coolly.

A moment's hesitation. Though spite was not his way, a part of him relished her uncertainty.

"What," she said faintly. "The next day, then?"

"Nay. Not then or the day after, or even the day after that."

His coolness rekindled her fire. "Explain yourself, if you please."

"Certainly. Cameron charged me with your care— with your protection—and I will see to it."

"There is no need."

"There is every need, since I was—"

"Aye, I know! Charged with my care! But I now discharge you of that obligation."

"My obligation was to Cameron, not you, Glenda. Even were it not so, I have an obligation to myself to see that you are safe."

"I *am* quite safe, and I am hardly alone. I have Bernard and Milburn, and Nessa and Jeannine."

"Nonetheless, I am staying."

Her mouth opened and closed. Egan was not about to back down, and perhaps she knew it. Still, it seemed she would have the last word.

"One night, Egan. You may stay this one night, and that is all."

She swept past him with nary a glance, the set of her small shoulders stiff with proud defiance. Egan waited until the echo of her footsteps had faded, then finally moved to close the door.

Did she truly think he would leave her in this place, such as it was? Why, the very idea was laughable!

I have Bernard and Milburn, and Nessa and Jeannine.

Egan shook his head in amazement. Did she really believe those four would insure her safety? A woman who was half crippled and another who was daft! A man who was half-blind and half-deaf and would not hear if an entire army crashed through the gates—and another who apparently was as fond of bathing in his ale as drinking it!

And did she truly think there was nothing between them?

He could not help but shake his head in disbelief. *We shall see, sweet lady,* he thought to himself. *We shall see.*

Chapter 5

As luck would have it, Egan was one of the first ones Glenda encountered when she ventured into the bailey the next morning. He stood just outside the stables talking to Milburn, who was mounted atop a gray gelding. Glenda could see that he was much more alert than he'd been yesterday when they arrived.

There were several large pouches looped across his saddle. She couldn't help but remember last eve, when she'd told Egan she would have food readied for his journey . . . but it appeared as if Milburn was the one prepared for a journey, not Egan . . .

Even as she watched, Egan said something to Milburn. Milburn squared his shoulders; his chest seemed to puff out. He gave a nod, wheeled the gelding, and galloped across the bailey toward the gate.

A frown pleated her brow. With a whirl of dust in his wake, he disappeared beneath the shadows of the gatehouse. Where was he going, she wondered, and what was it that he and Egan had been discussing so earnestly?

Her gaze slid back to Egan. If she could have

turned and scurried back into the keep, she would have, for he had seen her and was striding toward her. Glenda remained where she was. All at once her pulse was suddenly thudding.

"Good morning to you, Glenda." His greeting was calm, his gaze unerringly direct.

She found it rather irksome that he appeared so well rested and at ease. She, on the other hand, had hardy slept a wink. Her mind was amuddle . . . and all because of him!

Her fingers curled into her palms. Somewhere she found the courage to meet and match his ease of manner. "Good morning to you, Egan." She tipped her head toward the gatehouse. "That was Milburn, wasn't it?"

"It was."

"Ah. And where is he off to?"

"To Dunthorpe."

"To Dunthorpe!" Glenda's eyes narrowed suspiciously. "Whatever for?"

"To deliver a message."

"And may I be privy to this message?"

Her arch tone was not lost on him. He inclined his head, his features cool. "Indeed you may. I've informed Cameron that I intend to remain here at Blackstone indefinitely."

Glenda's temper began to simmer. "I thought we settled this last eve, Egan."

"We did not."

She glared at him. "Your behavior is most audacious."

"No doubt it is"—he startled her with his agreement—"but I have good reason. I would not leave any woman here under these circumstances."

"I meant what I said last night. There is no need for you to remain."

"Is it pride, or stubbornness, which lies behind your refusal? A little of both, methinks. And something else, too, I vow." His regard was steady. "Why are you so afraid of me, Glenda?"

"I am not!" Yet her heart began to thud almost wildly in her chest. It wasn't him, she told herself. It was *her*. The way he made her feel, so out of control, so unlike herself.

"Then why are you so set against it? So set against me? Is it because of last night?" A brow arched high. A smile curled his lips, a smile she suspected was rooted in lazy amusement. "Need I remind you that nothing happened?"

Glenda felt her entire body go hot, and it was not from the warmth of the spring sun beating down. "Of a certainty it didn't," she snapped, "so do not make sport of me, Egan MacBain. My father is gone. My uncle is gone. These are my people now, and I must set things to right here."

His smile was no more. "As well you should," he said almost grimly. "Still, there are some things which cannot be done alone. I pray you will not let your emotion sway your good judgment."

"You seem convinced I have no good judgment!"

"If I gave you that impression, I am heartily sorry, for in truth I do not know any woman more capable than you. Yet if someone is driving your people from their homes—burning them out—you cannot ignore it. *I* cannot ignore it. What of the castle's defense? What if someone should attack the keep itself? Your men-at-arms I can count on the fingers of one hand. And if it's true that Simon Ruthven is a lawless man, then it may well take a lawless man to bring him to heel."

"And you think you are that man?"

"Mayhap I am."

His tone had turned as hard as his gaze. "I meant no affront to your manhood," she said stiffly. Sweet heaven, never that. She eyed his lean, powerful form, the depth and broadness of his chest, the power of his legs as he stood with booted feet slightly apart. The sun turning his eyes to a silvery-blue hue nearly took her breath away. The planes of his cheeks and jaw were deeply bronzed, and the breeze lifted a black lock of hair from his forehead. All she could think was that she'd never seen him look quite so handsome as he did at this moment.

Everything inside her churned. She was wrong. She *was* afraid of him. What was she to do? she thought almost desperately. God help her, what was she to do?

Exactly what he said, a voice inside her prodded. She must be rational. She could not be a fool. She could not gamble with others' lives. She must put her feelings for him aside . . . she caught herself just in time.

What madness was this? Her feelings for him . . . she *had* no feelings for him save what she'd stated last night! This was Egan. Above all, she must ever bear that in mind . . .

This was Egan.

Dear God, how could she forget? And why was this decision so hard, when it should have been so easy?

She twisted her fingers in her skirts. "This is my home," she said, her voice very low, "not yours. The duty is hardly yours."

His gaze seemed to sharpen. "I am well aware of that, Glenda. Be assured, I have no intention of wresting control from you."

For the longest time she said nothing, aware that he watched her. Then: "How long will you stay?"

"As long as it takes. No more, no less." His inflection, like his features, was impassive.

Glenda nodded. When he had gone, she let out a long, uneven breath. She had denied that anything was happening between them. Indeed, she told herself, she would not allow it . . .

Yet she was very much afraid it was already too late.

By the end of the day, Glenda's head ached abominably. She spent the day inspecting every inch of the castle. Though she would never have admitted it to anyone, she was disheartened by all she found over the next few days. The castle stores were vastly depleted—whether from careless waste or sheer inattentiveness, she knew not, though she suspected the latter. In truth, it didn't matter either way. She must hope that the year's harvest would be a fruitful one, that provisions for the winter ahead could be acquired.

Nor was that the only worry. There were numerous repairs to be made. Egan had found several gaping holes in the castle walls and places where the stone had crumbled and fallen. The timbers that supported the rooms in the north tower were rotting and required replacement. And Egan was right. Black-stone Tower's defenses were deplorable.

It was Egan who found a mason to begin repairs. Their meals over the next few days were far better than the first as well. She suspected it was Egan who had gone out hunting, but he did not say, and Glenda did not ask. It was as if she'd convinced herself that the less she acknowledged him, the easier it would be to disavow his existence.

If only it were so easy.

Several days later, Simon Ruthven arrived just before the evening meal. Egan didn't know what he'd expected, but it was not the tall fair-haired man who strode into the hall. He carried himself with the graceful, commanding air of a man who was confident of himself in all things. Clothing of deep, rich burgundy complemented the gold of his hair. His eyes were the color of jade. Full lips smiled beneath a long, well-shaped nose that had clearly never sustained damage from the brunt of another man's knuckles. He was, Egan knew, the kind of man that women whispered about in hushed excitement, each longing to be his chosen one . . . the kind of man that he—Egan—was not.

He gritted his teeth. Glenda had crossed to the newcomer. The top of her head barely reached Simon's chin. Rosy lips were curved in a smile that Egan had seen but seldom these past few years. His only satisfaction came when Nessa curled her lips and declared her intention to take her meal elsewhere. He inclined his head in polite acknowledgment when Glenda introduced him. Simon deemed him unworthy of further attention by turning back to Glenda.

"Will you sup with us?" she asked.

"Dearest lady, I would be honored."

These past days, Egan had heard much of Simon Ruthven—none of which had been flattering. He'd been anxious to meet the Englishman face-to-face; indeed, he'd chafed when he'd learned Simon was away. Yet now that Simon was here at Blackstone, Egan found himself wishing Glenda would toss the bastard out on his ear! Still, he was well aware what must be done. He must put his feelings aside, put his annoyance aside and use the opportunity to watch and learn.

"You must forgive my tardiness in welcoming you back to Blackstone Tower," Simon was saying. "I have been in London and have only just returned. Have you ever been there?" He reached out and plucked a fat goose leg from a platter.

"To London? Nay." Glenda shook her head, her tone wistful. " 'Tis a long way from the Highlands?"

"The Highlands. Lord God, but I must tell you, Glenda—you look exactly the same as when you left here so many years ago to wed your Highlander . . . what was his name?"

A split second passed before she spoke. "Niall. His name was Niall."

"Niall! Ah, yes, that's right. I had heard of your loss, but I must know. Have you children?"

Her eyes darkened. The smile faded. Wordlessly she shook her head. She did not elaborate.

Egan took subtle note. After all this time, it was still difficult for her to speak of the bairn she'd lost.

Indeed, he'd never heard her speak of it, at least, not to him. The day was branded forever in his mind—the day when the heads of Niall and his father Ronald had been delivered to Dunthorpe. 'Twas a sight that sent many a man to his knees, sickened and retching. The shock had sent Glenda, heavy with Niall's babe, into labor.

Born too early, her son had survived but a few pitiful minutes.

That had been nearly three years ago. Perhaps, being a man, in particular a man who had never fathered a child—at least that he knew of—Egan could not fully comprehend her difficulty. Was it truly still so very painful?

The thought was cut abruptly short as Simon's hand came out to cover hers. "I, too, have seen the loss of one dear to my heart."

Egan curled and uncurled his fingers. He longed to leap across the table and rip out Simon's throat with his bare hands.

"Ah, yes. Your wife. I'd heard. How awful for you to have lost her during your first year of marriage." Glenda eased her hand from beneath his and reached for the ewer of wine. "More wine, Simon?"

"Yes, if you please."

In order to fill his goblet, Glenda had to lean forward slightly. Egan didn't miss the way Simon's gaze wandered lustfully down the arch of her throat, boldly evaluating the swell of her breasts beneath her gown.

When she was done, he murmured his thanks and glanced at Egan. "And what of you? Do you have lands in the Highlands?"

"Nay."

"A farm then?"

Did Simon intentionally belittle him? Egan would have given anything to strangle him then and there. "I know naught of farming," he said without thinking. He groped for something more to add, feeling very much the fool.

It was Glenda who said, "Egan lends his sword to the clan MacKay. Indeed, he is my brother-in-law Cameron's most trusted warrior, as well as his friend."

"A pity then, that he couldn't have saved your husband and his family."

Every muscle in Egan's body went taut. Did this bastard somehow know of the guilt that consumed him in those days that followed the massacre of the MacKays by the Munroes? He had agonized endlessly—at times he still did! Over and over he'd wondered . . . would the outcome have been the same if he had been there? Could he have saved Niall and the others?

He had to force himself to relax. "I do hope you meant no insult."

For an instant the air seemed charged with a pent-up tension. Then those perfectly arched golden brows shot high. Simon began to laugh. "Good God!" he erupted. "No need to be so defensive, man, or you'll have me believing it's true the Highlanders have the devil's own temper. 'Twas an idle remark, meant as neither insult nor challenge, I assure you."

Never had a meal progressed so slowly. Egan was smoldering inside. Was Glenda taken in by the Englishman's demeanor? Simon was strikingly handsome, but it wasn't just his god-like golden looks. His speech was cultured, glib and facile; he was well-mannered and well-dressed. Next to Simon Ruthven, Egan felt the lowliest churl.

"I have a question for you, Simon. Upon my arrival, I learned that Blackstone has seen troubled times aplenty since my father died and my uncle sickened."

Egan sucked in a breath, caught wholly off guard by Glenda's words. What in God's teeth was she doing? Surely she didn't mean to confront Simon with the rumors! Faith, but he could have throttled her. He would have warned her with a glance, but she had focused her attention wholly on Simon.

"Indeed—" calmly she folded her hands atop the table—"there have been nighttime raids on some of Blackstone's people."

Simon nodded. "So I'd heard! What blackguards, to attempt to roust those poor people from their homes."

Both Egan and Glenda gauged Simon's reaction closely, but the Englishman was completely composed.

Glenda's lips curved into a smile. "Can you imagine?" she said lightly. "Why, I've heard tell that even your name has been bandied about as the one responsible."

"No doubt because my own lands and tenants have not been harmed." Simon was as smooth as ever. "I've been lucky, it seems." He gazed at Glenda levelly. "Blackstone's lands are valuable. You must guard them well."

Egan's gaze narrowed. He had the feeling that

Simon was a man who coveted Blackstone . . . *and* its mistress.

"But the hour grows late," Simon was saying. "I've extended my welcome long enough."

Indeed, he never *was* welcome, Egan decided blackly. He rose as well, but kept his distance from the pair as they advanced toward the tall, carved doorway. He didn't want to make his presence too obvious, yet he was reluctant to leave Glenda alone with this man.

Simon raised a hand. "Egan, may you have a safe journey back to the Highlands."

For the first time since Simon Ruthven had entered the hall, Egan's smile was one of genuine pleasure. "I fear it won't be a journey I'll be making soon. Glenda has asked that I stay on and assist her with matters here for a while."

Did he imagine it—or did those pretty lips curl into a sneer that was swiftly masked? Nor did Glenda deny it—which pleased him even more.

" 'Tis good that you are here, then," Simon acknowledged. To Glenda he said, "However, since Egan here is not so fond of farming, I am only too happy to offer my assistance, should you need it."

Surely no smile had ever been as short-lived as the one that rimmed Egan's lips. With an effort he caught hold of his anger.

Simon had reached for Glenda's hand. "I trust we'll meet again soon."

"No doubt we will."

"I will look forward to the day, then. For now I bid you good-night." He raised Glenda's hand to his lips, then strode from the hall. Egan cursed to himself foully. No doubt the scoundrel was gloating at his triumph!

Glenda watched him disappear into the shadows, then turned. She jumped when she discovered Egan there before her. How the devil had he moved so silently and so quickly?

"Do not be alone with that man."

His tone was almost deadly quiet, yet within was an imperious note she found vastly irritating. Her reply was as blunt as his.

"I am not a child to be told what I can and cannot do."

His eyes flickered. Almost casually, he said, "When you leaned forward to pour his wine, he was staring at your breasts."

"What!" Glenda couldn't believe her ears.

"Aye, he was staring at your breasts. Quite lustfully."

"And you have *seen* my breasts!" Not until the words issued forth did Glenda realize what she'd blurted out.

"Aye," came his tight-lipped response. "Your breasts, and far more."

Such frankness made her gasp. "Egan, stop! Why do you persist in saying things you should not?"

"Things I should not? Mayhap you should expect it, for am I not a clod from the Highlands?"

Glenda blinked. Something flared high and bright in his eyes. Her mind was suddenly buzzing. 'Twas so quickly there, so quickly gone. Was he jealous? Nay. Surely not.

"Nonetheless, I must ask that you heed me in this, for you were entrusted to my care."

"Entrusted to your care! Egan, I am a woman full-grown—"

"As Simon can surely attest to. But I have seen you naked and did nothing. He might not be so generous, so do not trust him. And while I admire your daring, I must also warn you to guard your tongue when speaking of these raiders. 'Tis never wise to provoke a man unless you are prepared for the consequences. In short, you need no enemies."

Glenda expelled a sound of sheer frustration. He could state that he admired her in one instant, then berate her in the next? "Egan, you speak in riddles! You tell me not to trust him, and then you tell me not to make an enemy of him!"

"All I mean is this—do not test him, Glenda. He covets you. He may well covet Blackstone, but Blackstone has neither the men nor the provisions to handle a full-blown assault."

He was somberly intent. Her ire was no longer so ripe. For the first time, she began to truly grasp the gravity of the situation. Egan was right to warn her to be wary. There could be no open accusations without proof.

Despite Egan's observation, she could fault neither Simon's manner nor his speech. Yet when Simon had kissed her hand, she had longed to snatch it back and scrub it clean.

Her mind traveled back to the days of their youth. She hadn't known Simon particularly well; indeed, she hadn't wanted to, for on those occasions when she was with him, he'd struck her as a greedy sort of lad.

A prickle of unease trickled down her spine.

"You're right," she admitted slowly. "I will not be so careless again. And—I will be wary."

Chapter 6

Seeing Simon that day somehow solidified something deep within Glenda. She was all the more determined to restore Blackstone to its former state of prosperity. It was a daunting task, and of a certainty she was not about to give up.

The next day she pored over the accounts anew, flipping the parchment pages over and over as if it would somehow change the neatly etched letters and numerals there. She couldn't help but drop her quill in mute despair. There had been some coin locked away in the small chest used by her father and uncle; the contents of the storeroom was meager. The overlord here in this part of the Borders was the Earl of Whitley; he held lands both in Scotland and England, including those across the river. It was through the Earl that her family held charter to Blackstone, since the early 1100s. Simon held his lands through the earl as well.

But rents were due to the earl in just over a fortnight. The earl's men would be making the rounds and expecting payment and goods, of which, in either case, there was precious little.

There had to be a way through this, she told herself, but what? She prayed that night for a solution, but decided to say nothing to Egan about the rents. This was her burden, not his.

Just then there was a knock on the door of the solar. Jeannine opened it a crack. "My lady," she said, "there is someone here to see you."

Before Glenda could ask who it was, a peremptory hand pushed open the door. "Is she in there?" came an impatient male voice. A tall male figure brushed by Jeannine and stepped boldly within. "Ah, there you are, Glenda."

It was Simon.

"Good day, Simon." She remained where she was behind the table. Deliberately she smiled at Jeannine. "Thank you, Jeannine."

Jeannine gave a slight nod. Glenda made note of the way her eyes lowered immediately as she flattened her back against the door when Simon stepped past, lest he touch her.

As the door swung closed, Simon's lips carried a curl of distaste. "There is no babe in that swaddling."

Glenda's spine stiffened. "Nay," she confirmed.

"Then why does she persist in carrying it?"

Glenda wasn't particularly obliged to be gracious, but Egan's warning not to provoke him rang in her head.

"She lost her babe, and still misses him greatly."

"In the village they call her daft."

And in the village they call you "Simon the Lawless." The retort hovered on the tip of her tongue.

"She does no harm to anyone."

"I do not know how you abide having her about,

but no matter. I've come to let you know that I've given orders for a half-dozen of my men to patrol your lands each night. If I have aught to say about it, we will find the rogues responsible for your people's ills."

Glenda chose her words carefully. "Simon, that is not necessary."

"Of course it is. Why, I insist! We are neighbors, are we not? We must help each other as we can." He smiled. "I do hope you will feel safer."

It seemed her hands were tied. How could she refuse without appearing ungrateful? "Then I must thank you, Simon." She hoped he would not notice her reluctance.

Glenda was relieved that his visit was not so lengthy as his first. She didn't see Jeannine again until the evening meal, when she filled their cups with ale.

Egan crossed his legs at the ankle and leaned back. "How is your young one today, Jeannine?" he asked pleasantly.

Jeannine's dark eyes brightened as always upon such inquiry. She pressed a finger to her lips. "Sleeping quite soundly, my lord," she whispered.

Egan lowered his voice. "And it wouldn't do to wake him at such a late hour, would it?"

Glenda's mind sped straight to Simon's unkind words this afternoon. Thus far, she had yet to witness Egan issue even a single criticism of odd behavior. His manner had always been gentle and considerate. If she compared the two men, she could not help it.

Almost as if he'd known what she was thinking, Egan swung his attention to her. "I understand

Simon was here today." Little did she realize his jealousy was carefully guarded.

Glenda nodded. "He informed me he's sending some men out to find those responsible for plundering Blackstone lands."

Egan's features blackened. "Ah, but I should have expected it! How clever! Now his men have an excuse to be about at night." His lips thinned in self-deprecation. "Damn, if we but had the men to spare, I would have already seen to it myself!"

Glenda's reaction had been much the same. Yet it struck her how easily "we" had sprang to his lips. Should she be offended? Dismayed? Somehow, she was neither.

"You were not alone with him, were you?"

Glenda fought the impulse to squirm in her chair. "Nay," she lied, then wondered why she did so. It was just as she'd told him last eve—she was not a child to whom he could dictate.

Luckily, he questioned her no more.

Glenda's sleep that night was troubled, her mind fraught with worry. Should she have told Egan about the Earl's rents? Nay, she decided. When she had resolved to resume her life here at Blackstone Tower, she had known there might be difficult times ahead. She must be strong. Resourceful. Somehow she would find a way to pay the earl his due.

She woke at dawn the next morning. Though the hills were still shrouded in brooding mist, she ordered Druscilla saddled. She was restless and felt the need to be alone to think.

The land had just begun to stretch and yawn when

she headed back toward Blackstone Tower. There were shouts in the fields. Cattle lowed.

The sun was just breaking through the haze when she started to pass by a small cottage tucked into the hillside near the apple orchard. Outside were a shaggy-haired man, a woman, and three young children clustered around a small cart. Their features were shadowed and bleak. A funny feeling crowded her chest as the man heaved a sack into the cart and stuffed it beneath the legs of a chair. Was this yet another family packing their belongings and leaving? She whirled Druscilla and headed toward the hut.

They all looked up at the sound of hoofbeats. Glenda didn't imagine the fear that flashed across their faces until they saw it was a woman who approached. Still, the woman gathered the children close to her skirts. They stared at her with wide and wary eyes.

"Good day," she called as she reined Druscilla to a halt. "I am Glenda of Blackstone Tower."

The man swept his cap from his head to his chest. "Mistress. I am Buford. This is my wife Analise and our children."

Her smile encompassed all of them. "You are awake early this morn."

There was a slight hesitation, then he said, "Aye. We've a long journey ahead of us."

"I see. And where does your journey take you?"

"To Perth, mistress."

"I see. And when will you and your family return?"

A flush crept into Buford's thin cheeks. "We will

not, mistress. I am a freeman, and you cannot stop us."

"Indeed," Glenda said quietly. "May I ask why you're leaving?"

Buford and his wife exchanged glances.

"Do not be afraid to speak, Buford. I've only just returned from the Highlands, but I've heard tales of the raiders that plague our tenants. Is that why?"

"Aye," he said. "I fear we have no choice." He swept his hand toward a small patch of land that sloped beyond a crude pole fence. "Mistress, we have plowed and seeded. Our crops began to sprout and we thought 'twould be a good year. Then one night men came and trampled the field, and so we plowed and seeded again. Our crops sprouted anew." A shadowed bleakness crept into his face. "Then once again men came and trampled the field. They killed our goats and our sheep."

Glenda leaned forward in the saddle. "Who, Buford? Who did this? Did you see them?"

"Nay, lady. Always in the dead of night they came. Always." He paused. "There are those who blame Simon Ruthven," he said heavily, "Simon the Lawless. I fear I cannot say. Even if I knew, it changes nothing! We must have food. We must have food, or we cannot survive the winter."

Taking a deep breath, Glenda looked from Buford to his wife Analise. "Buford, I will not stop you from leaving. But I will help you, I swear."

"So you say, mistress, but how can you? We know of Egan, the Highlander. Indeed, we could trust in just such a man. But what will happen when he leaves? You are a woman. How can you defend us?

How can you protect us? And what if we stand behind you and you fall? What then? Simon the Lawless will have his revenge on *us!*" He shook his head. "Nay. I cannot. We go to join my brother."

His words were bitterly forthright. Glenda was aware there would be no persuading him otherwise. And indeed, what could she do? Take up the sword herself?

In the village the clatter of the mill-wheel reached her ears. Several men waved; her smile was distracted. In the bailey, a pair of hounds snarled and fought over a stringy bone outside the smithy's shed. Glenda never even noticed. She stepped inside the great hall, feeling both frustrated and helpless. Buford's words weighed heavily on her mind.

You are a woman. How can you defend us? How can you protect us?

If Blackstone's men-at-arms were at full strength, there would be no problem. Was Blackstone's defense truly beyond her capabilities? If only she had a fighting force! She had no choice but to rely on Egan to find and train men-at-arms, and fortify the keep to the point where she could at least defend her own.

So involved was she that she nearly barreled headlong into Jeannine. The girl looked over at her.

"Mistress, have you seen Egan this morn? Bernard is asking for him and no one has seen him yet."

Glenda's heart leaped. She couldn't withhold the thought that sped across her mind. She hadn't wanted Egan to stay and had protested most vehemently. Had he decided to leave as well? Sweet Mother of Mary, she prayed, please, no! For if he had, then she—and Blackstone Tower—was doomed.

She patted her shoulder. "Tend to your duties, Jeannine. I will find him."

On impulse, Glenda decided to check his chamber. Perhaps he'd slept overlong this morning.

As she approached, she noticed the door was ajar. She hesitated, then raised a hand to knock. As she did, she glanced within.

Egan stood with his back to her. Apparently he was not long from his bath. His hair was black and gleaming wetly. He did not wear his kilt; trews covered his legs, but he was bare to the waist. In all the years she'd known him, Glenda had never seen his naked torso. An unsettled heat descended into the pit of her belly, for it was disturbingly virile . . . disturbingly masculine. Somehow she had always known he was a powerful man—aye, and never more so than at this moment! His skin was sleek and brown, his shoulders and arms sculpted and keenly defined. His back was one long slab, thick with muscle and carrying no hint of fat.

He half-turned, and it was then she saw he was not alone. Belinda, a young and pretty serving girl with ample hips and breasts, stood before him. In her hands she held a length of linen. Belinda saw her before Egan did. She froze in the act of reaching for his chest with the linen, drawing back the cloth sharply. She dipped a curtsy and rushed past Glenda out into the passageway.

Glenda scarcely noticed. The soft line of her lips compressed. To think that this was the man she hoped might be her savior and salvation. Here she was, worried sick about the safety of her people, while Egan amused himself with one of the maids!

She was sorely vexed and she cared not if he knew it! When he turned to face her, she bestowed on him a withering look. "Well, you are ever at the ready, are you not?"

He cocked a brow. "What do you mean?"

"I think you know quite well what I mean!"

He was completely unfazed by the fire of her glare. A slow smile rimmed his lips. "Glenda, do you speak of my manly appetites?"

"Your words, sir, not mine," she snapped. Her resentment blazed higher with his amusement. "Though I must say, your appetite seems quite hearty!"

"And what of yours, Glenda?"

"Whatever do you mean?"

"You are a woman without a husband. A woman without a man. I am not a fool. Women . . . well, women have appetites, too. Especially those who know the pleasure that can be found in another's body."

And well she knew. She had lost her maidenhead on the marriage bed, but she had never found love-making a chore or a duty, as she'd heard some women were wont to do. Instead, she had found it a vastly pleasurable experience . . . all at once she was appalled. She couldn't believe what they were discussing! To speak of her lying with a man . . . of his lying with a woman . . . and to each other, yet!

He persisted. "Come, Glenda, what of you? I asked you once, and you would not answer. Do you not find yourself lonely? Do you not miss the closeness of a man's body, the heat of lips warm upon yours?"

Suddenly she was the one who was on the defensive. "Nay," she gasped.

"Nay?" He feigned astonishment. "What, Glenda! Did you not love Niall, then?"

Glenda's breath grew short; it seemed there was not enough air to breathe, for he was so close. *Too* close. So close that she could see the tiny droplets of water which glistened in the dense forest of hair on his chest. Niall's chest had been smooth and nearly void of hair, and it was all she could do not to stare in mingled shock and fascination.

She was certain her face flamed scarlet. "Of course I did! You know I did! But I"—she made a valiant stab at reasoning—"I have put aside such longings."

He did not take his eyes from her mouth. "Have you?" he said softly. "Have you indeed?"

A strong hand settled on her waist. In but a half-breath, it was joined by the other. His touch seemed to burn through the layers of clothing to the flesh beneath.

"Egan." She floundered. "Egan, please!"

"What, Glenda? What is it?"

She shook her head. Her eyes were wide and dark. Her head had lifted. Her lips hovered but a breath beneath his. The temptation to give in, to kiss her, to trap her lips beneath his and taste the fruit of her mouth was all-consuming. Almost more than he could stand.

She wanted it, too. He sensed it with every fiber of his being, but she was fighting it, damn her! Yet still he wanted to hear her say it. He *needed* it.

"Tell me, Glenda. What is it you want?"

She shook her head. Her hands came up between

them. Her fingers opened and closed on his chest . . . his *naked* chest. Dark, bristly hairs tickled her palm; to her the sensation was shockingly intimate. Yet she did not snatch back her hands—she did not push him away—as she should have.

As she could have.

"Egan? Are you here, lad?"

It was Bernard. They jerked apart. Egan moved first, stepping back from her. Did he curse beneath his breath? Glenda did not wait to find out.

She fled. Her heart was pounding and her lungs labored as if the devil himself nipped at her heels. Her feet did not stop until she was safe in her own chamber and the door was shut. 'Twas then that her strength deserted her. She pressed her back against it and slumped, landing in a heap on the floor.

Thrice now, Egan had almost kissed her. *Thrice.* What madness possessed him? Sweet heaven, what madness possessed *her*?

For Glenda could not deny the yearning that still burned deep in her heart. Just once she longed to feel the touch of his mouth on hers. *Just once . . .*

In the days that followed, she had only to look at him and she quivered inside. What was she feeling? A feeling unformed. Untamed. But no. She couldn't lie to herself. She was no innocent. She knew. *She knew.*

For the first time since she'd been married those many years ago, Glenda wondered what it would be like to lay with another man. With Egan.

The thought frightened her. Shamed her to the

depths of her being. She despised herself, for such was a betrayal to the memory of Niall.

Still it persisted, and she despaired her awareness of him.

Always he watched her. Always he was there, his expression impassive, his thoughts hidden behind the screen of his eyes.

Should she insist that he leave? Nay. Nay, she could not! She might as well cut her own throat. Though she hated to admit it, Blackstone's safety might well rest in his hands. Only yesterday Jeannine had confided that she slept much better, now that Egan was here. Her shoulders slumped. There was so much at stake to risk losing it all now. *Too* much.

Her demeanor was not eased by the presence of Simon. They crossed paths more than once in the next few days. She surveyed him closely, listened intently when he spoke of her tenants. But she could find no fault with him. She had taken to riding in the morning, and saw him several times. The last time they had come upon a cotter named Ellis just outside the village. It had rained heavily the night before, and the track was muddy and rutted. Ellis's haycart was stuck in the mud. It was Simon who dismounted and helped him dislodge the cart, though he was covered in mud by the time it was done. Ellis thanked him for his generosity, yet his tone was meek. He kept his head bowed low and not once did he meet Simon's eyes.

Glenda didn't know what to make of Simon. Oh, aye, he was always polite, ever courteous and gallant. Indeed, he was so earnest, so concerned about her troubles that she could almost have believed that everyone was mistaken; that Simon had naught to do with the rape of Blackstone lands. Yet something stopped her, a feeling she couldn't put a name to.

She said naught to Egan of their meetings. Indeed, she said naught to Egan about much of anything, for she was doing her best to avoid him. When he was near, she could not think.

In the solar the next afternoon, she pulled out the heavy leather bound book where the accounts were recorded. With a sigh, she pick up her quill and began to delete those tenants she had been informed had already left.

She'd not been working long before there came a knock on the door. She glanced up just as Simon stepped boldly within. He stopped short as he saw her bent over the book that lay open on the table. With a shake of his blond head, he planted his hands on hips.

"What is this?" he said in mock demand. "Glenda, you work far too hard. 'Tis a fine, warm day outside. Come, join me for a ride."

"I fear I cannot, Simon. You see, I've only just begun and there is much to do. When Uncle Rowan was sick, there was much neglected. It must now be tended to."

"Then I will keep you company." Simon made a move to shut the door, but she stopped him with a word.

"Please, Simon, leave it open. 'Tis overly warm in here."

"Precisely the reason you should leave!" His tone was hearty as he approached. "Now, I know a place where we might spend the afternoon beneath the shade of a stand of oak trees along the river."

"Tempting as it sounds, I must say nay." In truth she had been highly uncomfortable closeted alone with him the other day. She had no wish to repeat it, but softened the refusal with a faint smile.

By now, Glenda had risen to her feet as well. Simon's gaze fixed on the faint lines etched between slender chestnut brows. He glanced to the ledger, and back again.

"You are worried, aren't you?"

Glenda was not about to divulge anything to him. "Nay," she denied quickly.

"You do not fool me, Glenda. You work overmuch. You worry overmuch."

" 'Tis nothing. Truly."

Simon clasped her hand within his. With the table at her side, and the chair nudging the back of her knees, she could not avoid him. Panic flared briefly, but she reminded herself the door was open. Surely he would not do anything, for if someone should pass by, they could easily be seen.

The hands enfolding hers were soft and smooth, nearly as smooth as her own. Clearly Simon was not a laboring man. She could not withhold the thought that spun through her brain. No doubt Egan's hands would have felt nothing like Simon's. She'd glimpsed for herself the roughened calluses on the tips of his fingers, and there was little need to wonder why. Only yesterday he had lent a hand in the fields. She'd seen him from the tower window. And earlier this morn, he had been alongside the mason's helpers, carrying the rough, heavy bricks to the crumbling wall where the mason worked. Simon's hands, she suspected, were not at all like Egan's.

Simon's eyes narrowed. "Tell me," he said abruptly. "The Highlander, Egan. When does he return to Dunthorpe?"

Glenda blinked. Was it so obvious, then, where her mind dwelled? "I do not know."

"You have no need of him, Glenda."

"Ah, but I do," she said lightly. "Egan has proved invaluable. Bernard is old and can no longer do what he used to. But already Egan has begun to bring in men to replace those soldiers who deserted when Uncle died."

"But I could help you as well as he."

Why was he so insistent? She gave a tiny shake of her head. "Simon, I appreciate your offer, really. But I assure you it's not necessary—"

"Glenda . . . Glenda! We've known each other a long time, haven't we?"

"Aye." Glenda was beginning to grow uneasy.

"Then you know you can trust me. You do, don't you?"

"I . . . of course I do." Inside she cringed. Faith, but she prayed God was absorbed with someone else just now; that He would not reach down and smite her here and now for speaking such an untruth!

"Then hear me out. I've lost a wife. You've lost a husband. We have much in common. We share a bond, you and I!" His grip on her hand tightened. " 'Tis soon, I know that. But these past days, I've thought of no one but you." He edged nearer.

And I have thought of you, too, only not in a way that you would like! It was all she could do not to glance nervously toward the door. Was he asking what she thought he was? Och, but she should have known! Where was Nessa? Jeannine? Anyone, she decided desperately. Did she dare risk offending him?

She summoned a smile, striving for a light tone. "Simon," she began.

"I must speak with you, Glenda."

It was Egan. He filled the door, his shoulders so wide they blocked out the light.

Simon released her. "Can you not return later?"

"I cannot." He was as abrupt as Simon. "I fear 'tis a matter most urgent." When Simon did not move, black brows arose. " 'Tis for her ears alone, sir."

Anger sped across Simon's features, but it was swiftly gone. "Very well, then." He gave a terse bow. "Glenda, I trust I will see you soon."

Egan's expression was grim, so very grim. Her pulse began to thud. What? she thought, stricken. What was amiss? She'd heard a lone rider but a short time ago. Perhaps it was Milburn, returned from Dunthorpe. Perhaps something awful had happened to Cameron or Meredith.

The instant Simon made his exit she moved toward Egan. "Tell me what's wrong, Egan. Tell me!"

He made no answer. Calmly he inquired, "Have the two of you made plans to meet again?"

Her heart tripped over itself. There had been no need to speak with her, she realized dumbly. It had been naught but an excuse, and all at once a surge of pure indignation brought her upright, like a fist plowed into her back.

"How dare you frighten me like that!"

"How dare you be alone with him like that." His

eyes were cold, his expression remote. It was only through the most stringent effort of will that Egan stopped his rage from boiling over. The sight of her with Simon, her hand cradled snug within his ... the way she smiled into his face ...

Something snapped inside him. That Simon should touch her so ... that she should allow it!

Glenda stiffened. "The door was open," she pointed out coolly.

"And a good thing it was, or you might even now lie on that table beneath him, your gown hiked up to your waist and your thighs spread wide beneath his."

She gasped. What need was there to be so crude? Niall had never spoken to her thus. Nor any man with any respect for a gently born woman ... Ire surged afresh through her veins.

"Do not look at me like that! You are not a maid, Glenda. You know well and true what I refer to. Or did I mistake the situation?"

"Did I mistake the situation with you and Belinda?"

"You did indeed, but that is not the question here. The question is what you were doing alone with Simon ... yet again."

So he knew. She shouldn't have felt guilty, yet she did! But she would not allow him to know it. Sweetly she said, "Forgive me if memory fails me, but was it not you who advised me not to make an enemy of him?"

He made a sound of disgust. "Neither did I tell you to warm his bed!"

As he spoke, his eyes slid down the length of her,

a journey both bold and irreverent. His comment was as insolent as his regard, Glenda decided furiously. He had impugned Simon for daring to gaze at her thus, yet he dared far more himself. His gaze lingered with brazen insult on the thrust of her breasts, the place where her thighs joined together. She felt as if he'd stripped her naked! Hating the betraying rush of color in her cheeks, she drew herself up proudly.

Blue eyes clashed endlessly with gold. The very air between them seemed to pulse and seethe as the silence mounted.

It was Glenda who broke it. "Simon asked me when you were leaving! By God, I wish you would!" Sheer anger fueled the remark.

"Oh, you've made that quite clear," he taunted smoothly. "It occurs to me that mayhap Simon is the reason you did not want me to stay—the reason you are so eager for me to leave. Tell me, did Niall know of him—of the two of you?"

Glenda did not think. She simply reacted. Her hand shot out. Never had she slapped a man—never had she laid a hand on another in her life! Yet she knew intuitively that she would enjoy immensely the sting of her palm on his hard cheek.

Alas, there would be no satisfaction, for the blow was never allowed to fall. With the sharply honed senses of a warrior, Egan reached out and caught her wrist. Strong fingers wound tight about her flesh.

Glenda's head jerked up. A little shock went through her. Ah, but the burning of his eyes should have served as a warning. He was not calm. His jaw was knotted and clenched. He was furious, and she was stunned to realize that never before had she seen

Egan angry. Determined, aye. Brittle with resolve, as well. But angry? Nay. For Egan was a man who was ever in command of himself, ever and always.

Yet now the very flames of hell seemed alive in his eyes. Glenda felt as if she'd been scorched to her very soul.

His mouth was a thin, forbidding line. "Did you encourage him?" he asked tautly. His gaze stabbed into hers, relentless and piercing.

"What if I did? 'Tis no concern of yours." A righteous anger met and matched his. He was neither her keeper, nor her husband or father, or even her brother. What right did he have to use such a tone with her?

Egan's teeth came together. "Would you have let him kiss you?"—there came the smallest of pauses— "Did you?"

"You assume I would have allowed him to bed me! Why would I not allow him to kiss me? Indeed, what makes you think I have not? Now let me go, Egan."

He did not listen. He did not heed. A steely arm snared her about the waist and caught her against him.

With a gasp Glenda looked up at him. They were so close her breasts were crushed against the broadly forged plane of his chest, her feet wedged tight between his boots.

He stared down into her face, his features black as she had never seen them. "Damn you," he said in a voice that vibrated with something she had never heard before. "Damn you! Why do you deny me what you would give freely to him?"

There would be no reprieve this time. In her heart
Glenda knew it . . .

And then even that thought gave way as his mouth
came down on hers.

Chapter 7

In all her days, Glenda had kissed no other man but Niall. She had lain with no man but Niall. And so this was like that very first kiss—that first, wondering, yearning taste of a man's mouth . . .

Yet 'twas like nothing she'd imagined, this kiss . . . *Egan's* kiss. Merciful heavens, she could scarce believe it!

He was still angry. She could feel it in his iron hold. His hands on her waist stayed any movement she might have made—not that she tried, for she was stunned into immobility.

His lips were not hard and punishing, as she had anticipated. Ah, if only they were, for then she would have fought against him with all of her strength . . . Instead, his mouth was a fiery brand, consuming and hungry and hot as fire. He kissed her with blistering thoroughness. When her lips yielded beneath the demanding pressure of his, his tongue breached within, initiating a wild, plundering rhythm that made her senses spiral and her knees go weak. She could feel him, the iron-corded strength of his thighs braced wide apart as he pulled her snug into the vise of his thighs. The ridge of his manhood strained against her, unmistakably hard . . . unmistakably virile.

Her heart began to clamor in her breast. Deep within, a part of her was appalled that she allowed such liberty. Yet now that she had succumbed, his touch was like a drug that invaded every part of her. Addictively persuasive. So devastatingly tormenting that she felt herself carried away—and she cared not where! Perchance she'd known it would be like this. Perchance this was why she'd resisted. Perchance this was why she'd fought so hard against it . . .

But Egan was tired of fighting. Fighting against her. Fighting against himself. He'd felt the first forbidden stirrings of desire the moment she'd ridden into Dunthorpe alongside Niall all those years ago. No longer could he withhold the rush of desire that had gone unchecked and unsatisfied.

Until now.

A fierce exultation shot through him. This was the sweetest moment of his life. He'd never been so achingly aware of the feel of a woman. She was small and fragile, the slenderest reed in his arms, yet with a suppleness that excited him almost past bearing. The dizzying scent of her filled his nostrils. She smelled like lavender. She tasted of a heaven he'd always known existed . . .

Yet dared not dream would ever come to pass.

Yet now it had. Now it did. She radiated an earthy sensuality that called out to everything that was wild and primitive within him. With stark, painful clarity, he recalled the mesmerizing sight of her naked body. And now that he had her in his arms, his heart thundered. His rod pulsed with need of her. He could feel the softness of her breasts against his chest, and he ached to shape her fullness into his palm, to pluck that rosebud tip like the ripest of fruit.

Her head fell back, an invitation Egan could neither deny nor resist. His lips traced a scalding path down the slender arch of her throat, clear to the rounded neckline of her gown. He did not stop until he reached the valley between her breasts, the place where that succulent flesh quivered against his mouth with each and every breath. She felt what he did—oh, aye, for her hastened breath betrayed her. Yet did he dare trespass? By the bones of Christ, did he dare?

With a gasp her hands came up to his shoulders. Slowly Egan raised his head.

She gazed at him, golden eyes dark and glistening, her expression disbelieving. Even as he watched, a hot tide of color rushed into her cheeks.

Her hands curled against him. "Release me," came her ragged whisper. "Release me!"

The seconds spun out as he regarded her, his eyes dark and depthless. For one awful moment, Glenda feared he would not. Then at last his hands fell to his sides. His features were carefully controlled.

"Why do you do this? Why?" A soft cry of confusion erupted. "You said you were charged with protecting me, but you forget yourself, Egan. You forget yourself!"

He willed aside the sliver of guilt that pricked at him. His mouth twisted. "I forget nothing. And I am not your servant, Glenda."

"Neither are you my husband!"

The tension that simmered between them was palpable. It was alive in every breath, every heartbeat.

Blue eyes flickered. "This was meant to happen, Glenda. You know it as well as I."

"I know nothing of the sort. You-you should not touch me so! You should not kiss me, for . . . for what of Niall?" she cried. "What of Niall?"

There was a crackling silence. "What of him?" he said at last.

"He loved you as surely as he loved his own brothers, Egan! Indeed, he thought of you as one! And now you dare to make free with his wife!"

A tempest of fury brewed within him . . . that *she* should dare to throw this back at him! He cursed silently, long and blackly. Did she think to salvage her own conscience by placing the blame on him? Somehow he'd thought better of her.

A smile that held no mirth twisted his lips. "Ah, but you were not so unwilling, were you?" he said with cool, careless deliberation. "And Niall is dead, lass. He is *dead*."

Glenda stood mutely. An endless pain washed through her, but in the next instant it was numbed by a cold rage.

"God, but you are arrogant. You are vile and heartless and disgusting!" she flung at him. "And to think Niall called you his friend!" She drew herself up proudly to her full height. "I have no choice but to ask—nay, demand!—that you leave Blackstone."

His smile withered. His jaw clenched fiercely. For a moment, he looked as if he would explode, but then his expression was replaced by a cool remoteness. He gave a low, stiff bow. He met her gaze, his own icily distant. His lips barely moved as he spoke.

"You need not worry. I will make my way this very day."

He was right.

She was hardly unwilling. She had made him out to be the villain. Indeed, it was her own fault! Why had she told him that she had let Simon kiss her? Why, the very thought made her shudder in distaste.

Nay, she should never have challenged him. In truth, Glenda didn't know what had come over her.

It was but a kiss, she told herself after he had gone. Nothing had happened. But she felt as if it had. She felt guilty, and she could not bear it! It was as if with his kiss, a stranger had stirred to life inside her. She no longer knew herself.

God! she thought in anguish. Why couldn't she have felt nothing?

Niall is dead, Glenda. He is dead.

Those words still burned inside her. Ah, but he had been unspeakably cruel! Didn't he know she still mourned him? How much it still hurt to think of Niall, the emptiness of life without him? At times she still felt barren inside, as barren as she'd believed she had been those first few years of marriage.

When Niall had died, a part of her had died along with him—and their child.

A squall blustered inside her. She didn't understand the emotions tearing at her breast—at her very heart. She desperately needed time to think, time to compose herself. Yet it seemed Egan had no more swept from the room than Nessa shuffled inside.

Glenda had already sunk onto the chair behind the table. Nessa studied her, her eyes sharp despite her years. "The two o' ye had words, didn't ye?"

It was difficult to pretend that naught was amiss, when just now Glenda was certain that everything was amiss. She prayed she would be able to. She raised her head.

"Nay," she denied.

Nessa made a sound deep in her throat. "I've not spent as many years on this earth as I have and not be able to read what lies in a woman's heart—*and* a man's eyes." She leaned upon her staff and gazed at her former charge. "He did not look pleased, nor do ye."

When Glenda made no answer, Nessa tugged at the fingers of her coif. It had not taken long to discern what went on between the pair, reluctant though they both appeared.

"What troubles ye, lass?"

I have no choice but to ask—nay, demand!—that you leave Blackstone. Not until the words had passed her lips did Glenda realize what she'd just done. Now it was too late to retract them.

Go after him, urged a voice inside. *Stop him.*

Still another voice argued against it. How could she? How could she even face him after what had happened? It was pride that spurred her angry demand, she acknowledged. Yet there was no swell of satisfaction in the knowledge. It was that same foolish pride that kept her from going after him now. She would not beg or plead. She cared not if he left and she never saw him again!

Liar, taunted the voice.

Nay. *Nay!* She had no feelings for him, save relief that he would soon be gone and would trouble her no more. Nay, no longer would she feel this tug inside whene'er she saw him, and wonder what it was . . .

She might as well tell Nessa the truth. All would know soon enough anyway.

She took a deep, fortifying breath. "I sent Egan away."

"When will he be back?"

Glenda lowered her eyes. "He will not."

"What!" Gnarled fingers curled hard around the staff of ash. "Glenda! Tell me, lass, that ye didn't send him away for good!"

The censure in the old woman's voice startled her. "I should have thought that you would be pleased. I thought you did not like him."

The staff hit the floor with a resounding thump. "Never did I say that! Even if I did, is an old woman not allowed to change her mind?

"Oh, aye," she went on. "I am not so witless as everyone thinks. Egan says nothing. *You* say nothing. But many a time I've seen him gazing toward your solar."

Glenda's heart skipped a beat.

"As for ye, child, I've seen ye gazing at him when ye think that no one sees."

Glenda gasped. "I have not!"

"Och, but ye do, lassie! Your eyes follow him, as a lamb follows its mother."

Glenda gave a shake of her head. "Nay, Nessa, you are wrong. To do so would be a—a betrayal of my marriage vows."

"Yer husband is no longer here, lassie."

A fresh surge of resentment coursed through her.

First Egan, now Nessa! "Am I not allowed to grieve?" she cried. "While you did not witness it, I tell you now that I loved Niall with all my heart! I married because my father commanded it, Nessa. But I did not *love* because he commanded it."

"That is oft the way of love. It comes when you least expect it. Aye," Nessa agreed bluntly, "you loved your husband. But the time for grieving is past. You must look to the future."

"I have!" Glenda cried. "That is why I returned here, to Blackstone!"

"Is it?" Nessa's voice was quiet as the night. "I think you came here to forget."

Glenda's eyes opened wide. "How can you say that? And what would you know of love? You've never been married!"

For the space of a heartbeat, Nessa hurtled back in time. "Married, nay. But I loved a man once. Once"— there was a long, drawn out pause—"before you were born."

Glenda lapsed into silence. Her rashness came with a price, she discovered, for a spasm of pain flitted across Nessa's features. She had no wish to hurt the old woman, and it struck her that this was a side of Nessa never before glimpsed. As far back as she could remember, Nessa had taken care of her and her sister Eleanora; after the pair had grown to womanhood, Glenda had no doubt Nessa had then spent her days taking care of her father. Glenda well remembered the day her mother had been buried. It was in Nessa's arms she had sought solace, Nessa who had been there to soothe the hurts from that day onward.

Yet beyond that, the old woman's life was a mystery, and Glenda felt a pinprick of shame.

Shame. Ah, but it was a constant companion this day!

With that, Nessa left the room, her staff a hollow echo on the rough wood floor. She made her way to the great hall, where she questioned the first servant she saw. "You, there! Have ye seen Master Egan?"

"Nay—"

"I have," piped one of the pantler's boys. "He is in his chamber."

Despite her advanced years, despite her infirmity, Nessa moved with urgent compunction toward the tower stair. As the boy predicted, Egan was in his chamber.

She knocked once, waiting impatiently. When he bade her enter, she did and spoke without hesitation.

"You will not tell Glenda of this conversation."

Egan stuffed the last of his belongings into his pouch and straightened. His smile was grim as he beheld the old woman. "You need not worry. I will not be here."

"Stay. I pray you, stay."

Nessa was the last person he thought to expect such fervent words from, indeed, the last things he thought to hear from the old woman. He swung around fully to regard her. To his surprise, her regard held no hint of the wariness he'd come to expect.

His jaw thrust out. "You do not understand," he began.

"Ah, but I do. I know that she demanded you

leave—I know not why. But she will regret it later. We all will, methinks."

Egan gave a short, harsh laugh. His mood was not particularly easy just now. What would Nessa say if she knew Glenda had dismissed him as vile and disgusting?

"If she sees me, she will no doubt have me tossed from atop the highest tower." He did not jest.

"Then do this. Do not journey far. Stay near, but do not leave. There is a woodcutter's cottage in the forest. No one lives there. You can stay there. I will say naught to anyone."

His eyes narrowed. "Why would you ask such a thing of me? The day we arrived, I could have sworn you'd have liked to slit my throat."

"I did not know you then. I saw the way you looked at her, as if she belonged to you."

"Your sight fails you then," he stated coolly, "for you see what is not there."

"Do I? Even if that were true, there are some things that are felt as well as seen." As she spoke, she thumped her free hand to her scrawny breast meaningfully.

Egan stared at her, astounded, amazed, and annoyed all at once. "I cannot," he said flatly.

"Do not desert her."

"Desert her! 'Tis *her* wish, not mine!"

"Look after her."

Bitterness seared him. "She will not allow it."

"And so you will abandon her?"

"Abandon her! She demanded that I leave!"

"Protect her, for there is no one else to do it. She will regret her rashness."

Egan's jaw thrust out. "You cannot know that."

"I *feel* it."

His eyes narrowed. "What has she said to you?"

"She has said nothing. I told you—I *feel* it, as only another woman can feel."

Egan's mind turned furiously. Nessa offered little in the way of explanation, yet now that his anger had begun to abate, he could feel himself weakening.

God knew he did not wish to leave. God's bones, it was the last thing he wanted!

"Why?" He tipped his head to the side. "Why do you trust me?"

Nessa's answer was a long time in coming. "I do not know. I only know that I do. And indeed, 'tis far better that she be with you than him."

Him. Without ever speaking his name, they both knew the wretch to whom she referred.

"He wants her," he said slowly.

"I know. He is not what he seems. He is slippery as a greased eel."

Egan swore hotly. "How the devil am I to protect her, when she wants naught to do with me?"

"How? Must I do yer thinking for ye, man?" Faith, but men were sometimes the most helpless, hapless of creatures. "There must be a way. 'Tis up to you to find it!"

Egan was all at once reminded of Robin. If the rogue were of a mind to seek revenge, wouldn't he have done so by now? If only he could be certain!

Then there was Simon Ruthven. Blackness stole over him anew. He clamped his jaw tight. Nay, he decided, he could not go. If Glenda were to endure any harm, he would never forgive himself.

Nor, he suspected, would Nessa. She would guard Glenda's safety like a mother goose guarded her goslings.

He was unaware of Nessa's closely held scrutiny. Inside she held her breath. If she could sway him, then she might breathe easier. It was not her own welfare she was concerned with, for she had lived a long life. When God was ready to take her, she would not fight.

But she would battle to the ends of the earth for her beloved Glenda. Now that Glenda was home, Nessa viewed life with renewed vigor. She did not like that women were rarely granted respect and even less credit for their achievements. Home and hearth might run like a well-oiled lock through the wits and wisdom of its mistress, but it was the lord who gained—and claimed!—what credit was to be taken. Yet when it came to brawn and the might of the sword, she could not argue that it was much better to stand behind a strong arm.

She prayed he would relent, else all might be lost! Most Lowlanders were wary of Highlanders—and Englishmen! Such was the way of life here in the Borders. Her bones might be old and creaking, but she could spot a strong, powerful man as surely as any woman less than half her age.

She watched a brown, callused fingertip absently stroke the scar on his cheek. It lent him a dangerous, wicked look, but no matter. She uttered a silent, fervent prayer that Egan MacBain was a man who would give all for those whom he cared for.

For if not, then this effort might well be in vain—and she could not bear the thought.

"Stay," she pleaded one last time. "If all goes well and no danger comes this way, then you may leave, if that is what you wish."

"I will think on it."

"Do not think too long," she warned.

Egan remained where he was long after Nessa hobbled from the chamber.

Protect her, she urged. Protect the woman who scorned the sight of him and banished him from her home!

All because of a kiss.

He was tempted to laugh, and ended up groaning instead. Had he known the furor that would arise, would he have done it?

He could not regret it. By God, but he could not! Yet he could not help but wonder . . . If it had been but a fleeting, simple kiss—the wispiest brush of his lips against hers—would she have been so incensed?

Almost tiredly he dropped his pouch onto the floor. His anger at her had faded. When, he asked himself tiredly, would hers?

In the next breath, his shoulders straightened. He had sworn to protect her—whether or not she willed it, whether or not she wanted it. So he had vowed, and so he would.

He had only to find a way.

Chapter 8

When Glenda arose the next morning, her head was pounding. She had hoped a night's rest would ease her scrambled turmoil, but it was not to be. She could not rid her mind of him . . . Egan. A part of her could not believe he was gone. As the twilight shadows crept across the treetops, she had watched him pass beneath the gatehouse, watched until horse and rider were well beyond the wooden palisade. An odd feeling knotted her chest, making it difficult to breathe. She grappled with the certainty that she had made a horrible mistake.

No. *No.* She was stronger than that. She had only to get through each day, one at a time.

Pray God she did not have another like yesterday!

Her people would have to be told of his departure. At supper last night Jeannine had glanced more than once at the chair he usually occupied, but she didn't inquire as to his whereabouts. Glenda sighed and tied a ribbon around the end of her thick chestnut braid, flipping it over her shoulder. Bernard, in particular, would no doubt be searching for Egan this morning.

So caught up was she in recounting the day's on-
erous tasks that she didn't notice the strident blare
of the horn. It was Nessa who peered through the
window. "We have visitors," she announced.

Glenda frowned. "Who is it, Nessa?"

"I cannot be certain," Nessa murmured, "but I
think it's the earl's men. They wear his colors." Her
gaze sharpened. "And if I am not mistaken, there is
the earl himself."

All thoughts of Egan were driven from her mind.
Glenda fairly flew to the arched window and looked
down. Chickens flapped their wings and squawked,
teetering out of the way of flashing hooves as a half-
dozen men emerged from beneath the gatehouse.

She turned away with a smothered moan. "The
earl! Oh, I know why he is here. He comes to collect
the rents, but I cannot pay them. There is simply not
enough in the treasury."

"Calm yourself, Glenda. It cannot be so bad as all
that. Your father always believed the earl was a fair,
just man, and so must you."

How easy it was for her to say! Yet no hint of
Glenda's distress showed through, an hour later. The
earl sat at the head of the table in the great hall.
Glenda had ordered that food and wine be brought.

She studied him covertly. He was garbed in a tunic
of his colors—a rich, forest-green rimmed with gold.
A man of trim, compact build, no hint of paunch
hung over the belt that encircled his hips. Streaks of
silver swept back from his temples. An ornate, bejew-
eled ring adorned the third finger of his left hand.
Unremarkable of looks, his bearing, speech, and

grace of movement carried an aristocratic air that reflected his position and his title. His men, Glenda noted, were quick to do his bidding.

Glenda ate a few bites of bread and cheese, but could manage no more. Her stomach would have protested most heartily, and the last thing she wanted was to embarrass herself before the earl. This meeting was difficult enough as it was.

She motioned for Jeannine to step forward to refill the earl's cup. He declined with a wave of his hand and turned to her.

"I offer my regret on the passing of your father and uncle." There was a slight pause. "And your husband as well."

"Thank you, my lord." Her tone was quiet. She lowered her gaze. Her fingers caught nervously at each other in her lap; she stilled them, hoping against hope that Nessa was right, that the earl was truly a just, fair man.

Slowly she raised her head. "My lord, there is a matter which I would like to discuss with you. It concerns the rents."

"Oh?"

Of a certainty, she'd captured his interest. His eyes fixed on her, like a hawk's upon its prey.

Somehow Glenda willed the tremor from her voice. "I know my father respected you greatly, as do I, my lord, and everyone here at Blackstone Tower. Yet I must plead for your indulgence in the matter of the rents. Our circumstances are dire. I arrived from the Highlands to find the treasury nearly depleted. It seems the past twelve-month has not been a profitable one."

"And why is that? It has been bountiful elsewhere on my lands," he observed coolly. "Why not here at Blackstone Tower?"

Glenda took a deep breath. "I fear some of our tenants—both free and unfree—have gone elsewhere, my lord."

"Elsewhere!" he exclaimed. "Why?"

Quaking inside, her voice low, Glenda related much that had happened. Her mind raced as she spoke. Quickly she weighed and considered. Did she dare lay the blame at Simon's door? If only it were so simple! She sensed that the earl was not a man who would submit to such without proof—and she had none. Mayhap it was not Simon at all. Mayhap it was just as Nessa had stated that first day—men bent on making mischief. No, she decided, she could say nothing.

With his fingertips, the earl tapped out an impatient rhythm against the arm of the chair. "If some were bound to the land, then they are fugitives. Are they being sought?"

"Nay, my lord. My uncle had been ill and—and had not the men to spare." Inside she winced, for there was no doubt his expression was now dark with disapproval. "And so, my lord, there you have it. This is the reason our resources are scarce. Yet 'tis my hope that by year's end all will have changed. With God's grace the harvest will be bountiful and I may then repay all that is owed and more." She held her breath and waited.

That restless tapping continued. Light reflected off the jewels of his ring.

"I commend your directness." Above his thin, aquiline nose, the earl's eyes pinned hers. "However, that does not change my circumstances. I have obligations as well."

"I understand that, my lord." She spoke with painful dignity.

"I would be justified in stripping this keep and its lands from you, for your family has held them only because mine allowed it."

She cried out inside. Please, no! Blackstone Tower had always been her father's pride and joy. He would have been so disappointed—she had returned here to save her family's home, not to lose it!

"There must be order on my lands," the earl continued.

Her heartbeat quickened. For the life of him, what was he about? "Aye, my lord. That is my intention."

"The tenants look to their lord in times of strife. Their leader cannot be weak."

Glenda's chin came up a notch. "I am not weak, my lord."

"Perhaps not in will or spirit, but you are a woman."

Sheer resolve kept a biting retort clogged deep in her breast. She was both furious and dismayed. Did all men have so little faith in women? Did he have so little faith in her? Yet she dare not defy the earl, for if she did, it might very well result in losing Blackstone—and that was the one thing she wanted to avoid at all costs. She must find a way to fight to keep these lands, and so she made no reply.

"If your tenants desert, my coffers empty as well.

However, I recognize that fate has not been kind to you, and I am prepared to be generous. Therefore, I will delay the payment of your rents for half a year. But you must heed my advice, lady."

The relief that poured through her was immense. "I will do all that is necessary." Graciously she inclined her head, then looked up at him. "What is it you wish, my lord?"

"Find yourself a husband, and quickly," he stated grimly, "else I will choose one for you."

Egan had caught a glimpse of the earl, whose richness of garments gave away his identity, and his small troop of men earlier that morning from the side of the drove-road. He did not think twice about the earl making the rounds of his estates, but watched as the small assemblage turned toward Blackstone Tower. He gave it no further thought. No doubt the earl had learned of Rowan's death and come to visit Glenda.

He had done as Nessa suggested and spent the night in the woodcutter's cottage. As soon as the earl's men were no longer in sight, he turned his horse in the direction of the village alehouse. He would not skulk about in the dark like a thief afraid to be discovered. At the moment he did not particularly care if Glenda knew he lingered nearby. By God, he was free to do as he wanted and if she did not like it, then she would simply have to remove him herself.

In the alehouse he seated himself in the far corner. It was a tiny place, dark and dingy. What light there was came from the window near the fireplace, where someone had scraped aside the dirt and soot near the center.

An hour later the ale he'd ordered had done little to improve his mood. He glanced up only when he heard the clatter of hooves upon the wooden planks of the bridge, just outside the alehouse—the earl and his men again. It took no great powers of the mind to discern that the earl was now headed for Simon's keep.

Egan stared into his cup, then grimaced as he took a long draught. The brew was as clouded and stale as his temperament.

He'd been brooding since yesterday afternoon. Guilt had blunted the edges of his anger. He should not have spoken as he had to Glenda. He should not have reminded her of Niall's death. Yet it was true: Niall was dead. No matter how much she—or any-one—wished otherwise, Niall was gone. Never would he return.

You are arrogant. You are vile and heartless and dis-gusting! And to think Niall called you his friend.

Her words echoed through the chambers of his mind. Mayhap he was as arrogant as Glenda claimed. Clearly her devotion to Niall was as strong as ever. He chafed inside for he was not blind, nor was he a youth who knew naught of the ways of women.

The feel of her washed through him anew. He had not imagined the way her lips quivered beneath his; he'd felt for himself the wild thunder of her heart beneath his very fingertips! Oh, she could deny it all she wanted, but he was no tender youth to be taken aback by such a claim. The sweetness of her response was all he craved—ah, but far too fleeting!

So what was he to do? Stay, Nessa urged. Protect her. Ah, but he had watched from afar for too many years. To do so much longer, while she forever yearned for Niall . . . Darkness crept around his heart, like shadows over the sun. The thought was untenable. He might as well plunge a red-hot knife in his gut and twist it. Clearly he'd not been meant for the church, he decided with a faintly self-derisive smile. He was not so selfless as he should have been.

He was caught in a web, snared deep in its threads. How could he leave . . . yet how could he stay?

On and on his mind turned. Perhaps it was just as he'd suggested, and she was lonely. Could he make her want him? If only he could! But he was not like Niall. Wearily he reminded himself he wasn't the son of a chieftain, as Niall had been. As Simon had so cleverly needled, he possessed neither wealth nor lands, nothing that would make her want him . . . *need* him.

Unbidden, a fingertip came up to absently rub his scar. Nor was he as handsome as Niall . . .

And Glenda still loved him—that was the greatest hurdle of all.

How could he stay? Yet how could he leave her alone?

The sun began to sink below the treetops. Still he remained, though no answer to his dilemma revealed itself. He really should leave, he told himself a dozen times. Yet he could not summon the willpower to take himself to the door.

He barely glanced up when three men strode

boldly within. On their part, they gave no notice to the figure in the corner.

"It seems the earl was not pleased when the mistress of Blackstone was not able to pay the rents."

The earl ... Egan's head nearly jerked up. He stopped himself just in time. It was Glenda they spoke of! In light of the current state of affairs at Blackstone, he could not doubt the validity of the statement. Yet why the devil hadn't she confided in him? *Fool,* chided a voice inside, *you should have known. 'Tis plain how she feels about you! Why would she confide in you?*

Yet who else might she have confided in?

He did not like the answer that leaped to the fore ... Surely not Simon!

One of the men gave a grating laugh. "I know how I would have made her pay! A fine piece of womanhood, she is!"

The bald man across from him pinched his nostrils and made a face. "You? Why, methinks she would sooner lie with a rotting pig!"

"What!" said the first. "Why, she would welcome it! She's not been had for many a year, or so it's said."

"Och, but ye wouldn't know what to do with a woman like her!"

"And you would?"

"Can you doubt it?" With a boastful grin, the man was on his feet. Chest high, he swaggered forward, stopped, clapped his hand to his groin, and pumped obscenely.

Lewd laughter erupted.

"Perhaps we should place a wager on the next man to warm her bed," the third man chimed in. A few sparse, gray hairs sprouted atop his pate.

Egan was about to rise and throttle all three, but their next words caught him cold.

"That's not a wager I'll make," the first said promptly.

"Nor I," said the second. "We all know 'tis our own lord Simon who will have her."

So. They were Simon's men. Egan had suspected as much.

"Ah, but ye should have heard him crowing when he heard that the earl demanded she find a husband."

"What! Find a husband?"

What, indeed? Egan thought furiously. He had gone very still both inwardly and outwardly. Every inch of his being was focused on the three men.

The trio continued with gusto. "The earl told her she must marry. If she does not choose a husband soon, then he will find one for her."

"Aye, and all know that would be Simon. Who else would it be, for he at least pays his rents on time!"

"Aye," nodded the bald one. He drank deeply, then wiped his mouth with the back of his hand. "The earl has played right into Simon's hands. I heard him bragging to the steward. He said that mayhap if he takes the lady Glenda to his bed, 'twill hasten the inevitable and she will have no choice but to wed him." He went on to describe in base, bawdy detail precisely what Simon had said he would have her do. "Perhaps he does the deed even now!" he finished with a leer.

"Simon is at Blackstone?"

"I daresay he rode out just after we did. The stableboy was readying his horse."

"Then mayhap we should join him and give the Scots lass a ride she'll never forget!"

Egan was already on his feet. His blood was boiling and he longed to release his fury. But such anger would have been misplaced.

The trio never noticed as he made for the exit. His step was determined, his resolve both brittle and black. Nay, he decided anew, he'd not be heading back to Dunthorpe just yet.

Nor would he stand aside and allow Glenda to marry a wretch like Simon!

At Blackstone the watchman in the tower yelled in greeting. Egan lifted a hand in brief salute. In the bailey, when a groom scurried over to catch his reins, Egan couldn't help but note the muted air which prevailed.

His gaze seemed to stab through the air. He leaped from his horse with a great bound. Fury beat like wings in his breast at the sight of Simon's dark gray steed.

It was then he spied Nessa coming toward him. The old woman spared no time for greeting.

Nessa planted both hands around her staff and looked him up and down, her lips pursed thin with disapproval. "Where the devil have ye been? I sent a man after ye long ago! Och, and to think I was convinced ye could save my lassie!"

Egan's jaw hardened. He had no time for either explanations or recriminations. He had but one thing to say. "Where is he?"

Without a word, Nessa hitched her chin toward the great hall.

Egan mounted the wide stone stairs two at a time.

Voices drifted his way even before he saw the pair. From around the corner he heard Glenda's dulcet tones as she inquired, "More wine, Simon?"

Egan stopped short, gritting his teeth. What was this that she served the rogue wine, when what she should be serving him was the toe of her slipper on his arse!

" 'Tis not wine I want, but you. I would do anything for you, Glenda. Do you not know this? Nay, say nothing!" Simon went on. "I see by your expression that I have startled you. I pray you, do not be embarrassed. For you see, I know of your predicament. I know of the earl's . . . request, shall we say. I assure you, there is no cause for you to worry. I am, as ever, your humble servant, ready and waiting to accommodate you in this."

"Simon. Simon, please—"

"Nay, do not be shy, duckling. There should be no shyness between husband and wife."

Egan could stand it no longer. He stepped into the hall. Glenda's eyes found him first, across Simon's shoulder. As Simon gleaned another presence, he turned. Irritation was plainly writ on those perfect features.

Egan bristled as an overly familiar hand settled on the curve of Glenda's waist. Lean fingers bit into his palm. It was the only way he could keep his hands at his sides—and from giving in to the temptation of Simon's throat.

"Kindly remove your hand from the lady's person." Oh-so-pleasantly he spoke.

Simon scowled, but did as he was bid. "We wish to be alone," he said stiffly.

Egan inclined his head politely. "Indeed. Why is that?"

"Why else?" Simon snapped. "Because we wish to discuss our marriage plans!"

Egan smiled slowly. Even as he spoke, he reached for Glenda. Catching her fingers within his, he drew her to his side.

"Ah," he said, and his tone was almost whimsical. "Now that's where you're wrong, laddie. For you see, the lady has already consented to marry another."

"Another!" Simon's features twisted into a snarl. "Who the bloody hell would that be?"

Egan's smile widened a fraction. "Me," he said softly.

Chapter 9

In truth, Egan could not say what came over him. Until that very instant when he'd heard the words come forth from his own lips, he had not known what he would say . . . what he would do.

His heart thundered.

For years he'd had to stand back and watch her with his friend . . . with Niall. Oh, aye, he'd pretended he did not care. He'd carefully preserved his distance and masked his emotions, watching as the pair fell ever more deeply beneath the spell of love! No one had ever suspected his true feelings. Of a certainty not Niall. Not even Cameron, and most assuredly not Glenda! Oh, he'd despised himself for his jealousy. Yet scarce a day went by that it did not eat away inside him. It was like a blight upon his soul, the wrenching awareness that she would never belong to him. Knowing that she longed for another man. That she slept in the bed of his friend, clasped tight in Niall's arms . . . Niall, whom he loved like a brother! That she cared for another . . . and would never care for him.

Yet in that shattering instant between one heart-

133

beat and the next, he knew only that he could not stand by and watch her with another man yet again. By God, he *would* not!

And somehow—*somehow*—he had known what must be done.

What he must do.

Tensely he waited. Ah, but so much depended on her. *Everything* depended on her.

His heart thundered violently, in a way that had never happened before, for this was a fear unlike any other he had ever known—unlike any fear he had ever faced against any foe.

Beside him, he felt Glenda tremble. A tremor of shock, he wondered? Or a shudder of fear? Mayhap even revulsion . . . The small fingers within his grasp were icy-cold. But she did not denounce his statement . . . she did not denounce *him*.

Simon's features had turned a mottled red. He sputtered. "You—you have stolen her from me."

Egan's smile grew thin. "I have not."

"You have, you . . . you wretched Highlander!"

Egan's smile grew thin. He uttered a fervent, silent plea to the Heavens that Simon would not glean his dilemma, would not know that he was taking the risk of a lifetime!

"The lady makes her own choice," he said with soft deliberation, "but mayhap you should hear it from her lips, and not mine."

Two pairs of male eyes immediately swung to Glenda. Her head was lowered, her eyes downcast, her thoughts a mystery to both.

Egan took a breath, praying as never before. With a lightness that far belied the tumult in his soul, he said, "Whom will you wed, Glenda? Me? Or Simon?"

The seconds spun out endlessly. Just when he was convinced that all was for naught, that he'd gambled greatly and lost, she fixed her eyes upon him.

"You," she said, her voice so low he had to strain to hear her. "I will marry . . . you."

Something hotly primitive leaped in his breast. Unable to disguise his triumph, a brow climbed high. He glanced at Simon.

Simon gave a vile curse. Spinning around, he stormed to the door.

They were left alone. In the hearth, the fire snapped and hissed. The flames flared high, then burned low.

Glenda was still reeling. From his statement. From the day as a whole. Was it naught but a dream? By the blood of Christ, this could not be happening! She was still too stunned by all the day had wrought to do aught but stand there.

She spouted the first thing that vaulted into her mind. "I thought that you had gone. I watched you leave!"

Egan did not take his eyes from her. "I did not go far," he said simply.

Only then did she snatch her hand away. Proudly she drew herself up before him.

"Would that you had!"

Egan saw then that it was neither fear nor revulsion which had held sway her tongue. She was not afraid. She was angry—as angry as he had ever seen her.

His eyes narrowed. "If I had," he pointed out, "you would even now be planning your wedding vows to

Simon the Lawless. Or did I speak too soon? Is he the one you wish to wed? If so, why did you not say so?"

She ignored the question, as he thought she might. Instead she countered with one of her own. "Why?" she said, in a voice that shook as much as her body had but a moment earlier. "Why did you do this? Why would you say such a thing?"

Frustration gnawed at him. What was he to say? That he ached for her? Burned for her with a fever that ignited his very being? Nay. He could not. For Egan had his pride, too, and he would not bare his soul in the face of her unbridled fury.

"What the devil was I to do? I was at the alehouse, Glenda, when I heard Simon's men." Sparing no thought for her tender ears, he recounted precisely what Simon's men had said, taking a perverse satisfaction in the way her skin turned as white as fresh milk. "He meant to have you, Glenda. I knew it that first night he came here to Blackstone. And you admitted you needed to be wary."

"And so I was—and so I am!" she cried wildly, her emotions hopelessly distorted. "I will not have Simon. Indeed, I will have no man!"

"That is not what you said. From your own lips, you said you would marry me."

"Only because you trapped me! Because you knew I would not choose Simon over you. I-I do not see why I need marry either one of you!"

Egan was both outraged and incensed. "What, then? Were we wrong, both Simon and I? Perchance the earl did not advise that you take a husband after all. Perchance he did not tell you that if you did not make haste, he would choose a husband for you instead."

The blaze in her eyes flickered, then died out. She said nothing. Though he decried his tactics, he pressed home his advantage.

"Do you want to lose Blackstone to Simon?"

"Nay." Her gaze faltered, then fell. The word was a low, muted sound.

"To the earl, then?"

"Nay!"

"You have no choice, nor do I. Even if I had left— even if I departed now—the earl would choose a husband for you." He watched her closely. "And we both know he would choose Simon."

Glenda compressed her lips. She knew it, but something inside would not let her admit it. Not now. Resentment gathered full and ripe within her. She was too furious just now. To all of these men— Simon, the earl, and Egan—her life and her home were like a pair of dice, to be tossed in the air at whim and will, to fall where they would.

"At least you know you can trust me—"

"Trust?" she burst out. "How can you speak of trust, after what you have just done?" Her gaze was as blistering as her tone.

His regard sharpened. "You have known me for many a year, Glenda. Have you ever known me to lie?"

Glenda glared at him. Ah, but he was so damned smug! Was he so assured of victory, then? By the Rood, she would not oblige him further!

He moved before she knew what he was about. His

hands came down on her shoulders and pulled her close. He stared into her upturned face.

"Have you?" he demanded. "Have you ever known me to lie? Have you ever known me to commit a falsehood against anyone, man or woman?"

There was no escaping the determined glitter of those ice-fire eyes. Though she longed to answer in the affirmative, in the end, it was *she* who could not lie. "Nay," she admitted, her voice very low. "But if that is true, then tell me this, Egan. Why would you do this? Why would you sacrifice your freedom and take a wife? Is it truly to protect me? Because of your promise to Cameron?"

Everything shifted then. It was not she who was on the defensive, but he. Slowly he released her.

"That is a part of it." He hesitated. "But that is not all."

"I thought not." Her tone was arch.

"Do you think I will deceive you now? I will not," he stated evenly. "If I return to Dunthorpe, I will have naught but a place at Cameron's side, a bed beneath his roof." Nay, he would not lie. For so long now, it had been enough. But there was an emptiness that stretched inside him, a restlessness he had only just now begun to recognize. "This may well be an opportunity I will never have again. But if we are wed—"

"Then Blackstone is yours!"

"Aye. If we are wed, I will have a home and lands."

"Ah, what have we here? 'Tis not to protect me at all, but for your own gain!"

Egan regarded her tautly.

"You will find fault no matter what I say, Glenda," he stated knowingly. "With me as your husband, you and the people of Blackstone can be assured of protection. I have nothing to lose." A roguish black brow arched aloft. "Can you say the same?"

A stark, wrenching pain ripped through her. Glenda could summon no retort, because deep inside, she was aware that he was right.

If she delayed, the earl might well choose a husband for her—and what if that man was Simon? The thought of Simon's hands on her body, invading every corner of her life . . . She couldn't bear it! But was Egan any better? She felt as if he'd betrayed her no less than if he'd buried a knife in her back!

"You dare to speak to me of trust. Well, I trusted you, Egan. You told me you would stay until Blackstone was safe. Ah, but now the truth is out," she flung at him. "You will stay and help me, aye—but marriage is your price for helping me and my people!"

"This was not of my doing, Glenda."

"But it is of your choosing! My father devoted his entire life to Blackstone Tower and his people! I cannot lose it, not now!"

"So that's it, isn't it? I told you once I wouldn't wrest control of Blackstone from you, and I will not. Aye, when we are wed, Blackstone will be mine. But it is yours as well, and, God willing, it will ever be so."

"So you say now! But what will happen when we are wed . . . *if* we are wed?"

Egan's jaw clenched hard. There would be no reasoning with her, not now.

"If we are wed? You need me," he observed tightly, "far more than I need you. At least if we marry, we both profit, do we not?"

When she made no reply, his gaze pinned hers, ruthlessly direct, ruthlessly intent. "You have no choice," he reminded her harshly. "I have nothing to lose. Can you say the same?"

Unfairness raged inside her. Why, she wondered bitterly, must women ever bow to men? She felt as if the world were crumbling beneath her.

She had thought she'd been prepared to do anything to save Blackstone. Yet she had never dreamed what it would cost her. She'd never dreamed it would come to this! The price was far steeper than she had ever imagined. Yet she would do whatever she must to save Blackstone, no matter the cost, even to herself.

A wave of bleakness swept over her. Nothing could save her now. Egan was right. If she did not marry, the earl would simply see to it that she married another . . . and God help her, it would not be Simon.

Egan was the only one who could help her. Dear God, *Egan* . . .

Her voice was but a thread of sound. "So be it then. I will marry you." She did not look at him, but cast her eyes downward.

His scrutiny deepened. The tension remained as pulsing as ever, but his harshness waned. Glenda was too distraught to notice.

"Glenda," he said softly. He stretched out a hand. "Glenda, come here."

A reckless indignation washed over her. Her head

snapped up "I will not!" she said bitterly. "Aye, I will wed you, but the vows are not yet said, so I will thank you to keep your hands to yourself."

Egan's expression went utterly remote. He inclined his head. "As you wish, then," he intoned coolly. "I will send word to the earl that we will be married one week hence."

Chapter 10

There was little rest to be found that night. Glenda tossed and turned. Though she tried to blot her mind of all that had happened, she could not. She wavered between shock and outrage, outrage that Egan had dared to presume she would wed him! The misty colors of dawn had begun to wash the eastern sky before she finally slept from sheer exhaustion.

She woke to the sweetly melodious sound of a songbird outside in the bailey. At almost the same time, the door creaked. Glenda opened her eyes as Jeannine peered into the room.

"My lady!" came her whisper. "Are you awake?"

Glenda pushed her hair away from her face and sat up. "Aye. Please, Jeannine, come in." She'd been in no mood for company last eve. At supper she'd taken a tray in her room.

Yet she couldn't hide away forever. Summoning a faint smile, she patted the coverlet. "Come sit."

Jeannine did as she requested, carefully tucking the coverlet around the swaddling in her arm.

"Mistress, may I tell you something?"

"Of course you may."

Jeannine raised shining eyes to hers. "We are happy for you, mistress, all of us here at Blackstone. Egan . . . he will make a good husband, and a fine lord."

"Thank you, Jeannine. 'Tis good to know that all approve."

"Mayhap I should not speak so freely, but we are so verra relieved it is not Simon whom you will wed, all of us here . . . when we heard that the earl would have you marry, we were so afraid Simon would be our new lord. I-I am not one to tell tales, but I . . . oh, but I dinna like him! He is not kind, as Egan is kind. One day afore Simon rode out, he struck Martin the stableboy for dropping his reins on the ground."

The rogue! Somehow Glenda was not surprised.

"I pray that the two of you love each other the way Colin and I do."

Glenda's heart twisted. She had loved Niall. How could she ever love another? Yet Jeannine was so happy, she couldn't bear to tell her otherwise.

It struck her then. Sometime during the night she had resigned herself to her fate. And if the people of Blackstone were satisfied with Egan as their lord, then so must she be satisfied as well. Though she would have preferred to live her life as she chose it, that could never be.

"He will make a good husband, I know. And a good father," Jeannine said earnestly. The fingers of her free hand crept to the swaddling. A hint of shyness flitted across her face. "Mayhap within the year we will both have a babe in arms."

Glenda blanched. Everything inside her seemed to

freeze. A babe. Her mind screamed. *No*, she thought. *No!*

Her mind raced. Her stomach clenched. Throughout the long night she had put the thought at bay, but now she could not. Would Egan demand she lay with him? It was a husband's right. A wife's duty.

A babe, she echoed in despair. The thought veered where it would and she could not withhold it . . . Another *dead* babe?

When she and Niall had married, they had fully expected a babe within the year, for most nights found them together, limbs entwined and hearts a-pounding. A part of her soul had been chipped away, little by little, when her monthly flux continued to appear. She'd tried potion after potion, convinced that she was barren; though Niall had often assured her it did not matter that she didn't conceive, Glenda had sensed his disappointment. More than four years went by before she'd gotten with child.

Niall had been just as elated as she.

Yet now both father and son dwelled in the arms of the Lord.

There was a dull ache in the center of her breast. The prospect of a babe was too painful to perceive, and so Glenda did the only thing she could. To remember . . . was to hurt. Perhaps it was selfish of her, but throughout the next days, she put it from her mind. Put *him* from her mind . . . or tried to.

The day before the wedding, the earl sent over sacks of finely ground wheat, great bricks of cheese, fowl and fish from his estate for the wedding feast—a tacit sign of his approval, she realized. This wedding would take place, whether she willed it or no . . . whether she wanted it or not. Wearily she directed the carts to the storeroom.

The next afternoon Jeannine and a group of twittering maids arrived to help her bathe and dress. Glenda's lips parted. She would have dismissed them, preferring to see to the task alone, but Nessa gave a tiny shake of her head.

She stood quietly while they dressed her in a fine linen underdress. Her arms lifted to ease the way as a gown of scarlet was dropped over her head, finely embroidered about the rounded neckline and long, full sleeves. Her hair was brushed until it shone; it tumbled down her back, a cascade of gleaming chestnut.

Her heart caught painfully as a small, beribboned circlet of flowers was placed upon her head. She couldn't help but remember another time when she had stood thus, poised on the precipice of marriage, certain she would spend the rest of her days with the man she was about to wed. Niall's father Ronald and her own had known each other as youths and were great friends, so much so that they had pledged their firstborn son and daughter would marry. Glenda had not laid eyes on Niall until a sennight before they were wed. Niall had been dashing and laughing and gallant; as frightened as she was, she'd fallen in love with him just a wee bit that very first day . . .

At last she and Nessa were left alone. The old woman placed both gnarled hands on her staff and gazed at Glenda.

"There is not a sight more beauteous than you are now, child."

Glenda tipped her head to the side. A faint, wistful

smile curled her lips. "You said the very same thing the day I wed—"

Parchment-dry fingertips came to rest against her lips. "Hush, lass, do not say it. I do not mean to be cruel, but that day is forever gone. That man is forever gone."

Sudden, startling tears sprang to Glenda's eyes, tears she couldn't quite withhold. Her throat constricted. Nessa's arms came about her; she held her clasped tight against her frail form.

Yet she was dry of eye when she made her way to the door of the kirk a short time later. As she approached, several people turned. Glenda recognized one as the earl. She was not sure if she was more indignant or startled. Had he come to see that the deed was done? Suddenly the earl was forgotten as she felt her gaze drawn inevitably forward, as if beneath the powerful lure of some ancient spell.

It was Egan. He awaited her, a tall, formidable figure dressed in a dove-brown tunic and kilt. Never had she seen him so handsomely clad! Aware of his unrelenting perusal, she made her way toward him, feeling as if her legs were made of wood. She could not look at him just now—she could not! Yet before she closed the meager distance that separated them, she found herself impelled by an urge she couldn't overcome.

Their eyes collided. His features might have been etched from stone; they revealed naught of his thoughts, neither pleasure nor displeasure. His only reaction was the veriest lift of heavy black brows, a silent signal to face the priest. That last, final step brought her beside him. Glenda was careful not to touch him. In some far distant part of her mind, she had the sensation that if she did, her composure would surely shatter. Perversely, that very same part of her couldn't help but note his powerful ruggedness, the way her head scarcely reached the top of his shoulders.

Throughout the ceremony, she stood with her head held high, her spine straight and stiff as an arrow pointed skyward. Father Anselm's voice droned on so endlessly, she longed to scream at him to end it. Yet she knew she could not, so she focused her mind elsewhere. She was only half-aware as Egan spoke his vows, his tone strong and steadfast.

Father Anselm cleared his throat. With a start, she realized the priest—indeed, all those present—waited expectantly. A fleeting panic engulfed her. She longed to dart from the church—from him!—for she was suddenly terrified of all that lay before her. Yet such an action would be futile . . . and the act of a coward.

Her throat was as dry as bone. Her voice seemed to come from some lofty, faraway place. Dimly she heard herself speak. "To you, Egan, I give thee my troth, to have and hold thee for my lawful husband"—only then did she falter—"to my life's end."

Father Anselm gave the final blessing, asking that their union be long and fruitful and blessed with many children.

It was over.

Glenda stood dumbly. Behind her, someone let out a whoop, and then a loud cheer seemed to rumble the very earth beneath her feet. What she would have done then, she would never know, for a rock-hard arm locked tight about her waist, pulling her about. Her hands flew up, an attempt to maintain some distance between them—a pitiable effort, that!—for in the next instant she was caught tight against his chest.

His visage swam before her. Just before his head swooped low, there was an unmistakable flash in his eyes, something she could only discern as triumph.

Indeed, Egan couldn't help the feeling of heady pride that surged high like a tide, flooding his being. The mistress of Blackstone Tower might not be glad of his presence, but its people were—he could hear it in their cheers. This was his, he thought in sheer amazement . . . all of it. Well beyond the surrounding walls and the adjacent forest. He was a man who had seldom planned beyond the next day—there was no reason to, for he had simply accepted what would come with no further thought.

Yet he did so now, for suddenly all was different. Only yesterday he had almost nothing—his weapons, his horse, a bit of coin. Now he had Blackstone. Oh, aye, he resolved, he would nurture this land and its people, that they would prosper and grow . . . as he would. He was all at once determined as never before, determined to see Blackstone flourish, anxious to see the crops grow tall and fertile, eager for the autumn's bounty. For the first time, he truly understood what Glenda must feel . . . why she could not abandon her father's heritage . . . what her father had surely felt, this boundless connection to the land and its people. The Lord had smiled upon him this day, and God willing, there would someday be children who would share in all this.

Even the mutinous light in Glenda's eyes could not dampen his euphoria.

And indeed, Glenda could feel the fire, the rise of emotion inside him. Nor was this a mere brush of his lips on hers, a cursory acknowledgment of the vows between husband and wife. It was a raw, blistering kiss that spoke of possessive mastery.

Everything within her cried out starkly. Was this for the earl's benefit, or his own? She resented him fiercely, both him and the earl, yet there was no stopping him. The shouts and whistles all around faded to nothingness. When his tongue traced the seam of her lips, she gasped. He pressed home his advantage; his tongue dove deep, a plundering journey that plumbed the depths of her mouth. He kissed her until her senses were reeling and she was certain the only thing that held her upright was the brace of his arms about her back.

When at last he released her, she felt herself sway. Egan had already turned; he raised their joined hands high. A roar broke out anew. Yet she could not begrudge these people, any of them. She caught a glimpse of Jeannine, beaming. And there was Bernard, grinning from ear to ear. No doubt it had been a long time since there had been occasion to celebrate. And thanks to the earl, there was plenty to eat and drink.

Before she knew it, they were in the great hall. A crush of well-wishers gathered around them. Nessa appeared before them, but it was Egan she addressed: "Ye best take care o' her," was all she said.

A jet brow climbed aloft. "Oh, I will try, Nessa, but methinks the lady would rather take care of herself."

Glenda's chin came up a notch. Would that she had been allowed to! The biting retort hovered on her lips, but she did not give voice to it. Nessa was aware of her feelings about this marriage, but she would not disgrace either of them by allowing someone else to know the truth.

Mayhap that was why he'd kissed her with such brazen thoroughness!

Determined not to allow him to needle her so, her lips curved upward. She turned to find the earl standing before her. Despite her vexation with his dictate, she sank into a curtsy.

"My lord," she said breathlessly. "I must thank you for your generosity. The wedding feast will be bountiful indeed."

When she rose, the earl startled her by kissing her on both cheeks. " 'Twas no trouble, lass." He shifted his attention to Egan, who had taken note of his presence as well.

"My lord, may I present my"—the weight of a stone seemed to strike the center of her chest—"my husband, Egan MacBain."

"My lord, you honor us." Egan gave a low bow.

"I had to see you for myself." He winked at Egan. "Though I did make inquiries. I'd not have allowed this lovely lady to marry just anyone, you know."

"I should hope not."

Glenda stiffened. Did the faintest twinge of mockery taint his tone?

"However," the earl went on, " 'tis not an enviable situation you come to."

"Nay, my lord." Egan's smile faded. All at once he

was very earnest. "I will see that Blackstone prospers once again. You have my word on it."

The earl tipped his head. "I do believe you will," he said. His gaze slid to Glenda. "You have chosen well, lass. He is a good man."

Never had Glenda been so frustrated. It was not that she found fault with his statement. In her heart, she knew that Egan *was* a good man. Yet it somehow grated that everyone was singing his praises. If Blackstone prospered, it would be because of her own hard work as well as Egan's! If all turned out well, the credit should be equally shared!

Gritting her teeth, she graciously inquired, "Will you join us in our wedding feast, my lord?"

"Aye, I do believe I will."

The faces began to blur, until they all looked the same. Then all at once a tall figure stepped before her. Blond hair gleamed like a field of wheat. Glenda's heart lurched, for it was Simon. She hadn't realized that he was here!

"Simon! What do you here?"

"I missed your first wedding, Glenda. I could hardly miss the next, now could I?"

He did not kiss her hand, or her cheek, like so many of the others. Instead he placed both hands on the narrowness of her waist and kissed her full on the mouth.

His lips were cool and dry. There was no time to protest, no time to withdraw. She couldn't suppress a shiver of distaste. She could never have married him, never!

His boldness did not go unnoticed by Egan. Glenda felt the very instant the tension invaded his tall body. Simon's gaze flickered to Egan.

"I trust there are no hard feelings," Simon said smoothly.

Glenda held her breath and waited. Yet she should have known that Egan's response would be equally calm, for he was not one to give rise to fits of temper.

"Nary a one. Nay, it simply would not do if we were enemies. You are welcome here, Simon, just as you were before. We are neighbors, are we not? And I suppose now is as good a time as any to tell you that your men need not patrol Blackstone lands at night searching for marauders—we've intruded on your generosity long enough. I've several men in mind that are quite up to the task. Please be assured, however, that if ever I can return the favor, I pray you will not hesitate to come to me."

It was a warning. Whether anyone else knew it, it mattered not, for the three of them did. Something leaped in Simon's eyes, something Glenda feared was anger. Yet it was swiftly masked.

"Rest assured, I will," he said pleasantly. With a nod to both, he was gone.

In the hour that followed, Glenda's head began to spin. Egan, however, seemed to be having the time of his life. Ah, but he was in a fine humor! A ready smile curved his lips and never waned, Egan who smiled but rarely! Never had she known a smile could be so grating! The earl returned and claimed the spot next to him. Very soon they were engrossed in avid conversation, as if they had known each other for years! Listening to Egan's deeply resonant voice and the earl's laughing response, there could be no doubt the earl applauded her choice of husband.

Glenda wasn't sure if she was relieved or incensed! As for Simon, she saw no more of him, and for that she was heartily grateful.

There was a never-ending procession of food from the kitchens—roast peacock with its bright plume of tail feathers intact, capon, goose, a various assortment of meat pies, cheeses and breads. As the dishes were offered and served, she accepted but a few.

Egan leaned close. "Why do you not eat?" he asked bluntly.

"I had a hearty meal this morn," she murmured.

"You did not. I asked Nessa."

Caught in the lie, Glenda said nothing. His eyes pinioned her, his regard so unrelieving and so penetrating she grew even more uncomfortable.

"Are you ill?"

"You know I am not one to sicken easily." As if to prove it, she reached for a portion of mutton and chewed determinedly. Though it was juicy and tender, to Glenda it might have been boiled leather, for all she tasted of it.

He persisted. "Would you like to leave?"

"There is no need." Though she blanched inwardly, she was outwardly calm. "I am fine. Truly."

"Very well, then."

He turned aside, but not before her eyes came to rest on his mouth. Just now the cast of his lips was unsmiling, yet not stern. The shape of his mouth was sensuous, his lower lip slightly fuller than the upper. All at once Glenda couldn't help but remember how it felt on hers. Warm and smooth and resilient. So firm and relentlessly masculine.

A tight, heavy knot gathered in the pit of her stomach. She longed to be able to claim otherwise, but she was hardly unaware of him—a man who aroused feelings she'd never expected she would experience again. His scent was pleasant and clean; it swirled all around and filled her nostrils to the exclusion of all else. The fingers of one hand rested casually around his goblet as he glanced out across the hall at the revelers. His hands were lean and brown, so very much larger than her own. Panic engulfed her. What would happen when they were alone together? Her own curled in her lap. Her palms grew damp.

Jeannine started to pass by, only to be stopped by Egan. He beckoned her close, then leaned forward to whisper in her ear. Jeannine gave a nod, then moved around to Glenda and laid her free hand on her shoulder. "Come," she murmured with shining eyes. "Come."

Glenda shot him a fulminating look. Now she understood the reason for his whisper. The merest hint of a smile dallied about his lips, yet within the depths of his gaze lurked a wordless challenge.

Glenda longed to retire unnoticed. But as soon as she was on her feet, someone gave a shout. Her cheeks heated. Trying to close her ears to the bawdy remarks and boisterous laughter, she walked quickly toward the stairs.

Upstairs in her chamber, her clothes were drawn from her and a gossamer-thin gown drawn over her head and twitched into place. The transparency of the gown made her cheeks flush darker. Amidst giggles and knowing glances, the women withdrew. Yet alas, Glenda was allowed no time for sanctuary, no time to scarcely even draw breath, than Egan strolled through the door, as if it were his due . . . as if he had every right to be here!

As indeed he did.

The door clicked quietly shut. For a moment he simply stood there, tall and powerful, his shoulders nearly as wide as the door.

Silence prevailed. Their eyes locked. Hers were the first to fall away. Candles burned brightly behind her and Glenda was certain the outline of her body was clearly visible. She fought desperately to slow the frantic throb of her wildly thrumming pulse.

His gaze shifted to the table near the fireplace, where a tray with wine and two goblets had been placed, then back to her.

"Would you like some wine?"

She shook her head.

"Then will you pour for me?"

Glenda hesitated, then moved to comply. As she handed it to him, quickly she withdrew her fingers lest they touch. If Egan noticed, he gave no sign of it. His manner was easy and relaxed, while she felt like screaming from the tension that played like a string upon her body.

"The day was long," he remarked.

"But no longer than any other," she returned.

No different than any other. Though she did not say it, that was what her tone implied. So. This was what she thought of him. Of their wedding day. Through-out the day she would scarcely meet his gaze. He had noticed the paleness of her skin, yet no wounded doe was this! The incline of her chin told the tale only too well. And the slant of her mouth was fairly mutinous.

And indeed, now that they were alone, something

inside her rebelled. She was not yet ready to lay with another man—with Egan! To do so seemed the ultimate betrayal of her love for Niall.

Yet it was just as she'd told herself earlier. She must accept all the responsibilities of a woman . . . and a wife.

Nay, she would not live in dread of this night—in dread of this moment. It was better to feel nothing. Better to be done with it once and for all.

'Ere the thought sped through her mind, her hands were on the gown, dragging it from her shoulders. In one swift move she let it fall to the floor.

His breath hissed. Cool air rushed across her naked skin as she stepped from the gown. In some far distant corner of her mind, she was appalled at her audacity. What madness was this that she should taunt him so? She couldn't explain the reckless anger that provoked such daring, yet it was too late to recall it.

Egan's tone was tight. "What the devil do you think you're doing?"

Slowly Glenda raised her head. They stood so close he had only to lift a hand that he might touch her. But his hands remained close at his sides. If she'd thought he would be overcome with lust, she was sorely mistaken. His eyes blazed, but not with lust.

Their eyes locked. "I but oblige my husband. Need I remind you this is our wedding night?"

"I need no reminder, Glenda." The words were clipped and abrupt.

The burning of his gaze seemed to forge twin holes within her. Her chest rose and fell quickly with each breath. "Nor do I, so do what you will. I will not stop you."

Still he moved not a muscle. The air in the chamber was suddenly stifling and close.

Wildly she said the first thing that came into her head. "What is it? I stand before you naked . . . naked and willing!"

Egan could not help it. Slowly he looked the length of her, a scorching appraisal that left no part of her untouched. Did she truly think he was so noble that he would not? If she did, then she had woefully underestimated him. Indeed, he was hardly unmoved by the sweetness of her feminine charms displayed in their entirety. Aye, he'd seen her naked before, but not like this. Never so close at hand . . . the very sight of her made his blood run thick and his heart pound, his loins swell painfully hard and erect.

Her hair hung well below her buttocks, a rippling cascade the color of honey. Her skin was pale and unblemished; in the flickering candlelight, it gleamed with the luster of a pearl. Impudent, coral nipples crowned breasts that were delightfully round and alluring; he yearned to weigh their unbridled fullness in his palms, to taste those budding tips and suck hard and long until she cried out in wanton ecstasy. Her hips flared below the nip of her waist. He longed to thread his fingers through the golden thatch at the joinder of her legs and spread wide the pinkness of her core.

It was agony, knowing she was indeed within his grasp . . . yet never had she been so disdainfully aloof! He saw the way she swallowed; sensed her struggle as she fought to keep her hands at her sides and refrain from shielding herself. Egan did not touch her, though his hands itched to. He ached to catch a handful of her hair and bind it around his fist, bringing it to his mouth, to taste it and feel for himself if it was as soft as her lips. But he was neither blind nor a fool. No doubt she had disrobed on her own so that she need not suffer his hands on her body!

His jaw clenched tight. "Willing, is it?" His laugh was brittle and short. He bent, snatched up the bedgown and flung it at her. "Cover yourself!"

Stung by his fierceness, for an instant Glenda gaped at him. Then a rallying anger rose like a tide within her. "What do you expect? The earl demanded that I marry. I have done so. But I do not have to like it."

"Tell me then, and tell me true: would you rather be with Simon? I saw you when he kissed you, Glenda. You shuddered, and I daresay 'twas not in ecstasy. Yet now you dare to taunt me, with words and with this bold display of flesh! Do you think I do not know what you are about? You think to stir my wrath, to make me take you in anger, that you might then condemn me." His lips thinned. " 'Tis not like you to scheme, Glenda. 'Tis not like you to be so petty!"

"I do not scheme!" she flared. Petty, was she! Why, the oaf! Did he treat bedding a woman so lightly then? Would she have been just another tumble like . . . like the maids he'd taken at Dunthorpe? Oh, but it was just like him! Bitterly she confronted him. "I might add that 'tis not like you to gloat!"

"I do not gloat," he said flatly.

"Didn't you? I watched you. I watched you throughout the day, and you did gloat! You gained much today, Egan. A wife. Lands aplenty. This keep."

"Aye, I gained lands, lands whose tenants have fled! And this keep . . . a keep that needs a goodly amount of repairs and fortification. Oh, aye," he mocked, "I gained much this day—this keep, and all the burdens that come with it!" Egan was starkly, bitterly furious, and cared not if she knew it! He stepped to the bed and swept the coverlet aside.

"In with you," he ordered curtly.

"I will not! Aye, you are right—Simon's kiss did make me shudder—and so did yours! I did not want this. I did not want you!"

Her defiance rankled. "You lie, Glenda."

"I do not!"

Egan's response was instantaneous—and uncontrollable. Boldly he clamped her breasts with both hands, raking his thumbs across both peaks until they sprang eager and taut with longing. Dismayed by her body's involuntary response, she looked up at him with a gasp. The gaze he leveled on her was one of fearsome intensity.

"Will you deny what you are?" he demanded. "What you feel? You are not a woman who is cold as a grave lined in winter's frost. You are not a woman without passion! I've felt it for myself! By God, I feel it now."

The suddenness of the action—and aye, the possessive hold of strong brown hands upon that part of her—wrung a choked sound from deep in her throat. She tore herself away.

"You pretend to know the secrets of my heart," she cried, "but you know nothing of me!"

His eyes rained blue fire. "Nothing, is it? I know you pine for Niall. Even after all this time, you pine for him. But Niall is dead, Glenda. Dead. He will never come back. Why can you not see it?"

"No one knows it better than I!" She let loose the storm in her heart. "Damn you, Egan, damn you! Why must you do this? Why must you hurt me? You cannot know the pain I live with, the heartache that cleaves me in two!"

And you cannot know the pain I feel in watching you, he almost said. Yet something held him back.

She straightened her shoulders proudly. "I do not want to lay with you," she announced.

"We are wed, Glenda."

"Aye, we are wed!" The words were fairly flung at him. "But I do not want your seed! Do you hear me? *I do not want your seed!*"

Egan went utterly still, both inside and out. The words scalded him, burning through him like a raw, blistering wind. He could barely check the impulse to snatch her to him, to smother her mouth with his and show her what rubbish she spoke!

Blackness stole over him, a shroud of darkest midnight. That she dared accuse him of hurting her! By God, it was she who dealt a punishing blow to the very center of his soul. But he would not allow her to know the depth of his hurt. He masked his pain with the fury that still simmered just below the surface.

His posture rigid, he gestured to the bed. "Get in," he said between his teeth.

His expression was all at once so darkly forbidding, she nearly shrank back. Desperately she shook her head. "Nay," she said faintly. "I told you, Egan. I will—"

"I heard what you said, Glenda, but you will not make a fool of me. We are expected to share a bed this night, and by God, we will. Oh, you need not worry that I will lay a hand on you. I would not take you for Blackstone Keep and a thousand others like it."

His lip curled as he went on. "It is your desire that our marriage remain unconsummated. So be it. But I do not worry that you will tell. And indeed, who will know, for there will be no virgin blood expected from a woman who is not a maid." He spoke the words as if they were a curse. "Nay, I do not fret. You will not cross the earl. If you refuse this marriage, he will see that you make another—and your next husband might not be as considerate as I."

Nor was he finished. His features were rigid and stony. Bending over her, he caught her chin between thumb and forefinger, allowing no retreat. Her heart pounding wildly, Glenda found herself staring into eyes that impaled her with the fierceness of their glow.

"But know this, wife, for I make you a promise I will not forsake. When I want you, you will know it. And when I take you"—a cold smile touched the hardness of his lips—"when I take you, Glenda, you will want it as much as I."

Chapter 11

I do not want your seed.

Even now, a sennight later, those words had the power to lacerate his heart. He felt like shoving his fist through the curtain wall whenever he thought of it. Such imperiousness was wholly unlike her, for in truth, Glenda was one of the most warm, giving women he'd ever encountered in his life. Why, then, was she so opposed to giving herself to him in their marriage bed? Was it him? he wondered. Did she find the prospect of lying with him so unappealing? He couldn't help but be affronted. Was it his scar? He hurled wordless curses at the fates that had so marked him for life. Yet was he truly so very odious in appearance? There were some who had even called him handsome.

Or was it the fact that the choice had been stripped from her? Now that was something he could understand. Yet he couldn't help but think of her union with Niall—their marriage had been arranged for many years, and she'd had little choice in the matter.

But she had quickly grown to love Niall, needled a voice within him. *Indeed, by the time the pair had arrived*

162

at Dunthorpe, mere days after they were wed, she had been
madly in love with her husband. It was there in the melding of their eyes.

Something squeezed inside his chest. He pushed
the remembrance aside, chafing bitterly. She'd had to
choose between him and Simon. Yet Niall still stood
between them. Niall . . . the name reared high before
he could stop it. Guilt seeped at his insides like slow
poison. He'd loved Niall like a brother—still loved
him—yet there were times when he'd almost hated
him . . .

His soul cried out the injustice. Glenda was now
his wife. By all the saints, *his wife*. She was so very
near . . . yet tantalizingly out of reach. Aye, she continued to remain as elusive as ever . . . the one
woman in the world he'd ever truly longed for . . .

Still he could not have her.

A sennight passed, and then another.

*When I want you, you will know it. And when I take
you, you will want it as much as I.*

His wicked promise was all the more dire for the
very softness of his tone. It pricked her deeply, like
a thistle imbedded deep in her skin. She couldn't
deny the tumult that raged inside her. She despised
herself for her weakness, for being drawn to Egan,
her husband's friend.

I do not want your seed.

Until the instant she'd blurted those words, she
hadn't known she would say them. Glenda cringed
whenever she thought of what she'd said. She had
spoken rashly, in the heat of the moment . . . but
would she recant them if she could?

She knew not.

In truth, there had been no time to consider, no time to adapt, no time to come to terms with all that marriage entailed. Sharing not just a home . . . but a bed.

For hers was a desperate fear that transcended all else. A fear unlike any she had ever known. Egan didn't know of the alarm that raced through her at the thought of what might happen if they lay together . . . he couldn't know! How could any man truly know? A man did not carry a babe beneath his heart, nourish its body with his, protect it and shelter it from the world those many months. He did not feel it grow, or feel it kick and roll, so tiny yet so alive . . . only to cradle its limp, tiny body tight against her breast, to will it to live though life was already gone. Oh, but her arms had been so empty . . .

Aye, the thought of another babe terrified her as nothing else. The pain of losing a child was too great—she could not stand to do it again!

She could not give . . . not the way a wife should give. Oh, but they should never have wed. But they had, and she had no choice but to make the best of it.

She told herself it was better this way. Better that he should despise her. Better to hold her distance . . . better to keep *him* at a distance.

But for that very first night, he'd not slept in her bed, but his own.

Aye, his behavior toward her was decidedly cool. He was neither solicitous nor callous. Instead he treated her with polite indifference, keeping his vow not to touch her. Indeed, he seemed to take great pains to avoid any contact with her, even the merest brush of their fingers! What little time they spent together was marked with strain and tension.

She should have been relieved, yet in the days that passed, Glenda found herself utterly confused. Thoughts of him tormented her. Could it be that his desire had waned? Perchance he did not want her that way. Odd, for she had been so convinced that he did . . .

Or was there another reason? Mayhap now that he was the lord of Blackstone, she had served her purpose. She should have been glad. Relieved beyond measure that he did not share her bed. Yet somehow she couldn't stifle a pinprick of hurt.

As he strode through the bailey, greeting this one and that, his manner was easy and carefree; there was always a word and a smile for anyone who approached or came near. It struck her then . . . it was as if he thrived as never before.

Indeed, Egan embraced his role with an enthusiasm she'd never expected—and for the first time Glenda saw him in a role never before imagined. That first night here with Simon, he admitted he knew naught of farming; yet she saw him one morning as she was out riding in the fields of Godfrey Fyfe. Egan stood behind the plow handles, guiding the colter as it cut through the ground and broke it; Godfrey stood to the left, driving the oxen forward with his goad, while his boys trailed behind scattering seed in the damp furrows.

On this particular morn, Glenda stepped around the corner of the donjon. Lifting the hem of her skirt, she prepared to cross the bailey, only to look up at the ringing of steel against steel.

A pair of men were engaged in swordplay, while a line of others observed. Egan stood near the pair, shouting encouragement and directions to both. Intrigued in spite of herself, Glenda paused to watch.

The fighting between the pair intensified. Their swords came together time and time again. Then suddenly one lunged forward and sent the other man's weapon spinning away. It landed in the dirt, sending a spray of dust high. The victor spun around and heaved sword and shield high above his head with a whoop of triumph.

"Well done, Graham." This came from Egan. "But you must remember, 'tis not just might and brawn and the strength to wield a sword that make a formidable opponent. The battle must also be fought here." With a fingertip he tapped his temple. "Even as you must be ever on guard, you must be one step ahead, anticipating your opponent's next move so that you are ready to parry and thrust." He gestured to a youth, who obediently trotted forward carrying his sword and shield. Egan plucked them from the boy's hands, then turned to Graham. "Now, let's see if you're up to a trifle more challenge."

For a moment the young man looked decidedly wary. Then he nodded and resumed his defensive stance.

It was Egan who struck the first blow. In the seconds that followed, it appeared Graham had all he could handle to defend himself, let alone initiate any offensive moves. Sunlight flashed off Egan's sword as it whirred through the air. Graham lifted both sword and shield to his efforts to ward off Egan's blows—clearly Egan was the superior swordsman. He wielded his sword with speed and accuracy; his feet were agile and swift. Graham's expression was harried. Her heart leaped as Egan's sword crashed against the other man's shield, a particularly mighty blow. She couldn't withhold the cry that tore from her throat.

It was then he saw her. His gaze flitted over Graham's shoulder to where she stood on the edge of the grass. In that split second, his attention shifted just enough that Graham was able to attack. Distracted by her presence, his reaction skewed by a fraction of a second, he was slow in lifting his shield. Graham's blow knocked him off balance. He landed heavily on his back.

Glenda wasn't quite aware of moving. The next thing she knew, she was standing above him. She tipped her head to the side and regarded him, the veriest smile upon her lips.

"I should say, sir," she murmured demurely, "that Graham is certainly up to the challenge. The question is . . . are you?"

A ruddy color flushed his cheeks. Getting to his feet, Egan scowled at her. "Perhaps you would like to try, madam."

"Certainly not," she replied crisply. "I've not the strength."

Egan smiled slowly, his eyes agleam.

"Nor," she added, "does it seem that you do either."

His smile was wiped clean. "Could it be you require a bit more might and brawn? Or mayhap you should hone your skill here." She tapped her temple as he had done. "Or mayhap your calling is in the fields as a plowman," she added sweetly, then shook her head. "Alas, if my present husband cannot protect this keep, I fear I shall have to find one who can."

He scowled anew. "Mayhap you should keep to the accounts and your sewing."

It was Glenda's turn to smile. On that note, she turned and departed the bailey.

The men were much amused by his humbling defeat before his wife. Egan bore their good-natured ribbing well, but resolved not to let it happen again. Though Glenda had never suffered from an overabundance of vanity, he decided it wouldn't hurt her to have a taste of humility. Nor could he help but be a trifle uncertain of her comment that she should find another husband. She was jesting, wasn't she?

The opportunity came the very next day. As he returned from the village near noonday, he came upon a family of peasants. Mother and children walked before a lumbering cart piled high with a table and chairs, and various sacks of grain, driven by the father.

Egan greeted them. "Good day!" he called out.

"Good day," the man atop the cart returned. He reined his oxen to a halt. "Would ye happen to be the Highlander known as Egan?"

"That I am." Egan inclined his head. "And who might all of you be?"

"I am Randolph, and this is my wife Mary . . ."

He left them a short time later. The children waved as they continued on their way.

Just before he entered the gate, he chanced to see

Glenda poised on the wall-walk, staring down at him. "Good morning, wife!" He raised a hand in greeting. She didn't return his greeting; instead her head disappeared from view.

By the time he got to the stable, she was there, awaiting him. The sunlight picked out strands of gold in her chestnut mane, untamed now, for the wind had snatched away the ribbon that bound it.

Desire struck him like a fist to the belly, powerful and relentless. Egan felt his blood surge hot and molten through his veins. But he was still smarting from the day before when he'd been training the sentries in the bailey.

Her expression was filled with distress; he soon discovered why. "Tell me, Egan. The people with the cart . . . are they leaving, too? God knows, we can afford no more . . ."

When Egan had first spotted the family, his head stood still, for he'd thought that very thing. "Ah, you mean the Murrays, Randolph and Mary."

"The Murrays. Yes, yes!" She could barely restrain her impatience. "Tell me, are they leaving?"

He pretended to consider. "Nay," he said finally, then said no more.

She stared up at him, her agitation plain to see. "Nay?" she echoed.

"Nay," he affirmed.

"But . . . their cart was filled with their belongings, was it not?"

"Oh, aye."

"Then what are they doing if they are not leaving?" Her eyes were anxious and pleading and filled with frustration, all at once.

"The Murrays?"

"Aye!" If her features were any indication, she longed to throttle him.

He decided to put an end to her misery. "They are returning," he said simply.

"Returning?" she echoed. "To Blackstone?"

"Aye. Randolph told me their cottage lies a mile north of the village." Calmly he said, "Oh, and I suppose you might be interested in this as well. They told me of three other families who will be returning within the week as well."

Aware that she gaped, he started to saunter off, only to turn back.

"Oh, and Glenda?"

"Aye?" she said weakly.

"I saw you watching as I worked with the sentries this morn. Six worthy men and they could not take me."

Oh, the swaggering oaf! Glenda decided. Yet just now she couldn't even summon the mildest irritation. Her chest was filled with too much gladness. Blackstone's tenants had begun to return!

"It seems you will simply have to be content with your present husband, does it not?" He spoke with a wicked smile, then departed.

But thus began the contest between them. If he leveled a challenge, she was certain to return it in full measure.

One evening at dinner, their exchange was particularly tart—it seemed neither would allow the other to have the last word. Finally Egan rose, gave a stiff bow and left.

Nessa's gaze drilled into his back as he made for

the stairs, rife with disapproval. Glenda couldn't resist one last remark. "A veritable prize to be treasured, is he not?"

Nessa whirled on her. Her glower had not softened in the least. "I am ashamed of ye both! What ails the two of ye that ye should snipe at each other so?"

Glenda was taken aback by her nursemaid's biting censure. Shame made a brief appearance, but then she squared her shoulders defensively. "We should never have wed," she said quietly.

"And have ye tried, either of ye? I know not what to expect of Egan. But ye, lassie . . . when ye were a child, ye had a stubborn streak. Oh, 'twas seldom that we saw it, but when we did . . . well, yer poor dear mother would say that ye might as well have been rooted in the earth, like a tree that refused to be fallen. 'Twould seem ye have not changed!" She thumped her staff on the floor. "Tell me, lassie—do you wish to live your entire life like this? Would you always have it so between you and yer husband?"

Glenda raised her chin. "This should never have happened, Nessa. I sent him away."

"And it was I who asked him to stay!" Nessa's sunken lips thinned further.

Glenda blinked. "What! You mean to say that you—"

"Aye! I asked him to stay and protect you. I asked him not to abandon you . . . not to abandon Blackstone! I asked him to stay and watch over all of us."

"Nessa, how could you? You—you cost me my freedom!"

"Yer freedom!" Nessa scoffed. "Ye are hardly the first woman to marry when you did not wish to.

Why, I should think ye would be countin' yer bless-
ings, for if I had not, ye might well be wed to Simon
the Lawless this very moment and not Egan."

"You cannot know that, Nessa. I might have convinced the earl there was no need for me to wed!"

Nessa snorted. "If that's what you believe, you fool
no one but yerself, lassie. As fer me, I've no wish to
spend my last days in the midst of a squabble between husband and wife simply because they are
each as stubborn as an ass! Perhaps *I* will be the one
to leave!" she finished with a sniff. With that she
marched off as fast as her aging legs would allow.

Glenda did not go after her, not just yet. She was
furious at both Nessa and Egan for keeping from her
the fact that Nessa had asked him to stay on. It was
not that it truly made any difference either way—it
was simply that neither of them had been honest
with her.

By the next day her anger had cooled. Glenda was
out walking in the orchard when she chanced to see
Egan's huge black stallion. Ah, there was his master!
He stood with one booted foot braced upon an out-
cropping of rock. The clean lines of his profile revealed his lips turned up at the corners ever so
slightly. He gazed out upon the fields that dipped
and rolled, no longer fallow. Crisp new shoots of oats
and barley had pushed through the earth, straining
toward the summer sun. Glenda sensed his satisfaction with all that she possessed. It was there in that
wretched smile and the swell of his chest.

In that instant, her resentment surfaced. It was then
she remembered she'd idly plucked an apple from
one of the trees but a few steps before she glimpsed

Egan. Her gaze lowered; it traveled from Egan's figure to the plump, unripe fruit in her hand, then back to Egan's figure . . .

The next thing she knew, the apple was flying through the air. What possessed her to hurl it, she knew not. Indeed, she was not thinking at all . . . she simply acted without thought or reason.

The apple glanced off his shoulder. He turned abruptly. Glenda had already retreated and ducked beneath a low-hanging branch and hunkered down. All at once she was laughing as she hadn't since she was a child, her hands covering her mouth and smothering the sound. A moment later, she crept forward and peeped out. Egan had turned back and resumed his pose.

Biting her lip, amazed at her audacity, she plucked another apple from the branch . . . and let loose her next missile.

This one struck the middle of his back.

He whirled. He strode forward, his mouth a straight, forbidding line.

Glenda didn't hesitate. She grabbed her gown and ran as fast as her legs would carry her. Her lungs began to burn as she weaved through the orchard, making for the meadow and the path that led back to Blackstone.

Then all at once he loomed before her. In her frenzied state of mind, it was as if he was as tall as the stoutest oak that grew near the river and just as broad.

She stopped short with a gasp.

Egan leisurely crossed his arms over his chest. A smile dallied about his lips. "Well, well," he said lightly. "I had no idea I'd married such a skilled warrior. But here is a lesson in tactics, wife. Let not your enemy see you."

Glenda had already begun to back away. "What!" she rallied breathlessly. "I am not skilled, sir! Indeed I need more practice." She already clutched one last apple in her hand. Acting sheerly on impulse, she launched it anew.

It hit him squarely in the temple. His eyes reflected his shock. He took one tottering step forward . . . and dropped limply to the ground.

Chapter 12

What had she done! God in heaven, she'd meant him no harm, only to make a little mischief and repay but a measure of the trouble he'd caused her. She flew to his side and sank down beside him.

"Egan!" she cried. She grasped his shoulder and shook him. "Egan, please, wake up!"

There was nothing. His lashes fanned thick and long on his cheekbones. Glenda gave a stricken little moan. "Egan—" Her voice began to wobble. "Egan, do not die! I-I could not live with myself if you did!"

She bent her head to his lips, straining to feel some wisp of air from his lips. Her heart lurched. Did he yet breathe? Saints above, she could not tell! Lifting her head, she thumped her fists on his chest. "Egan!" she screamed. Squeezing her eyes shut, she lifted her face heavenward and began to pray.

"Dear God, your aim is straight and true. Will you beat me as well? Tell me, wife . . . did you thus abuse Niall?"

Glenda didn't recognize the voice as the one shooting through her mind. It was laced with lazy laughter, that deep, masculine drawl. Her eyes opened, then slowly lowered.

Blue eyes glimmered up at her. He was smiling, the rogue . . . smiling!

Her screech was one of outrage. "Do not speak to me of Niall! You are not half the man he was!"

"But Niall is not here, and I am," he stated smoothly. He shook his head, as if in regret. "Ah, but how much better I should feel had you said you could not live without me."

Bristling, Glenda leaped to her feet. Her hands clenched into fists at her sides. "You wretch! You vile rodent! How *dare* you frighten me like that!"

A strong brown hand darted beneath the hem of her gown. His fingers skimmed up her calf, smoothing the tender skin behind her knee. He pretended to leer up her skirts.

"A most tempting view, I daresay."

Glenda heaved a breath of sheer frustration. Faith, but he was the most exasperating man in the world! She would not give him the satisfaction of a reply— nay, she would not venture where he would lead her . . . she would not play his game!

Her chin came up. Her lips compressed. Her spine went stiff and her muscles tightened as she prepared to tug her leg from his grasp that she might leave.

Somehow he guessed her intention. When she would have turned, that accursed hand descended to her ankle just as she would have stepped away. Her balance compromised, she felt herself wobbling precariously. She flung out her arms . . . and then felt herself tumbling downward. To her utter mortification, she did not land on the ground . . . she landed atop Egan!

'Ere she could take even a breath, arms of steel

banded tight about her back. Glenda managed to raise herself slightly on her elbows. In so doing the rounded neckline of her gown gaped, only she was unaware of it until she took a deep, ragged breath.

Egan's gaze tracked the rise and fall of the mounds of her breasts. "Oh, aye," he said again, "a most tempting view. Have all those who covet you seen your charms to such advantage?"

Glenda gasped when she realized where his eyes dwelled—and the reason for it. So he was well amused, was he?

"No one covets me!" she retorted. "Of a certainty not you!" She sought to push herself away, but his arms cinched tighter, so tightly she could hardly move.

"Ah, now, *that's* where you're wrong, lass." His smile widened—a wolfish grin now!

"You do not covet me! You mock me!"

In a heartbeat their positions were reversed. Egan lay straddled above her. Her wrists were shackled in one large hand and held over her head. In his eyes gleamed the reflection of victory.

"Oh, aye, dearest wife, but I *do* covet thee. The sweetness of thy lips, though I've been given but a miserly taste of all I crave. You smell of roses, and the scent of you lingers so that I can scarcely think. The softness of your skin, the color of cream. I long to touch it, feel its softness for myself, though I already know 'twill be as finely spun silk from the East."

There was naught of triumph in his voice. It had fled, along with the laughter. Nay, he was solemnly intent, his tone low and mesmerizing. It wrapped around her like a mantle of softest fleece.

"Egan." His name broke from her lips, a sound that trembled as she had begun to tremble. "Egan, you should not say such things."

"Why not? And if not to you, then to whom if not my wife? I should think 'twould be a good thing, that a man should think only of his wife. Am I wrong then?"

Glenda could summon no answer. Indeed, she could summon no resistance, for she was afraid to move, afraid even to breathe for fear of falling still further 'neath his spell.

She gave a tiny shake of her head. Her eyes locked helplessly on his face. It gave her no measure of ease to discover that his were locked on her lips.

He came nearer. She felt the weight of his chest settle over hers; his weight was heavy but not so great a burden that she could not bear it. Desperation filled her chest, for she knew what he would do . . . what he wanted. Yet still she could not move. It was as if a stranger had taken over her body and she could do naught but accept whatever was to happen . . .

It began with the most subtle of pressure, his kiss. Her lids fluttered shut as his mouth closed over hers. Warm breath filled her mouth. He was in no hurry, it seemed. His kiss was one of leisurely exploration, as piercingly slow as his last—that raw, possessive stamp of ownership on their wedding day—had been fierce. Oh, aye, it was wickedly seductive, this kiss. Treacherously languorous, leeching from her what little will and strength she possessed.

At some point he'd released her hands. Glenda

scarcely noticed, not until her hands crept round his neck to tangle in the dark hair that grew low on his nape. It was as if she were tumbling down a well, tumbling into some vast unknown place. Something fluttered inside her, only to disappear as his mouth grew hungrier, the contact deeper, intimate and fervent now. She shivered as his tongue touched the seam of her lips; her lips parted for the gliding probe of his tongue. She felt it rake across the edge of her teeth; her fingers curled into the muscled flesh of his shoulders. If only he would not kiss her! But it felt so good . . . *he* felt so good, so strong and lean and male . . . and impossibly hard to resist . . .

Taunting fingertips circled her nipples; they hardened and fairly leaped into his palms, tingling and aching. Scalding heat flashed in waves through her body. When his thumbs raked the budding crests, she moaned, a sound of yearning. Once before she'd felt the touch of that lean, dark hand upon that part of her without benefit of clothing; she ached to feel it anew. Ached for that and more . . . the feel of his mouth, hot and wet and tugging at the tip . . .

Her thighs weakened. Her knees drifted apart. With a growl deep in his throat, he caught her to him, his hips wedged between her legs. Even through the barrier of their clothing, she could feel the bold urgency of his arousal, the rigid brand of his maleness swollen and taut against her secret font . . .

She reeled. Mother of Christ, what had she done? What was happening? She was lying with Egan . . . *lying* with him . . . and nary a thought of Niall had intruded.

Sanity returned with a vengeance. Scorching

shame shot all through her. Her guilt knew no bounds.

She tore her mouth away from his with a strangled moan. A painful ache constricted her throat. "Egan"— his name was low and choked—"Egan, I beg you, please stop!"

The hard male body above hers went very still. Slowly he raised his head. Twin embers of fire rained down on her.

She pleaded mutely with her eyes. Still clamped against his form from breast to belly, she took a jagged breath, anxious to free herself. "Egan," she said waveringly.

"Cease!" he hissed. "Surely you know me well enough to know I will do nothing you do not want! But you must give me a moment."

His tone was as quelling as his regard.

Closing his eyes, he raised his face to the sky. Glenda couldn't tear her gaze away from his face. His features were lined and strained. The tendons in his neck stood out tautly. Time dragged by, until at last she felt the tension drain from his body.

He rose, his posture stiff. Glenda knew then what the effort cost him. Regret poured through her, as well as shame. More guilt.

He did not look at her as she scrambled to her feet, brushing at her skirts. "I'm sorry, Egan. I'm sorry!" Helplessly she floundered. "I know not how to explain, only that I cannot give . . . what you deserve . . . what a husband deserves."

He looked at her then. A harsh smile twisted his lips. "Oh, you can, Glenda. 'Tis simply that you won't."

With that he turned and whistled for his mount. When the stallion appeared with a toss of his head, he snatched the reins and leaped into the saddle. Never did he look back.

Egan did not appear at supper that night. Glenda couldn't help but be relieved at not having to face him again so soon. Nonetheless, he allowed her no peace. Always he trespassed. In her mind. In her thoughts. Even in the dark of night when she crawled alone into bed, there was no escaping him, for her dreams that night were wild and wanton.

She dreamed they were back in the apple orchard, lying on the grass beneath the trees. The breeze carried the scent of wildflowers from the neighboring meadow, fragrant and sweet. The noonday sun blazed down from the sky, sending spears of golden light shooting through the branches.

They were naked, both of them, for in this dream, there were no cares, no inhibitions, no shame. His mouth was everywhere . . . even there at the secret place between her thighs. And then . . . it was not he who straddled her, but she who straddled him. Glenda saw herself as if through the eyes of another. She was laughing, sitting on him . . . *sitting!* . . . her loins nesting with his. Gathering her streaming hair in both hands, she arched her back. Her breasts jutted forth, pink-tipped and full. Boldly she displayed her nakedness for him . . . for *him*.

His hands ran over her. Everywhere. He cupped her breasts in his hands like plump fruit and leaned forward, suckling first one quivering peak, and then the other. Finally his hands caught at her hips. Her buttocks filled his palm as he lifted her, guiding her down over his shaft . . .

She awoke with a gasp. Her eyes snapped open and she stared at the beams that stretched over her head, panting as if she'd run a very great distance. Her body felt as if it were on fire. Indeed, the coverlet was twisted about her ankles. Reaching down to pull it up, she was horrified to discover that dampness gathered there between her thighs. Glenda was wholly shocked. Never had such a thing happened before, even with Niall.

There was no sleep for her the rest of the night. Her temperament was not the best the next morning. She took one of the maids to task for not starting to remove the rushes in the hall earlier in the morn. Almost instantly she regretted her sharpness, but the girl had already fled.

With a sigh she turned. Nessa stood before her. The old woman raised an iron-gray brow. "Does yer temper this morn have aught to do with your husband?"

"No, it does not." Glenda was not yet ready for another dressing-down by her nursemaid. "Where is he, by the way?"

"He has not yet come down."

Glenda's heart lurched. She couldn't help the panic that flared. Egan had been so angry when he left the orchard yesterday. And then he hadn't been at supper . . . Dear God! Had she finally succeeded in doing what she truly did not want—only she didn't even know it until now! Had she driven him away from Blackstone?

Lines of worry knit her brow as she spun around

and left the hall. Her step was quick as she climbed the stairs that led to the east wing. As she breached the last step, a distinctly feminine voice drifted to her ears, followed by a low male baritone. Her body went stiff. She paused on the landing, then gazed down the passageway.

Her heartbeat stumbled. There was a pinch in the region of her heart. Nay, her husband had not yet come down, Glenda noted furiously. Why should he when he had so much to occupy him here?

Even as she watched, Egan slipped an arm around Belinda's shoulders and slid his knuckles beneath her chin. Tilting her face up to his, he gazed down at her and said something. Belinda nodded in response. Then all at once, the girl lifted herself on tiptoe and pressed her lips against Egan's.

Glenda moved without conscious volition. Her heels rapped out sharply as she approached the pair.

It was Belinda who stepped away first. Her eyes flew wide and she bobbed a curtsy. "Good morning to you, my lady."

Glenda didn't even look at her. "Belinda, you are needed in the hall."

"Aye, mistress."

Belinda fled, leaving her alone with her husband. He was utterly calm; his expression betrayed no hint of either guilt or regret. Glenda fumed. Had he no conscience? No morals that he would flaunt his relationship with his mistress openly before his wife?

"Did you wish to see me?"

The polite inquiry but further kindled her ire. "I did. 'Tis late and Nessa said you had not yet come down."

"I fear I did not sleep well."

"Do not complain to me if you found no sleep. Mayhap 'tis the company you keep! You did not appear at supper last night. Why, no doubt you left me and went straight to her."

His eyes flickered. "So the lady is angry. Come now, out with it, Glenda. 'Tis not like you to bandy words."

"Then I will not! I came after you, yet what do I find? The fair Belinda kissing my husband!" She let loose the storm in her heart. "Could the two of you at least exercise some discretion? Must you carry on your activities outside your chamber?"

He had the audacity to smile, the wretch! "The kiss you saw was not as it seem—"

"Not as it seemed? I'm glad you find this so amusing! But tell me, then. The press of one's lips upon another's . . . is that not a kiss?"

"Aye, but it was to thank me. I but gave the girl comfort."

"Comfort! Is that what it's called?" Baldly she confronted him. "How dare you? How dare you rut with the servants!"

"I was not rutting with the servants!"

"Let me say it again then. If the term 'rut' offends you, here is another: I believe it's called adultery."

"Adultery?" His jaw tightened. His smile vanished. "Our marriage remains unconsummated," he pointed out coolly. "In truth, ours has yet to be a valid marriage. We could still have it annulled."

"And perhaps we shall."

"We will not," he countered immediately. "As for

the reasons why, I do believe we've had this discussion before."

Glenda glared. She could find no suitable retort. "You are a womanizing rogue, Egan. Never did I realize how much of one until now!"

So. She thought him a rogue, did she? He took a curious delight in knowing that her mood was surely foul, for he'd been feeling rather sorry for himself—sorry and neglected. Was the kiss responsible? Nay. Surely not. A part of him scoffed. She spurned him, ever and always. Just when he thought she would yield—surrender all—a shield of iron went up, a shield he had no hope of penetrating.

"It did not take you long to find a mistress, Egan. Or is Belinda already one of many, like the pretty maids you left behind at Dunthorpe?" Glenda's anger overrode all pretense of control. "What was it you said yesterday in the orchard? Ah, yes, I remember. You said 'twould be a good thing, that a man should think only of his wife. But clearly you haven't the slightest regard for your wife. Well, I tell you now, Egan, I will not let you make a fool of me!"

Egan's eyes glittered. His hands shot out, winding around her wrists and snatching her against him. "What! You are the one who dares much, methinks! You refuse me outright. You scorn me as if I were the lowliest of men. And yet you would have me be a husband, when you refuse to be a wife! Nay, do not dare to chastise me, Glenda. Do not dare to take me to task, for you are not the one wronged here!"

His lips were ominously thin, his expression awful to behold. Deep inside alarm clamored within her, warning her that he was not a man to toy with, but

Glenda was beyond caution. She struggled to free herself, but his grip only tightened.

"Oh, but you are a knave! Niall would never have done what you have done. He would never have treated me the way you do!"

It was a mistake, the wrong thing to say. Glenda knew it the instant the words left her mouth, for she felt the rigid fury that invaded every part of him. His dark features froze. He stared down at her, his face a cold, hard mask.

"Niall. Niall!" he said fiercely. "I am sick of hearing his name, do you hear? 'Tis *me* you are wed to, Glenda, and I am not Niall. I am Egan!"

Her gaze flew wide. Whatever she might have said, his seething expression jammed it back in her throat. Too late she realized she'd pushed him too far. Nay, there was no escaping the determined glitter in his eyes. There was no time to react, no time for speech. His features filled her vision, dark and terrible.

And then his mouth crushed hers.

Chapter 13

There was something dangerous about him just now, something reckless, almost ruthless. Seized fast in his embrace, she decided almost hysterically that she possessed a knack no one else did . . . the ability to rouse the demons of anger inside him.

Lean fingers threaded through the length of her hair; they burrowed against her scalp, keeping her mouth captive beneath his in searing fusion. The corded muscle of his thighs bulged against her own . . . and so did the burgeoning swell of his manhood.

On and on he kissed her. Hotly. He kissed her as she'd never been kissed. Madly. With ravaging intent, as if he were starved and she were the most bounteous of feasts. He kissed her until the world eroded and she clutched at him as the only solid object in a wildly spinning universe.

He released her mouth . . . but he did not release her.

"Tell me who I am," came the hoarse rush of his voice against her ear. "Tell me I am your husband."

Her lips still throbbed. "You—you are my husband," she gasped.

"What is my name?" His head moved so that he stared down at her. His expression was implacable. She could read neither fury nor triumph in it, naught but the fiery demand she sensed he would not forswear.

She swallowed. A hot ache filled her throat, making it nearly impossible to speak.

Egan's jaw locked. "Say it," he ordered roughly. "Say my name."

The breath she drew was deep and shuddering. "Egan," she said, her voice barely audible. "You are . . . Egan."

Something snapped inside him then. A tide of scalding possessiveness shot through him. In one swift move he captured her in his arms. Four steps took him into his chamber. He slammed the door shut with his heel. Carrying her to the bed, his big body followed her down.

His heart thundered. Heat streaked through him. His rod felt ready to burst, thick and pulsing, straining to be free. With his eyes he sampled what would soon be his, carving a deliberate pathway down her body—lingering on breasts, belly, and the place where her thighs met. By God, she *would* be his. He ached with the need to mold his shaft against her, thrust deep inside her clinging heat. Soon, he promised himself, he would have her naked and writhing in his arms.

Raising himself slightly, he ripped off his tunic and trews and flung them aside. A hand alongside her face, his thumb beneath her chin, he urged her lips to his. His mouth was devouring and consuming, a stark testament to the tumultuous emotions gone wild and ungoverned within him.

It was then he tasted the salty warmth of tears. Locked in the throes of desire that tightened every part of his body, he wanted to deny it. To ignore it and tell himself they did not exist. But something caught at his conscience, something that made his head come up.

Her cheeks were glistening and wet, her lips swollen and damp. Her chest heaved. Her breath came thin and shallow.

He bit back a scathing oath. "Why do you cry, Glenda?"

His tone was grimly demanding. Glenda sought to evade his regard—to evade him!—by turning her face aside. Egan's grip on her chin tightened so that she could not.

"Tell me, Glenda."

She gave a tiny shake of her head. "I do not know," she said faintly, and then it was a cry: "I do not know!" And indeed, she did not. In all truth, she didn't know she wept until a tear leaked down to the shell of her ear. Lifting a hand, she dashed it away.

Egan's jaw clenched. His regard was relentless, his temper unconcealed. "You want me," he said fiercely. "You want me as much as I want you. Oh, you may claim differently, but I *know* differently. I've felt your lips part beneath mine. I've felt your very heart tumbling against mine! If it is not so, if you do not want me, if you feel nothing for me, then tell me—but tell me now!"

Time yawned, time with no end. The tension spiraled ever higher as they stared into one another's eyes.

"I cannot," she said at last, her voice half-strangled, "for I do . . . feel something for you." Her chest felt hollow and empty. She sought to rally the words, but none would come! "Don't you see, I-I know not what to do!"

Oddly, Egan did understand. He knew then that he could not do this. He could not take her like this, not with anger and tears between them . . . and the shadow of Niall. She would hate him forever!

Then there was his promise to her. It was made in the heat of anger, but a promise nonetheless. He'd promised her that when he took her, she would want it as much as he.

Clearly she did not.

He was tired. Tired of losing. Tired of fighting a battle that could not be won. She did not want him. His lips twisted in self-derision. She would never want him, he thought blackly. Even as he told himself sternly he must accept it, he resented her bitterly for ever keeping him at bay.

Yet his desire remained unchecked . . . unquenched. His heart was pounding, roaring in his ears. His blood still rushed hot and scalding, pooling hot and heavy in his loins.

The taste of acrid bitterness was like some vile brew. "You know not what to do . . . well, I do, Glenda. *I do.* Ah, but I should have known what to expect. A woman reluctantly wed . . . will be bedded just as reluctantly! Deny me then. Deny me forever. But since you desist from giving as a wife should, then at least I will have this."

He rolled to his side, bringing her with him, an arm about her back, even as strong fingers caught at hers. With unwavering intent she felt her palm dragged across the hair-roughened grid of his belly. He pulsed against her palm . . . into it. There was no withdrawing, for his hand clamped tight around hers, and hers tight around his burning shaft.

Her breath departed her lungs in a hiss. "Egan . . ."

His gaze cleaved into hers. "What! Do not be shocked, Glenda. Surely you know of such things! The night you first came to Dunthorpe . . . I wanted you then. Christ, all I could think of was you. All I wanted was you. But you were in Niall's arms, in Niall's bed! And so I did what a man must do when no other woman will do . . . when his body craves release . . . when he must gain his pleasure in the only way he can . . ."

The words were stark and raw. What he was doing was stark and raw. She was shocked to the core, stunned by what he'd said . . . by what he was doing . . . the way he moved her hand up and down his swollen, throbbing rod in a frenzied, shattering rhythm. His hips picked up the same frantic tempo . . .

"Christ," he whispered. "Christ!"

His eyes squeezed shut. The cords in his neck stood out. His features were contorted, whether in pain or pleasure she couldn't be sure. His breath harsh and scraping, all at once he reached for her hips, binding them tight against his own.

His back arched. A convulsive shudder wracked his body. Glenda buried her face against his neck, aware his passion had spent itself.

He sat up, swinging his legs to the floor in a jerky motion. Glenda sat up as well, pushing her heavy hair away from her face. She saw that the skin of his shoulders was covered with a damp sheen. Uncertain, she reached out and tentatively touched his forearm.

He jerked away from her. With a vile curse he was on his feet. In one swift move he donned his trews . . . and with them a stoic distance.

He strode to the door and flung it open. "Leave," he said without looking at her. His voice was flat; it contained naught but a glacial calm.

Confused, Glenda stared at him, at the starkness of his profile etched in bitter reproof.

He swung back to her. "Dammit," he said grittily, "is your hearing no better than Bernard's? I want you to leave!"

Her heart constricted. There was a sharp, rending pain in her breast, but this time there was no hesitation. Smothering a jagged cry, she ran from the chamber to her own.

Though she longed to hide away in her chamber, Glenda did not. There was much to be seen to—the planning of tomorrow's meals, beating the dust from the wall hangings, replacing the rushes with fresh ones from the marshes. Though she caught Nessa peering at her oddly once, the woman did not query her further. Indeed, what would she have said if she had! She got through the day by busying her hands that her mind would not dwell on . . . other things. She managed to steer clear of Egan, though late in the afternoon, she heard him shouting in the bailey.

It seemed his mood was little improved. With a feeling of dread coiling her middle, she went down to the evening meal.

Once again he was absent.

She was not inclined to linger afterward, but made her excuses and sought her chamber. She was exhausted, both mentally and from the physical toils of the day, and sought refuge in sleep.

Sleep . . . there was none!

Hours later, as wide awake as ever, she flung off the covers and moved to the window. Throwing open the shutters, she watched as moonlight showered down from the sky, washing the distant hills in a pale, silvery glow.

The morning's encounter crept into her mind. She winced, thinking about it . . . and then she could not stop.

She could still feel the sharpness of jealousy, like a falcon's talon tearing into her skin. Had he lied to her? All at once she wanted desperately to believe him, to believe that Belinda meant nothing to him, that he had indeed meant only to comfort her. Besides, he'd said he wanted her . . . Glenda . . . And the passion in his flaming kisses had not lied . . .

Aye, it hurt to think of Egan with Belinda—it hurt unbearably!—with any other woman! That was why she'd been so incensed. Otherwise, if she cared nothing about him, it shouldn't have bothered her in the slightest.

There. She'd admitted it. She was jealous.

Of Belinda. Of Patsy, the night of Daniel's wedding at Dunthorpe. She cared about him. She could not help it, for it was just as she'd admitted the night

they had arrived here at Blackstone. She admired
him. She respected him. His pride. His honor. His
skill as a warrior. All of those things, and more . . .
there was no man more loyal to the clan MacKay
than Egan. No man more dependable, or trustworthy
. . . no man more *worthy* of trust.

What was it he'd said? *The two of us . . . 'tis not the
same as before.* He was right, she confessed, her heart
knocking crazily. When had it begun? she asked herself dazedly. Perhaps 'twas then, the night of Daniel's
wedding . . . that moment in the dance when they'd
come face to face . . .

Oh, aye, she cared about him. Far more than she
should have . . .

Her conscience lent her no ease. Even now, she
could feel his anger all through her. Even as the encounter had unfolded, she told herself she'd been
wronged. That she was furious he would dare to im-
pose his will over hers. And why? Because she was
afraid. Oh, not of him, not of his power and strength.
Nay, she was afraid of the way he made her feel.
Because he made her feel things she'd never thought
to feel for another man . . . for a man other than Niall!

She couldn't forget what he'd said this morn. His
voice thrummed through her brain.

*You refuse me . . . You scorn me . . . You would have me
be a husband, when you refuse to be a wife . . . You desist
from giving as a wife should.*

Glenda cringed inside. Each word was an angry,
bruising blow. Shame poured through her like boiling oil. Always he had been there for her. On their
journey to Blackstone, he'd rescued her from Robin's

clutches. It was then that she had confided she was beholden to him.

And aye, she was.

For whether she willed it, whether she wanted it, he had rescued her from the earl's demand. From marriage to Simon, a man she neither wanted nor trusted. What did it matter that Nessa asked him to stay? True, he had gained much. But now he had far more to lose. Yet still he dared to risk all . . . and how had she repaid him?

It was just as he had said. She'd scorned him. Refused him.

An odd little pain clamped about her heart. She could not blame him. He was right, she acknowledged piercingly. She did desire him. Why, then, did she deny him? Why did she deny herself?

She felt as if she were in the midst of some violent battle, and knew not which way to turn. Should she stand her ground? Or surrender? And what then? What if she should regret it?

For if she yielded her body, what if he should demand her heart and soul?

Yet one thing stood out above all others. The boundary between them was of her choosing—a boundary that was proving intolerable, no matter how much she might have wished otherwise. They could not go on like this, either of them. She sensed he was like a brittle twig that would snap with the slightest pressure. Nor could she live with the thickening tension that mounted with every passing day.

Her mind made up, Glenda summoned all her strength, banished the demons of fear which threatened to rise up and steal her courage.

*   *   *

She approached his door and knocked, her heart thudding so that she feared it would surely give her away.

There was no answer. Yet she knew he was within, for she could see the flickering candlelight from beneath the door. She knocked again, this time more firmly.

The door opened. He was clad as he'd been when she left him that morning, only in trews. His chest was bare, matted darkly with a dense pelt of hair. Her mouth went dry, but she did not avert her eyes.

The skin on the back of her neck prickled suddenly. There was no smile in his eyes, only a chill that nearly sent her running back to her chamber.

But no. She'd come this far. "May I come in?"

"No," he said bluntly.

Her eyes flew wide when he made as if to close the door. "Egan, please!" Pleading eyes lifted to his. "There is something we need to discuss, you and I."

"What?"

"Our marriage." In the face of his coldness, she floundered. "About . . . what happened this morning."

He wanted to refuse. She could see it in the way his mouth compressed. Yet in the end he relented. Wordlessly he held the door wide.

Glenda stepped within. The heavy oaken panel creaked shut behind her. Even as she spied several bottles of wine on the table near the hearth, she was assailed by a strong scent.

When she turned, he stood directly behind her. "You've been drinking," she said without thinking.

"Drinking, aye. But I am not sotted." Would that

he was, he thought darkly. Would that it would take away the pain in his breast.

His gaze ran over her. Her hair tumbled about her shoulders, loose and free. Her mantle reached nearly to the floor, completely covering her clothes. He frowned. Had she been outside, then?

Glenda clutched the edges of her mantle together. There was a sinking flutter in the pit of her belly. Never had he been so aloof! It was her fault, she knew, yet how was she to explain what she didn't fully understand herself? From the look of him, he was not even disposed to listen! Yet she had to try. She had to!

Swallowing, she focused on the squareness of his jaw, for she could look no higher. Her voice but a wisp of sound, she began.

"I am ashamed, Egan, deeply ashamed. You are right. I have treated you as . . . as no wife should treat a husband. I was wrong to—to refuse you. To deny you as I did. But before God, I will not do so again." Her fingers fumbled with the laces at her throat. A flush stained her cheeks, but she did not stop. "I am yours, Egan. Yours to do with . . . as you will."

The mantle fluttered to the floor. It lay in a dark pool about her ankles.

Beneath it she was naked.

There was a ringing silence. He said nothing. Eyes of ice-blue fire pored over her, a scorching appraisal that made her quiver both inside and out. Did she please him? Oh, if only she knew! His lips were drawn in a relentless line. He stood like a fortress of stone, his expression shielded behind a wall that stretched clear to the Heavens. The strain was almost more than Glenda could stand. A hundred doubts crowded through her mind. She was no longer as young as she'd once been. She'd carried a babe, and bore the marks on her belly and hips to prove it.

Still there was nothing.

"Egan," she said faintly. "The night I first rode into Dunthorpe"—her voice began to wobble—"you said you wanted me, even then—"

"I know what I said."

She flinched from the bite in his tone.

He took a step forward, only to stop short. His hands clenched into fists as his sides. "Damn you," he said feelingly. "Why do you taunt me?"

She saw him through a misty blur. "I do not taunt you!" she cried.

He was suddenly reminded of what he'd done— the crude way in which he'd used her this morn. Lord, he was the one who was ashamed!

Realization dawned suddenly. He gave her no chance to respond. "You pity me, don't you?"

"Nay!" Glenda was stunned.

His lips twisted. "What then? In truth, I don't know what you think of me!"

Her lips parted. She gave a shake of her head. "How can you not when I stand before you naked . . . naked and willing?"

"You said that before," he accused.

Secretly shattered inside, she wanted to weep. He would reject her! Perhaps this was his way of paying her back—of making her feel what he had felt.

" 'Tis different, I swear." Silently she beseeched him, to no avail. "Egan, I thought you wanted me!"

It was a stricken cry. Shamed and degraded, she bent to retrieve her mantle.

He stopped her, his fingers winding around her wrist and bringing her upright.

"I do want you," he said tightly. "God above, you know I want you!" His eyes pinned hers. Within his gaze glittered a searing demand. "But what of you, Glenda? What do *you* want?"

"I want . . . this. I want . . . you . . ." She gazed at him, with quavering heart and limbs atremble.

Egan's eyes darkened. Having her so near, dainty and bare in all her glory, was a temptation beyond bearing. His release this morn had been no release at all! Indeed, it but deepened the frenzied longing that stirred his blood to a molten heat. The urge to drag her against him, to plunge his hardness in her furrowed channel and feel her moist heat clamp tight around his rod surged high in his mind. But they had come so close before. . . . He was a man, not a monk, and he could not be turned aside again. He had to know for certain this was what she wanted.

"And what if I do not believe you?"

There was a heartbeat of silence. When her voice came, it was but a thread of sound.

"Then it appears I have no choice . . . but to show you."

Chapter 14

Glenda had hoped he would make this easy for her. He did not. He *would* not. Ah, but she could not blame him! He was wary. She knew it was a test. He was asking her to prove the truth of her claim—her claim that she wanted him.

In all her days, Glenda didn't know when she'd been so afraid. Her pulse was pounding so that she could scarcely breathe. Her throat was parched and dry.

Candlelight bathed his form in golden silhouette. He stood before her, vital and strong. Fierce and compelling. Dark hair matted the broadness of his chest, the hard plane of his belly. His arms were knotted and lean, cleanly sculpted with muscle. He wore his pride like a targe of iron, so intensely masculine he drove the very breath from her lungs.

His eyes barely flickered as she stepped before him. His expression was unreadable. With her eyes she traced the squareness of his jaw, the flare of a brow both noble and arresting. The journey ended with his mouth; it spun through her mind that she'd always thought his mouth was beautifully shaped, though stern and a bit thin just now. Gathering all her courage, she eased upward, closed her eyes and kissed him.

His lips remained closed and tight. He might have been a statue carved in marble for all the effect it had on him.

Glenda frowned. Tentatively she splayed her hands across his chest. It was hardly the first time she'd touched a man's chest, but Niall's had been smooth and void of hair. Since the day she'd first seen Egan working alongside the mason, naked to the waist, his chest had held a forbidden fascination for her. Responding to an unbidden call within her, she twined her fingers through the dense, curly fur; it was startlingly soft, springing against her palms. Beneath it, his flesh was resilient and warm, almost hot.

"You must do better than that, wife, if you are to convince me."

"You did not seem to like my kiss." Glenda couldn't help it. His coolness hurt.

A roguish brow climbed high. "Then mayhap you should kiss me again."

Hesitating for a moment, Glenda did as she was bid. This time his mouth moved ever so slightly beneath hers. Encouraged, she pressed her tongue to the very center of his lower lip. She felt more than heard his indrawn breath. His arms started to come up, tensed . . . then fell to his sides.

Scarcely daring to breathe, she slipped her arms around his neck. She kissed him, opening her mouth against his, melding her body against him so that the pelt on his chest tickled her nipples...aye, even there at the apex of her thighs.

In all truth, Glenda did not know what came over her then. As always with Egan, she lost track of her senses, of her very self. Succumbing to the pulsebeat of desire that throbbed in her veins—and with a daring she hadn't known she possessed—she arched her woman's mound against that part of him that was so very different from her own feminine softness.

And now he was not so indifferent. Everything inside her began to sing, for his body betrayed him. His rod swelled, an iron prod against the hollow of her belly.

Something snapped inside him. The arms around her constricted; for a perilous instant she thought he would crush her, for his embrace was almost frighteningly strong. Then with a groan that vibrated deep in the cavern of her mouth, he lifted her clear from her feet.

"Are we done talking?" His voice was strangely thick.

Her fingers coiled in the hair that grew low on his nape. "Aye," she said faintly.

"Good, for I have never been one for pretty speeches."

Suddenly it was no longer she who directed their play, but he. He captured her mouth in a long, fevered kiss that made the world turn over, letting her slide against his body as he lowered her to the floor. He released her long enough to strip off his trews and kick them aside.

When he turned back to her, he was as gloriously naked as she. She had but one mind-spinning glimpse of his body—long, virile limbs liberally net-ted with a layer of silky dark hair. Between his legs the spear of his arousal stood stiffly, rigidly erect; its size widened her eyes and left no doubt that her de-sire was returned in full measure . . . and more.

All at once his arms engulfed her. His eyes were hot and glittering; they sheared directly into hers. "If you would stop me, do it now, or by God, I'll not be stopped."

Her fingers curled and uncurled against his chest. Her pulse knocked wildly. Shyly she laid her fingers against the bristly hollow of his cheek.

"I cannot," she whispered. "I *will* not."

Something flared in his eyes. Triumph? Victory? She knew not. She cared not.

"Put your arms around my neck, the way you just did."

His urgent whisper rushed past her ear. Her arms closed about his neck, and when they did, he braced his legs wide apart. Lean hands curved beneath her buttocks until her thighs were braced upon his.

She could feel him, all of him. Her gaze was drawn down . . . ever down. She saw him . . . jutting hard and thick and straining . . . She saw herself, poised on the very crown of his staff. Neither could look away as his velvety tip breached her damp golden nest. With one burning, scalding stroke he made her his, stretching her flesh, driving deep . . . deep within her velvet portal, so deep there was no more of him left to give. A shivering cry of sheer pleasure tore from her throat.

His head jerked up at the sound. "Are you all right?"

"Aye," she whispered, the sound but a breath. His girth nearly made her gasp. She was immeasurably full of him, there where her satin channel fitted tight around his swollen flesh—he was not a small man, and his shaft was buried within her to the hilt. Yet there was no pain. Smiling slightly, she traced her fingers over the shape of his mouth.

He groaned and kissed each tip in turn. "Wrap your legs around my waist."

She complied with no hesitation.

He nearly spilled himself in that instant.

His eyes never left her face as he lifted her—he almost left her completely, but not quite. His arms grew taut. His gaze roved the delicate features upturned to his. And then she was coming down ... down on his rod as the long, erotic friction began anew ...

Her smile faded.

Thunder crashed inside her.

He kissed her with stark, raw possessiveness, the demands of his mouth hot and fierce. Her head fell back as his lips slid down the slender column of her neck. Kissing. Licking. His tongue darting like living flame along the throbbing vein at the side of her throat. He held her almost desperately, fallen victim to a tormented hunger. He held her as if this were the end of the world and they were the only two left, giving in to the gut-twisting desire. Forever he'd wanted her. Forever he'd waited. And now to finally have her here in his arms ... it was too much. He shuddered with the pleasure of being inside her at last, knowing that if he allowed it, but a few quick thrusts and his climax would explode. But he didn't want it to end. Not yet. Not so soon. He wanted to make it last forever. He nearly moaned, in sweet satisfaction or sheer frustration, he knew not. But his body succumbed to an urge more powerful than he could command. With hot passion swirling abrim, he could hold nothing back.

Nor could she.

The world was tilting, spinning all awhirl. Dizzy and breathless, she gasped as his dark head dipped low. His lips closed around the burgeoning tip of one breast; with his tongue he circled it again and again, lashed it to quivering erectness, then took it between his lips and sucked strongly.

She ran her hands over the heavy satin of his shoulders, thrilling to the powerful flexion of muscle beneath her fingertips as he lifted her again and again. Somehow she'd always known it would be like this with Egan—raw and explosive and fiercely primitive.

Their hips churned faster and faster. Again and again he plunged into the hot cave of her womanhood, so deep he touched her very womb. Glenda dug her nails into the binding of his shoulders in wild abandon. She felt wicked. Wantonly erotic as his eyes locked on the fullness of her breasts, bobbing with the fierceness of each thrust.

His features were rigid with strain and passion. His hands locked almost convulsively on her hips. He buried his head in the scented hollow of her throat.

"Glenda"—her name was a hoarse, shivering cry, tearing from deep in his chest—and then again: "*Glenda!*"

Slowly he raised his head, his eyes glittering in the candlelight. "You belong to me," he said fiercely. "You belong to me now."

The storm inside her quickened, driving her toward the edge in a great torrent, like the rush of the river toward the sea.

He lunged inside her, a rending force, frenzied and torrid. Once. Twice. Thrice. As if he'd lost all pretense of control . . .

He gritted his teeth, holding on by a thread. "Say it," he commanded gratingly. "Say my name."

His name trembled on her lips. He gazed down at her, his features tense, his eyes searing. Something held her back . . . something . . . she knew not what . . .

"Say it," came his fiery demand anew. *"Say my name"* . . . And within that torrid sound was a tortured plea she could no longer deny . . .

Something gave way inside her. "Egan," she whispered, and all at once it was as if a dam burst free inside her, as if everything broke apart. His name spilled from her lips. "Egan," she cried softly, the sound laden with the hazy blur of desire. "Egan . . . Egan . . ."

Her body convulsed almost violently around his. Feeling the spasms that shook her, Egan groaned. One last piercing lunge and his seed spewed against the very gates of her womb, a release more scalding and intense than any he had ever known.

"Yes," he breathed. "Yes." He flung back his dark head and cried his ecstasy aloud. "God, yes!"

*   *   *

Lulled to wakefulness by the sunlight glancing through the shutters, Egan woke with his mouth as dry as ashes. Turning his head, he saw that the candle at the bedside table had burned to a stub. His first thought was that he'd consumed more wine than he'd realized . . . his second was that his body was unaccountably warm. He started to stir, only to freeze. His blood seemed to clog in his veins. His heart surely stopped. For Glenda was here.

Here in his bed.

Long skeins of chestnut and gold streamed across his belly, a thick, satin cloud shot through with morning sunlight. Her head was pillowed against his shoulder. A dainty hand lay upturned in the center of his chest. She was sleeping deeply, the lushness of her form draped against his side, her breath a warm mist against his skin.

It came back to him slowly, tiny snatches of remembrance. His anger at Glenda for denying him . . . her startling appearance in his chamber. Naked beneath her mantle . . . so brave . . . so enticing . . . He remembered the tremulous way she had kissed him, the feel of her small, delicate frame in his arms, the sweet heat of her passage seizing hold of him as he thrust inside her . . .

Christ, he'd thought he dreamed it! The most wondrously erotic dream of his life . . .

An incredible pride washed over him. No other woman but Glenda would have possessed the courage to come to him as she had done. Yet in that instant between one heartbeat and the next, he felt himself slung to the depths of a shame blacker than any he'd ever known.

He'd taken her like a slut. On his feet. Her legs wrapped around his waist. Jesu, but he'd stormed the gates of her womanhood like . . . like a battering ram!

Where before, his senses had been dulled by sleep and drink, now his mind turned furiously. She should hate him. Yet she was still here—in his bed! And . . . was it a wholly misbegotten swell of masculine pride and prowess that reared its head here? He could have sworn she'd been as aroused as he— as needy as he. Or was it merely his inebriated state that rendered it so?

He swallowed. Christ! Why had she stayed? Why had she given herself to him?

Her nearness swarmed his senses. Shifting slightly, he eased the sheet from the bare slope of her shoulder to gaze at her more fully. Relaxed in sleep, she still possessed a sensual allure that made his mouth go dry all over again. The mounds of her breasts, plump and full, rose and fell evenly. Her nipples were of deepest rose—he well remembered the taste of those roseate peaks, the way they had puckered and surged into his mouth. Her skin was like palest cream, flawless and unmarred—against his own bronzed hardness, he felt like a heathen.

She shifted, and he froze, for now one slender leg lay intimately entwined between the length of his own.

"Egan?"

His name was the wispiest of murmurs.

"Aye." His heart pounded. A wary dread knotted his stomach. He paused, awaiting the censure he was sure would follow.

" 'Tis late, isn't it?" Her voice was still husky from sleep.

The beat of his heart ceased its clamor, returning to normal—as normal as could be with soft, feminine flesh plied along the length of him as she was.

"Aye." His voice was nearly as soft as hers.

"We should rise."

"We should," he agreed.

Neither of them did. The twin sounds of their breath filled the air, accompanied by the whirr of insects outside the window, the echo of a distant hammer.

There was a subtle tightening of powerful arms around his tender prey. His fingers weaved through hers, dark against fair, coming to rest there amidst the tangled fur on his chest. Something slipped over him then. Something beyond words, beyond feeling, beyond description . . . something akin to contentment, but much deeper . . . It had naught to do with passion's play, the satiation of physical pleasures. Egan knew it as surely as the sun had risen this very morn.

This, he thought, this was what he'd been waiting for all his life. Wanting it without knowing it.

Reluctantly he eased back so that he could see her face. "We must talk, lass."

Glenda, too, had enjoyed the quiet peace of the morn, the security she felt while lying snug in his embrace. Tipping her head, she saw that his expression was one of guarded watchfulness. He sounded so serious—and she was not yet ready to be serious.

She smiled slightly. "You were not in the mood for speech last night, as I recall."

"True," he admitted. There was a small pause. "But there is something you must know, something I should have told you last night."

All at once Glenda was not sure she *wanted* to know. Propping herself on her forearm, she tucked the sheet against her naked breasts. "What? What is it?"

Egan took a deep breath. "I did not lie with her. I did not lie with Belinda."

Glenda inhaled sharply, for his confession was not what she'd expected. But it pleased her. It pleased her mightily.

She searched his face—endlessly, it seemed! Oddly, her eyes were the first to falter. "Egan"—her voice was half-stifled—"I would not blame you if you did. Truly—"

Warm fingers captured her chin. His gaze trapped hers. "I did not. Not before we were wed, or after. Nor will I," he vowed. "I would not have this come between us, Glenda."

"Nor would I." Her breath tumbled out in a rush.

He had yet to release her eyes. "Indeed"—there was an uncharacteristic huskiness to his low voice— "I would like to please you as I did not last night."

Glenda blushed. "You did please me," she said faintly.

"Nay. It was too fast. Too rushed."

True, she had been a little overwhelmed by the force of his passion. But not disappointed. The night returned in scorching remembrance—the stunning thickness of his shaft imbedded deep inside her. Nay, she thought vaguely. Never that . . .

"Too . . . hard."

A teasing light glimmered in her eyes. "Well," she said gravely, "you were that."

Egan caught his breath. God, but the sweetness of her smile made him feel like frumenty pudding inside.

His eyes caught the flame in hers. "Ah, would that I could savor all I could not see last night." A hard arm swept the covers back in one swift move.

Color warmed the whole of her body, but she didn't flinch from his scouring gaze. Lingering on the bountiful curves of her breasts and the golden brown fleece between her legs, his eyes seemed to sizzle. She was suddenly proud that her figure had not gone to mush after the babe. He'd said he wanted to please her; but she liked knowing that her body pleased him far more . . .

She shivered when a callused fingertip traced a flaming line down the flare of her hip. Her nipples were taut and tingling even before he bent to feast greedily on first one, and then the other. She bit back a cry when at last his lance thrust home inside her.

But when she came hurtling back from the heavens, she found she could not look at him.

Fingers that were incredibly tender brushed the damp hairs from her cheek.

"Glenda. Glenda, tell me, what is it?" He was suddenly petrified. "Did I hurt you?"

She shook her head, then hid her face against the hollow of his throat. "Egan, please!" she said in a choked little voice. "Do not make me tell you!"

"Now I fear you must!" His laugh was shaky. Sitting up, he pulled her upright as well, curling his knuckles beneath her chin. "Glenda, tell me. What is it?"

Her gaze shied away. "I thought I was wrong," she said jerkily. "I thought I must have imagined it last night . . ."

"Imagined what?"

"I cannot tell you. You will be angry."

"I won't."

"You will!"

To his shock, her voice wobbled traitorously. And there was a suspicious glaze in her beautiful golden eyes . . .

"Tell me, Glenda. Tell me now."

"All right, all right then . . .'tis different with you than it was with . . . with Niall," she blurted.

If it hadn't been for her tears, he would have snatched back his hand. "Different . . . how?" The pitch of his voice was very low.

"With him, 'twas like the calm of the loch near Dunthorpe on a windless day. With you, 'tis as if a storm rages inside. Like—like fire burns through me."

The relief that swept through him was so great, he felt like weeping. Instead he smothered a laugh. "Where? Let me guess," he said before she could answer. He tapped her forehead. "Here?"

"Nay!"

He tweaked a curl that lay over her arm and spoke with hearty certainty. "Ah. Here then."

His teasing had the desired effect. She glared at him, her eyes just as bright, but now with indignation.

"No?" He feigned the greatest exasperation, a dark

brow arching high. "Well then, where?"

"You—you know where!" Her gaze both accused and pleaded.

Lazy amusement glimmered in his eyes. "I do indeed. And do you know what? It pleases me to know you feel the same as I." His mouth closed over mutinous lips. He coaxed them apart with the tip of his tongue. Her lashes fluttered shut and she sighed.

There was a sudden pounding on the door. "Is my lassie in there?"

It was Nessa.

Glenda dove for the sheet. Egan had no such qualms regarding modesty—his or anyone else's, it seemed! Naked, he strode to the door and threw it wide.

"Come see for yourself."

Nessa entered, bold as you please, her staff resounding on the floor. But if Egan thought to shock the old woman, he was sorely disappointed. Nessa gazed calmly at the rumpled mound of bedclothes.

"Will ye be needin' a bath this morn, mistress?"

The form beneath the coverlet moved, yet no answer was forthcoming.

Egan folded his hands across his chest. His mouth quirked as he addressed himself to Nessa. "You must forgive your mistress. The morning's activities seem to have stolen her voice, but aye—she would indeed like a bath."

Nessa's head swivelled back to him. For an instant it appeared she wished to throttle him with her bare, gnarled hands. But all she said was, "I'll see to it, then."

Not until the door had closed did Glenda deign to

show her face. Her head popped free. "Egan! How could you say such a thing?"

"Nessa has been on this earth a good many years. I suspect she's heard a good many things far more shocking."

Glenda moaned and ducked beneath the covers again. She didn't emerge until the tub had been wrestled out from behind a screen and filled with water. Egan leaned back against the pillows, decently covered again. A fiery blush proclaimed her embarrassment as she slipped from the sheets, yet she made no attempt to cover herself as she walked to the tub, then sank beneath the water.

She felt his scrutiny with every ounce of her being. Aware that he watched, her heart thumped. With a nonchalance she was far from feeling, she dipped her cloth into the water.

Behind her there was a rustle. She glanced back over her shoulder. Her eyes widened.

Egan had pushed the sheet aside and was on his feet. If she had thought him splendid before, in the sheer light of day, he was even more so.

His body was all sleek, animal hardness. Muscles rippled between dark, golden skin as he approached. Captivated by the power and grace of that stark masculine form, she couldn't look away.

She expected him to kneel beside her.

Not so.

One long, virile limb lifted over the edge of the tub. Water sloshed precariously as the other joined it. Glenda's heart lurched. She saw the hair-matted landscape of his chest . . . and much more.

Hard flesh slid against hers, wet and warm.

Without a word he took the cloth from her hands. Slowly he began to wash her. The cloth glided down her neck, the slope of her shoulder, breasts and belly. Oddly, she could have sworn there was nothing sexual in his ministrations. When he'd finished, he transferred the cloth to his own body. Instead it was Glenda whose heartbeat quickened. The sight of his flesh, wet and glistening, made her feel all hot and fluttery inside. She couldn't help but wish he would allow her the same privilege—to wash him as he had washed her.

She wanted to. She wanted to quite badly, and the realization shocked her to her core. She wanted to run her hands all over him, explore the satin heat of his shoulders, thrill to the solidness of muscle and sinew.

At last he finished, he folded the cloth into a neat square and laid it over the edge of the tub.

Only then did he speak.

"What are you looking at?"

Her stomach clenched. Her heart beat high in her throat. "You," she whispered in awe.

In order to accommodate them both, he'd drawn his legs toward his body, letting his knees rest against the side of the tub.

Her gaze was trained between his legs. The sight of his manhood widened her eyes and made her breath catch. He was swollen and thick, rigid with arousal.

Egan nearly groaned. Knowing she stared at him thus and did not look away made him swell still further.

The smile he offered was crooked. "I want you, sweet. I fear I cannot hide it."

The breath she drew was ragged. She dragged her gaze back to his face. The way he looked at her—the longing he made no attempt to disguise—made her feel humble and perilously close to tears. Suddenly his words the night before resounded in her head.

The night you first came to Dunthorpe . . . I wanted you then. Christ, all I could think of was you. All I wanted was you.

What had he meant? Surely he hadn't wanted her all that time. Something inside her balked. God above, that was *years*! Nay, her ears had deceived her. Surely it was so.

"Why?" It was a soft cry, half-strangled. "Why do you want me? Egan, I . . . I am old!"

His smile faded. Leaning forward, he curled his hand around her neck, beneath the fall of her hair, urging her toward him.

He rested his forehead against hers. "If you do not know, then 'twould seem it's my turn to show *you*."

His head bent. He kissed her, long and sweetly—and with mounting urgency. All at once she feared the moment it would end; her hands came up and caught at his bare shoulders. She yielded her mouth with a moan she couldn't withhold.

In a surge of power, he was on his feet, his wife in his arms.

Their bath was forgotten.

Chapter 15

Summer came to Blackstone Keep with days of warmth and sunshine that sent the crops surging skyward. A deep, verdant green, the fields bowed to the winds that rippled through the valley and the showering rays of the sun. The people of Blackstone went about their work with the fervent hope that summer's endeavors would be the bounty that sustained the long winter months ahead—that, and the prayer that relief from the midnight raids would continue.

All had been quiet since Egan had begun sending out nighttime patrols, yet it was not so easy to forget. Oh, smiles abounded readily and fear no longer prevailed; while the cloud of menace had lifted, the threat that the raiders might stir havoc anew had not been fully extinguished. One had only to mention the marauders to know it—smiles quickly faltered. All talk would cease, and those present exchanged uneasy glances.

Egan sometimes accompanied his men on their nightly patrols. Glenda hated it, yet she would not ask him to stay; she knew he would not ask his men to do something that he himself was not willing to do. On those nights she tossed and turned, for there was no rest until the moment he slid into bed beside her.

So it was that many a morn found the lord and lady of Blackstone Keep locked fast in the arms of the other. Thus began many a day . . . and thus began many a night.

That very first time, Glenda avowed it was duty that compelled her to lie with him. His right as a husband. Her obligation as wife, just as it was to see to his clothing and his comfort.

She did not blame Egan. Yet neither could she deny him, any more than she could deny her own treacherous longing. 'Twas she who had given herself to him. Yet many a time she wondered . . . should she have tried harder to resist?

She knew not. She *could* not.

She despaired her own weakness, for she was powerless to fight his masculine allure. She could not deny him, any more than she could deny herself. It felt good to feel the strength of his arms hard about her form in the darkness of night. No longer did she feel so—so empty, as she had those last months at Dunthorpe, so very alone!

Perchance it *was* duty that sent her to his bed.

That was not what kept her there.

It was something else. Something far different.

A fire of the flesh . . . a fire in the heart? Nay. Not love. Surely not love. Love was what she'd felt for Niall. With Niall, love had blossomed slowly, steadfast and true. Yet he had never made her feel as Egan did, as if a tempest swept through her—inside her—

with naught but a look. A hike of his brow . . .

Desire. Passion. Lust. And yet, by whatever name it was called, it was just as she confided that very first night . . . it seared her veins like a sword of molten steel. He had only to enter a room and the murmur of her pulse began to clamor. Ah, but he commanded her senses, the very rhythm of her heart! A restless hunger quested inside her. Heat seeped beneath her skin. Wanton urges surged within her. She could not control them. She could not withhold them.

'Twas a battle she could neither fight . . . nor win.

Yet neither did she lose.

Beyond that, she refused to examine.

Indeed, she could find no fault with him. He was strong and loyal and protective. He knew all the tenants by name—even she did not! Though she told herself it was her lands that he coveted, he was as determined as she that Blackstone should prosper and thrive.

Yet she was learning much about him that she had never truly known. He made her laugh, even when she did not expect it! There was nothing he would not try; no task he deemed below him. On her way to visit the chandler one day, she paused to watch him alongside Edgar, the swineherd.

Several squealing little piglets had escaped their pen. All but one had been captured—and this one proved most elusive! Glenda's mouth quirked. Egan's expression was grimly determined as he stalked the wee creature who sniffed and squealed and ran about the bailey at will. Every time Egan paused and drew close, the piglet darted out of reach, as if he scented captivity. Swearing and red-faced,

Egan was wholly unaware of her regard.

It had rained before dawn, and the morning sun had yet to dry the puddles that filled the ruts left by the tanner's cart. Just then the piglet paused. On silent feet, Egan came near the little beast, who rubbed his snout in the damp grass, seemingly oblivious to the man who crouched behind him.

Anticipating victory, Egan's eyes gleamed. His chest expanded as he took a breath.

The piglet scampered forward, but Egan was not to be dissuaded. He leaned forward and grabbed his quarry.

With a high-pitched squeal, the piglet bolted from his grasp and leaped through the spoke of a wheel.

Egan was left sprawled head first in the mud. It was Edgar who finally seized the little piglet. Cursing hotly beneath his breath, Egan lumbered to his feet.

When he turned, his wife stood before him. She looked him up and down, wrinkling her nose as water dripped from his nose onto his chest.

"You, sir, need a bath."

Egan was undaunted. He reached out and seized her, hauling her up against his chest.

"Egan!" Now as filthy as he, she screeched her outrage as loudly as the piglet. "Egan, nay!"

Not so lofty now, was she, he thought in satisfaction. His smile was wicked. "What a pity," he remarked in lazy amusement, "but it seems I'm not the only one in need of a bath, now, am I?"

The bony shoulders of Edgar the swineherd heaved in laughter. Several soldiers near Bernard and Milburn called out ribald encouragement. Amidst her protests, Egan swept his wife high in his arms and toward the tower stairs . . .

They were not seen for some time to come.

Egan had honored his vow not to wrest control of the keep from her. Glenda continued to see to the immediate matters of the household, while he saw to Blackstone's defense. Initially Glenda had been a trifle reluctant to involve him on other matters, yet all this was new to her, too; she did so gradually, and found herself admitting his insight and observations were enormously helpful. Soon the decisions being made were done jointly, with mutual consent.

Where justice was concerned, Glenda also came to realize that Egan could not long remain an observer; else he—and she—might well risk putting his authority in jeopardy. He seemed surprised when she asked that he join her to adjudge those matters that arose. Thus far, he had proved both fair, lenient and impartial in his judgment.

On this particular day, a young couple stood before them, an arm's length separating them. When Bernard gestured, the pair stepped forward.

The young man cleared his throat. "Good day, my lord, my lady. I am Alfred, and this is my wife Annabelle."

Egan inclined his head. "Good day to both of you. What brings you here?"

The young man shot a sullen look at his wife, who had maintained the distance between them and stood with eyes downcast. " 'Tis not I, my lord, but my wife who insisted we come here." He clamped his mouth shut as if determined to say no more.

"Indeed. Annabelle, would you explain why?"

Annabelle wiped her face with the corner of her apron, then slowly raised her head. Her eyes were red-rimmed and swollen from weeping. "I wish to return to—to my mother and my father, my lord, my lady. Alfred will not allow it." Her wounded tone took on an indignant note. "He said he will chain me with the goats if I try!"

Glenda's heart went out to her, for even now, the girl's lip trembled anew. Why, her husband was surely a brute to threaten her so! Her back stiffened, and she prepared to tell him so in no uncertain terms, but Egan's hand was on her forearm. The slightest pressure from his fingertips compelled her silence.

"How long have the two of you been wed?"

It was Alfred who answered. "Two days, sir."

"I see. Was this marriage arranged between your families?"

"Nay, milord. We . . . we wished it, Annabelle and I."

Egan shifted his attention to Annabelle. "Annabelle, is this true?"

Annabelle looked uncomfortable. Finally she gave a nod.

"So it was your wish as well?"

She said nothing.

"Why, she insisted, she did!" said Alfred. "Why, she would not even . . ." All at once he stopped short. He seemed to have recalled that he stood not only before his lord and lady, but various others as well.

Egan cocked a brow. "Annabelle, is this true? You went to the marriage of your own free will?"

"Aye, milord," she answered finally, her voice very small.

"And you, Alfred? You entered the marriage of your own free will?"

"Aye, milord." Alfred's voice rang out clearly.

"I see." Egan nodded thoughtfully. "I wonder, then, why Annabelle wishes to return to her father and her mother?"

"Oh, I do not wonder, milord. 'Tis because we quarreled!"

"I see. Is this true, Annabelle?"

Annabelle's lips trembled. 'Twas clear to see that speech was impossible, Glenda decided. Her eyes flitted away. Her head dipped low.

"Annabelle, have you and your husband quarreled often since you've been wed?"

Alfred started to answer. "But, milord, 'tis only two da—" Egan help up a hand, signaling him to halt.

"Nay, my lord"—her voice quavered—" 'tis the first time."

"Then I must ask the nature of this quarrel."

Annabelle's head came up. Her eyes flew wide. Her ruddy cheeks turned scarlet—and so had her husband's. She cast a pleading look at her husband, who for the first time was unwilling to speak.

"My lord. I canna say, truly . . ."

"It is of a private nature?"

"Oh, aye!" she gasped.

"A matter between man and woman . . . say, a matter between husband and wife?"

Her head bobbed furiously.

Egan pretended to ponder. "Annabelle, I would not embarrass you, but I must ask . . . does your husband desire another woman?"

"N-nay, milord."

"Does he beat you?"

"Nay!"

Egan glanced at Alfred. "Alfred, would you set this marriage aside if you could?"

Alfred was startled at the question, then lifted his chin. "Nay, my lord."

"Then come closer, both of you."

They did as they were bid, but both appeared rather tentative.

"You made a solemn vow before God," Egan said sternly, "a vow you must honor. Annabelle, it is not a vow you can put aside, to run willy-nilly home to your mother and father at the first sign of trouble."

Annabelle began to blubber.

"Whatever comes between you must be settled between the two of you. Is that understood?"

Alfred's head came up. "Aye, my lord."

"You are to stay within your hut for three whole days, both of you, and you are not to come out."

The makings of a smile appeared at the corners of Alfred's lips. "We understand, my lord, and we submit to your good judgment." He reached for his wife's hand. "Come along, Annabelle," he announced.

Annabelle was wailing as they left the hall.

Egan reached for his wife's hand as well. Once they were out of view of the others, she snatched it from his grasp. Egan shrugged, but kept pace behind her as she marched toward the stairs. She was smoldering so that she never even noticed when he waylaid a passing maid and told her they would take their meal in his chamber. The moment they were alone, she whirled on him.

"How could you do such a thing?" she demanded. "Didn't you see the way that poor girl wept? That wretch has made her miserable!"

He let her rant, watching calmly as she paced before the hearth.

"Why did you even bother to ask why they quarreled? You had only to look at Annabelle to know why!"

Egan defended himself smoothly. "How could I know when she would not tell me—and neither would he?"

"Of course they didn't! I've no doubt he asked her to perform some lewd perversion!"

Lewd? Perverted? Egan shook his head. "More than likely she was just shocked."

"Of course she was. She probably came to the marriage a maid!"

Egan shrugged. "Perhaps," he agreed. "If that's so, then probably her shock blossomed into outrage, and her outrage into a quarrel." A glint appeared in his eye. "Now, if she were just more willing to accept what her husband knows of such things—"

Glenda halted in a swirl of skirts. "That a man knows better?" she snapped.

Egan spread his hands wide. "If you say so," he began.

"If I say so!" Glenda glared. "Do not grin at me like that! I do not approve, Egan. You asked him if he wished to remain wed. You didn't even ask Annabelle!"

"There was no need. I knew what her answer

would be . . . if only poor Alfred is given the chance to prove himself."

Glenda's mouth turned down. "Poor Alfred?"

Egan had never had such a difficult time keeping a straight face. "I can think of worse things than to be shut away with one's husband for three days."

Glenda was still muttering when the maid knocked and delivered their meal. "Three days! Lord knows what he will do to her!"

Three days. Perhaps he *had* gone too far. Ah, but no wonder Alfred had been grinning from ear to ear. He suppressed a groan of envy. Ah, but he could only imagine . . . he envied Alfred—not for his choice of bride—but for the time *spent* with his bride.

"Wait and see," he predicted mildly. "Their marriage will be the stronger for it."

"Let me guess. A man knows best . . . a *husband* knows best?"

His smile reflected his acknowledgment. He walked to the table where their food awaited and pulled out a chair. "Come. Let us eat."

Glenda moved stiffly to the table and sat down. Though she was determined to say no more, she was still smarting. So a man knew best, did he? She chewed furiously. Her gaze chanced to light upon a small spiced tart filled with almonds and currants. Her temper, still simmering and not yet eased, spiked anew. Even the cook bowed to him!

"I see the cook has made your favorite. Are you hungry still?"

"I am."

A pause, and she arose. "Would you like for me to feed you?"

Egan had seen the gleam enter his wife's eyes. He was well pleased by the seductive sway of her hips and the sweet melody of her tone—along with her attentiveness when she moved to sit upon his lap.

"I would." Hungrily he eyed the graceful sweep of her throat. He would have availed himself of a greedy taste, but already the tip of the spoon was poised before him.

"Open," she whispered.

Egan complied.

The spoon dipped within the crock, then returned, again and again, faster and faster, until his lips had barely parted and more tart was dumped into his mouth.

He coughed. "I'm choking—"

"What, on your own words? Then chew, my lord, do not speak."

"Glenda, please—"

"Please? Do you not know your own mind, husband?"

She was on her feet like an arrow shooting high through the air. Dumbfounded, Egan could only watch as the remainder of the contents of the crock was overturned in his lap. It began to ooze over his thighs, a thick, gooey mess.

"Glenda! What the devil . . . sweet, why are you so angry?"

"You tell me, sirrah." Her smile was sweet, but her eyes flashed fire. "A man knows best, does he not?" In a swirl of skirts, she was gone.

Egan stumbled to his feet and flung out a hand. The sticky mess dripped to the floor, beneath his boots. He slipped and nearly fell. Curses spewed from his mouth, along with the crumbs of the tart.

"Glenda. Glenda, wait!"

It was only later that they both were able to laugh about it. Like the quarrel between Alfred and Annabelle, it was a quarrel that did not last the night. Arrogant though he was, Glenda could neither deplore nor argue his logic, particularly once she permitted him the chance to expound upon it.

" 'Tis far more than providing Alfred the chance to lay with his wife!" he had said. "If I seemed cruel to her, I did not mean to be. Annabelle must understand that marriage is a bond, an alliance that is not to be taken lightly. 'Tis an alliance that should be neither entered into nor broken with capricious whimsy, as she would have done had I allowed it!"

Glenda listened intently. And in so doing, she gained a deeper glimpse of the emotions that resided deep within her husband, of the feelings that drove him. Not for the first time, she realized . . .

He was not a man to take his own so lightly. But then, she'd known it for a long, long time. She had only to think of his loyalty to Niall. To Cameron and the clan MacKay . . . to Blackstone . . . and its people. His determination to keep them safe from all harm . . .

He did tease her unmercifully, though, when they spied Alfred and Annabelle a fortnight later—for now the pair strolled hand in hand.

He lay in bed one night, propped on an elbow, watching her as she brushed her hair. He'd drawn the sheet up to the jutting ridge of his hip, but it barely covered his maleness. Even unaroused, she could see the long, ridged shape of him outlined beneath the cloth, the impressive fullness beneath. Under the dense layer of dark, curling hair, his chest was thick with muscle. His shoulders and arms were as hard as they looked, gleaming like oiled walnut, bronzed from the summer sun. Just the sight of him made an odd little quiver run through her.

Aware that his eyes never left her, she rose and walked barefoot to the bed, sliding in beside him. He slept naked and somehow always saw to it that she did as well. Now she no longer bothered with a bedgown.

Easing back on the pillows, she discovered that he had yet to relieve her of his regard. "What is it?" she said breathlessly. "Why do you watch me so?"

"I am speculating."

"About what?"

"About whether you have fantasies."

"Fantasies!"

"Aye, fantasies. Surely you know . . . the kind like women have."

She glowered. "You mean the kind like men have," she said crossly.

His lips quirked. "What would you know of men's fantasies?"

"I heard two of my father's men talking in the stables once. Long ago, when I was a girl."

"What! And who was more wicked? The men, for talking so frankly . . . or you, for listening?"

His teasing quickly earned him a jab in the ribs. "I was in the stall with my mare, just after she'd birthed a foal! They didn't know I was there, and obviously I couldn't leave without calling attention to the fact that I was there! It would have embarrassed all of us."

"I see your point. But tell me—what did they say?"

"They seemed to have quite a fascination with the breasts of the miller's eldest daughter." Her mouth turned down. "In particular, their . . . abundant size, and what they would do if they had her alone."

"A fascination I can well understand." Beneath the sheet, an impudent finger traced a taunting circle around an equally impudent nipple.

"Stop that." She slapped at his hand.

There was an unholy glimmer in his eyes. "Continue. What about this girl's breasts?"

"They did not refer to them as breasts," she said heatedly. "And they envisioned using them for—for a use other than what God—and most men—intended!"

All at once Egan had a very good idea what she meant . . . her heatedness made him smother a laugh. For a woman who professed to be old, she was as innocent as a maid! He couldn't resist teasing her further.

"Indeed," he said gravely. "And were there . . . male bodily parts involved?"

"Aye."

"Dare I ask what male bodily parts were involved?"

Her eyes flashed. "The one most men seem to regard as the one of prime importance!"

Egan chuckled. Lord, she was precious! He bent his head and kissed her, then ran his thumb over the rosy flesh of her mouth.

"That was their fantasy. But what of yours?"

"I have none."

She was so quick he almost believed her . . . almost, but not quite.

"All right then. Have you ever had dreams . . . erotic dreams?"

Glenda's heart lurched. She had—and all of him! The dream of the two of them in the orchard rose high aloft in her mind.

"What?" she said faintly. "Would you make me tell you that, too?"

His hand cupped the slope of one bare shoulder, then slid down. Strong brown fingers curled around her arm; his hand lightly caressed, his knuckles skimming the side of her breast, sending a ripple of sensation all through her, making her nipples stand hard and taut, ripe and straining.

"Would you?" Softly he encouraged her.

Glenda swallowed. "I cannot."

"Why not?"

She shook her head. " 'Twas not here . . ."

A brow arched in silent query.

" 'Twas not here . . . in this bed." Her face flamed. "Or indeed, in any bed."

He kissed the corner of her mouth. "Where, then?" he whispered.

"The orchard," she said weakly.

"Was there a man in this dream?"

"Y-yes."

"Who?"

The world seemed to come to a halt. "You," she whispered.

His eyes seemed to blaze. Too late she recognized

the folly of her confession. The sheet slipped down to her waist.

"You are right, sweet. I would rather you not tell me. I would rather you *showed* me."

Blessed be, he meant it.

In the orchard the following day, he pulled her from her horse. For a time they merely walked in lazy companionship, for it was just such a day— warm, but not hot, the air pleasantly cool as it played among the treetops. Egan paused to watch a hawk as it surged high towards the clouds and was lost from sight; Glenda sank down beneath the gnarled, out-stretched branches of an ancient apple tree, tucking her knees beneath her.

"I'm exhausted," she complained. "Come sit."

Egan shook his head. "How can you be tired? Nessa told me you slept half the morn away."

"There'd be no need to sleep the morn away if someone did not keep me awake half the night!"

"And who would that be?" He shook his head in mock outrage. "I'll have to find the rogue and see that it does not happen again."

"Ho! You need not look far to find him then!" Laughing, she laced her hands on her skirts. Tipping her head to one side, she regarded him.

He advanced toward her. "You," he accused with-out heat, "are a temptress."

Her chin angled high that she might see him, re-vealing the long, graceful arch of her throat. She peered up at him through long, curling lashes. "And do I tempt you?"

Egan sucked in a breath. His gaze roved slowly over her features. She'd never been more beautiful to him than she was at that moment, her lips enticingly pink, her hair unbound and streaming over her shoulders like banners of silk, the laughter turning her eyes to sheer gold.

"Lady," he said with soft deliberation, "you do, indeed." Without a word he knelt before her.

"You've yet to tell me of your dream," he said softly. "Were we near this spot?"

"We were here"—her gaze locked helplessly on his rugged features—"beneath this very tree."

"A good start, I should say then. What were you wearing?"

Her tongue came out to moisten her lips, darkening them to deepest rose. "Nothing. 'Twas an erotic dream, if you remember."

"Ah. How could I forget?" Easing his hands beneath the neckline of her gown, he peeled it away from her shoulders. Full, creamy flesh spilled free. Her gown dropped in a heap about her knees.

Slowly he drew back to look at her. On her knees before him as she was, her breasts jutted forth, the dusky peaks deeply rouged, trembling before him as if in offering. The sight made the blood surge hot and heavy in his loins.

"Did I touch you here?" His palms brushed across the quivering peaks, relishing the way they surged stiff and tight against him.

"Aye. But with . . . your mouth."

His mouth slid with slow heat down the side of her neck. Guessing his intention, her ragged inhalation but aided him further. His tongue curled around the swollen tip.

Her fingers came up to tangle at the back of his

head. She pressed him against her. "Harder," she whispered.

His mouth opened. Torrid and greedy, he feasted on honey-brown nipples, first one and then the other. Her breath began to fray.

With an effort he dragged his mouth back to hers. "And here, lass?" His knuckles skimmed her belly. Long fingers tangled in her fleece; his fingertips traced an elusive path along her furrowed channel, coming close to but never quite touching the bud of her desire. "Did I touch you here?"

Her hands came out to grasp the binding of his arms; her eyes half-closed. "Aye," she whispered.

Egan gritted his teeth. He could feel her liquid dew, glistening and damp. One long, strong finger plunged within her silken depths, and then another. His thumb joined the play, tormenting and evocative, circling again and again around that tiny nubbin of flesh centered deep within tight gold curls.

She began to writhe against his hand.

Against her lips, he grated out, "Did I touch you here, sweet? With my mouth? Did I touch you with my lips? With my tongue?" The words were stark and raw and wanton.

"Aye," she cried. "Aye!"

Her soft panting excited him to a fine frenzy. His eyes burning, he nudged her to her back. She gasped aloud as he parted her knees with the width of his shoulders. He pressed his open mouth against her belly, the soft, pale inside of one slender thigh . . . then the other.

With his tongue he touched her swollen rosebud, her flowering core.

Her body jerked. Her hips came off the ground, again and again.

He pleasured her until his head was pounding and his blood was aboil, his manhood engorged as never before; demanding, even as he gave of himself as he'd never done before, reveling in her soft, panting breaths. He knew the moment she yielded, a whimpering cry of shivering surrender.

Flinging his clothing aside, he dragged himself over her, shaking with need of her. Freeing his rod, he guided it through, gasping as pink, creamy folds closed tight around his swollen flesh. Her eyes opened, dark and smoky with passion. He weaved his fingers through hers, clasping them together alongside her head as he plunged hard and deep, filling her with himself, with his passion.

"Kiss me," he muttered. Her head turned. Soft lips sought his with an urgency that made him soar high as the hawk he'd glimpsed earlier. He felt his seed searing through his loins, but he did not want such blistering ecstasy to end so soon. Not yet. Not now.

Shuddering with the need that thundered through him, he rolled.

She was astride him now, seated upon his burning shaft. "I dreamed of this," she gasped.

"So did I."

Her eyes darkened. Bracing herself against their hands, still clasped so tightly together, she lifted her body so that she was poised on the very tip of him. Then all at once she thrust down . . . down. Spearing him with her velvet heat. He stared down where the two of them joined . . . him to her . . . or her to him . . . he cared not. It mattered not.

Encased in tightness and fire and warmth, he lunged inside her with shattering force, desperately seeking that pinnacle of pleasure.

Suddenly her back arched. She cast back her head. The walls of her passage contracted around his turgid shaft, again and again.

"Egan," she cried. "Egan!"

The sound of his name sent him over the edge. His release was scalding. He exploded inside her, his seed hot and thick and drenching her with fire.

In the wake of such intensity, a blissful peace descended like a curtain around them both. They dozed, then woke and made love again, their caresses more mellow and leisurely this time, but with no less satisfaction.

It was late when at last they arose. Egan helped Glenda up, brushing dried grass and leaves from her form.

It happened without volition, without thought. A tug upon her heart, a chain upon her soul. It was as if a curtain of gray had parted, as if she saw the world anew . . . and him.

Framed before sun and sky, his teeth were very white against his skin. The squareness of his jaw was rough and dark with the day's growth of beard. An unruly lock of hair tumbled over his forehead. All combined to lend him an air of rugged virility. Never had she seen a man more striking or arresting, and all at once, her heart seemed to stumble.

Her fingers came to rest on the plane of his cheek. They moved, the veriest caress.

"Your eyes are so blue," she whispered. "So very, very blue. Oh, God . . . why did I never notice? Why did I never see?" The stricken little cry slipped out before she could stop it.

The answer came from some corner deep inside. *Mayhap because you did not want to. Mayhap because you did not look.*

She gazed at him anew, but naught had changed. His eyes, ringed by a fringe of thick, black lashes, were a soft, clear blue flecked with tiny silver lights, a blue more pure than the sky on a cloudless summer day.

Her heart squeezed. Pain tore through her, a wrenching blade from throat to groin.

She began to cry.

Egan was stunned. "Glenda. Glenda, what's wrong?"

His arms closed around her. Tender fingers brushed the dampness from her cheeks. She clung to him and he held her, aware of the sudden shift in her emotions, but not understanding.

Nor did she. She knew only that in that moment, something stirred inside her . . . a tumult that rocked her to the depths of her being.

She was suddenly terrified as never before.

Chapter 16

Did she love him?
Nay. She dared not. She *did* not.

Yet, alas, he was like a stone in her slipper. A thistle beneath her nail. Always he trespassed. In her thoughts. In her heart . . .

Ah, but her heart had already been taken for all eternity. Hadn't it? Her mind screamed. *Hadn't it?*

What she felt was vastly different than what she'd felt for Niall. Love had been like a lilting, wispy breeze to lift the spirit. But what she felt for Egan was . . . demanding. Consuming. A storm quested inside her whene'er he was near.

She had only to gaze at him and feel herself afire. To experience a jolt of hungry longing that sent her senses aflame and desire abrim through every part of her . . . to know a terrible fear that surpassed any other.

She tried not to think of it. She tried so very hard not to remember the husband and son she'd left behind, buried in the rocky hilltop that overlooked Dunthorpe. Oh, the rending ache in her heart had faded, yet the starkness of that memory was a torment that would burn inside her forever.

She had loved Niall . . . but he had died. She had loved their child, longed for him to live with every fiber of her being . . . yet he had died too. She'd loved them both—and lost them both. Yet now there was Egan, creeping into every corner of her heart and soul . . .

She didn't want to hurt like that again. She couldn't *feel* that way again.

She was afraid to love him. Afraid to lose him.

Afraid of the pain known so keenly when Niall and their son had died.

Over and over she sought to convince herself she didn't love him, to hold herself distant. If she didn't love him, should she lose him, it wouldn't hurt so much.

Yet just as there was a stirring in her heart, just as nature would follow its course and men would have their way, life had already stirred and caught hold deep in her womb.

And this, too, was different. Oh, aye, her breasts blossomed round and full and plump, her nipples plumbed large and dark and were on occasion tender—indeed, she told herself, it was no wonder, for her appetite had been so hearty of late. She did not sicken, her belly pitching and heaving when she woke. Nor did her waist and hips thicken. She was not so tired her lids drooped when it was scarcely noonday. She was still slender, but for that slight protuberance that began to burgeon 'neath her navel. With her first babe, she had begun to round almost from the first.

The harvest came in, as bountiful as all had prayed

for. The earl was paid his due and more—werthers of mutton, beef, and honey, and a bulging purse full of coin. The vaults in the storeroom were full.

Her courses had come but once in the spring, just after they wed. Three months passed. Four. Soon it would be five. Still Glenda did not speak of it. She dared not think of it, but fleetingly!—and then only so quickly it was as if she could not catch hold of the thought—like a fugitive, bent on escape.

To acknowledge that she carried a babe was to believe. And to believe was to hope . . .

And Glenda was desperately afraid to hope.

If Nessa knew, she said naught as well.

With the advent of the harvest, she rose early, often earlier than Egan. Today, however, he was gone when she arose. Quickly she bathed and dried herself. Moving to the cupboard, she reached inside, searching for a shift until she found it. Raising her arms high, it billowed high before sailing down over her body.

That was how Egan came upon her that morn. Busy before the cupboard, she didn't hear the click of the door as it opened and closed behind him. In the instant between one and the next, he clearly saw the silhouette of her form—full, high breasts, delectably round. He smiled, his gaze continuing their journey down her body . . .

He froze.

A faint, choked sound wedged midway up his chest. He sucked in a breath. His heart soared. He thought . . . oh, a hundred things! It was inevitable. He marveled that he hadn't guessed sooner. God knew he should have! Since the time she had first gone to his chamber, she had lain with him nearly every night since . . .

His smile withered. His temples began to pound. His mind sped back.

Not once had she pleaded her woman's time. *Not once.*

She hadn't told him. Yet how could she not have known? This wasn't the first time she'd carried a child.

A searing pain reamed his brain.

When Glenda turned, Egan stood directly before her. His gaze was riveted to her middle.

She blanched. *No*, she thought in horror. *Oh, no.* His features were drawn and tight, his mouth a thin, relentless line. A muscle jumped, there near his scar. Never had he been so ominous or forbidding.

"Have you something to tell me, sweet?"

Sweet. The word was a brittle condemnation. Beneath his unyielding gaze, she cringed. Her arms started to move around herself, an instinctive, self-protective gesture. He didn't allow it.

His hands captured her wrists like iron manacles. He held them fast to her sides.

"You knew."

Uncertainty roiled within her like a churning sea. All she could do was nod.

"How long? How long have you known? Weeks? Months?"

Again that pitiful nod.

"Why did you not tell me?" he demanded.

Glenda drew a shuddering breath. Wincing, she glanced away, anywhere but at the scathing reproach she knew resided on his face.

"I should have."

"Aye, you should have!" His voice was like a clap of thunder. "Does a man not have the right to know? Do *I* not have the right to know?"

Glenda floundered. What was she to say? " 'Twas not that," she said helplessly.

"What, then? Did you think I would not care?"

The fierceness of his glare discouraged any answer she might have made—and indeed, what defense had she? She could not plead innocence, for it was not true.

"Your silence these many weeks, both then and now. Ah, but it says so very much!"

Glenda could not speak for the hot tears that stung the back of her throat.

"Still she says nothing. Do I accuse when I should not, Glenda? Do I wrong you?"

Hot tears stung the back of her throat. She blinked them back. "You do not wrong me." Her voice wobbled traitorously. "But you wound me."

"I wound you . . . that you should know what it's like to be wounded! How far gone are you?"

He gave her little chance to respond. A lean hand threw up the hem of her shift. She gasped and tried to push his hands aside, but he was insistently determined to assess. Imperious fingers splayed across the smoothness of her belly, the small, hard mound the size of a fist.

His hands left her, but not his icy glare. "How far, Glenda? Four months?"

She swallowed painfully. Her voice, when it came, was very low. "Nearer to five, I think."

"Five!" It was a blistering curse. "Ah, I begin to see

why now—why you rise before me! Why you douse the candle before coming to bed! But it was you who came to me that first time," he reminded her, "you who came to me!"

" 'Tis a wife's duty to—to lay with her husband."

"Duty! Is that what brought you to my bed? I felt you come against my mouth. My lips. I felt you come while I lay deep inside you! Duty! Is duty what *kept* you in my bed?"

Nay, she thought. *Nay!* Yet somehow no sound passed the constriction in her throat.

He'd gone white about the mouth. "I wanted you, aye!" he charged. "I wouldn't have let you go, not after that first night! But never did I force you, Glenda, never!"

Glenda's eyes widened. "I know that." Wildly she shook her head. "You do not understand. At first I did not realize . . . I thought I would be barren. You know that with Niall I was barren those many years!"

"But in time you did conceive, Glenda. Or was your child not his?"

Glenda gave a little scream of rage. "Oh, but you are cruel to say such a thing! You know I loved Niall!"

His mouth twisted. "Ah, yes, I know! I well remember the night at the table when you told Niall you were most likely with child. You cared not who listened. You cared not who knew! Indeed, within the hour, everyone at Dunthorpe was aware of your condition."

Ah, yes, her eyes had been shining, alight with pure joy. The remembrance battered him, for now her eyes were dark and shadowed—the news something to be hidden away, even from him! Oh, aye, he decided blackly, but with him it was different. It was as if she were ashamed to carry his bairn, and everything within him cried out the depth of his fury and his pain. The hurt was excruciating . . . unending.

His grip merciless, he caught her chin between thumb and forefinger and prodded her face up to his. "Are you pleased about this babe?" he demanded.

Her gaze cleaved to his. She groped for an answer . . . an answer that eluded her.

His hand fell away from her, as if in disgust.

Glenda's lungs were burning with the effort it took not to break down. "Egan. Egan, try to—"

He paid no heed, but lashed out in bitter anger. "Forgive my foolish question! How quickly I forget! You did not want my seed. 'Twas Niall's child you wanted. Not mine. Never mine."

Pierced to the quick, she raised shimmering eyes to his. "Must you mock me?"

"I do not mock you! I but state the truth!"

"The truth. The truth! You cannot begin to know what I feel, the tangle in my heart," she choked out. "I was afraid to say a word to anyone . . . afraid to be glad, for what if I miscarried? Would you have me be filled with joy, only to feel the life gush from my body? I could not stand that. I-I thought 'twas better to feel nothing—to think not of this child at all! All those years of yearning . . . of watching other women cradle their babes against their breast . . . my arms were empty. My womb was empty! And then when it finally happened, I-I was delirious with pleasure—and now you would fault me for it. You would fault me for it!"

Though she longed to scream and rage, her voice emerged a tremulous, broken whisper . . . with heart-rending candor.

"It was all that filled my thoughts, my heart, night and day! A child lived inside me, the child I'd longed for for so long! My strength was his own. I wanted my babe so much, and then I—I lost him! I held his wee, limp body against me. He died in my arms, Egan. He died in my arms! You cannot know what it's like to lose a child, a piece of my heart, a piece of my soul!" She gave a jagged sob. "I was afraid to risk again—I am still afraid! How can you not see? How can you not know?"

She looked at him then, her face so very pale, her lovely mouth tremulous, her eyes huge and glittering with tears. But Egan was blind to her anguish, deaf to her pleas, numbed by his own fury, his heart raw and bleeding.

How can you not see, she had cried.

How could *she* not see that she sheared his very heart?

How can you not know?

How could *she* not know that he loved her? That he'd loved her for so long now.

But it was a love that was blighted . . . blighted by a ghost.

The ghost of her husband.

He feared it would ever be so. Through all the days of his life.

But no. Niall was dead. That was what he'd wanted her to see all along. Niall was dead. And *he* was her husband now. He . . . Egan.

And by God, she would know it.

His hands closed about her arms, dragging her close, so close that his breath pelted her like angry blows.

"This is what I see. This is what I know, from your own lips! That was Niall's babe. Not mine. *Not mine!* Indeed, I wonder that you've not tried to rid yourself of this child—my child!" He loomed over her. "Do not," he warned, "for if any harm comes to this babe, I promise you'll regret it."

For one awful moment, their eyes collided—his were filled with a terrible light, his jaw clenched so tight she was certain it would snap.

He released her and spun around, slamming the portal shut with a force that resounded in her ears long after.

Her breath emerged in a rush. Shocked and stunned, Glenda made her way shakily to the bed. Her knees were aquiver, her legs so weak she feared they would no longer hold her. For the first time, she felt a flicker of fear of this man whose stony features were a mask she scarcely recognized.

God help her, she thought numbly, should anything happen to this babe.

He announced her condition to all at dinner. Immediately there was a collective gasp, and then all eyes fell upon her—including his.

Within glimmered a challenge. Did he think she would deny it? Glenda was not sure whether she was more angry or hurt.

"When did you say the child will arrive, sweet?"

She longed to screech that she had not! She raised her chin. "Sometime early in the year."

Immediately there was a great crush around her. Somehow she managed to smile and say all the right things, aware that Egan watched—and listened—all the while. Finally, pleading tiredness, she escaped to her chamber.

It was Nessa, not Egan, who followed.

"Well, I daresay 'tis about time." Nessa's tone was cheerful as she bent to drape her mistress's gown over the chair. She had interfered once before where this pair was concerned, and though she'd had to bite her tongue many a time, she'd decided that this time she'd let the two of them find their own way.

Ah, but this was a rocky and treacherous path the two of them chose! If they but joined forces, 'twas a journey she suspected would be made with far less trouble . . . and even a bit of happiness.

"He is angry that I did not tell him sooner."

Nessa snorted. "He should have guessed far sooner!"

"How would he know? He has never before fathered a child." Jealousy flared within her as she thought of the women he'd had at Dunthorpe— Patsy, Anna, Mary, Louise. "That I am aware of," she added darkly. Yet not until it was out did Glenda realize she defended him! The lout! After all he'd dared say to her, she defended him! What the devil was wrong with her?

Hobbling to the bedside, Nessa stole a glance at her. "Nonetheless," she added, "he appeared pleased."

"Aye. And why shouldn't he be? He has lands and a keep, and an heir on the way."

"He is not the only one to win here, lass."

"I know." Glenda's voice was very small. The tears that were still perilously close to the surface threatened to reappear. "I-I just pray this babe will be healthy and whole . . ."

As the other was not. But she could not say it aloud.

Nessa's arms came around her. "And we will see that it is. I've never borne a bairn meself, but I've brought many into this world and seen many a woman through it."

Glenda clung to her, then drew back with a sheepish smile.

"Nessa?"

"Aye, lass?" Busy stirring the fire, Nessa glanced back over her shoulder.

"Why did you never have children?"

"Mayhap because I've never had a husband!"

Glenda studied her quietly. She knew that Nessa had been born on Blackstone, and to her knowledge, had never left. Though Nessa's hair was sparse and gray as storm clouds, her limbs brittle with age, her skin lined with myriad wrinkles, Glenda imagined what her old nursemaid might have looked like when she was of an age with herself, with hair shiny and dark as the wings of a raven. Nor had Nessa always been crippled with the ague that nearly bent her double now. Glenda recalled the days of her own childhood, when Nessa had been stout and strong, her legs straight as the beech trees that grew near the river. Indeed, Nessa must have been quite fetching.

She waited until the old woman had turned and set aside the poker. "You told me you were in love once," she reminded her quietly, "before I was born."

For an instant, Nessa said nothing. She felt herself

hurtled far back in time, to the days when she had been as young and slim as the beauty before her. Aye, she had loved once . . . loved a man far beyond her reach . . . yet ever within reach. With a faint smile, she gazed into her charge's eyes, eyes that were so like another . . .

"Aye," Nessa admitted slowly, "but we could not be together."

"Why not?"

Something wistful—something that might have been regret—sped across the old woman's face. Yet in the very next heartbeat, she said simply, "He married another."

And somehow Glenda knew . . . it was not so simple at all.

"Now"—gnarled fingers drew the covers up to Glenda's breast"—rest and do not worry, lass. Whatever troubles ye have, they will soon pass."

Glenda smiled slightly. A pang bit deep. As much as she loved Nessa, she couldn't help but wish that small comfort had come from another . . .

But Egan did not come to her that night. Nor in the days that followed.

Oh, he inquired daily as to her health, but he made no attempt to renew their intimacy. All along Glenda had told herself it wasn't really her that Egan wanted—it was her home, her lands. Indeed, he'd made no secret of it.

She didn't want to believe it.

His body had not lied. The tempest of passion that lit their nights to a raging conflagration had not lied. Yet now, when his eyes, so breathtakingly blue, chanced to rest upon her, they were as chill as the

mists that clung to the loftiest peaks of the Highlands.

She lay alone in her bed at night, thinking of him,
remembering that wondrous day in the orchard
when the colors had been so vivid and bright; when
happiness washed over her in waves of mellow yellow, and passion was the flame of a fiery crimson
blossom.

Yet now the bleakness in her was the gray of a
wintry, leaden sky. And despair was an endless
black, the color of her heart.

The closeness—the tenderness—was glaringly absent. If he was distant and indifferent, needled a niggling little voice, could she blame him? It was
through her own folly that it had come to this; she'd
been stung by her own shame, stung by his pride.

She'd thought she could hold herself aloof—what
a fool she was! Her mind was filled with bitter self-
disparagement.

He wanted his child . . . but it seemed he no longer
wanted her! Indeed, how could he desire her now?
'Twas as if, now that he'd been discovered, the babe
within had finally decided to show the world of his
presence. Her belly began to mound, hard and firm.

She'd been so convinced a part of her had died
along with that first babe, with Niall's son . . .

And then she felt the life within her quicken. The
merest flutter . . .

She was alone when it first happened. With a gasp
she pressed a hand to her middle, wanting it to happen again . . . willing it! And it did, like the wings of
a butterfly tucked within her womb. Her mind sped
straight to Egan. She wanted to press his hands to

her belly that he might feel, too. She longed to share it with him, and hurried to the hall to find him.

It was Jeannine who told her he had ridden out and wouldn't be back until nightfall.

Her steps slowed. The moment was gone. She shut herself away in her chamber and wept in fear and frustration, her misery crowding her chest until she could scarcely breathe.

Yet by morn she was filled with fresh resolve. She could not give up. Her child needed her. This babe was alive . . . and she would fight to keep it so.

Autumn brought brilliant hues of gold and russet to the Borderlands. In the garden, the flowers lost the blush of summer; vines withered and grew yellow, twisting limply across the ground. The air began to chill and carried with it the promise of a long, hard winter.

In deference to her condition, Glenda had taken to walking, both within the walls of the keep and without. Today, however, she stood atop the wall-walk, shivering a little beneath her mantle. Far below, she saw Egan striding across the bailey. He stopped short, shielding his eyes and looking up at her. She could have sworn he glowered, but she paid no heed. Very soon day would give way to night, and she had already spent much of the day indoors; she and Jeannine had spent the afternoon sewing window cushions to guard against the cold in the coming months. But she was not yet ready to go inside, despite Egan's disapproval.

The clouds hung low, spread out like giant wings, nearly black as soot. A flutter of snow drifted from the sky, and she sighed, knowing that soon she would have to go in.

She'd noticed earlier the small black dot that punctuated the far distance. Her idle gaze caught it anew, and she realized that it was a horse and rider—and they were fast approaching. Curious, she stayed where she was, though far below, she heard Egan hail her.

"Glenda! Come down! 'Tis far too cold for you there!"

"Wait!" she called down, then pointed in the distance toward the rider.

Just then the sentry in the tower caught sight of the horse as well. "Someone comes!" he shouted.

By the time she descended to the bailey, the horse, a huge black beast as big as Egan's, cantered through the gatehouse.

Her gaze sharpened. The man turned his head then. The folds of his plaid parted, and a small head with hair of ebony popped out.

Her eyes widened. "Mary, mother of God," she breathed. "It's Cameron and Brodie!"

Chapter 17

Glenda tore across the uneven ground as fast as she was able. Cameron enveloped her in a massive hug. "Glenda! Lord, 'tis good to see you!"

Glenda blinked back tears, a tremulous smile on her lips. "And you, Cameron, and you." She clung to his hands, amazed and disbelieving.

Egan looked on as his wife smiled with unabashed joy up at the man with hair as dark as midnight and eyes of crystalline gray, aware of an odd sting in the middle of his chest. If he had been the one returned from afar, would his wife's greeting have been so warm?

Ah, but no doubt she would have rejoiced had he never returned!

Brodie had decided he'd been neglected long enough. Egan had lifted him from atop Fortune, Cameron's steed. Now he tugged upon Glenda's skirt, gazing up at her mutely.

Glenda bent and would have lifted him, but suddenly Egan was there, sweeping the lad from the ground and placing him in her arms. Impish blue eyes glowed happily. The boy framed her face with chubby palms and gave her a wet, sloppy kiss.

"I missed you!"

Glenda's heart melted. "And I missed you, too, Brodie!" She hugged him, then drew back. "I didn't think you would even remember me!"

"Of course he did. He's as clever as his father!"

Naturally the claim came from his father. Glenda wrinkled her nose at him. "I happen to hold a different opinion. I think he's as clever as his mother!"

"So I've lost favor already, have I?"

Glenda laughed and lowered Brodie to the ground. When she straightened, Cameron was busy looking her up and down.

"Good lord, woman, what happened to you?"

Egan's gaze sharpened. Was it his imagination, or did her smile falter?

Cameron clapped a hand on Egan's broad shoulders. "You waste no time, do you, man?"

Egan felt the tightness in his muscles ease. He cocked a brow. "I could say the same of you," he said easily, reminded how quickly Meredith had gotten with child. Only with Cameron and Meredith, the babe had been well on the way before the wedding ever took place. "That reminds me . . . where is your wife?"

"Alas, she sends her regrets that she could not come as well. Nor, I fear, would Aileen ever be still long enough to make so long a trip on horseback or even in a cart."

"Aileen!" Glenda echoed eagerly. "How is the babe?"

"Hardly a babe any longer, and grown so that I vow you'd never know her." He pretended to pull a

face. "It does no good to swaddle her. She's just begun to crawl and seems to feel it her duty to know
every inch of Dunthorpe—and all at once!"

Glenda's smile held a trace of wistfulness. "Ah, but
I wish they had come with you!"

Cameron nodded. "I know you do, lass." He
paused, then added mildly, "But, as I'm certain you
know, travel is not always wise for women with your
particular affliction."

As Glenda's eyes widened, a grin played about the
corners of his handsome mouth. His gaze dropped
meaningfully to the swell of her belly. Cameron
chuckled as Egan's brows shot high in a show of surprise. Glenda's response was not so subtle.

"You cannot mean to say that Meredith is with
child again!"

"I can and do."

"Another babe—so soon after Aileen?" Meredith
was aghast. "Why, the poor woman will have no
rest!"

His grin was utterly wicked . . . utterly Cameron.
"What can I say?" he murmured. "The nights are
long in the Highlands."

"The nights are long everywhere!"

Cameron chuckled. "So I see, lass. So I see."

Glenda blushed fiercely. Her eyes strayed helplessly to Egan, only to discover that a trace of color
had crept beneath his skin as well.

Cameron's grin widened. "And methinks my wife
will be immensely pleased when she learns *your*
news as well!"

Glenda couldn't help it. She could hardly chastise
the man for loving his wife, could she? Her mouth

twitched with an answering smile. Even the lines around Egan's mouth had softened.

There was much boisterous laughter that evening while they dined. Cameron got to his feet when Nessa shuffled into the hall—it mattered not that she was a servant. Cameron recognized her not only as his elder, but as one who carried an air of wisdom sought by many and attained by few. When the old woman stopped and fixed her eyes on the newcomer, Glenda started to make the introductions.

Nessa stopped her. Boldly she assessed the visitor, though she had to tip her head far back in order to see his face, the same way she did with Egan.

"I remember ye," she stated flatly. "Ye're Cameron, the one with eyes of steel. Now sit, lad. Ye're makin' me back ache, standin' so tall."

Glenda smothered a laugh. Cameron blinked and muttered, "Aye," clearly taken aback by Nessa's candidness as Egan had never been.

Brodie ate stoutly, moving from his father's lap, to Egan's, to Glenda's. Invigorated by the meal as well as the attention lavished upon him by all, young Brodie lost his shyness among the strangers and proved himself quite the jester. Before long he slid from Cameron's lap to walk before the fire roaring in the hearth, back and forth, back and forth.

Cameron suddenly noticed that nearly every eye in the hall had fastened on his son. He stopped what he was saying and frowned over at him.

"Brodie, what are you doing?"

"Look, Papa! I can walk like you!"

With strides as long as his little legs would allow, the boy strutted back and forth with his small chest puffed out, his chin hitched high and sturdy shoulders jutting forward, first one and then the other in an exaggerated swagger.

Everyone roared.

Cameron sputtered. "Why do you laugh? I do not walk like that!"

"Oh, but you do." Egan couldn't hide his amusement.

Cameron scowled. "Brodie, come here, lad!"

Blue eyes sparkled. A dimple flashed. "I'm going to hide. Come find me, Papa!" He dived beneath the table.

Cameron groaned. "Brodie, no! Come here!"

"I begin to see why Meredith did not come with you," Egan said dryly. "She sought some much needed rest."

Before long, Brodie clambered up onto Egan's lap. He sat facing Egan, tipping his small head first to one side, then the other, peering at Egan until all three adults watched him curiously.

"Egan?"

"Aye, lad?" The boy's tone was earnest; it accorded Egan's undivided attention.

"When I am a man, will I have thistles on my face like you?" He leaned forward and rubbed his palms against the dark stubble on Egan's cheeks and jaw.

Egan's expression was such that now it was Cameron who availed himself of a long, mirthful laugh.

It was late when Glenda pushed herself back from the table. Brodie had fallen asleep on the bench beside his father. Most of the others had retired as well. Egan started to rise, but she stopped him with a word.

"Nay," she said. "Stay and talk."

Indeed, Egan thought darkly, why shouldn't he stay? It was not as if the two of them would be sleeping together!

Glenda smiled at Cameron, her expression fondly tender as it moved from him to Brodie. "I'll take Brodie and put him to bed in my chamber. You can fetch him later."

Cameron nodded and wished her good-night. A maid was summoned to carry the slumbering child up the stairs to the tower.

Egan's gaze never left her as she bent to kiss Cameron's cheek. Lean fingers tightened ever so slightly on his cup. An odd feeling knotted his insides. She had not been sickly, thank the Lord. There was a lush luminescence to her hair, her lips and skin. Whether she wanted it or no, carrying this child suited her. Looking at her now with Cameron, he could almost feel that velvet caress against his own heated skin . . .

A rending ache cut through him. Christ, but it had been so long! A slow burn simmered in his veins, of desire or jealousy, he knew not! A part of him envied Cameron, for her smile had scarcely left her this night. He felt . . . cheated. It rankled, the readiness of her laughter, their teasing banter and the ease in which it was traded.

It was not like that when they supped together. The tension hung between them, as thick as roiling storm clouds.

His disquiet ripened—his uncertainty along with it. Seeing Cameron again . . . did she think of Niall? In truth, there was something of Niall in Cameron's profile, the blade of his nose, the patrician shape of his brow ... the deep resonance of his voice.

Did Glenda see it? Did she hear it, too? Was she reminded of the love they had shared—and lost? Did she mourn anew? Fervently wish that the babe inside her was Niall's and not his?

Guilt slipped over him, a shroud of midnight. He'd claimed his friend's wife. As Glenda's husband, he now owned her lands and her home. Jesu, he was no better than Simon!

He'd gone a little mad the day he'd realized she was with child. He'd been so angry that she hadn't told him—so jealous of Niall ... of the man who had once been her husband.

Bleakly he wondered what it must be like for her. Bound to one man ... still loving another.

One who was gone to her forever.

He was abruptly angry with himself. Ashamed. So very ashamed. It was good to see Cameron again, yet dread coiled heavy on his breast. The fact that it *was* Cameron only made it all the more difficult. He felt vulnerable and naked as never before.

It was not a feeling he liked. He couldn't remember a time when he'd felt so awkward. Their friendship was such that they had an almost uncanny awareness of each other's thoughts.

He glanced across the table at Cameron, lifting his tankard to his lips. "I hope the fact that I didn't return posed no hardship for you."

"Nay, of course not. When you left Dunthorpe, I asked that you take care of Glenda." There was a pause. "What I never expected was that you would marry her!"

Egan nearly choked on a mouthful of ale. So much for guarding his feelings!

"But you must tell me of things. The letters you wrote left much to be desired."

That was something Egan did not doubt. He was afraid to say too much, just as afraid to reveal too little. That was why he hadn't written to say he and Glenda expected a child.

With much trepidation, he met Cameron's eyes. His friend's gaze was steady on his face. Little by little, the rigidness seeped from his limbs. Grimacing, he told Cameron of all that had transpired.

When he'd finished, Cameron leaned back. "What of the raids?"

"There have been none of late," Egan said slowly, "yet I am reluctant to be complacent. It seems there have been other times when there was no sign of the raiders for many weeks—then, just when all began to feel safe, they returned anew. 'Tis not something so easily forgotten, and I know there are still some who remain uneasy."

"And this man, Simon Ruthven?"

Simon the Lawless. "He was angry when I announced I would wed Glenda. Yet he was present at the ceremony, and displayed no rancor. In truth, since that time I've seen little of him," he admitted. "I've heard tales of his temper and his treatment of others, but I've yet to witness it myself."

"Mayhap he's tamed his ways."

"Mayhap," Egan allowed. "He has given me no reason to distrust him, yet neither do I trust him." He mulled for a moment. "Maybe the raiders have simply moved on."

"Let us hope so." Cameron touched the edge of his cup to Egan's. "But methinks you are wise to remain cautious."

Egan sipped the brew, his expression pondering. " 'Tis an awesome task," he said after a moment, "and one that I never fully appreciated until now."

"What task is that?"

"Knowing that others look to me for guidance. Knowing that not only am I responsible for the care and safety and protection of Glenda and myself, but others as well."

"And soon a babe, too."

"Aye. And soon a babe."

"You've shoulders broad enough to bear it."

Egan was quiet for a moment. "What if I fail?"

"You won't."

If only he was as certain as Cameron. "You do not understand," he said briefly. "I haven't made a very good start."

"But you have! All was in a shambles, you said. When you arrived, there were no men to guard the keep. When *I* arrived, I saw men on every tower, and unless I'm very much mistaken, men who are well trained indeed! The walls are strong and intact. The fields were clearly well tended, your household is well tended and your table plentiful."

"Not that, Cameron." Egan swallowed. The pitch of his voice dropped. "I mean my marriage. Glenda . . . sometimes I'm certain she would just as soon see me in hell."

"Oh, I doubt that," Cameron said cheerfully. He eyed Egan across the rim of his cup. "My old friend Egan, a husband. A father! Why, I remember the days when I was certain no maid would ever steal your heart!" He laughed softly. "Would that Meredith could see you now!"

Egan smiled slightly. "She must have been surprised when she learned Glenda and I had wed," he murmured.

"Surprised! She was beside herself with joy. You know how it was with her. She didn't want Glenda to spend the rest of her days alone."

"But what of you, Cameron?" Everything inside compelled that he speak, even as he dreaded the answer. "Were you as glad as Meredith? Or were you"—God's teeth, he swore to himself, but this was hard!—"were you angry?"

"Angry? Why should I be angry?"

Egan hauled in a deep breath. "I married your brother's widow."

Something flickered across Cameron's features, something he couldn't decipher for once. He watched tensely as Cameron slowly lowered his tankard to the table.

His smile ebbed. He appeared very grave, almost somber.

"I know, Egan," he said very softly. "*I know.*"

Egan looked at him. What he saw made him brace himself inside. "What do you mean?"

"I know that you didn't marry Glenda for what she could bring you. I know that you didn't marry her to keep her from Simon's clutches. I know . . . that it's always been her. That you've loved her for a long, long time."

Even before Niall had died.

Those words unspoken vibrated between them, tipping Egan's world on end.

Egan felt himself pale. "How?" he whispered. "How do you know?"

Cameron gave a slight shake of his head. "When you sent word that you had wed Glenda, I felt something stir inside me—I know not how to explain it! But I didn't know for certain," he admitted, "until I saw you this day. Suddenly it all made sense. I remembered how, at times, when Niall and Glenda were together, you sometimes looked away . . ."

An awful sensation crowded Egan's chest. He gripped the edge of the table. "Dear God. Did Niall know?"

"Nay. I would stake my life on it."

"Does Meredith?"

"Nay."

"Tell no one, Cameron."

"You needn't worry," Cameron spoke gently. "I won't."

Egan's gaze flitted away. "You must hate me." His voice was as raw as he felt inside. "I coveted your brother's wife. I *took* your brother's wife."

"No," Cameron said. "She was his widow. And now she is *your* wife."

Egan's gaze swung back. Almost fiercely he ground out, "You *should* hate me!"

"Never in this life. Never on this earth." Stretching out a lean hand, he laid it on Egan's shoulder. "Egan," he said softly, "I wish you only happiness, for you are my brother as surely as Niall ever was. Nay, not in blood . . . but in spirit."

Egan's eyes stung. His chest ached. He could not

speak for all he heard—all he glimpsed in Cameron's face—for the emotion that swelled his throat. Instead he reached up and briefly squeezed his friend's bicep, a wordless conveyance of all he felt.

For the span of a heartbeat, they regarded each other.

It was Cameron who finally gave a rusty laugh. "Here we sit, man to man, yet with women's tears misting our eyes! God forbid that the rest of the household should see us like this!"

A corner of Egan's mouth curled upward, yet a trace of bleakness bled onto his soul. "I could be happy, if I thought Glenda cared for me."

"Cared for you!" Cameron tipped his face heavenward. "Lord, man, she's heavy with your child. She does care for you!"

"She does not. She wed me, for there was naught else to do. The earl insisted she have a strong arm here at Blackstone."

"Sometimes others see what we do not. Indeed, if not for Glenda, I might never have married Meredith when I did—and alas, she made me feel quite the wretch for not having done so much sooner."

"Am I a fool, Cameron?"

"Nay, not a fool. You are in love. If you are a fool, then so am I!" Cameron raised his tankard high. "To fools everywhere, and the women who make them so!"

Both men drank deeply. Before long, the effects of the ale had begun to show.

"You know," Egan said with a gleam in his eye, " 'tis not Glenda but me you should thank for Meredith and your children."

"You? 'Twas *you* who argued against taking her from the nunnery. But when I did . . . why, you would have much rather murdered her, not once, but twice!"

"She was a Munro!" Egan defended himself staunchly. "I but defended your honor after the massacre of your family, for I did not think a Munro deserved to live! And you did as you pleased with her anyway. So you see, I deserve your gratitude."

"Ah, but then you were convinced she tried to poison me! Why should I thank you?"

"Because I did not act upon it! Besides, I did not know her as well as you!"

"That was good, for I think I'd have killed you if you had!"

It was a long time later before they stumbled up the tower stairs. Hearing the ruckus in the hall, Glenda tugged the door open.

Both nearly fell inside—and then erupted into hoarse, male laughter.

Glenda jammed her hands on her hips and glared. "Hush!" she admonished sternly. "Brodie is asleep, and he is exhausted from the journey."

Cameron peered within the shadowed chamber. "Where is he?"

Glenda pointed. "There, on the bed."

He weaved toward it. There was a crash, followed by a black curse.

"You kicked the stool. Here, let me get the candle." Egan snatched a tallow candle from the spike on the wall. Yellow light undulated on the far wall.

Glenda's eyes widened. Cameron was bent low,

rubbing his shin. Egan had nearly caught his tunic afire.

The unmistakable odor of ale now permeated the room. "Och!" she cried. "You're sotted, both of you!"

Cameron picked up Brodie and turned. "Not so!"

With a mutinous glare, she pressed a finger to her lips and indicated his slumbering son.

"Sorry, I forgot." Cameron's whisper was still overly loud. Smiling crookedly down at his son, he pressed a decidedly sloppy kiss on Brodie's cheek.

Egan pulled a face. "You're slobbering on the poor lad!"

"I do not slobber," Cameron informed him with a scowl. "Babes slobber. Aileen slobbers. The new babe will slobber. Without question, yours will . . ."

"For pity's sake! I should have known this would happen with the two of you together again!" Try though she might, Glenda couldn't be angry with the pair.

"Cameron, put your son to bed"—she marched to the door and held it wide—"and yourself along with him."

"Aye, lady."

His tone duly chastened, Cameron cradled his son in his arms and ducked through the door. Glenda remained where she was, expecting Egan to follow.

He did not. With a surety that belied his drunken state, he replaced the taper on its spike. A single step brought him alongside her.

With the heel of his hand, he closed the door.

" 'Tis a good thing you weren't sleeping naked. I would have been furious if Cameron had seen you unclothed. So, I think, would Meredith."

Glenda blinked. This was the last thing she'd expected him to say! All at once she was flustered without knowing quite why. "I cannot think why you would be jealous. I'm fat as a sow."

"No, you're not. You're beautiful." His gaze wandered slowly down her form. "But you should only be naked with me, Glenda."

"I am not naked at all!"

"Nay, sweet. Not yet."

Heat flooded her. The huskiness in his voice made her breath catch. Even drunk, he made her shiver inside. And when he gazed at her the way he was just now, she couldn't even think.

"Egan." Tentatively she spoke his name. " 'Tis late. We should be abed—"

"We should indeed."

Strong arms came hard around her, lifting her high aloft, as if she weighed no more than the down of a thistle. With a swiftness that startled her, the candle was blown out and he was striding toward the bed. She flung her arms about his neck.

"Egan, be careful!"

Already she was being lowered to the mattress. Her gown was whisked over her head. Almost before she could draw breath, he'd shucked his own clothes. Lean, hair-roughened limbs slid against her own softness.

Her heart lurched. "Egan, what are you doing?"

"A husband and wife should not sleep apart."

Her lungs emptied. Once again she was caught snug within the binding circle of his embrace. Oh, but he was as arrogant as ever!

There was a perilous coil of heat low in her belly.

Her fingers curled against his shoulders—in denial or invitation? " 'Twas you who chose to sleep elsewhere," she said shakily.

"Cameron and Meredith do not sleep apart. They sleep together. So should we."

"Oh!" she cried. "Because they do, so must we? That is why you're here?"

His arms tightened. "Nay," he muttered. "That has nothing to do with us. With you . . ."

His eyes glimmered above her, blue fire in the night . . . crimson flames in her heart. His mouth took command of hers in a long, unbroken kiss. A thrill shot through her. He still wanted her! Her heart sang. Did he truly think she was beautiful? He made her feel beautiful, when he kissed her with such sweet, ardent persuasion.

Warm lips traced the arch of her throat. Her hands ran wild over his back, skimming straining muscles beneath sleek satin skin. He nuzzled the hollow between her breasts. A sinewy thigh inserted itself between her legs.

In fevered abandon, she breathed his name.

There was no response, not aloud nor otherwise. Gradually she felt the iron strength seep from the arms that held her.

"Egan?" she whispered again.

A gentle snore was her only answer. Glenda didn't know whether to laugh or cry. Whatever amorous intentions her husband had harbored—whatever intentions *she* might have had—they'd gone the way of the wind.

Her husband was fast asleep.

Chapter 18

When Glenda roused the next morning, he was gone. She couldn't help but feel bereft. Unbidden, her hand crept out to the spot where he'd lain. The sheet still bore the imprint of his body. It didn't matter that they had slept chastely. When he'd come to her room last night, the cool, hard edge that had marked his manner of late had vanished. She missed him desperately; missed the heat of his body in the chill of the night, the strength of his arms about her back.

A stark yearning surged within her. Her throat swelled with the memory. For a while last night, she hadn't felt so empty, so very alone.

Just before the noonday meal, she came upon him in the hall. Her gaze was full and direct; Egan's eyes but grazed hers. They were quickly averted, as were his steps.

Glenda's soul cried out. Inside she was devastated. Did he regret the hours spent with her in her bed?

He did not speak of it, even when they found themselves alone in the hall later that eve, waiting for Cameron and Brodie.

Nor would she, for it was just as she'd told him last night. She swung between the depths of despair and a righteous outrage. He'd taken himself from their bed . . . it was up to him to return. She would not beg or plead, for she had her pride as well.

The next evening, the scenario was similar. All of them remained at table for a long time. Brodie fell asleep against his father's legs. Tired, Glenda excused herself, taking the lad upstairs with her. Yet despite her weariness and her earlier vow, she made herself stay awake.

Egan and Cameron remained in the hall for a long time. When she heard their footsteps in the passage outside, she held her breath.

This time they were not sotted.

Nor did Egan remain.

In her chamber the next morning, she pushed the shutters aside and glanced out into the bailey. Egan had just dismounted from his stallion. A small figure ran toward him—Brodie. Egan caught him and lifted him high in his arms. Even from here, Glenda could see the laughter that blunted his rough-hewn features. A lean hand smoothed the back of Brodie's dark head. Such strength. Such gentleness, she found herself musing . . . Her heart wrenched. She, too, had known the gentle touch of that hand, and its powerful strength as well. But now there was so much distance between them . . .

Egan placed the lad upon his stallion. Taking the reins from the stableboy, he began to lead the horse across the grass.

Her hand slipped to the mound of her belly. What would their child be like? she found herself pondering. Dark like Egan, with long-lashed eyes as blue as a sunlit sky? Or with her own golden coloring? She did not mind whether the child was lad or lassie.

"Grow strong, little one," she murmured aloud, "as strong as the stoutest oak tree." Her eyes closed. She directed a fervent prayer heavenward that she would remain well—that their child would be healthy and sound as her first had not. As if the babe heard her, her belly rippled as the child rolled vigorously in her womb.

Glenda smiled.

That night as she prepared for bed, there was a sudden clamor in the bailey. Glenda looked up from where she sat brushing her hair before the warmth of the fire.

"What is it?" she asked. Jeannine had moved to the window and stood looking out.

Jeannine shook her head, a slight crease between her brows. "I know not. But the groom is bringing out Egan's horse."

Glenda flew to the window to see for herself. Several men carrying torches strode toward the guardhouse. Egan stood near the entrance to the tower, talking to a sentry, his features grim. An odd shiver played over her skin.

The brush fell from her fingers. She hastened from the chamber and down the stairs. Outside, a frigid blast of air hit her like an icy brine, but she paid no heed. A fierce gust sent her hair streaming, whipping about her face. She dragged it aside and began to run, unable to see her path, but plunging ahead anyway. In her haste, she tripped on her gown. A shrill cry tore from her throat, for she felt herself tumbling forward. She flung out her hands to catch her fall, that she would not land on her belly.

There was no need. Strong hands caught her and brought her upright.

With a gasp she looked up into Egan's face. Somehow, she thought with a pang, he was always there when she needed him. Always . . .

"Glenda! What are you doing here? Where is your mantle?" His frame of mind was unconcealed. The harsh line of his mouth exactly matched his voice.

She glanced past him, where a stableboy held the reins to his stallion, now fully saddled.

"Where are you going, Egan? What's wrong?"

His jaw thrust forward. For a moment she thought he would refuse to answer. "The miller's boy just rode in. He saw men riding in the forest. They wore cloth tied about their faces."

A full-fledged panic assailed her. The raiders! "You cannot go alone!"

"Cameron goes with me," he said tersely. "I've men out, but there's no telling where they are. I'm taking others with me. We'll ride in parties of two so we can cover more ground. Now go inside."

Her pulse was clamoring. What if they were outnumbered? What if he was hurt? Caught in the rampage of the wind—in the rampage of her heart—she remained where she was.

She wanted him to kiss her, she realized. Wanted it with a desperation that made her long to reach out to him, to draw his mouth down to hers for his kiss, however brief it might be. She twisted her hands in her skirts to stop from doing precisely that.

"Egan—"

He whirled, his countenance black and scowling. "Have you no thought for the babe? Go inside!"

His sharpness stung. There was no mention of her. It was the babe he cared about, not her. Pierced by a bittersweet pang, tears burned her throat, her eyes. But she would not cry before him, she vowed, she would not!

There was a hand on her arm. It was Cameron. "Will you stay with Brodie?"

"Aye. Aye, of course."

"Good. I asked a maid to take him to your chamber."

She nodded. Egan was already atop his stallion, his reins in hand.

"Cameron!"

Cameron hesitated. His gaze slid from her to Egan, and back again. "He'll be all right, Glenda. Do not fret." Already he was striding away.

She drew a deep breath. "May God be with you both," she called.

Cameron waved. Egan gave no sign that he even heard. He rode off without a word, without a kiss, without a touch . . . without even a farewell.

It was only later that she told herself it was foolish to feel so abandoned. No doubt the raiders consumed his attention—and his concentration. Yet somehow she couldn't quite erase the hurt she felt.

In her chamber, she slipped into bed and gathered Brodie's small body against her. After a while he shifted restlessly, whimpering a little. He sat up, rubbing his eyes. Glenda had left a candle burning so that if he awoke, he would not be alarmed.

Tears welled in his eyes. "Where is Papa?"

Gazing down into his forlorn little features, Glenda felt her heart turn over. Brodie was such a sweet-natured child; it was unlike him to cry and complain.

"He and Egan had to ride out, I'm afraid." She smoothed the black hair that tangled on his forehead. With a smile she sought to reassure him. "He'll be back."

His lower lip trembled. "When?"

"Soon, Brodie. Very soon. When you awaken, he will be here." She hoped. Dear God, she prayed . . . !

"You are such a brave little lad, love," she said cheerfully, then shivered apurpose. "Will you help me to keep warm?" She held out her arms.

Brodie came into them and nestled against her. Glenda hugged his stout little body tight, soothing him back to sleep. Within minutes he was asleep again, his cheek curled against her shoulder, a chubby hand fisted against his chest.

There was no such ease for Glenda. She stared at the shifting shadows of the firelight dancing on the ceiling, her ears straining for some sign that the men had returned.

Hours passed, an eternity.

The embers in the fire were no longer toasty and warm. The meager ray of light from the stub of candle flickered, then went out. There was a sudden chill in the room, a chill that crept round her heart, invaded every corner of her being. She shivered, but not with cold. Nay, not with cold.

Tucking the covers tight around Brodie, she slipped from the bed. Moving to the window, she eased the shutters aside.

There was no sign of movement, no sign of Egan.

The bailey was dark and deserted. Beyond the walls, the earth lay utterly still. Clouds scuttled across the pale sliver of moon, and then even that frail light was gone.

The memory revived. Unbidden. Unwanted. With vivid clarity, she recalled another time at Dunthorpe when she had been watching. Watching and waiting anxiously for her husband to return . . .

Pray God the outcome was not the same.

A half-sob wedged in her throat. She smothered it by pressing the back of her hand to her lips.

Brodie whimpered in his sleep. She crawled back into the softness of the bed, though she knew there would be no rest, no sleep until Egan and Cameron were back unharmed.

She started at each shout of the sentry, the echo of hoofbeats, darting to the window to look outside. Over the next several hours, the men returned, two by two.

All but Egan and Cameron.

The usual commotion of the household had already begun. A cock crowed. Voices came from a distance. Glenda began to truly despair when at last the pair appeared beneath the gatehouse. They were both back, alive and well, thank God!

Footsteps thumped on the stairs a short time later. It was Cameron, come to retrieve Brodie. She stifled her disappointment, for Egan was not with him.

His expression sober, Cameron relayed that no one had found any trace of men on horseback, masked or otherwise. There were tracks in the mud, but they could have been from their own men. Nor had anyone discovered signs of any villainy, but Glenda knew it might be later in the day before that was known.

"Simon is here," Nessa told her some time later.

Glenda arched a thoughtful brow. "Indeed," she murmured. "We've seen little of him since the wedding. I wonder what brings him." She paused. "Is Egan here?"

"I know not. Cameron and Brodie and some of the other men went out hunting, but I did not notice if Egan was with them."

"Well, then, I have no choice but to see him." In truth, she was rather uncomfortable at the idea of seeing Simon without Egan present. But she could hardly leave him alone. Putting aside her sewing, she descended to the hall.

Simon stood warming his limbs before the fire.

He turned and spied her, his greeting hearty. "Glenda! You're looking well!" His gaze ran down her body. There was a nearly imperceptible pause on her midriff.

"I am, thank you." Glenda inclined her head. "And you, Simon?"

"Well enough, I suppose, considering this beastly cold!"

"Then perhaps you'd like some hot, spiced wine to warm you." She beckoned to a maid, who went to fetch it.

When the girl was gone, he turned to her with a half-smile. "Ah, Glenda," he said with a sigh. " 'Tis not pleasure that brings me here, I fear."

"If not pleasure, then what?"

It was Egan. He stood just behind her. She felt his presence even before she heard him. For a split second, a hard light shone in Simon's eyes—or did it? It vanished so quickly she wondered if she'd imagined it. Not that she could blame him, she realized. Egan's tone was curt; she'd been brought up to be gracious, and in her mind, such rudeness was not warranted.

"Egan! How are you, man?"

"Well." Egan was downright grim. "What brings you here, Simon?"

"I heard tell there was some trouble last night."

"No trouble. But some strangers were seen, aye."

"Masked riders?"

"Aye."

Beside her, Glenda had felt Egan stiffen. The admission came reluctantly, it seemed.

"I knew it! Without doubt they are the very same, then."

"The very same?"

"Indeed. I came to warn you, you see. These men were seen on my lands as well."

Perhaps because they came from your lands. Egan couldn't help the thought that tolled through his mind.

"Was any harm done?"

"Nay, nay! For that, I am thankful." Simon tipped his head to the side. "But I understand you and your friend from the Highlands rode out to investigate."

Egan's eyes flickered. "Cameron. Aye, we did."

"And you found nothing? No trace of these men?"

"Nay."

Glenda didn't dare look at Egan. She could feel the tension emanating from him.

Simon paused. "I know not how to say this . . . but, if you've need for more men . . ."

Egan cursed silently. Oh, but the rogue would still do his damndest to belittle him and make him appear small—and always before his wife!

He forced a thin smile. "I do hope that you do not imply that my men are less capable than yours?"

Simon spread his hands wide. "You need not take offense—"

"And none is taken."

" 'Tis simply that all know how Blackstone's resources have been tested—"

Egan wanted to grind his teeth in impotent rage. Faith, but the man knew not when to quit!

His smile did not waver. "A problem which has been resolved, I assure you."

Simon's lips compressed, but he had no comeback. Pleased, Egan took the other man's arm and started toward the door. "Had I known you were here, I would have arrived much sooner. Please let us know the next time you wish to visit and I shall allot more time. As it is, well, I fear I've much to do this morn, and so does my wife."

With that Simon was hustled through the door.

"Well, if he wasn't your enemy before now, I've no doubt it won't be long before he is."

Turning to face her, Egan took exception to the bite in her tone. "Would you have me be like you? Offer him wine and comfort and warmth?"

His mockery cut deep. "I would have you be civil, or do I ask too much?"

"However much you decry it, this is my home, too. Simon is not welcome to come and go as he pleases."

By God, if she would criticize, then so would he.

For pity's sake . . . "He does not come and go as he pleases!"

"I'm in no mood to be charitable," Egan said abruptly. "I've just learned that Annabelle's parents— her brothers and sisters—were rousted from their hut last night."

Her heart leaped. "Were they hurt?"

"Nay. They were left bound and gagged in the pigsty. They were half-frozen with cold, but otherwise unharmed."

"You told Simon there was no trouble. Why didn't you tell him?"

"Why should I when he already knows?"

She hesitated. "We don't know that for certain."

"Don't we?" He stared at her long and hard, the plane of his jaw inflexible. "You defend him again, Glenda. Why?"

"I do not defend him, nor did I ever!"

"All right then. Even if he is not responsible, he'll find out soon enough. I'm not about to make him privy to all that goes on here. I do not need his advice or his men. Or do you think me incapable of defending your lands?"

There was no denying that he was in a fine temper. She had no desire to quarrel, yet here they were.

"They are your lands, too!" The protest was made in half-irritation, half-frustration.

"Aye," he stated coldly, "they are. Annabelle's family was lucky. My guess is that these raiders pursued no further deviltry so they would not be discovered. But if it begins anew, I will do whatever I must to protect Blackstone's people." His expression was taut, the words dismissive. He spun around and was gone, leaving her standing alone in the hall.

Supper that night was subdued. Even Brodie was less buoyant than usual. Egan scarcely deigned to look at her, let alone speak. Glenda tried not to let her misery show, yet throughout the meal, the threat of tears loomed perilously close. Before she embarrassed all of them, she made her excuses and left. Though she suspected Cameron was well aware of the true state of their marriage, he'd said nothing. She could feel his eyes following her as she left the hall.

The next morning Cameron announced his intention to return to Dunthorpe the following day. "Brodie is missing his mother—and so am I," he admitted with a wistful half-smile.

Glenda nodded. "We'll miss you, but I'm sure Meredith is just as anxious for you to return."

Egan agreed. "Of that, there is no doubt."

At least they were in agreement about something, Cameron thought. Mounting the stairs to prepare for the journey, he shook his head. He was tempted to return to the hall and shake some sense into the pair! They loved each other. Cameron knew it. He'd heard it in Egan's voice that very first night. It was there in Glenda's eyes, in every look bestowed upon Egan. Each had only to admit it—to themselves, and to each other. Yet, in truth, he reminded himself, the path to love for himself and Meredith had been no less rocky.

Nay, he would not interfere.

When it came time to take his leave, Glenda hugged Brodie, then turned to him. He winced at the tear-bright sheen of her eyes, but he was proud that she summoned a wisp of a smile.

"Have a safe journey home, and tell Meredith my heart is with her."

His eyes softened. "As hers is with you." His lips quirked. "Make certain your husband does not forget the way to Dunthorpe. Meredith will be anxious to see the new babe, and with three young ones in tow, I fear I'll never get beyond the gates."

Gently he kissed both cheeks. Then, succumbing to impulse, he slid an arm around her shoulders and hugged her. She ducked her head low, and he could have sworn he felt her shoulders heave.

Damn, he thought raggedly. _Damn_!

"All will be well," he whispered against her temple. "Believe it, and it will be."

Just then the babe in her womb gave a vigorous kick. Cameron drew back with a chuckle, welcoming the chance to lighten the air. "You see, I'm being sent on my way. Now I know it's time I left!"

Standing near, but not touching, Egan saw the way his wife clung to Cameron, the glaze in her beautiful golden eyes. She seemed so unhappy . . . he longed to reach out and comfort her.

But she had Cameron. Niall's brother. _Niall_, he thought. _Niall_! His insides squeezed. He stood stiff and silent, rooted in despair.

Would she always love Niall? Would she never love him? Ah, but he'd been a fool! he thought bleakly. She had come to him. _To him_. And he had allowed himself to hope . . . to believe that once he'd possessed her body, her heart would surely follow.

It was all for naught.

"Did you hear what I told Glenda? Do not forget the way to Dunthorpe, or Meredith will never forgive either of us."

Egan smiled, when he'd never felt less like smiling.

Cameron was suddenly sober as well. "Egan, if you are ever in need of anything, you have only to send word."

Their eyes met. A message passed between them, an unspoken bond.

"I know," Egan said softly, "and I will."

With a jaunty wave and a whoop from Brodie, Cameron was gone.

For the space of a heartbeat, neither Egan nor Glenda moved. A stifling tension descended; it was as if an impenetrable wall loomed high and unscalable between them. They did not speak, nor did their eyes meet. Egan went one way . . . Glenda the other.

Never had the gulf between them seemed greater. Both felt it keenly . . . yet neither knew how to breach it.

Chapter 19

With Cameron and Brodie's departure, it was as if all the laughter had been extinguished as well. Glenda felt as if a pall had fallen over her—and Blackstone Tower.

There was another raid that very night; this time there was true violence done. A man was so badly beaten it was not yet known if he would live or die. According to Nessa, he clung to life by the merest thread.

For indeed, it was just as Nessa had relayed the day of their arrival, Glenda reflected. Just when all began to feel safe, turmoil threatened anew. Mayhap it was her melancholic state, yet Glenda couldn't banish the certainty that it would not end here.

She awoke one morning to the sound of shouting in the bailey. Rising, she saw one of the cotters and the miller having what appeared to be a decidedly vehement exchange. Fists punched the air. There was a shove, then one tackled the other and both tumbled to the ground. It took four guards to separate them. Unease abounded. Tensions ran high and tempers short . . . including her own.

She sat on a stool in her chamber one day, winding newly dyed wool around the distaff. Outside a ferocious wind and sheets of rain pounded the walls; flames hissed and sizzled with the wetness that leaked through the chimney. Though the hour was not yet noon, the weather but deepened the gloom which hovered over all.

Glenda's fingers were clumsy, her mind askew, and all at once there was a tangle of yarn about her feet. Jeannine sat in the opposite corner. Glenda called for her assistance.

"A moment, my lady. Thomas is fretful today." Jeannine's brow was puckered in consternation; she plucked at the swaddling tucked in her elbow.

Glenda lost patience. "Jeannine, stop fussing! Thomas is gone! He died last winter!"

Jeannine's head jerked up. She stumbled to her feet. "You are cruel," she choked out. "Your babe died, and so you wish mine dead, too?"

Glenda froze, recoiling as much from the girl's words as her own. Aye, her babe had died, but she had another. One who surged so strongly within her that at times she woke from a sound sleep. But Jeannine had nothing. Nothing to look forward to in the days to come, in the years ahead . . .

"Oh, God," she whispered. By the time sanity returned, Jeannine had fled. The echo of the girl's dry sobs went through her like a lance. She was ashamed as never before.

Pushing aside her guilt, she went in search of her. She found her huddled in a corner in a small storeroom off the hall. Kneeling down, she touched Jeannine's shoulder.

"Jeannine," she whispered. "I'm sorry. I'm so, so sorry . . . I shouldn't have said what I did."

Jeannine raised her face. The girl's eyes were puffy and swollen from weeping, so empty that Glenda could have wept herself. At her words, tears filled Jeannine's eyes and overflowed. Glenda's arms stole around her. She rocked her back and forth while Jeannine wept her heart out.

Yet when at last they arose, Jeannine clung tighter than ever to her bundle. What was she to do? Glenda wondered helplessly. She'd begun to believe it did more harm than good, allowing Jeannine to believe her babe still lived. Yet how was she to reach her? Indeed, she asked herself achingly, how could anyone?

Never had she been as weary as she was when she sought her bed that night; it was a weariness not only of the body, but of the mind, for the day had been a trying one. She closed her eyes, anxious for the healing balm of sleep.

It came, but alas, it was not healing, not this night. Her dreams were dark and disturbing. She dreamed of the horror of the past . . . the dread of the future. She was at Dunthorpe again, in the bailey. The stench of death was sickeningly cloying, for seven lifeless bodies lay in the dirt, all in a row; their limbs were mangled and slashed, their clothing torn and streaked with crimson. The first was Niall. His brothers Burke and Oswald, young Thomas. The burly form of his father.

She backed away, recoiling in horror. Even as she watched, Niall's body arose. He got to his feet, and she began to scream and scream.

His head was gone.

Blood poured from his neck, the gaping hollow where his head should have been. He raised a hand. Pointing. Accusing.

"You killed my son. *You killed my son.*"

As if through a shrouded mist, she looked down and saw herself. She was on her knees in the bailey. In her arms was the limp, shriveled form of her infant son.

The mists swirled and shifted. Suddenly she was here at Blackstone. A swarm of people clustered around. Nessa. Jeannine. Bernard and Milburn.

Egan stepped forward, much as Niall had done, his eyes sizzling with icy blue fire. "You did not want me," he accused. "You did not want my seed. Will you kill this babe the way you killed the other?"

Everyone stared at her. Silently condemning. And then suddenly they were all moving closer, until she was being smothered. She turned and whirled, but there was nowhere to go. She lifted her arms to ward them off . . .'twas then she noticed.

Her hands were stained with blood.

In the distance, someone was screaming, the sound shrill and bloodcurdling.

Hands closed over her shoulders. She felt herself being shaken. Her throat felt raw. It took a moment for her frantic senses to realize those horrible sounds were coming from her.

Her eyes opened. The wavering yellow glow of a candle came into view . . . and Egan. He bent over her, his features taut and grim and almost forbidding. She wanted to scream anew. But her stomach was roiling, churning like the frothing sea.

She pushed him aside and tried to rise, only to fall hard to her knees in the rushes.

"Glenda!"

She clamped a hand to her mouth. "I'm going to be sick," she moaned.

Swearing, Egan yanked the chamberpot from the cupboard. It appeared before her just in time. She retched violently, as violently as she had when the heads of Niall and his father had been delivered to Dunthorpe that horrible day. When she finished, she sagged upon her arms, too weak to do otherwise.

An arm slid around her waist, bearing her that small distance to the bed. Her head was still spinning when he pressed a cup against her lips and bid her rinse and spit. Glenda did as she was told, then leaned back against the pillows. She was dimly aware of him rising and crossing the room. The sound of water being poured into a basin reached her ears. Feeling weary beyond measure, she closed her eyes.

They opened when a cool, wet cloth passed over her cheeks. Egan sat beside her, somberly intent as he bathed her face and throat. At length he set the basin aside.

"Christ, I feared there was someone in here with you." He paused. "Were you dreaming?"

Glenda nodded. The remembrance made her stomach rebel, but she took a long, deep breath. Mercifully, the spasm eased.

A tremor shot through her. She discerned no hint of coldness in his manner. Her gaze strayed to his chest, virile and bare.

In truth, Egan marveled that he'd heard her, for

his chamber was the floor below hers. "Of what did you dream?" he asked quietly.

She averted her head. "I cannot say."

Yet somehow he knew. He knew. Though he no longer touched her, she could feel the stiffness that invaded him. Yet he did not withdraw, as she thought he would . . . feared he would.

"You dreamed of Niall."

"Aye," she said tonelessly. "He was dead. He and the babe."

There was a never-ending silence.

"You must think I despise him."

Glenda hesitated. She would never forget the day she had recklessly—and aye, so foolishly!—compared him to Niall. He'd been so consumed with rage. It was for that very reason that she had since guarded her tongue with far more care and closeness. Nay, since that day, the name of Niall had not passed between them . . .

Until now.

"I don't hate him," he said suddenly. "Christ, how could I? Yet I cannot deny my jealousy. Whenever I lay with you, I wondered if you thought of Niall . . . if you wished you were with Niall. . . . I know how you loved him . . ." His voice trailed away. His jaw tensed. "The night Niall and the others were slain—I hated myself. I hated myself for not being there with them!"

Glenda drew a sharp breath. Her gaze locked on his features. She was stunned by the ravaging bleakness reflected there.

"No, Egan, no. There was nothing to be done.

Cameron was lucky to escape with his life—he almost did not!"

"If I had been there, maybe I could have stopped it."

She shook her head wildly. "No one could have stopped it, Egan. No one."

His eyes darkened. "I'll never forget your face that day, Glenda. I looked at you and it was like a knife twisting and turning . . ." Slowly he raised a hand. She felt the sweep of his fingers as he traced the contours of her cheeks, the line of her jaw. As achingly gentle as his touch was, his expression was all at once very fierce.

"I would have bartered my soul to the devil himself," he said fervently, "if only I had been the one to die, not Niall. I shall never forgive myself. Never."

The anguish she heard pierced her to the bone.

"What is there to forgive?" Her voice was low and unsteady. "I praise God you were not with them that day, Egan, for then you would not be here with me now."

Egan went very still inside. "I will not be angry," he said quietly. "I will not blame you. But can you look at me now—and tell me from the depths of your heart—that you do not wish that *I* had been the one to die instead of Niall?"

"I can, and I do." She shook her head, a soft cry breaking from her lips. "I would never wish you dead, Egan, never!"

Their eyes clung. His gaze roved over her features, deep and intense, as if he sought to see clear inside her. "Truly?"

"Aye," she whispered through a faint smile. "Egan,

you are so hard on yourself, both then and now. Blackstone has prospered through your efforts. The people love you. They respect you. We have supplies laid in for the winter. The earl's rents have been paid. It's all because of you, Egan. Don't you know how much everyone needs you?"

His heart contracted. Even as her words brought him no small measure of satisfaction, he couldn't help but wonder . . . what of her? Uncertainty gnawed within him, a vast, gaping emptiness. Did *she* need him?

He was afraid to ask . . . for fear of the answer he would receive. With bittersweet irony, he decided mayhap it was better if he did not know. It would be best—God knew it would be easier—if he returned to his own bed . . .

Yet a niggling voice of conscience battered him. How could he leave her alone this night, when the demons of the night and the past still haunted her?

Rising swiftly, he shed the rest of his clothing, blew out the candle and crawled in beside her.

She startled him by turning into his arms and melting against his side. Her lips grazed the smooth hardness of his shoulder. "Don't leave me," she said in a tiny little voice.

His arms locked tight about her form. He laid his cheek against her hair, inhaling of the clean, fresh scent of her. He felt the softness of her form, the way she clung to him, her breasts rising and falling in gentle tempo against his side. His arms tightened protectively. It had been torture, having her so near at hand, near enough to touch, yet knowing she would not welcome it. Having her turn to him, nestling against him as if he were all that she sought, made his chest swell and his heart fill.

No other woman had ever made him forget about Glenda. He'd made that discovery long ago at Dunthorpe.

No other ever would.

He discovered then that his motives were not entirely unselfish. His body responded in a way he could neither will nor control ... It had been many weeks since they'd lain together; he would not sully her—or himself—by going to another woman. Shame pricked him, even as longing shot through him, a sizzle of lightning. His blood scalded him. Desire flamed and swelled his loins to full, aching hardness.

'Twas his strength she sought, he told himself harshly, not his weakness. 'Twas his comfort she needed, not his lust. How could he take her without damning himself for a randy oaf?

It was a decision he did not have to make.

Glenda burrowed against his encompassing warmth, reveling in the sweep of his arms hard about her back. She'd felt so lost and alone, and so very frightened ... Was it her dreams of death? It mattered not. He was warm. Vital. Alive. Power and strength. She longed to run her hand down his lean, muscled frame, to slide her palms down his chest with its curling mass of dense, dark hair.

Unable to overrule the dictates of her mind, her hands followed suit. Her mouth grew dry, for his skin was hot as fire. Her fingertips crept down the ridged tautness of his belly, journeyed down to hairroughened thighs that might have been forged of

iron . . . it was on this plundering, upward journey
that her fingertips chanced to graze the jutting lance
of his arousal.

Her breath caught. She dared not look down to
know that he was rigid and thick and straining.

"Look at me, sweet."

His velvet whisper demanded compliance. Her
heart pounding, Glenda looked up into stark, hungry
features.

He lowered his head. Their lips just barely
brushed. "I want you," he said.

No protest would he find in her. No further invitation did he need. She wound her arms around his
neck and wordlessly offered her lips.

A tremor shook her. It was heady, that kiss, as
heated and shattering and raw as his whisper had
been. It was everything, that kiss . . . deep and searing and long and tender. She wanted to weep with
relief, cry out with the dizzying passion that surged
like a tide inside her when his hands slid over her,
stealing her gown from her and leaving her as naked
as he.

She felt the span of his fingers, wide upon the taut
curve of her belly, and gloried in the stark possessiveness that flared in his eyes. With hands and lips
and tongue exploring the rounded shape of her, he
sucked the deep, straining centers of her nipples into
his mouth until she whimpered and thrashed and
twisted her fingers in his hair.

But he was not yet finished. Lean fingers threaded
through her curling nest, parting her wide. Her heart
skittered into a frenzy. That wanton finger dipped
and circled and taunted, a torrid, tormenting caress

that rendered her slick and damp and nearly delirious. Half-mad with desire, she writhed against him,
aching for him as never before.

"Egan," she cried softly. "Egan!"

Scorching heat filled her . . . as he filled her, hot
and smooth and hard, his shaft buried so deep that
she could take no more of him. His eyes glittering,
he raised himself above her and whispered her name,
a ragged harshness to his breath and a sound that
betrayed a need as desperate as her own. When she
reached for him, he caught her hands and locked
their fingers in a searing clasp. She arched her back
for the driving power of his thrust, and when it came,
she cried out in glorious, fevered splendor.

He kissed her mouth, the arch of her throat. He
praised her beauty, whispered of the longing that
raged in his veins like a fever, the slaking of desire
that only she could quench. And when she felt the
pulsing spasms of his seed explode within her, pleasure surged, all the more intense because of his. Her
body abrim, she hurtled toward that pinnacle of rap-
ture, casting back her head, screaming her joy aloud.

When at last it was over, she opened her eyes to
find his long form stretched beside her. A tender
hand smoothed the damp tendrils of hair from her
cheek. He peered at her oddly.

"What is it? Did I hurt you?"

She pressed her hot face against his shoulder, embarrassed at her abandon. "Nay," she said, the sound
half-strangled, "nay!" She caught his hand and
pressed it to the hardness of her belly, where it
seemed the babe had awoke from a sound sleep. Her
skin rippled as he tumbled and surged.

Egan's eyes widened, for there was an unmistakable kick. "Dear God! Does it not hurt?"

"Nay. He is often thus."

He looked so astonished, she couldn't help but smile. He bent his head, and laid his ear to her belly.

"His heart!" he said in wonderment. "I can hear it!"

She laughed. " 'Tis mine you hear, not the babe's."

"It is not!"

So emphatic was his pronouncement that she began to doubt her own certainty. It struck her then . . . she felt as if a very great weight had been lifted from her shoulders. Oh, but it felt good to laugh again! It felt so good to hear Egan laugh.

Her sleep the remainder of the night was blessedly undisturbed. Egan was gone when she arose, but he kissed her and ran a fingertip down her nose and whispered that she was to rest.

The day was a reflection of her mood, brighter than it had been for days. The hills were edged with a white, feathery fringe of clouds; though the air was crisp, the sky was a clear, brilliant blue. Humming, she decided to see the cook about the menu for the morrow's meals—but first, she must check the spices. He'd been complaining that some were old and stale, and she decided she had best check for herself first.

It was then she felt it—a cool, sticky wetness between her thighs, there where they touched when she walked . . . it pulled her up short. She halted in the midst of her descent to the storeroom. Surely she hadn't wet herself! True, nature's call now came many a time throughout the day—and night—but she had always been aware of it. Yet this seemed somehow different.

Frowning, she cast a look up and down the stairs. There was no one about, so she pulled up a corner of her gown and touched her fingertips to the inside of one thigh.

They came away sticky with blood.

Her breath came fast, then slow. "Egan," she whispered, and then it was a scream: *"Egan!"*

Chapter 20

As Egan left the smithy's hut, the clang of metal upon metal resounded in his head. So it was that at first he thought he was hearing something that was not there . . .

Then it came again.

It was a frightened scream, a shivering scream of breath and body and sound. The world seemed to give way beneath his feet. All else faded to oblivion. His head came up. In but a heartbeat, he had sought and found his wife.

She was standing at the top of the stairs near the entrance to the hall. Her face was white as linen, her gaze frantic as it scanned the faces in the bailey.

He broke into a dead run.

"What is it? What's wrong?" He caught her by the elbows at the top of the stairs, and whisked her into the hall and out of the cold, for she was shaking from head to toe.

"I'm bleeding," she said frantically. "I'm bleeding!" Her eyes huge, she raised a trembling hand for him to see. The other clutched protectively at her belly. She welded her thighs together, as if to keep the babe locked tight within her womb.

Egan stared numbly at the crimson that stained her fingertips. For an instant his mind was slow to fathom . . . a chill ran down the length of his spine.

"Christ," he breathed. "Christ!" He bent and carefully lifted her in his arms. "Hold tight to me, sweet!" He bore her through the hall toward the tower stairs, barking over his shoulder for Nessa.

In her chamber, he deposited her gently onto the bed.

She reached for him. "Don't go!"

Her little cry tore at his heart. Her hands were like ice. He warmed them between his own.

"It's just like before," she said tonelessly. "The blood . . . Soon the pains will begin . . . It's too early. Too early!"

By then Nessa had appeared. "We need a midwife!" he growled the instant he saw her.

Wrinkled lips mashed together until none could be seen. Her sunken eyes blazed like coals. Aye, if looks could burn, he would be naught but a pile of ashes.

"There is no better midwife than me in all the Borderlands!" she hissed. "Now take yerself from this room that I may examine her!"

Egan's jaw thrust out. A ready argument surged to the fore, yet was quickly supplanted. She was right. He must let her work.

Banished to the hallway, he could do naught but sag against the wall. He dragged a hand down his face, feeling haggard inside. He was a warrior, hale and whole and hearty. Yet never had he felt so weak and helpless.

Egan had little experience with childbirth. Oh, he had clapped other men on the shoulder in cheerful congratulations; he'd shared a dram when their eyes darted fearfully to the place where their woman labored to bring forth their child. It was a woman's domain, and like most men, he preferred to keep his distance. But Glenda's reaction had told him all he needed to know.

She was right. It was too early. There were weeks to go before the babe should have been born, nearly two months.

No child who arrived so early could ever survive.

Every minute he waited was like a torment. A dozen times he nearly threw open the door and barged within. A dozen times he checked himself. Finally he began to pace in a tight circle, for it was the only way to leash his impatience.

When Nessa stepped outside, he pounced upon her.

"How is she? Does the babe come?"

" 'Tis too soon to tell."

"But she's bleeding!"

"Not so much as I had feared," Nessa admitted.

"Can you stop it?"

Nessa's faded blue eyes slipped away. She shook her head. " 'Tis not good when a woman with child bleeds like this," she said.

Egan paled. A cold sweat dotted his forehead. "Is she in danger?"

"I think not," the old woman said heavily. "But as for the babe . . . we can only pray the child decides to wait."

Egan's gaze bored into hers. "I don't care about the babe. Just save her, Nessa. *Save her.*"

Neither realized the door was ajar. Both turned when Glenda let out a piercing cry.

Egan rushed to the bedside. She looked at him, her mouth tremulous. "No. No! Don't let my babe die, Egan." She began to cry, dry, wrenching sobs that tore him apart. "Don't let my babe die!"

He was stunned and shaken. She was always so strong, to see her break down like this pierced him to the soul. Yet it shouldn't have, he suddenly realized. For this was her deepest fear, to lose another child, even this one he'd been so convinced she did not want! He'd thought she didn't care, that she didn't want *his* child.

Guilt seized hold of him like a clamp. He should never have touched her last night, no matter that she was tempting beyond all reason, beyond all will! Desire ruled, and he'd cared not. He'd taken her. In lust. In love. God's bones! What did it matter?

"Calm yourself, sweet," he said raggedly. "This can do you no good, either of you. Nessa said the bleeding is not so much as she had feared."

"This is how it began before," she wept. She could say no more, for it was past all bearing—past all telling.

His arms encircled her. He gathered her close and tight against him. His mouth grazed the fine hairs of her temple, the curve of her cheeks, the dainty hollow just behind her ear. He whispered comfortingly, he knew not what.

She buried her face against the side of his neck. Hot tears trickled against his skin—his very heart.

The life in her womb fluttered.

They both felt it. In shock, their eyes locked.

It was Egan who reacted first. A strong hand tenderly imprisoned hers, urging it down to her belly. "Feel," he said intently. He trapped her gaze with his—her hand with his. "This babe lives, Glenda. Our child still lives."

Uncaring that Nessa stood near, he cradled her face between his palms and kissed her full on the lips. "You must rest," he said softly. He ran his knuckles across the downy curve of her cheek, marveling at its softness. "I want you well again, you and the babe."

"Will you be with me?"

"I am with you, sweet."

"Nay," she said, and her voice broke. "I mean when . . ."

Egan frowned, not understanding. "When the babe is born?"

She nodded. "I-I cannot bear to be alone again." Her gaze slipped. Her voice was so low he had to strain to hear.

In that instant, Egan's heart surely stopped beating. Comprehension washed through him. All at once he understood what he'd never truly understood before. The rending heartache she had felt, bearing Niall's son alone, when her husband already lay still and cold.

With his thumbs, he brushed away the wetness from her cheeks. His tone was very grave. "Look at me, Glenda."

Her eyes were huge and clouded, misted by the unmistakable glitter of tears. Egan nearly came undone.

"I will be there," he said fervently.

He felt the deep, shuddering breath her lungs drew.

"Do you promise?"

"I do. I promise I will be with you when our child is born."

The smile she returned was but a glimmer . . . a smile nonetheless.

Nessa silently nodded her approval. She'd been about to sniff indignantly that this was no place for a man. Indeed, her staff was half-raised, prepared to sweep him from the chamber! Yet seeing how this tall, lean Highlander was able to calm her lassie, she quickly banished the impulse. Instead she limped to the door and swung it shut. She suspected Egan would not be leaving soon.

Throughout the day and night they waited, the three of them, tense and silent. The child moved no more, but the pains Glenda had feared did not come.

The days passed. A sennight. Then a fortnight. The situation remained the same. The bleeding did not subside.

Yet neither did her body seek to expel the tiny life within her. A watchful caution was maintained.

They had discovered early on that when she arose, the bleeding worsened. Nessa's voice cracked sharply as she ordered her back to bed; Glenda scurried to obey. Still, as the days dragged on, the inactivity chafed at her. She hated being dependent, but she would do whatever was required of her. She forced herself to eat, though the constant worry stole her appetite. It was not the matters of the household that concerned her; she knew they would be tended to, perhaps not in the same, careful way that she was

wont to do, but tended to nonetheless. Nay, it was
the babe that commanded her concern . . . and
Egan's.

He came and sat with her daily, yet he seemed . . .
not distant, mayhap, but she sensed a kind of reserve.
Oh, he held her hand; he kissed her chastely on the
cheek. But Glenda wanted more. She wished desperately that he would return to their bed, for she longed
to feel his arms steal around her in the night, warm
and sheltering. She ached to hear the drum of his
heart echo beneath her ear in the quiet of the dawn.
Oh, she knew there could be no passionate pursuits
of the flesh. Though she almost hated herself for the
uncertainty, she wondered if it was because she was
no longer slim and desirable.

He looked so tired. There were deep grooves
etched into his cheeks. When she inquired about the
raids, he tried to put her off, but she was insistent.
He confided that there had been several more. He
had doubled the men on night patrols and spent long
hours on the watch tower himself.

She did not know that despite his assurances, Egan
was horribly afraid, in a way that transcended all
others, knowing their babe might still die . . . that she
could die! All of a sudden, he remembered every tale
he'd ever heard of women who had died in childbed.
Though he was loath to admit it, this was a matter
that resided solely in God's hands, and he was powerless to do aught but stand by. She was pale and
wan, yet the babe in her belly continued to grow.
There were deep mauve shadows beneath her eyes—
at times he had to force himself to meet her gaze! She

did not complain nor rage nor cry, but he knew her fear was never completely assuaged.

The guilt that swamped him was like a red-hot sword twisting in his belly, again and again. If this babe died, she would blame him. She had never really wanted him, not really. He had cast aside her wishes and taken her, planted his seed inside her. She had every right to blame him, for he had not been able to control his desire. If anything happened to her—to their child!—she would never forgive him.

He would never forgive himself.

He loved her. It was something he'd known for years.

He hadn't known how much until now.

For in those days, Egan sealed a vow within his own heart. He swore that never again would he burden her with such worry, frighten her as she was afeared these many days. Never again would he place her in such danger. If it meant that never again would he lay with her—claim her as his own with lips and hands and body—then so be it.

It would be enough, he told himself. For he loved her . . . too much to lose her.

Glenda awoke one morning in late February to a commotion outside in the bailey. Though she longed to rise and peer out to see the cause of the din, she remained where she was. When Jeannine delivered the tray with her morning meal, Glenda queried her.

"I heard shouts in the bailey earlier, Jeannine. Is something amiss?"

Jeannine paled. "I know not, mistress." Hastily she averted her gaze and fled.

An odd shiver played down Glenda's spine.

Nessa was the next to enter. Glenda watched as she placed a basin of hot water on the bedside table for her bath.

"Nessa," she said quietly. "Something happened this morning. What is it?" An awful fear gripped her heart. "Dear God, never say it is Egan!"

"He is well, child. Do not fret."

"I cannot help it. There is something wrong. I feel it."

Nessa said nothing. Her gnarled hands squeezed water from the sponge.

The soft line of Glenda's mouth compressed. "No," she said.

"But the water grows cold. Let me bathe you."

"Not until I know what's wrong."

The old woman's silence was stoic.

"Nessa, I have a right to know. If you will not tell me"—beneath her quiet tone lurked an unyielding, iron determination—"I shall rise and find out for myself."

Nessa glared her disapproval. " 'Tis for your own good. Ye need to rest, not worry."

"Nessa—"

"There is naught ye can do!"

Glenda sat up and shoved the covers aside.

"Stop!" Nessa pressed her back. "I will tell ye, then. Two of the guards sent out on night patrol, Murphy and Holmes, have not yet returned."

Her eyes closed, then opened. "God, no." An ominous sense of foreboding slipped over her.

"Where is Egan?"

"Here."

Bold as ever, her husband strode through the doorway, tall and vital and so strikingly masculine, an almost painful wave of pride washed through her just looking at him. But her heart constricted, for he was dressed for battle, his sword and dirk strapped to his waist.

One look at his wife's distraught features and his gaze bounced to Nessa for confirmation. Nessa gave a slight nod and retreated, closing the door and leaving them alone.

The mattress dipped beneath his weight. He took both her hands in his. He said nothing, merely gazed at her.

Her eyes were wide and distressed. "Must you go?"

"Aye."

"Can't you send someone else?" A crushing dread settled on her chest. She couldn't quell the sensation that if he left, something would happen, something terrible.

His gaze softened. " 'Tis only right that I go," he said gently. He shook his head. "Murphy and Holmes must be found." He did not weigh the possibilities—that they could be hurt. Even dead.

Yet they both knew it. Deep inside, Glenda knew he had no choice. Deep inside, she raged against the fates that would take him from her.

She bent her head low. Her lips trembled. Tears scalded her throat. Somehow she held them back. "How long will you be gone?" she heard herself murmur.

"Until we find Murphy and Holmes." As always, his reply was unerringly direct.

For the longest time she said nothing . . .

"Why did you never marry?" The question spilled from her lips before she could stop it; indeed, she knew not where it came from. Only that she had to know . . .

She'd startled him. She felt it in the way his big body had gone so very still.

She stared at the long brown fingers knotted around her own. "You could have, you know. Anna. Louise. Mary." She wet her lips, her voice but a whisper. "All those years at Dunthorpe, and you never married . . ."

Slowly she raised her head. He did not flinch, yet neither did he answer. A faint smile touched the hardness of his lips, yet she glimpsed something almost sad within the depths of his eyes.

"Tell me, Egan. *Why did you never marry?*"

His smile ebbed. His voice fell gently through the silence.

"Don't you know?"

Unable to speak, unable to tear her gaze from his, she shook her head.

"Because," he said softly, "you were the only one I ever wanted."

Chapter 21

You were the only one I ever wanted.

Glenda was wholly undone. She was afraid to hope. Afraid to believe . . . reaching up, she placed her fingers on the lean hardness of his cheek.

"Egan—" She choked back a sob.

There was a thunderous crashing on the door. "My lord!"

He cursed beneath his breath. "I must go."

"Egan . . . come back safely!"

His eyes darkened. "I will." A kiss into her palm, and he was gone.

With the closing of the door, she could no longer contain the storm in her heart.

For Glenda had a secret of her own.

She had said nothing to either Egan or Nessa, but she had not felt the babe stir since noonday yesterday. Now an excruciating pain passed through her, a blade through the heart. She wanted to cry and curse, scream and rage. Was she cursed, forever destined to lose both child and husband?

She could bear it if the babe were to die, she realized suddenly. With the first, there had been no one, no one to hold her, no one to mourn as she did. Oh, it would be hard, a bruise upon her soul to wear for many a day. But aye, she could bear it, if only Egan were here to hold her, to share the loss as only a husband could share.

But what if she should lose *him*?

She turned her face into the pillow. Hot, bitter tears streamed from her eyes, but she made not a sound.

Throughout the day the people of Blackstone waited tensely, including their mistress. Night cloaked the world in darkness, and still Egan did not return.

It was early into the next morn when Glenda felt a subtle, cramplike drawing low in her belly. She gasped, her hands flying to her belly. For one frozen instant, it sped through her consciousness that it was her time. Yet the sensation was gone almost instantly.

It came again, but an hour later.

By noon, there could be no doubt . . . for this, too, was something Glenda had experienced once before. Dead or alive, her bairn was about to be born.

And once again, without her husband near.

Early in the day, Murphy and Holmes were discovered deep in the forest.

Their throats had been slashed.

It was a grim-faced party that returned to Blackstone Tower. The bodies of Murphy and Holmes were slung over the backs of two horses.

"My lord." Two servants ran up to where he paced in the stables, tugging at his sleeve.

Egan shook them off. He was in the grip of the most vile rage he had ever known. Murphy had left behind a wife and two little ones. Holmes was not yet wed, but his mother's wails still echoed in his ears.

If Simon had done this, by God, he would pay. All that had gone before was bad enough, but murder ... Frustration roiled within him, for the same dilemma still plagued him! He couldn't go to the earl with unfounded charges, but he had no evidence! If only there was a way to make this man reveal himself!

He needed to think, to weigh and consider, for he would not act on the vengeful wrath that seared his veins; therein might lay the path of ruin and regret. Whoever had done this was clever. He must be careful.

"My lord," quavered the other man.

"Not now, dammit!"

The two men quailed. The glare bestowed on them was so fierce they instinctively fell back.

It was a young groom who finally braved his anger. The lad stepped forward, clearing his throat. "My lord."

Egan whirled on him, fists clenched at his side. "What?" he thundered.

" 'Tis your lady," the boy said. "The babe comes."

Egan's eyes turned toward the tower. "What?" he said dumbly. "Now?"

"Aye, my lord."

The two servants looked at each other. Never in all their days had they seen a man turn white as a lamb's belly—and such a fearsome one as their lord, yet!

Egan was already halfway to the tower. He burst

through the door to Glenda's chamber, his insides tied in knots.

Nessa was at the bedside, bathing Glenda's forehead with a cool cloth. At the crash of the door, the old woman's head swiveled to regard him in a baleful glare. The birthing of babes was women's work, but it seemed this one was to be the exception, like it or no.

" 'Tis high time you arrived!" she snapped.

He faltered. "But Nessa," he whispered. "I thought it was still too soo—"

She gave a quick shake of her head—a warning, he realized suddenly.

"Ah, but this babe should have been here by now," the old woman said stoutly, "but Glenda is stubborn! She bites back the pain. She insists that you must be here, that the child would not be born until you were. But this child will wait no longer!"

Egan swallowed. He stared hard at Glenda. She lay in the center of the bed. Her skin was ashen, her lips swollen and torn and bloodied. Her eyes were glazed; he sensed she was unaware of his presence. Never had he seen her so frail and weak! For one terrifying moment, he feared he might lose her forever.

Then a hand fluttered limply toward the mound of her belly. "Nay," she said feebly. "Not yet, little one. Not yet."

Three strides took him to her side. He sank to his knees. "Glenda!" he said raggedly.

Through the fog that surrounded her, Glenda sensed that something was different. Egan's voice called to her. She glimpsed his craggy features, like the sun blazing through the mist.

Strong hands captured hers, mating their fingers together. Bending his head, he rubbed the bristly roughness of his cheek against the back of her hand. The wordless tenderness of the gesture wrenched at her. He was unshaven and gaunt, but never had he looked so dear! He was here, as he had promised. She needed him, and he was here. Taking care of her, as always.

"I told Nessa you would come," she breathed. "She doubted you."

Egan stole a glance at Nessa, who had hobbled to the foot of the bed. "I am not surprised," he said dryly. "I've yet to win your nursemaid's approval." He shook his head. "I fear I am at a loss as to how it might be done."

Glenda smiled faintly. Egan felt his heart squeeze. She was so strong, so brave. Yet all at once she shuddered. His big hands trembled around hers. He prayed she wouldn't feel it, yet she clung to him so tightly her nails dug into his palm.

"Nessa," she gasped. "I think it will not be long now." Throughout the afternoon, the spasms of her womb had grown closer together, with mounting strength and urgency. With each and every pain that seized her, she hadn't been able to stop her gaze from straying to the door. But now there was no need to fight any longer . . .

From the foot of the bed, Nessa nodded. "I think ye're right, lassie."

Her back arched. She moaned, the sound tearing from her throat, so great was the pressure that surged between her thighs. It appeared that now her husband was here, her body was one with her mind after all, and there was no need to wait any longer.

Nessa gave encouragement. "Aye, lassie, that's the way! I can see the head. Breathe now, girl!"

Anxious, tired and afraid all at once, Glenda obeyed. Her lungs filled with air. With a deep, racking breath, her belly heaved, straining to be rid of the burden it had carried for so long now.

The babe spilled from her in a rush. She sank back upon the pillows, exhausted.

"A girl"—through a haze, she heard Nessa—"a wee lassie!"

But Glenda had heard the break in her voice. She raised her head from the pillow, unable to mask her fear. "Does she live? Tell me, does she live?" She caught just a glimpse of a slippery, wet head in Nessa's hands . . . saw the glaze of tears in her nursemaid's eyes.

"No!" she cried. "No!"

A tiny fist flailed. A thin, wavering cry filled the air.

Glenda burst into dry, wrenching sobs. "Let me hold her. Let me hold her!"

"A moment, lass. She must be cleaned and swaddled." Glenda was still sobbing when Nessa laid the tiny bundle into her upraised arms.

Egan rose to his feet. He stood awkwardly for a moment, then finally stumbled toward the door. In the hall, every eye turned upon him. A dozen figures rushed toward him.

"My lord!"

"All is well?"

He nodded.

"The babe?"

"A girl," he heard himself say.

A hand at his shoulder urged him onto a stool. Someone brought him ale. He downed it in a gulp, then another and another. Time passed in a haze. The next thing he knew, the hall was deserted, and Nessa stood before him.

"You've yet to see yer child," she announced. Gnarled fingers parted the swaddling so he could see.

Egan rose slowly to his feet. He stared. Dear God, he thought in amazement, in all his days, he'd never seen a creature so small.

"Take her," Nessa prompted.

Egan started to reach for her. All at once he stopped. Awareness struck. One of his hands was nearly as big as her entire body!

He swallowed, suddenly very much in awe of this wee creature. "I cannot. What if I hurt her?"

The corner of Nessa's mouth turned down. "You'll not."

Before he knew what was about, he stared down at the tiny being nestled in the curve of his elbow.

Nessa stepped back with a sniff. "Let us hope she does not have such a liking for ale as her father!"

The ghost of a smile sped across his lips. "Aye," he agreed. She weighed no more than a goose feather! he realized in amazement.

"She is well?"

"Possessed of a full and healthy set of limbs and lungs, I assure you."

"Glenda will be pleased," he murmured. Entranced, he regarded his daughter. She was asleep, a wee fist curled against the curve of her cheek. Her hair, what little there was of it, was sleek and dark. The babe was unmistakably his.

The emotion that rushed through him nearly buckled his knees. Suddenly his smile froze.

"Oh, Christ," he said hoarsely.

"What!" Nessa demanded. "Are ye disappointed with a daughter, then? If ye are, ye'd best keep it to yerself!"

" 'Tis not that." His gaze lifted slowly to Nessa's face.

"What then?" The sting faded from Nessa's tone. His expression was most odd. She knew not what to make of it.

Egan's mouth was dry. Gently, almost reverently, he touched the babe's fist. "Nessa, I know not how to explain. I never thought to have . . . her. Glenda. Any of this. A keep like Blackstone. Lands. A child. And now that I do . . . 'tis humbling. Frightening at times, for so very much depends on me . . ."

Nessa tipped her head to the side. Most men would never admit to such, for fear it might be perceived as a weakness.

Yet Nessa saw it only as strength. Strength of a kind that could not be seen in stamina, prowess, or the might of the sword.

A strength that came from within.

"I would put my faith in ye before any other," she stated bluntly.

Egan's eyes widened. Could it be that the approval he'd never thought to gain was his after all? He smiled slightly.

Nessa gazed at him steadily. "I know ye love her, lad. Ye should tell her."

His smile withered.

"Do ye deny it?"

"Nay." He hesitated, his voice very low. "You do not know how it is. How I feel—"

"I can. I do."

"What do you mean, Nessa?"

"I loved from afar once. But I thought . . . he was far above me in station, ye see. And so I watched while he loved another, while he married another."

Egan inhaled. Nessa in love! Yet was it really so strange? Nessa was a woman who would have loved without question, without reservation. 'Twas then that the strangest notion sped through his mind . . . but no, he thought. It could not be . . .

"I held his wee ones in my arms, as if they were my own. I watched them grow as if they were my own! Indeed, I was a mother to them when their own died. And I was the one who held tight to his hand when he breathed his last."

Egan spoke very quietly. "It was Royce, Glenda's father, wasn't it?"

Nessa said nothing. But Egan gleaned the answer from the way tears stood high and bright in her faded eyes.

"You never told him, did you?"

"Naught would have come of it. He was never within reach, and I knew it. I understood that, and so I said nothing." It was a painful truth that Nessa acknowledged. " 'Tis different for ye, lad."

Silence drifted between them. Egan's throat closed

tight, thinking about all she said. She made it sound so easy—but easy it was not!

At length Nessa reached for the babe. "Ye should tell her," Nessa said again before she left him alone.

A short time later, Egan made his way to her chamber. Glenda was propped up against the pillows, her head dipped low over the babe. She was clad in a fresh, clean gown; her hair had been combed and lay in a cloud about her shoulders. His gaze trickled slowly over her, drinking in the sight of her, more dear to him than anything in the world. The bodice of the gown was unlaced, baring the generous swell of one bare breast. Their daughter suckled at the rosy-tipped fullness. Egan couldn't help but note how the skin of her breast was almost translucent, pale and gleaming and invitingly full.

Yet for a timeless moment he stood there, feeling very much the intruder. He was afraid to move. Afraid to destroy the moment, reminded keenly of how she'd waited so long for this, the chance to hold her infant in her arms. Years. He hated to rob her of any of it . . .

Then Glenda glanced up and spied him standing on the threshold. Their eyes meshed. A hot possessiveness swept over him then. This was his wife. His child. *His.* A flush colored her cheeks and crept down her lovely throat and into her naked breasts, but she did not avert her gaze. Nor did she seek to cover herself, even when he moved to sit directly beside her, the stretch of his muscled thigh riding gently against the softness of her form.

"I looked for you earlier, but you were gone," she

confided breathlessly. "Have you met your daughter yet?"

His gaze roved her face. The skin beneath her eyes looked almost bruised. She was pale and looked incredibly weary, yet a glow surrounded her that had been absent before.

"Nessa brought her down to me," he murmured. "I must say, she terrified me."

"You . . . terrified! Why?"

"She's so tiny," he said ruefully. "And I am not exactly that."

He trailed a finger down the infant's cheek, his skin very dark against the little one's.

The babe's mouth stopped working. Tiny black brows drew together in a frown of displeasure. Then all at once she latched onto her mother's nipple anew, so fiercely that Glenda started.

The laugh they shared was husky.

Her smile abrim with joy, Glenda traced the arch of tiny black brows. "She looks like you," she mused, then sighed. "She's beautiful, isn't she?"

"Aye," he agreed, but now his gaze was only for his wife. His mouth quirked. "Though I wonder that you can say she resembles me and then call her beautiful."

"Oh, stop! You are quite handsome, and well you know it."

Egan considered his scarred countenance, not certain he could agree with her. Still, it pleased him that she would say it—it pleased him greatly.

"We need a name, Egan. And I must tell you now, I will not consider Patsy. Or Anna or Mary—"

"Ah. Perhaps Louise, then."

His grave deviltry earned him a surprisingly solid thump in the chest.

"I was thinking . . . Elizabeth." She regarded him with mock suspicion. "Or is there a woman named Elizabeth in your past?"

Lord, no, he thought. *There's only you, Glenda. It's always been you . . .*

"I like the name Elizabeth."

"Excellent. We shall call her Elizabeth, then." Her smile was filled with the brilliance of a thousand suns. The babe had finished nursing and now slept against her breast. Much to Egan's regret, Glenda tugged her gown back over her shoulder. She gazed raptly at the sleeping infant, but very soon her lashes began to droop.

Egan could see her battle to remain awake. A tender hand smoothed a tangle of hairs from her temple. "Glenda," he murmured, "you need to rest."

"I know." Her arm tightened around her precious bundle. " 'Tis silly of me, but I don't want to let her go. Egan, please, not just yet—"

"She can sleep beside you for now." Holding her—holding them both—he eased her down so their daughter lay nestled against her side.

Glenda's hand crept to the babe's crown. She looked up at him suddenly. "She's so small."

He felt the fear in her. "Healthy, though, Nessa assures me."

She trembled. "Egan, when the pains began, I was so afraid she might be stillborn . . ."

His heart twisted. "I was afraid, too," he said huskily. "But you are here, and she is here, and I am thankful for both of you."

"Egan—" She gazed at him, searching his face, her lips parted. He bent close, thinking she wanted to say something, but her exhaustion overcame her. Her lids fluttered closed and she spun away into the netherworld of sleep.

A tremor went through him. He straightened, but he did not leave. Instead he watched the pair sleep. Mother and daughter. Wife and child.

His mind churned, along with his heart. Was Nessa right? Should he reveal his love for her, a love that seared his soul to ashes?

I have not the words, he thought. *I have not the heart. I have not the courage*, he admitted at last. For what if his love was not returned?

What if she still loved Niall?

He sighed. His gaze returned to his wife and child. They slept on peacefully, unaware of the turmoil in his soul, the turmoil in the keep.

He was on his knees beside them, unaware of even moving. With his knuckles he traced the curve of Glenda's cheek, down the graceful line of her jaw. A powerful hand cradled the head of his newly born daughter.

A fierce protectiveness shot through him. He would allow no harm to befall them, he vowed, either of them. He'd gladly forfeit his own life in order to save theirs . . .

Though he prayed it would never come to that.

Chapter 22

🪆 Glenda's recovery from the birth was not as swift as she would have liked. Lying abed for so long had left her weak and depleted. She would scarcely allow Elizabeth out of her arms those first few days—most assuredly not out of her sight! Nor would she permit a wet nurse to feed the bairn.

When she held her child, such love and happiness brimmed within her that she felt she could burst with it. It was as if pure, brilliant sunshine poured into her. Though Elizabeth was healthy and thriving—and seemed to grow daily—there was still a dark, hidden corner where that shining brightness could not reach—a part of her that was still so horribly afraid of losing her child.

Egan visited daily, even if only for a few minutes. Was he disappointed that she had borne him a daughter and not a son? The notion soon left her. Her heart turned over when he confided his clumsiness about holding the child. Indeed, 'twas a sight to behold, the huge warrior with a tiny babe whose body seemed smaller than his hands! Yet it was also a sight that moved her to the core. In the evening sometimes, the babe slept on the long, lean stretch of his legs. When the infant awoke, Egan was clearly as loath to release her as she always was.

Glenda was shocked when she learned that Murphy and Holmes had been murdered. Egan looked so tired, his features lined with fatigue and strain; Glenda knew he was burdened. He had ridden out to speak with each and every tenant, that he might find some clue as to the identity of the murderers. He was determined to catch these knaves who had plundered their land and people.

It was to no avail. Even though there was no further trouble or bloodshed, the cloud that hung over Blackstone remained, dimming her joy. She was concerned for their people. What it must be like for them, seeking their bed at night and wondering if this would be the night they were rousted from their homes.

Along with that fear came another. During those days after Elizabeth's birth, a battle warred deep within her heart and soul. She feared it was already too late . . . that she loved Egan. Loved him wildly and desperately. Almost bitterly she wondered if she'd been cursed. Niall was dead. Their babe was dead. Her father was gone, too . . . was she forever destined to lose those she loved most?

She didn't want to love him . . . if only she didn't! For she could not banish the heartbreaking fear that if she loved him . . . then he would die, too.

She didn't want to hurt like that again. She couldn't face such a loss again. She couldn't *feel* it again.

Yet she couldn't forget what he'd said the night of

Elizabeth's birth. *You were the only one I ever wanted.*
Her pulse knocked wildly whenever she thought of
it. For so long now, she'd convinced herself he'd married her only for what it would bring him. Yet what
did it mean . . . truly? Did he speak only of passion?
She was afraid to ask—afraid of the answer. Afraid
to peer within her heart for fear of what it would
reveal . . .

Nay, she could not love Egan. She dared not.

A fortnight after Elizabeth's birth, Glenda was startled to see the Earl of Whitley ride in. Glenda quickly
put aside the little robe she'd been sewing for Elizabeth and joined Egan in the hall.

Simon was also with the earl, she saw, along with
a bearded, potbellied man dressed in rough peasant
wool. Her pulse leaped, but she told herself there was
no reason to panic. Still, she couldn't quite banish the
feeling that all was not well.

She knew it for certain when she paused before the
earl. His expression was sternly somber. Forcing a
smile, she stepped beside Egan and greeted both
Simon and the earl.

"My lord, has my husband offered you some repast?"

"He has, but I must decline. I've not come for food
or drink."

Egan lifted his chin. Like Glenda, he suspected that
something was amiss. "Why, then, have you come,
my lord?"

"I'll not bandy words," the earl said bluntly.
"Simon of Ruthven has come to me about a matter
most disturbing."

Simon! A quick assessment revealed Simon's

smirk. Ah, but he was up to no good, Egan decided blackly, though like the earl, the wretch had assumed a posture and expression of utmost gravity.

The earl beckoned for the bearded stranger to come forward. "This is William, a crofter from across the river."

Across the river—Simon's lands!

"Simon brought him to me that I might hear his story. He told me that you and your men attacked his family and burned his hut two nights past. What do you say to this?"

"I did not burn his hut." Egan was unfaltering. "Nor have I seen this man before this night."

"Why, then, would William go to Simon with such a story? Why would he tell me such a tale?"

A tale, indeed! Mayhap because the man had been amply paid by Simon to make that very claim! Egan chafed bitterly. Simon and this man might be willing to make false accusations, but he would not stoop to their level and make empty ones.

He glanced at Simon. Ah, but he could almost see Simon gloating! He knew then that Simon was responsible; no doubt the Englishman sought to discredit him before the earl. He opened his mouth to flatly deny it again, but before he could say a word, he felt Glenda step forward.

"My lord," she stated calmly, "I know not why this man William would make such accusations, but I do know this—it was not Egan who made this attack. My husband was with me that night . . . the entire night."

"He could not lay with you that night! You've just had a child!" It was Simon who made the outburst.

"Do you think that's the only use a man has for a woman—a husband for his wife?" With quiet dignity, she spoke. "A man can give comfort, lend his strength to his wife when she is in need of it."

Simon's jaw thrust out. "Do you call my man a liar, then?"

"I do not call him a liar. But the attack was at night, was it not?"

"Yes."

Glenda folded her hands demurely before her. "Then, in the dark, perhaps William was mistaken. Mayhap the men who attacked him covered their faces that he could not see them clearly. Mayhap, with the frenzy of the fire, he mistook Egan for some other knave."

Dear God! Egan wasn't sure if he should kiss her or throttle her. Did she know what she dared? Simon's self-satisfied smile had frozen. Egan didn't miss the tightness about Simon's mouth.

"Mayhap the fiends who burned William's hut are the same who have been terrorizing Blackstone lands these many months."

"Let us not forget, now mine as well!"

Coolly Glenda's gaze resided on him. "Odd, is it not, Simon, that your lands have only recently begun to be razed? Indeed, 'tis ridiculous to lay the blame at my husband's feet, when two of his own men were found murdered. And let us not forget, these attacks began while my Uncle Rowan was ill, long before Egan's arrival."

Egan's voice joined hers. "I would lay odds that the rogue behind these attacks believes he is cunning and clever. Yet I say he is weak, afraid to show his face. What true man would stoop to preying on others—harried, defenseless people? Whoever does this is a coward."

"I quite agree," the earl said grimly. "If this waste does not end soon, I may consider sending my own men to roust the man responsible—and when I do, he will regret the day he ran afoul of me!"

"You will not find him here, my lord." Glenda slipped her fingers into Egan's elbow. "I tell you again, my husband was with me that night."

The earl nodded. He raised a hand, a signal to one of his men to bring forth his mantle.

Simon's face had turned a mottled red. "What of William? I tell you he saw this man!"

William had turned a pasty white. " 'Tis just as the lady said," he whined. " 'Twas dark and I fear my eyes may have betrayed me."

Simon cursed. The earl whirled on him. "That is enough, Simon! I will hear no more. I do not doubt this woman, nor should you."

In seconds, Simon, the earl, and his men had gone from the hall, leaving a rush of cold air swirling in their wake.

After the others left, Egan turned to Glenda. A brow arched high. "You," he accused without heat, "are quite an accomplished liar."

" 'Twas not entirely a lie. A man can give comfort and strength to his wife"—her eyes grazed his—"and you have."

In truth, Egan was touched beyond measure by the way his wife had stood up for him.

"But not that night. You know not where I was."

Glenda shook her head. "Oh, but I do. You were

in your bed"—she gathered all her courage—"when you could have been in mine."

Egan's eyes darkened. A hard arm caught her beneath her knees. She felt herself borne high in his arms and carried toward the stairs. She was set on her feet in her chamber. His hands were warm upon her waist.

"Lady, you may regret inviting me back."

"I have no regrets," she said, and knew it for the truth. Almost shyly, she placed her fingertips on the broad sweep of his shoulders.

Egan sucked in a harsh breath. When she looked at him like that . . . Tangling his fingers in her hair, he turned her mouth up to his.

For Glenda, it was heaven. This was the first time he'd kissed her, really kissed her for weeks now, and the sweetly fierce pressure of his lips upon hers made her spine turn to water. A wailing little cry from the cradle in the corner finally broke them apart.

Glenda nursed Elizabeth in the chair before the fire, aware of Egan watching from the bed. After lulling the babe back to sleep, she crawled in to join him.

Strong arms engulfed her. Glenda melted against him with a breathy little sigh. Egan rested his chin against the shining cloud of her hair. He knew there could be no intimacy between them this night—it was too soon after Elizabeth's birth—but it was enough to hold her close, to feel the yielding surrender of her form pressed tight against the hardness of his.

It was the same for Glenda. She gloried in the power of his arms tight about her back, the steel-edged muscle of his chest beneath her cheek. Yet all at once a shudder coursed through her.

Egan felt it. "What is it?" he murmured, turning her face to his.

"Simon killed Murphy and Holmes, didn't he?"

For the longest time, Egan was silent. "I know not if he did the deed with his own hand," he said slowly, "but aye, I believe he was responsible. I feel it in my bones."

Her gaze was cloudy. "It was foolish of me to have baited him. I was just so angry that he dared to bring his man forward and accuse you of such a horrible thing—and before the earl yet."

"He didn't count on you coming to my defense the way you did," Egan admitted.

"He was furious. I could see it."

Simon was more dangerous than Egan had ever foreseen. The deaths of Murphy and Holmes had proved that. "We may have forced his hand." He voiced his thoughts aloud. "Mayhap it's just as well. I think the earl has finally begun to see him for the snake he is."

Glenda shivered, suddenly as cold as death. The foreboding had not left her; indeed, all at once she found herself pierced by the sensation that something awful was going to happen . . .

"Egan . . ." She clutched at him.

"Hush, sweet. All will be well, you'll see. I won't let any harm come to you."

His concern made her want to cry. " 'Tis not me," she told him raggedly. "I fear for you, Egan. Murphy and Holmes are gone. What if Simon decides you will be next?"

He suspected Simon had already decided he would be well rid of him. But this was something he decided was best kept to himself. He passed it off with a shrug and a false lightness. " 'Tis better to know one's foes, sweet, for it makes it far easier to guard against them."

"I hate this!" she cried suddenly. "I hate this waiting. Not knowing what will happen . . . or when . . ."

"Hush, sweet. It will pass. Now sleep, for soon it will be morn." With lips and arms he soothed her, until at last they both slept.

The wait was not so very long after all.

The evening meal had just been concluded when Alfred rode through the gates two nights later. He leaped down from the nag he was riding. "Where is Egan?" he cried.

A guard gestured over his shoulder toward the keep. "In the counting room, I believe."

Alfred bounded up the steep stone stairs two at a time. Egan was just striding into the great hall when he burst inside.

"Have you heard the news?" he cried. "The Sutherland farm was rousted. But the Sutherland boys were able to catch the leader. They're holding him there!"

Egan grasped his shoulders. "Where did you hear this, Alfred?"

"In the village. A man just rode in."

Egan's heart leaped. They had him, they had him at last! He shouted for his horse and men and weapons. Within seconds a dozen figures were darting across the hall toward the bailey. He whirled to find

Glenda standing near, holding Elizabeth in her arms.

"What is it? What's wrong?"

He went to her and gripped her hands. "We may have him. We may finally have him!" He told her the news Alfred had relayed.

She wet her lips. A huge lump had lodged in her throat, so that she could scarcely speak. "You're going to the Sutherland farm?"

"Aye."

Though she ducked her head, he didn't miss the sudden tears that misted the beautiful gold of her eyes.

Her distress made him groan. His arms came around her. He held her within the protective binding of his embrace. "Glenda, don't! 'Tis almost over."

"I know." With her free hand she curled her fingers into the front of his tunic, struggling for composure, seeking to be brave, as he was brave. Though she longed to throw herself against him, keep him here through whatever means it took, she sensed his impatience to be off.

Her hand stole to his mouth. "Egan," she whispered. "Be careful."

"I will, love. But methinks the danger is past." He kissed the tips of her fingers, her lips, the top of the babe's dark scalp, then spun away.

She watched him tear through the gates and down the muddied track, he and his men. As she turned away, a desolate wave of bleakness broke over her. He was gone . . . he was her husband and she loved him, loved him desperately . . .

And she'd never even told him.

*   *   *

Hard as she tried, Glenda couldn't rid herself of the feeling that all was not right. Elizabeth must have sensed her mother's anxiety and began to fuss as well, even though she'd just been put to the breast. Glenda managed to lull her back to sleep and put her in her cradle; then she made her way back to the hall. She knew better than to try to sleep. She would not rest until Egan had returned, safe and unharmed.

The hall was deserted. She was making her way toward the hearth to warm herself, when the doors swung open.

Simon strode in, bold as you please. Glenda squared her shoulders and fixed him with a glare.

"You are no longer welcome here, Simon."

"Oh? And why is that?"

Oh, but she itched to slap the arrogance from his face! "You know very well why. I suggest you leave forthwith."

Her demand met with grating laughter. "Oh, I think not. Not just yet."

There was something in his smile, something that sent a prickle of alarm up her spine. She glanced around, but there were no servants about.

He stepped close. "Your mantle," he said pleasantly. "You'll be needing it for the journey."

"What journey? I'll go nowhere with you!"

Ruthless fingers bit into the flesh of her arm. He jerked her against him. "Oh, but you will. You're going to England, a journey you make for your own safety. I'm taking you under my protection. Your husband has gone quite mad, you see. Terrorizing the countryside. Murdering his own guards."

In shock Glenda stared into his eyes. They flamed

with a light she could not begin to understand. He was the one who was mad, she thought faintly.

She tried to bring her fists up between them, to pummel his face. His arms tightened so that she feared her bones would surely be crushed. Suddenly she could scarcely breathe. Yet somehow she managed to tilt her head back. "You cannot think to get away with this! Egan will not allow it—"

"Your husband is already dead."

"No! He is on his way to the Sutherland—"

Simon was shaking his head. "No," he said calmly.

Glenda froze. "Dear God. 'Tis a trap—"

"No doubt my men have killed him by now—'tis most fortuitous that they should rid us all of this vermin from the north, eh?" Satisfaction rimmed his twisted smile. "But your daughter, Glenda. Where is she? In your chamber?"

Her eyes sparked. "What do you want with Elizabeth?" She opened her mouth to scream.

Brutal fingers clamped around her mouth. "Do not," he warned silkily. "I know she's in your chamber. If you scream, by the time help arrives, I'll have her throat slit."

He made the prediction with chilling coldness. Glenda saw that in his twisted, ugly smile, which made her blood curdle. Sickly she acknowledged that he was wild and crazed—that her premonition had been of this moment. His arms loosened, but he jerked her up hard against his side. Firelight glinted off the dagger in his free hand.

Glenda's heart sank. She had no choice but to do as he'd commanded.

Mutely she led the way to her chamber. Taking a

deep, serrated breath, she reached for Elizabeth.

The cradle was empty.

Glenda stared down in horror. "My babe," she gasped. "Elizabeth!"

In an instant Simon was beside her. He flung the blankets to the floor and whirled on her.

"Where is she?"

Glenda's eyes were streaming. She began to shake helplessly. "I do not know!"

Simon released a long, violent curse. "I'll not waste time looking for the brat! Come!" He nearly wrenched her arm from the socket and dragged her toward the stairs.

But the hall was not deserted. Nessa was just about to climb the winding steps.

Glenda's eyes flew wide. "Nessa, run!" Even as she realized the futility of the command, Simon seized the old woman's staff and dealt her a stunning blow to the head.

The old woman crumpled to the rushes.

"Nessa!" Glenda gave a strangled cry and would have rushed forward, but Simon stopped her.

"Leave the old witch be!" he snarled.

His dagger pressed against the small of her back, Glenda moved numbly into the chill night air.

Chapter 23

"Stop!" The word whistled quietly through Egan's teeth. He reined his stallion to an abrupt halt. The men behind him followed suit.

The clouds shifted and surged, revealing a full, perfect moon. Silvery beams spilled down from the sky, so that it was nearly as light as day.

Milburn's mount let out a snort. He leaned close. His face held a watchful calm. "What is it?" he murmured.

Their eyes met. It flitted through Egan's mind that much had changed since the day he and Glenda had first passed through the gates of Blackstone Tower. Milburn was no longer a sotted guard who swilled his ale so freely. The hours of training had rendered his body muscled and toned, his sword arm capable and adept. Egan now counted him as his most capable man.

They had not ridden far. In all truth, Egan could not say what came over him in that instant. The hair on the back of his neck rose as if in warning, alerting his every senses.

Danger lurked just ahead.

His fingers curled around the handle of his sword. It slipped from its scabbard with nary a hiss of sound. A silent nod indicated the road just ahead. There was a curve where the embankment dipped low and led to the wandering stream below.

By now Milburn's sword was in hand as well, as were those of his men.

Guttural shouts erupted, shattering the silence of the night. A horde of men surged from the ditch, brandishing their weapons high aloft. Steel rang against steel. There were moans and screams, but the men lying in wait for Egan were no match for his men.

They met their end with swiftness and little mercy.

Milburn leaped down from his horse and strode to a heavy-jowled man who lay sprawled on his back. "This is Simon's man. I recognize him." With the tip of his sword, he pointed to another, and another. Steel arced through the air. "All of them."

Egan shifted in his saddle. "They knew we were coming."

"You think it was a trap?"

Egan set his jaw. "Aye."

A flicker of disquiet knotted in his belly. His unease mounted with every beat of his pulse. His mind turned furiously. All at once he couldn't stifle the feeling that Glenda might be in danger as well.

"I will take no chances, Milburn. Will you take the men and ride on to the Sutherlands to make certain that all is well there?"

Milburn's chest swelled. He was honored that Egan would entrust him so. "Aye. But what of you?"

Egan gritted his teeth. "I'm going back to Blackstone."

The night sentry saluted him when he arrived at the gatehouse.

"Have you admitted anyone since I left?"

"Only Simon Ruthven, my lord. Your lady then departed with him."

Simon—with Glenda! A jolt ran through him. Egan could have howled his rage aloud, yet he couldn't blame the guard. He'd been careless. He'd left few of his men here at Blackstone. He'd been so certain it was Simon who'd been captured at the Sutherland farm.

The guard frowned. "My lord? My lord!" The guard's cries were lost in the thunder of hoofbeats.

Egan had already wheeled and raced away, his features utterly grim.

Glenda was terrified. Not for herself, but for Nessa and Egan—for their daughter. She could not bear to think that Simon's men had slain Egan; to think that his body lay still upon the earth, bloodied and unmoving . . . nay! She would not allow herself to believe it!

But where was Elizabeth? Most everyone in the keep had been abed. She didn't believe in faeries and witches, but her mind and heart were all awhirl. Had some demon snatched her babe away? No. It wasn't possible. Yet who could have taken the babe from her bed . . . and why? It was all she could do to stop her heart from plummeting to an endless depth of despair, yet she forced herself to cling to a gossamer thread of hope.

Simon had set her on his horse before him. She held herself stiffly erect, not wanting to touch him, any part of him. It was then she heard it . . .

The thunder of hoofbeats . . . her ears strained. In her desperation, did she only imagine it? The hour was late. Had Simon heard it? she wondered. Nay. His pace remained steady, but not urgent. They were headed toward his keep; it seemed he was in no hurry. The wind picked up, sending a scattering of leaves across the ground.

Her mind raced. If indeed a rider approached, she could call out for help, if she could only get Simon to halt. Aye, she had to think of something. Somehow she had to get away. She had to do . . . something!

"Simon, you must stop!"

"Not yet."

"Simon, I-I beg you! We must halt for a while." The plea cost her, but he slowed his horse, leading it to a copse of trees just off the road.

He dismounted, then lifted her down. His gaze ran over her. Aware of his perusal, deliberately she hobbled toward a stout oak tree.

He followed her. "What's wrong?" he asked with a scowl.

"Use your imagination," she said irritably. "My child was born but a fortnight past. I'm not yet ready to ride a horse."

His stare turned brazen. With a sly smile, he ran a finger down the shape of one breast. "Before long you'll be riding me."

His crudity made her flush. She pushed his hand away. The thought of his hands on her made her skin crawl.

"My people will never believe I left willingly."

He laughed outright. "Lady, the guard at the gate saw you go willingly," he boasted. "Your lands will be mine one way or another, and so will you."

"Is that why you did this? Harried my people? Set fire to their homes and drove them away?"

He smirked. "When your uncle sickened, it was then I began to think . . . Blackstone lands might easily be mine!"

"But for months you did nothing! Once Egan and I wed—"

"I knew I could never be so obvious. The earl would never have allowed me to take your lands by force. I had to bide my time—and find another way."

"Another way?" she cried. "*Deceit* was your way! You and your men hid your faces. You were afraid of Egan, afraid to face him outright, afraid of being beaten!"

His smile faded. He glowered, but said nothing. Glenda knew then she was right. "What about Murphy and Holmes? Why did you murder them?"

His smirk returned in full measure. "They had to die. They saw me and one of my men one night."

Glenda felt sick inside. "Someone will find out, Simon. The earl—"

"Will believe what I tell him, I assure you. As for you, you'll do exactly as I say, as long as I have your daughter."

Glenda felt the blood drain from her face.

"Ah, I see you take my meaning," he taunted. "You'll do whatever I want, whenever I want."

"I know not where she is," she said quickly.

"That I do not believe, lady. Even if you do not, someone does."

In this, she could only hope that he was right . . .

"I've no qualms about gaining what I want—in any way I want."

Glenda raised her chin. She had no doubt the tales of his cruelty were true.

" 'Tis just as Egan said. You prey on those who are weaker than you, because *you* are weak! You are a coward, Simon. You set your men on him because you are afraid to face him yourself!"

"Watch your tongue, else I'll cut it out." For an instant, anger transformed his features into a distorted mask. Then suddenly he was smiling, a smile that sent a chill the length of her. "No," he pretended to muse, "I do believe I'd regret it. I can think of many other uses for your tongue—all pertaining to my pleasure." He leered.

"I'll bring you no pleasure. You disgust me!" She raised her hand to strike him.

He caught it and dragged it behind her back. His grip merciless, he yanked her against him. His mouth came down on hers, hot and open and wet. He thrust her against the tree so that she cried out. When she did, his tongue stabbed at hers, gouging deep; she gagged. Hard hands caught at her hips and dragged her skirts high.

"No!" she screeched. "You will not do this!" She raised her fists high to pummel him.

Once again she failed. He caught her wrists and jammed them against her sides. He wedged his weight between her thighs and ground himself against her; Glenda was suddenly certain he did not care that her woman's flesh was still swollen and tender and healing from the rigors of childbirth.

He panted against her throat. "You're mine—"

"Nay, Simon, she's mine, and I grow weary of this battle. What say we settle this here and now?"

That voice, coolly imperious . . . It was Egan! Even as joy bounded high, she wondered how he had delivered himself so silently that neither she nor Simon had heard him. Then she realized that Simon had been so intent on his lust, and she on fighting him off, that an army could have passed by and neither of them would have noticed.

Simon's hands fell away from her. He turned and gaped, yet despite his astonishment, his recovery was speedy.

"You bastard," he sneered. "You should have stayed in the Highlands!"

Egan's eyes were steady on his foe, but it was Glenda that his quiet tone encompassed. "Stand clear, sweet."

But Glenda could not move. A dagger had appeared in Simon's hands. A scream welled in her throat as he bared his teeth and charged toward Egan, his arm raised high.

The dagger never fell. In his rage, he failed to see the glint of steel at Egan's side. Egan had only to raise his arm . . .

Impaled on his sword, Simon slumped to the earth without a sound.

It was over in but a heartbeat . . . yet for Glenda, 'twas never-ending.

She swayed unsteadily, then all at once strong arms enveloped her.

"Egan." She choked out his name and sagged against him, overcome with emotion. "Oh, God, Simon said you were dead—"

"I know. I heard. Ah, but 'twould take a better man than Simon to see me to my grave."

"I knew you would come. You always do ... whenever I need you, you're always near." She clutched at him, trying desperately to contain the tumult of emotion tearing through her breast. She longed to cry that she loved him ... demand that he love her in return! But all that emerged was a dry, jagged sob. Hot tears began to slide down her cheeks.

"Hush, love. It's over. We're safe and unharmed."

She shook her head, unable to quell her anguish. "Did you come from Blackstone?"

"Aye."

"Elizabeth ... did you see her?"

He frowned.

Her tears only flowed the harder. "No," she said brokenly. "God, no!"

"Glenda, what is wrong?"

She raised her face to his. "She was gone, Egan. She was gone!"

Egan stared at her. A trickle of unease creeped along his spine. "What do you mean?"

"She was not in her cradle, Egan. Simon intended to take her as well, but she was gone!"

His mind balked. There had to be some reason ... 'twas not as if the babe could walk away!

"Sweet, calm yourself. Perhaps in the dark, you were mistaken—"

"I was not. She was gone, I tell you!"

"Then surely Nessa has her—"

"She does not. Simon struck her when we left, and I fear she may be dead, too!"

There was a cramping tightness in his chest. Elizabeth ... gone, he thought vaguely. It could not be. For an instant he couldn't move. The terror in Glenda's eyes pierced him to the soul, for he knew this was her deepest fear. To lose her child ... *their* child.

Perhaps it was Glenda's tears, but he was suddenly unable to still the alarm that leaped in his breast. Turning abruptly, he whistled for his stallion. Without a word he swung Glenda up before him in the saddle.

They raced frantically back to Blackstone.

Her cheeks were still damp when the walls of Blackstone Tower came into view. A shout went up when the guard raised the gate and they passed into the bailey. A small body of soldiers and horses were gathered near the stables; apparently they had readied themselves to ride after him.

Someone spied Egan and called out. "My lord!"

Egan raised a hand. "Simon is dead," he shouted.

A deafening cheer went up; Simon the Lawless would not be missed here at Blackstone.

Assisting Glenda to the ground, he glimpsed Nessa hobbling toward them. A massive bruise welled on her temple, but at least she was alive. Glenda saw her then as well. Crying out, Glenda ran to her. Egan joined them, stunned when the old woman turned and hugged him as fiercely as her aging arms would allow. Glenda smiled, but her expression was still fraught with anxiety.

She reached for Nessa's gnarled hands. "Where is Elizabeth? Have you seen her?"

Iron-gray brows raised in confusion. "Why, surely the wee lamb is still asleep in your chamber—"

"Nay, she is not! Simon would have taken her, too, but she was gone!" Glenda raised tear-bright eyes to Egan. "I want my babe! Where is my babe?"

His arm stole around her. He was nearly as pale as his wife.

"We will find her," was all he said. "*We will find her.*"

Egan caught Glenda's hand and brought her close to his side. At his urgent command, others began to search for the missing infant.

And indeed, Elizabeth was not in her cradle. The sight of that empty nest wrung a moan from Glenda, but she made no further outcry when Egan drew her from the chamber to search first the north tower, then the south. The air was stale and thick with dust, for the rooms there had not been used in many a year. Though Glenda tried hard to take comfort from Egan's staunchness, when no cry that Elizabeth had been found was forthcoming, her spirit grew ever more leaden.

They were just about to leave the uppermost chamber when Egan suddenly stopped. Glenda's gaze swung to his face. She saw that he was staring intently at the cupboard jammed against the far wall.

Were it not for the first faint glimmer of dawn peeping through the shutters, lending its light to their candle, she might never have seen the bit of cloth sticking out from the bottom edge of the cupboard. In but a heartbeat he'd crossed the room anew and swung the door wide.

There was a small figure hunched inside. With a gasp the figure looked up at Egan, her eyes dark and wide and frantic.

It was Jeannine. In all the furor, Glenda had failed to notice that Jeannine was not present.

Egan cocked his head. "Jeannine?" he queried gently. "Are you hiding?"

Jeannine's head bobbed in affirmation. Then she whispered, "Is he still here?"

Egan frowned. "Who? Simon?" he guessed.

"Aye!"

Egan shook his head. "Nay. Simon is gone. Dead. He'll never trouble us again." His expression softened. "You may come out now, lass. 'Tis safe."

Glenda watched as Egan extended a hand and pulled the girl to her feet. Jeannine carefully cradled the ever-present bundle in her elbow. Absently noting it, Glenda slid her gaze back to Egan.

"Egan," she murmured, "we really should—"

The swaddling shifted.

Glenda caught the movement in the corner of her eye. She broke off her words as her eyes widened in shock. God above, this time there really *was* a babe in the swaddling!

Just then there came a pitiful little cry. Glenda knew that cry, knew it well, indeed . . .

It was her daughter's.

"Jeannine," she said helplessly. "Oh, Jeannine . . ."

"Simon wanted to take the babe," Jeannine said tentatively. "I heard him. So I took the babe and hid."

Her chin lifted proudly. A faint smile appeared. "I-I saved the babe."

"Aye, dear, you did," she said in amazement. "You did indeed." She bit her lip, then reached for Elizabeth.

Jeannine's arms tightened. Two pair of eyes collided, one pleading, the other suddenly uncertain. Did Jeannine believe it was her own child that she'd rescued? Even as Glenda's heart filled to overflowing, something twisted inside her.

"Jeannine," she reminded gently, "you know this babe is Elizabeth."

"I know," Jeannine stated quietly. "I'm not daft like they say, ye know." Carefully she surrendered the bundle into Glenda's waiting arms, her smile reappearing as Glenda murmured her heartfelt thanks.

It wavered. A stark, stricken look passed over her features. "My babe," she said quaveringly. "Thomas . . . he's dead, isn't he?"

She began to weep. Glenda slipped her free arm around her, a bittersweet ache inside. "Aye, love. But, God willing, there will be others—look at me." She held her while she wept, and so did Nessa. They were tears of grief, those tears—but they were also tears of gladness . . . and tears of hope.

The haze of dawn crept across the treetops when Glenda finally laid Elizabeth in her cradle. For the longest time she gazed at her daughter, who slept with her wee fist tucked beneath the folds of her chin. She gave a fervent prayer of thanks that Jeannine had heard Simon's threat against the babe and had acted upon it.

But there was a wistful yearning within her as Egan turned her in his arms. It must have shown, for he tipped his head to the side.

"What are you thinking of?" he murmured.

Glenda released a long sigh. "Poor Jeannine. Egan, for so long now, I knew not whether it was a blessing or a curse that she refused to accept Thomas's death. But now that she has, I-I almost wish she had not! I hurt so badly for her, knowing she has no one to comfort her."

His lips twitched. "I think it will not be that way for long."

"What do you mean? Why do you smile like that?"

"Have you not seen Culbert the wainwright making calf's eyes at her? When we left the hall, I saw him with her, holding both her hands within his."

Glenda was stunned. "Really?"

"Indeed." He smiled at her, and in that instant, a rush of emotion surged inside her, so intense it nearly brought her to her knees.

Her lovely smile faded. Her eyes were huge and glistening. Egan felt her tremble.

He exclaimed softly, "Glenda! Sweet, do not cry! The danger is behind us. Our daughter is safe and the future holds naught but promise for us!"

"I know that. But, Egan . . . there is so much to be said."

"What, sweet, what?" The sight of her tears speared his heart.

She lifted her face. "I love you . . . I love you! I did not want to . . . I was afraid to love you for fear of losing you . . . but I've loved you for so long now. Egan, oh, Egan, I love you so . . ."

There was not enough room in her for all she felt. It spilled from her soul, unleashed. Unbidden. It spilled from her eyes, a torrent of tears. It spilled from her lips, the chant of his name.

For the space of a heartbeat, Egan could only stare. His eyes scoured hers, but no shadows lurked in those beautiful golden depths; there was naught but a love so pure and shining he felt he would surely burst.

His arms tightened, possessively tender. He lowered his forehead to hers so that their lips were but a breath apart. "And I love you, sweet. I always have."

She twined her arms about his neck. Their lips met and clung, a kiss that was long and infinitely tender.

She was smiling through her tears when at last he released her mouth.

"Oh, Egan," she said breathlessly. "I think I knew it since the time I asked why you never married—but I was almost afraid to believe it!"

He laughed huskily. "Believe it, love, for you were the only one I ever wanted."

Epilogue

With summer nigh, the days had begun to grow longer, the air drier and warmer and filled with the promise of another prosperous year. The high stone walls of Blackstone Keep sparkled in the sunlight that poured down from an azure sky. Voices drifted on the warm spring breeze—along with lilting laughter and childish squeals.

'Twas a lazy afternoon, and the four of them, Cameron and Meredith, Egan and Glenda, sat upon the lush green grass, looking after their little ones as they played beneath the gnarled branches of the ancient oak tree that grew near the bend in the river.

Brodie was tall for a lad of his years, his limbs long, his shoulders sturdy. His sister Aileen, but an infant when Glenda and Egan departed Dunthorpe, was the image of her mother with her halo of fiery red curls and huge, sparkling eyes; much to Cameron's good-natured vexation, she had adopted her brother's habit of darting into places to hide, then imploring her father to come find her. Elizabeth, now just over a year old, possessed her father's thick, dark hair and her mother's wide golden eyes. With dimpled cheeks

347

and a ready, impish smile, she was a beautiful child.

But Elizabeth was not the only one whose lusty cries had filled the towering walls of the keep in the past year. Not long after Simon's death, Jeannine had wed Culbert; for a time it had seemed almost odd to see her empty arms. Yet within the year she carried anew a swaddled little bundle, this time full of a squirming little lad . . . It was Nessa who had delivered the bairn . . . and Nessa who would no doubt deliver still another before summer's end . . .

The second child of the lord and lady of Blackstone Keep.

A smile of contentment curling her lips, Glenda laced her fingers atop the curve of her belly. Egan had propped himself on an elbow beside his wife. Meredith sat next to Glenda, with Cameron stretched out beside her. Aileen sought to stand on her head, her plump little bottom stuck high in the air. Brodie dropped down beside his father, whereupon Elizabeth beamed and squealed with delight at finding Brodie on her own level. Flinging her arms around him, she pressed a sloppy wet kiss on young Brodie's cheek.

Brodie howled and scrubbed the spot fiercely with his knuckles.

"Mama. Papa . . . make Elizabeth stop!"

Egan chuckled. "She's very fond of you, Brodie."

"But must she always follow me? And must she always *kiss* me?"

"You should be glad that she finds you such a handsome young lad," Cameron chimed in. "Why, there may even come a time when *you* will be the one chasing Elizabeth."

Brodie hardly looked convinced. Yet despite his complaints, when Elizabeth tumbled forward in the grass, it was Brodie who reached her, hauled her to her feet with a grunt and brushed the dirt from her tiny gown. She swayed for an instant, then proceeded to follow in his wake when he ambled away. In truth, during the week since the MacKays' arrival, Brodie was quick to aid the little girl who forever toddled after him, for Elizabeth was still a trifle unsteady on her feet.

In the meantime, the two men had exchanged glances, their thoughts clearly reflecting the other's. It was Egan who said in a voice of dawning wonder, "God above, wouldn't it be something if Brodie and Elizabeth were to marry someday?"

"It would indeed." Cameron sat up.

"I would not be opposed if Elizabeth wished to marry Brodie. He is a good lad. Already he takes care of his own."

Cameron nodded. "Their children would likely have dark hair," he mused, thoughtfully eyeing the pair in question, "wouldn't you say?"

"Oh, I should think so, indeed." Egan nodded his certainty.

"We could have the wedding at Dunthorpe." Cameron's tone took on a note of excitement.

"But Elizabeth is the bride. The wedding should be here at Blackstone!"

Now it was Glenda and Meredith who looked at each other. "Blackstone. Dunthorpe," Glenda echoed in astonishment, then shook her head. "Do the two of you not hear yourselves? Already you discuss your grandchildren, but I would remind you, Elizabeth is hardly ready to become a bride, and Brodie is scarcely of an age to be a husband!"

Again that look between the men. Their eyes gleamed. "We could betroth them," said one.

"Nay!" chorused two female voices in unison.

"If they are to find each other, it must be on their own," said Glenda. "The two of you cannot make them fall in love."

"Aye," Meredith pronounced with mock sternness. "If it is to be, it will be, and not because the two of you say it will be so. We shall just have to wait and see, and the two of you must simply content yourselves with that!"

It was not long thereafter that they made their way back to the keep. Egan cradled a sleepy Elizabeth in his arms, while Aileen already slumbered against Cameron's shoulder. In the hall, Cameron proceeded up the stairs to put the little girl to bed. Brodie marched after him. Meredith glanced over at Egan and Glenda, just as the pair chanced to exchange a tender look above their daughter's head.

She smiled. Reaching out, she took Glenda's hand and squeezed it. "I cannot tell you how it fills my heart to see the two of you so happy," she said softly, then turned to Egan. " 'Tis just as Cameron once told me. You belong together." Stretching up on tiptoe, she pressed a kiss upon Egan's cheek before making her way after Cameron.

Later that night Glenda nestled close against the side of her husband. A fire burned cozily in the hearth, and the bed was snug and warm.

Peering up at him, Glenda arched a brow. With a fingertip she traced the place on his cheek where

Meredith had kissed him. "The women of Dunthorpe do seem to harbor a fancy for you, sir," she told him tartly. "I wonder . . . should I be jealous?"

Egan caught her hand and kissed her fingertips. Weaving his fingers through hers, he laid it on the mound of her belly. He laughed, the sound husky.

"Only one woman will ever hold my heart in her hands," he told her.

"Ah. And who might that be?" Glenda's tone was grave, but her eyes held the light of a thousand stars.

Egan laughed, the sound husky. "The woman I hold right here in my arms."

She smiled. "Perhaps you could show me as well, sir."

"Perhaps I will."

And, indeed . . . he did.

Welcome to the world of the Avon Romance Superleader Where anything is possible . . . and dreams really do come true

We all know there are unspoken rules that govern the acts of courtship. There are the rules of today (if he doesn't call by Wednesday he won't, even if he says he will!) and the rules of days gone by (a lady should never dance more than three times with a gentleman).

But often, what is expected is at odds with what is longed for . . . and how you're allowed to act is different from the way you feel. Heaven help you if you take a wrong step . . . but sometimes it's better to toss the rules away, take matters into your own hands—just as the heroines of these upcoming Avon Romance Superleaders are about to do.

~

HERE COMES THE BRIDE
Pamela Morsi

JULY AVON ROMANCE SUPERLEADER

Gussie Mudd, the proprietor of a small ice business in Cottonwood, Texas, has determined that at some point in a woman's life she must get herself a man, or give up on the idea entirely. To get her man she decides to play by the rules . . . the rules of business. And she makes a business proposition to her employee, Mr. Rome Akers.

"PEOPLE, MR. AKERS, ARE JUST LIKE BUSINESSES. THEY act and think and evolve in the same way as commercial enterprise. People want and need things. But when they are vastly available, they prize them differently."

"Well, yes, I guess so," Rome agreed.

"So when we consider Mr. Dewey's hesitancy to marry me," she continued, "we must avoid emotionalism and try to consider the situation logically."

"Logically?"

Rome was not sure that logic was a big consideration when it came to love.

"Mr. Dewey has been on his own for some time now," she said. "He has a nice home, a hired woman to cook and clean, a satisfying business venture, good friends and myself, a pleasant companion to escort to community events. Basically all his needs as a man are met. He has a virtual monopoly on the things that he requires."

Rome was not certain that *all* of a man's *needs* had been stated, but after his embarrassing foray in that direction, he chose not to comment.

"He is quite comfortable with his life as it is," Miss Gussie continued. "Whyever should he change?"

"Why indeed?" Rome agreed.

She smiled then. That smile that he'd seen often before. That smile that meant a new idea, a clever innovation, an expansion of the company. He had long admired Miss Gussie's good business sense and the very best of her money-making notions came with this smile.

"I can do nothing about Mr. Dewey's nice home, the woman hired to cook and clean, his business, or his friends," Miss Gussie said. "But I can see that he no longer has a monopoly upon my pleasant companionship."

"I'm not sure I understand you," Rome said.

"In our business if Purdy Ice began delivering smaller blocks twice a week, we would be forced to do the same."

Rome nodded. "Yes, I suppose you are right about that."

"We would be forced to change, compelled to provide more service for the same money," she said.

"Yes, I suppose that's right."

"That's exactly what we're going to do to Amos Dewey," she declared.

Rome was listening, but still skeptical.

"You are going to pretend to be in love with me," she said as if that were going to be the simplest thing in the world. "You will escort me about town. Sit evenings on this porch with me. Accompany me to civic events."

That seemed not too difficult, Rome thought. He did not normally attend a lot of public functions, but, of course, he could.

"I don't see how that will change Dewey's mind," he told her honestly.

"You will also let it be known that you are madly in love with me," she said, "and that you are determined to get me to the altar as soon as possible."

Rome got a queasy feeling in his stomach.

"Amos Dewey will no longer have a monopoly. *You* will be the competition that will force him to provide the service he is not so willing to provide—marrying me."

Gussie raised her hands in a gesture that said that the outcome was virtually assured.

Rome had his doubts.

"I'm not sure this will work, Miss Gussie," he told her. "Men . . . men don't always behave like businesses. They are not all that susceptible to the law of supply and demand."

"Don't be silly," she said. "Of course they are."

"I'm not sure I'm the right man to be doing this. Perhaps you should think of someone who would seem more . . . well more suited to the task."

Her response was crisp and cool.

"I was hoping for a late-spring wedding," she told

him. "When the flowers are at their peak. But I suppose, in this instance midsummer would be fine. Let's say the Fourth of July; that sounds like an auspicious day for a wedding. It is going to be absolutely perfect. The most perfect wedding this town has ever seen. I do hope you will be there, Mr. Akers."

❧

HEAVEN ON EARTH
Constance O'Day-Flannery

August Avon Romance Superleader

For Casey O'Reilly the world was supposed to be an orderly place where you met, married, and had children with the man you love. But nothing had gone according to plan. Mr. Right never made an appearance, and now, at "thirtysomething," Casey figured she had a better chance at being struck by lightning than struck by love . . . but then the unthinkable happened . . .

SHE WAS MAKING THIS UP. WHATEVER WAS HAPPENING was all in her mind. *It had to be!*

Desperately, Casey rubbed at her eyes and then cupped her hands around them to shelter her face as more lightning, familiar narrow streaks, flashed around her and thunder rumbled.

There was no time for questions as a man slowly, deliberately, walked closer, as though he had no fear of the lightning or the sandstorm. Casey's voice was stuck in her throat. She wanted to ask him who he was, but only garbled noises emerged from her mouth as she watched him unbutton his dark coat above her. His face was hidden by a wide turned-up collar and the cowboy hat pulled low over his brow, but somehow the closer he came, the less she feared him.

He knelt before her and, without a word, wrapped the edges of the raincoat around her, pulling her to his chest and sheltering her from the sandstorm. She could feel the strength of his arms around her back, and immediately sensed peace as she was gathered into the sanctuary of his body. She felt the strong beat of his heart reverberating against her face. She smelled something citrusy, very earthy, about him, and lifted her hand to cling to his soft shirt.

"You are all right, Casey O'Reilly."

She almost jumped at the close proximity of his voice resonating from his chest and into her ear. The low soothing tone sent shivers throughout her body and she found herself clinging even more tightly to his shirt.

"Who . . . Who are you?" she managed to mutter.

"I've come to help," he answered, holding her tighter as another crash of thunder made the ground shake violently beneath them.

"Thank heavens," she sobbed.

Somehow she felt incredibly safe, more so than she had ever felt in her life. Her body was tingling with some strange and powerful energy that was unfamiliar and yet . . . so perfectly wonderful. She felt a renewed strength welling up in her muscles, spreading through her body down to her burning foot. Her chest stopped aching and her headache eased as she held this man who had just walked out of a bolt of lightning and into her life . . .

~

HIS WICKED PROMISE
Samantha James

SEPTEMBER AVON ROMANCE SUPERLEADER

Glenda knew what was expected of a Highland lass—she must wed a man bold and strong enough to protect her. Love could come later . . . if it came at all. But although she was now without a husband, she had once known the joy of the marriage bed . . . and the pleasure that Laird Egan was willing to reacquaint her with . . .

"WELL, YOU ARE EVER AT THE READY, ARE YOU NOT?"

He cocked a brow. "What do you mean?"

"I think you know quite well what I mean!"

He was completely unfazed by the fire of her glare. A slow smile rimmed his lips. "Glenda, do you speak of my manly appetites?"

"Your words, sir, not mine," she snapped. Her resentment blazed higher with his amusement. "Though I must say, your appetite seems quite hearty!"

"And what of yours, Glenda?"

"Whatever do you mean?"

"You are a woman without a husband. A woman

without a man. I am not a fool. Women . . . well,
women have appetites, too. Especially those who
know the pleasure that can be found in another's
body."

And well she knew. She had lost her maidenhead on
the marriage bed, but she had never found lovemaking
a chore or a duty, as she'd heard some women were
wont to do. Instead, she had found it a vastly pleasurable experience . . . All at once she was appalled. She
couldn't believe what they were discussing! To speak
of her lying with a man . . . of his lying with a
woman . . . and to each other yet!

He persisted. "Come, Glenda, what of you? I asked
you once and you would not answer. Do you not find
yourself lonely? Do you not miss the closeness of a
man's body, the heat of lips warm upon yours?"

Suddenly she was the one who was on the defensive. "Nay," she gasped.

"Nay?" he feigned astonishment. "What, Glenda!
Did you not love Niall then?"

Glenda's breath grew short; it seemed there was not
enough air to breathe, for he was so close. *Too* close.
So close that she could see the tiny droplets of water
which glistened in the dense forest of hair on his
chest. Niall's chest had been smooth and nearly void
of hair, and it was all she could do not to stare in mingled shock and fascination.

She was certain her face flamed scarlet. "Of course I
did! You know I did! But I"—she made a valiant stab
at reasoning—"I have put aside such longings."

He did not take his eyes from her mouth. "Have
you?" he said softly. "Have you indeed?"

A strong hand settled on her waist. In but a half
breath, it was joined by the other. His touch seemed to

burn through the layers of clothing to the flesh beneath.

"Egan," she floundered. "Egan, please!"

"What, Glenda? What is it?"

She shook her head. Her eyes were wide and dark. Her head had lifted. Her lips hovered but a breath beneath his. The temptation to give in, to kiss her, to trap her lips beneath his and taste the fruit of her mouth was all-consuming. Almost more than he could stand.

She wanted it, too. He sensed it with every fiber of his being, but she was fighting it, damn her! Yet still he wanted to hear her say it. He *needed* it.

"Tell me, Glenda. What is it you want?"

She shook her head. Her hands came up between them. Her fingers opened and closed on his chest . . . his *naked* chest. Dark, bristly hairs tickled her palm; to her the sensation was shockingly intimate. Yet she did not snatch back her hands—she did not push him away—as she should have.

As she could have.

"Egan? Are you here, lad?"

It was Bernard. They jerked apart. Egan moved first, stepping back from her. Did he curse beneath his breath? Glenda did not wait to find out.

She fled. Her heart was pounding and her lungs labored as if the devil himself nipped at her heels. Her feet did not stop until she was safe in her own chamber and the door was shut.

'Twas then that her strength deserted her. She pressed her back against it and slumped, landing in a heap on the floor.

Thrice now, Egan had almost kissed her. *Thrice.*

What madness possessed him? Sweet heaven, what madness possessed *her*?

For Glenda could not deny the yearning that still burned deep in her heart. Just once she longed to feel the touch of his mouth on hers. Just once . . .

RULES OF ENGAGEMENT
Christina Dodd
OCTOBER AVON ROMANCE SUPERLEADER

Miss Pamela Lockhart knew that proper behavior could guide a governess through any trying situation. The rules were straightforward: never become too familiar with your employer, always take your meals upstairs on a tray, and remember your station at all times. But what happens when your employer is devastatingly handsome . . . and his behavior is anything but proper?

"YOU CONSIDER MARRIAGE THE SURE ROUTE TO MISERY."

"Not really." He stroked his chin, a gesture he had adopted from his grandfather. "The trick to marriage is not letting expectations get in the way. A man needs to understand why women get married, that's all."

Her mouth drew down in typical Miss Lockhart censure. "Why, pray tell, do women get married?"

"For money, usually." He could tell she was offended again, but with Miss Lockhart he didn't have to worry overly much about offense. After all, she didn't. Besides, he thought his assessment quite fair. "I don't blame them. The world is not fair to a spinster.

She has no recourse but to work or starve. So if she's asked, she marries."

Obviously, *Miss Lockhart* did not consider his assessment fair. She slapped her mug on the table so hard the crockery rattled. "Do you have any idea how insulting you are? To think a woman is single because she has never been asked, or if she is married she has done so for monetary security?"

He found himself entertained and very, very interested. "Ah, I've touched a nerve. Are you telling me there is a man alive who dared to propose to you?"

"I am not telling you anything." But swept along by her passion, she did. "A man can convey financial security, but whither thou goest, I shall go, and all that rot. A woman has to live where her husband wishes, let him waste her money, watch as he humiliates her with other women, and never say a word."

"Men are not the only ones who break their vows."

"So fidelity is a vow *you* intend to keep?"

Of course he had no intention of keeping that vow when he was forced to make it, and falling into that trap which had so neatly snared his father. "I've supported more women than Madame Beauchard's best corset maker. If I let marriage stop me, think of the poor actresses who would be without a patron."

She wasn't amused. "So nothing about your wife would be sacrosanct, not even her body. Your wife will cherish dreams that you never know about, and even if you did they would be less than a puff of wind to you."

Women had dreams? About *what*? A new pair of shoes? Seeing a rival fail? Dancing with a foreign prince? But Miss Lockhart wasn't speaking of the trivial, and he found himself asking, "What are your dreams?"

"You don't care. Until I spoke, it never occurred to you that a woman could have her dreams."

"That's true, but you are a teacher, and already you have taught me otherwise." Leaning back in his chair, he gazed at her and with absolute sincerity, and then said the most powerful words in the universe. "Tell me what you want. I want to know about you."

She had no defense to withstand him. She leaned back, too, and closed her eyes as if she could see her fantasy before her. "I want a house in the country. Just a cottage, with a fence and cat to sit in my lap and a dog to sleep at my feet. A spot of earth for a garden with flowers as well as vegetables, food on the table, and a little leisure time in which to read the books I've not had time to read or just sit . . . in the sunshine."

The candles softened the stark contrast between her white complexion and that hideous rouge. Light and shadow delineated her pale lips, showing them in their fullness. Her thick lashes formed a ruffled half-circle on her skin. When she was talking like this, imagining her perfect life, she looked almost . . . pretty. "That's all?"

"Oh, yes."

"That's simple enough."

"Yes, very simple. And mine."

Careful not to break into her reverie, he quietly placed his mug next to hers. "Why do you want that?"

"That's what I had before—"

She stopped speaking so suddenly he knew what she had been about to say. Moving to the side of her chair, he knelt on the carpet. "Before your father left?"

At the sound of his voice, her eyes flew open and she stared at him in dismay. She *had* been dreaming, he realized, seeing that cottage, those pets, that garden, and imagining a time when she could sit in the sunshine. Her countenance was open and vulnerable, and his instincts were strong. As gently as a whisper he placed his fingertips on her cheek. "There's one dream you didn't mention, and I can make it come true." Slowly, giving her time to turn if she wished, he leaned forward . . . and kissed her.

~❧

JUST THE WAY YOU ARE
Barbara Freethy
November Avon Romance Superleader

Allison Tucker knew that today's women were supposed to face their ex-husbands in a modern way—cordially, friendly, and with the attitude that you didn't have a care in the world. But every time she looked into Sam's eyes, she still felt a longing for what might have been if they stayed together—and what could still be . . .

"Did you ever love Mommy?"

Allison Tucker caught her breath at the simple, heartfelt question that had come from her seven-year-old daughter's lips. She took a step back from the doorway and leaned against the wall, her heart racing in anticipation of the answer. She'd thought she'd explained the separation to her daughter, the reasons why Mommy and Daddy couldn't live together anymore; but apparently Kelly still had some questions, and this time it was up to Sam to answer.

Alli held her breath as she heard Sam clear his throat, obviously stalling for time. In that second she wished herself a million miles away. She hadn't meant to eavesdrop, but when she'd arrived to pick Kelly up after her weekend with her father, she had been caught by the cozy scene in the family room. Even now she could see Sam sprawled in the brown leather reclining chair looking endearingly handsome in his faded blue jeans and navy blue rugby shirt. Kelly was on his lap, her blond hair a mess in mismatched braids, her clothes exactly the same as Sam's, faded blue jeans and a navy blue T-shirt. Kelly adored dressing like her father.

"Did I show you the picture of Mommy when she dressed up like a giant pumpkin for the Halloween dance?" Sam asked.

They were looking at a yearbook, Alli realized with dismay. She'd hidden them away years ago because there weren't just pictures of Sam and Alli in the yearbook, there were other people in there, too, people she didn't want Kelly to know anything about. Why on earth had Sam dragged out the yearbook now?

"Did you, Daddy? Did you ever love Mommy?" Kelly persisted.

Answer the question, Sam. Tell her you never really loved me, that you only married me because I was pregnant.

Alli held her breath, waiting for Sam's answer, knowing the bitter truth, but wondering, hopelessly, impossibly wondering . . .

"I love your mother very much—for giving me you," Sam replied.

Alli closed her eyes against a rush of emotion. It wasn't an answer, but an evasion. She didn't know why she felt even the tiniest bit of surprise. Sam would never admit to loving her. She couldn't remember ever hearing those three simple words cross his lips, not even after Kelly's birth, after the long hours of labor and frantic minutes of delivery.

He hadn't said the words then. Or later in the days and weeks and years that followed, not even when they made love, when they shared a passion that was perhaps the only honest part of their relationship.

Alli clenched her fists, wanting to feel anger, not pain. She'd spent more than half of her entire twenty-six years of life in love with Sam Tucker, but he didn't love her.

∾

THE VISCOUNT WHO LOVED ME
Julia Quinn
December Avon Romance Superleader

If there's one place a proper young lady should not be, it's in an unmarried gentleman's private study . . . crouched under his desk, desperate to escape discovery. Yet that's exactly where (and in what position) Kate Sheffield finds herself. Even worse, Anthony Bridgerton has brought a potential paramour back with him, and Kate is forced to wait out the entire encounter . . .

ANTHONY KNEW HE HAD TO BE A FOOL. HERE HE WAS, pouring a glass of whiskey for Maria Rosso, one of the few women of his acquaintance who knew how to appreciate both a fine whiskey and the devilish intoxication that followed, and all he could smell was the damned lilies-and-soap scent of Kate Sheffield. He knew she was in the house—he was half ready to kill his mother for inviting her to the musicale—but this was ridiculous.

And then he saw Kate.

Under his desk.

It was impossible.

Surely this was a nightmare. Surely if he closed his eyes and opened them again, she'd be gone.

He blinked. She was still there.

Kate Sheffield, the most maddening, irritating, diabolical woman in all England, was crouching like a frog under his desk.

"Maria," he said smoothly, moving forward toward the desk until he was stepping on Kate's hand. He didn't step hard, but he heard her wince.

This gave him immense satisfaction.

"Maria," he repeated, "I have suddenly remembered an urgent matter of business that must be dealt with immediately."

"This very night?" she asked, sounding dubious.

"I'm afraid so. *Euf!*"

Maria blinked. "Did you just grunt?"

"No," Anthony lied, trying not to choke on the word. Kate had removed her glove and wrapped her hand around his knee, digging her nails straight through his breeches and into his skin. Hard.

At least he hoped it was her nails. It could have been her teeth.

Maria's eyes were curious. "Anthony, is there an animal under your desk?"

Anthony let out a bark of laughter. "You could say that."

Kate let go of his leg, and her fist came down on his foot.

Anthony took advantage of his release to step quickly out from behind the desk. "Would I be unforgivably rude," he asked, striding to Maria's side and taking her arm, "if I merely walked you to the door and not back to the music room?"

She laughed, a low, sultry sound that should have seduced him. "I am a grown woman, my lord. I believe I can manage the short distance."

She floated out, and Anthony shut the door with a decisive click. "You," he boomed, eliminating the distance to the desk in four long strides. "Show yourself."

When Kate didn't scramble out quickly enough, he reached down, clamped his hand around her upper arm, and hauled her to her feet.

"It was an accident," she said, grabbing onto the edge of the desk for support.

"Funny how those words seem to emerge from your mouth with startling frequency."

"It's true!" she gulped. He had stepped forward and was now very, very close. "I was sitting in the hall," she said, her voice sounding crackly and hoarse, "and I heard you coming. I was just trying to avoid you."

"And so you invaded my private office?"

"I didn't know it was your office. I—" Kate sucked in her breath. He'd moved even closer, his crisp, wide lapels now only inches from the bodice of her dress. She knew his proximity was deliberate, that he sought to intimidate rather than seduce, but that didn't do anything to quell the frantic beating of her heart.

"I think perhaps you did know that this was my office," he murmured, letting his forefinger trail down the side of her cheek. "Perhaps you did not seek to avoid me at all."

Kate's lips parted, but she couldn't have uttered a word if her life had depended on it. She breathed when he paused, stopped when he moved. She had no doubt that her heart was beating in time to his pulse.

"Maybe," he whispered, so close now that his breath kissed her lips, "you desired something else altogether."